T0155435

SHOTGUN

DEVIANT MAGIC

BOOK TWO

Scott Colby

DEVIANT MAGIC BOOK TWO: SHOTGUN
Copyright © 2021 Scott Colby. All rights reserved.

Published by Outland Entertainment LLC
3119 Gillham Road
Kansas City, MO 64109

Founder/Creative Director: Jeremy D. Mohler
Editor-in-Chief: Alana Joli Abbott

ISBN: 978-1-954255-01-2
EBOOK ISBN: 978-1-947659-92-6
Worldwide Rights
Created in the United States of America

Editor: Gwendolyn N. Nix
Cover Illustration: Ann Marie Cochran
Cover Design: Jeremy D. Mohler
Interior Layout: Mikael Brodu

The characters and events portrayed in this book are fictitious or fictitious recreations of actual historical persons. Any similarity to real persons, living or dead, is coincidental and not intended by the authors unless otherwise specified. This book or any portion thereof may not be reproduced or used in any manner whatsoever without the express written permission of the publisher except for the use of brief quotations in a book review.

Printed and bound in the United States of America.

Visit **outlandentertainment.com** to see more, or follow us on our Facebook Page **facebook.com/outlandentertainment/**

This is a work of fiction.
Any resemblance to real people
or places is all in your head.
For best results, serve with a can
of local craft beer.

— CHAPTER ONE —

How would you like to help me change the world?"

Roger had never confronted a burglar before, but he was pretty sure no trespasser in the history of time had ever answered the question "What the hell are you doing in my house?" in quite that way.

The intruder leaned forward from her perch among the empty takeout containers piled high atop his kitchen counter, her black dress rustling against the tile. She was a long, spindly thing, her porcelain skin made even whiter by the long locks of jet-black hair framing her face. "Come on, Roger," she cooed. "I know you've got a good heart. I know you want to help people." How did she know his name? He'd certainly never met her before. Roger shifted his grip on his old shotgun and took a couple tentative steps closer. His slippers squeaked on the cracked linoleum. They were only a few feet apart now. "Who are you and what are you doing in my house?" he asked, fighting to keep his voice stern and mostly succeeding. Although the sickly-sweet smile with which she'd greeted him remained, she clicked her black nails across the counter in irritation. "Roger, this isn't about me. This is about you. Are you interested or not?"

"No," he croaked. He never should've come downstairs to investigate that strange, childish laughter. He should've stayed in bed, rolled over, pulled the covers over his face, and pretended nothing was happening.

The tall woman's smile faded and she shook her head. "Are you sure?" She pouted, staring out at him from under her bangs with eyes suddenly gone soft. It was exactly the way Roger's daughter looked at him when she wanted something.

He hesitated before answering. Was this some sort of test? Would things turn nasty if she didn't like his response? "I'm sure," he finally said.

She lowered herself to the kitchen floor like a snake slithering down a tree. Roger stood frozen in place as she confidently closed the gap between them. She took his hand gently in her own and led him into the hallway. He didn't fight it; he couldn't, not because he was afraid, but because her icy touch somehow put him completely at ease. They stopped before the big round mirror Roger's wife often used to check her appearance before leaving for work. Not once did the strange woman so much as glance at his shotgun.

"See how good we look together?" she hissed. "Just the two of us against the world."

What Roger saw was a gorgeous young woman making a man in his late thirties look even older than he felt. She made his brown hair seem grayer and thinner, the crow's feet by his blue eyes the size of railroad tracks, his lean build fat and sloppy, his firm jaw a trio of jiggling jowls. And her simple but elegant dress made his flannel robe and fur slippers look positively stupid.

"Roger," she cooed, turning his face so her shimmering red lips were less than an inch from his chin, "don't tell me you've never wanted to be something. Where's your ambition?" She capped that last sentence with an impetuous giggle.

His heart broke all over again. Those were the last words Virginia had said to him before she drove off with the kids six months ago, taking them to some mysterious new suitor who could better provide the kind of lifestyle she needed. Food and a roof bought with a high school janitor's salary had been more than enough for twenty years. Roger hadn't seen her change of heart coming, and he still couldn't figure out what had caused it.

But whereas Virginia had immediately swung herself into the car and peeled out of the driveway, the strange woman in his kitchen appeared to be waiting anxiously for an answer. Once again, he felt as if he were being tested. Had she been spying on his family? Had she watched his wife abandon him? The answers to those questions were obvious, he decided, and downright chilling—not to mention thoroughly confusing. How the heck was he supposed to help her change the world? He could barely change the ink in his printer.

It was all a trick. It had to be. She'd come to the kitchen to distract him, to mess with his head, to distract him or set him up or otherwise take advantage of him. Roger lowered his eyes to avoid her intense stare. He opened his mouth to demand that she leave, but the words wouldn't come. Opportunity loomed before him. No, more than that—a second chance. A chance to properly answer the question that had been torturing his days and his nights ever since it was first asked of him. Maybe doing so would give him some peace. So where *was* his ambition?

"I did what I had to do," he said, his voice quivering. Roger didn't explain how he could've been a baseball player. Scouts from seven different major league teams watched every game he'd played in his senior year. Consensus pegged him as a good-but-not-great prospect, a solid bench player at worst and a decent regular at best. But then Virginia had gotten pregnant, and the idea of being on the road while she raised their first child alone hadn't been one he could stomach. That jagged hole in his heart where his family had always lived began to throb. He closed his eyes, wishing even more that this damn woman would just go away.

The back of a cold hand caressed his cheek, sending a shiver down his spine. "If you ever feel the need to be more," the woman whispered, her breath hot in his ear, "just look in the silverware drawer."

When he opened his eyes, she was gone. Roger abandoned all pretense of calm or bravery, dashing immediately to the back door beside the refrigerator. It was still locked, as was the tiny window above the sink. He sprinted into the living room, vaulting the mess of old photo albums and empty beer bottles he'd left scattered across the fraying carpet, and tested each of the three bay windows. Locked, locked, and locked. The deadbolt on the front door was shut tight. The windows in the bathroom and the dining room were similarly secured. She couldn't have come in through the basement; the iron bolt on that door could only be opened from inside the house.

He retraced his footsteps through every room on the first floor, searching for things that had been taken. Nothing was missing. The mortgage and his family's birth certificates and Social Security cards were still in the safe under the bookshelf. Nothing was missing from Virginia's jewelry box in the bathroom—not that she'd left much of value. The old green rug in the hall, which usually held footprints for days, showed no sign of tracks smaller than his own. The counter from which the woman had teased him showed no evidence she'd ever been there.

Which left the silverware drawer. Roger stared at it in absolute terror for a few minutes before a small laugh squeaked through his lips. He'd been sleepwalking—that was it. Wouldn't be the first time. After all, what could such a strange woman possibly have wanted with him? And how could she have broken into his locked-up house and then disappeared without a trace? It had been a dream, he decided, a manifestation of his stress and loneliness and perhaps a subconscious need for the approval of an attractive woman. That last part made him feel kind of gross. He looked down at his shotgun and sighed, thinking how lucky he was that he never kept it loaded. Sleepwalking was dangerous enough; sleepwalking with a loaded weapon in his hands was something he didn't want to think about. He flipped the chamber open, relieved to see that it was still empty.

Roger headed for the stairs and his bedroom, telling himself that the drawer wasn't worth investigating. He wasn't a child who couldn't sleep unless someone checked the closet for monsters. The thought made his heart ache, even though neither Samantha nor Ricky had asked him to do that in years. One night, when his daughter was just four, he decided it would be entertaining to pretend like he'd actually found something. Sam spent the next week sleeping between Roger and Virginia.

The stairs squeaked in protest against his heavy, plodding footsteps. Worn out from his frenzied inspection of the house, he fought to keep his eyes open as sleep tried to reclaim him. A good night's rest, he knew, would go a long way toward helping him put this night behind him. Roger reached the second floor and turned left toward the master bedroom. He stopped in front of Ricky's room to check on his son—then remembered yet again that the little guy was gone. Roger shook his head and stumbled on, wondering if he'd ever break that habit.

He was about to open the door to the master bedroom when a low, guttural snarl stopped him in his tracks. Wood squealed as a dresser drawer was yanked open. Fabric swished as someone rummaged through his clothing.

"Here somewhere," hissed a scratchy, serpentine voice. "Must find it!"

Roger peered around the door, which he'd left slightly ajar. In the darkness, he could just discern a bulky, humanoid shape tearing apart the dresser beside his bed. Moonlight streaming through the window beyond glinted off a scaly hide. Wide hips and a proportionally narrower waist revealed the burglar to be a woman. Roger guessed she was about six and a half feet tall and over 250 pounds—more than big enough to wipe the floor with him. *That's a leather jacket*, he thought. *She's one of those assholes from the biker bar up the highway.* He wondered if his previous sleepwalking dream had been a subconscious warning of some sort or if he were still stuck in the same nightmare. Either way, the meager courage he'd shown in confronting the spindly woman in his dream wasn't enough to make him want to risk dealing with someone larger and probably better armed. A quick call to 9-1-1 would solve this problem. He slowly backed away from the door, his heart pounding in his chest.

In the bedroom, old hinges squealed in protest as the intruder turned her attention to the closet. Roger shook his head at the unintelligible muttering that accompanied the flutter of clothing being tossed every which way. *Drugs*, he thought.

Halfway to the stairs, a sharp corner jabbed his kidney. He spun and righted the table he'd backed into, but the framed photographs it so proudly displayed tumbled to the floor. Roger watched in horror as Virginia, Ricky, Samantha, and their trip to Cape Cod betrayed him in a cacophony of shattering glass and wood.

The sounds coming from the bedroom ceased. Roger raised his shotgun and took aim at the door. The old twelve gauge was a fearsome weapon and there was no way for the intruder to know it wasn't loaded. Roger hoped he'd have the confidence to pull off the deception. He'd never had a particularly good poker face.

Heavy footsteps thudded across the floorboards as the intruder approached the bedroom door. Roger fought the urge to wipe the sweat from his brow, knowing he'd have to make the first move.

The top of the door exploded in a shower of wood and smoke. A ball of flame zipped over Roger's shoulder, colliding with the far wall and setting it ablaze. Three red eyes glared from the master bedroom. The thought of being brave ran screaming from Roger's mind just as quickly as his bladder emptied into his pajamas. A hissing laugh followed close behind as he scrambled for the stairs and slid over the top step. He grabbed at the railing to try to right himself, which threw off his momentum, and he wound up tumbling down to the first floor. His useless weapon flew from his hands, bounced off the walls a few times, and disappeared around the corner, sliding in the general direction of the front door. Roger grunted as he collided with the opposite wall at the bottom of the stairs. Leaning heavily against the wall, he groaned at the pain in his ribs and back as he hauled himself to his feet. He needed to get to the phone in the family room so he could call the police and the fire department and—

The cold tingle of something metallic and sharp pressing itself to his throat extinguished his thoughts. "Do not move," said a male voice to Roger's left. "Tell me what you saw up there."

Roger took a deep breath, trying to slow his pulse so his quivering carotid wouldn't slice itself open on the blade. "I don't know. It had red eyes, and it spat fire...and I think it had scales."

"I thought so. You've just survived an encounter with one of the most dangerous creatures in the Western Hemisphere," the man explained slowly, as if giving a lecture. "That creature is looking for something very important. She knows it's somewhere in your home, but her limited ESP cannot narrow the search further. If we find what she's looking for first, we get to keep our lives. If we don't..."

Time seemed to freeze as terrible realization dawned on Roger. "It's in the kitchen," he said quickly. Smoke tickled his nose, reminding him of his other immediate problem. "And my house is on fire."

The blade pulled away. "Show me."

Roger nodded and turned toward the kitchen, risking a quick glance at this latest intruder. The man was tall and lean and clothed in black military fatigues. A pair of green eyes burned brightly between high cheekbones and a tight brown crew cut.

His posture was stiff and straight, his pace steady and purposeful. *Military*, Roger thought, *maybe Special Forces*. He carried a pair of wicked-looking blades, like Bowie knives with bigger guards. The tops of his ears ended in sharp points. Although he didn't seem like he wanted to do Roger any harm, he certainly looked capable of doing so if the mood struck.

Roger flicked a switch on the wall as he shuffled into the kitchen, bathing the room in harsh fluorescent light. He stopped just shy of the cabinets, deeply frightened of whatever was in his silverware drawer. Turning to face the pointy-eared man, Roger spoke in a sad, quivering voice. "Top drawer, to the right of the dishwasher."

"Thank you," the commando replied politely. He stowed his blades in sheaths at his hips and yanked the drawer open.

A golden globe of roiling energy, like a miniature sun, rose up from within the drawer. Thin tendrils of power flared outward from its surface and crashed back down in blinding arcs. Roger stared at it in awe as it continued to rise until it hovered just below the kitchen ceiling. He had no idea what he was looking at, but something told him it was as important as the pointy-eared man claimed.

And then the globe suddenly zipped away from them and streaked down the hallway. It came to an abrupt stop above Roger's shotgun and then lowered itself into the weapon, melted into the steel of the barrels and the wood of the stock, and disappeared.

Jaw agape, Roger turned to the pointy-eared man in search of an answer—but the other merely shrugged. "That certainly wasn't the way this was supposed to go—"

Before he could continue, the ceiling above him exploded downward in a torrent of shattered drywall and lumber. Roger dropped to the floor and covered his head with his arms, cringing as shrapnel pelted his back, coughing against the scratchy dust that filled his mouth and nose. He wondered if the pointy-eared man was all right—not out of any concern for the man's well-being, but because he didn't like the thought of facing the thing in his bedroom alone.

As the dust began to clear, something heavy landed behind him with a dull thud. A predatory snarl sent a tremor through Roger's soul. He was on his feet without thinking, racing down the hall toward the empty weapon he assumed was his only chance. That ball of plasma in the silverware drawer had to have done something to it. Hot smoke streaming down from the fire upstairs burned his eyes and lungs, but he pressed onward. The creature's footsteps followed him like a shadow.

He dove for the hazy shape he thought was his shotgun, gasping as his damaged ribs protested their collision with the hard oak floor. His hands scrabbled across that floor, searching, searching— had the shape just been an illusion of the smoke? —and then his fingers found purchase on the familiar wood of the shotgun's worn stock. He rolled onto his back and brought his weapon to bear on the dark form and the red eyes pouncing upon him, and something in the back of his mind, something he swore came from the weapon itself, told him to pull both triggers.

The smoky room was suddenly and violently illuminated as his shotgun kicked hard into his shoulder. The report was like thunder as a thick ball of blue flame exploded from both barrels. For a brief moment, he could clearly discern the reptilian features of his attacker—bronze scales rippling across a vaguely feminine form, a long snout, a ferocious mouth lined with razor-sharp fangs, a spiky crest of exposed bone where her hair should've been—and then the blue fire slammed into the creature's chest and hurled her back into the kitchen.

Roger dismissed his shock with a quick shake of his head. His home was on fire, and he had to get out before the entire place burned down. He darted for the front door and yanked it open, hoping the creature he'd shot was good and dead and not about to jump him from behind. A dozen scrambling paces later he collapsed on the frozen ground of his front lawn and turned to watch the fire take his small home. The flames roared into the night, hiding the moon and stars behind a curtain of evil black smoke. The harsh siren of a fire truck blared in the distance, but Roger knew there was no hope. He'd lost everything—his family, his home, his every possession except his pee-stained pajamas and the old shotgun in his lap. His lip quivered with rage. Somehow, he knew this was all that strange woman's fault.

Glass shattered as a dark shape crashed through one of the windows on the side of his house. Roger leapt to his feet, weapon ready. It had worked once without any ammunition, so he assumed it would again.

The pointy-eared man stood and dusted himself off, smiling gently. "You've nothing to fear from me, friend," he said with a cough. "That was excellent work."

Roger kept his shotgun trained on the man. "What the hell is going on?" he demanded.

"I'm afraid an otherwise secret affair has spilled painfully out into the public," the man said, casually strolling closer. He glanced at the burning home sadly. "I apologize for the damage."

"You apologize for the damage?" Roger was incredulous. "Tell me what the hell is going on or I'm going to blow your head off!"

The man sighed and stuck his hands in his pockets. He stopped his approach mere inches from the barrel of Roger's weapon.

"Though I'm ashamed to say it, I really don't know why this is happening. My name is Aeric. If you come with me, maybe we can find out."

"I'm not going anywhe—"

Aeric's right hand jerked upward from his pocket and unleashed a handful of silver dust in Roger's face. Roger gasped and turned away, but he inhaled a mouthful of the stuff. It tasted like burnt bread. The world around him spun and went black, and the last thing he remembered as he collapsed was a pointy-eared man slowly prying his shotgun from his paralyzed hands.

— CHAPTER TWO —

C onsciousness slammed into her like a speeding car colliding with a cement wall. A soft moan creaked through her dry, cracked lips. The back of her head throbbed like someone had bashed it with a sledgehammer. Pins and needles quivered through her fingers and toes and flashes of red exploded against the inside of her tightly closed eyelids. She rolled from her back to her side, the hard edges of whatever she was lying on digging through the thin fabric she could feel wrapped around her body. Though her skin was as cold as ice, her insides broiled. Breath came in quick, ragged gasps, and her heart raced so violently she feared it would explode. Her skin tingled with grime and sweat. Her scalp itched at the base of her antlers. Her body was a flurry of frantic activity, but the world beyond was silent.

Something was missing. Something important. Something she shouldn't have been without. Something that called out to her desperately, tragically, begging pathetically to be found, like a child that had wandered too far from its parents in a strange, new place. Something she shouldn't have been able to lose in the first place.

And then she realized what was missing. It wasn't something.

It was *everything*.

She raced through the dark, empty corridors of her mind, searching for any sign of someone or something or sometime. All she found was knowledge. She knew how to walk and talk and eat and sleep, but she had no recollection of ever actually doing any of those things.

And she was pretty sure those antlers weren't supposed to be there.

But then...she found something, faint and ethereal and perhaps beyond her reach. She lunged for it as a drowning man would for a rope, taking it in both hands and clutching it tight so it couldn't escape. It was a name. Her name. *Talora*. It didn't seem to fit; it felt like a nickname, or maybe an alias. But it was all she had, and she wasn't about to let it go.

The physical shock of suddenly popping into the world faded and Talora's body began to calm itself. Her mind, however, picked up the pace, searching the blackness over and over again for any hint that she had ever actually existed. Though she had no other events with which to compare her situation, she sensed intuitively that something strange had happened to her, though she had no clue what. The next logical step would've been to open her eyes and examine her surroundings, but she was afraid. She could feel something terrible lurking out there, something dark and hideous and full of sharp teeth that thirsted for blood. It was watching her. Maybe if she didn't watch it back, it would leave her alone.

A burst of soft laughter wafted through the blackness, warm and reassuring and feminine. It was the sound of a child greeting the ice cream truck, of young lovers reuniting, of a proud father at his daughter's wedding. *Everything is all right,* it seemed to say. *Open your eyes and you'll see.* Talora didn't trust it. It was a trick. It was a trap. She knew better than to fall for such an obvious ploy, even though she couldn't explain how or why she knew better. She pulled her knees up tight to her chest, wrapped her arms around them, and prepared for the worst.

But then someone's fingers snapped. Talora's eyes jerked open like a pair of rubber bands springing back into place. She was in a park, lying on a rickety wooden bench. It was dark, but street lamps spaced every thirty feet or so carved the area into islands of light, one of which surrounded her perch. Asphalt walkways crisscrossed between tall oak trees and patches of impeccably manicured lawn. It was not at all what she was expecting. It was too innocent, too serene. No crickets or frogs, no hooting night birds. The silence was deafening.

Then the laughter returned, a longer burst this time, bringing with it the touch of a cool spring breeze and the sticky-sweet smell of cotton candy. Talora tried to close her eyes, but the muscles that would've hidden the world wouldn't respond.

A dark figure appeared beneath the trees, seemingly materializing from everywhere at once, like a vast cloud of invisible gas coalescing into a single visible solid. A shiver ran up Talora's spine. The grass made odd crunching sounds as the humanoid form slowly sauntered toward the lamp's glow. It was a woman, about six feet tall with a figure like a flagpole. Black hair tumbled to her shoulders in a thick mane. A sleeveless black dress hung loosely from her spare form, covering even her feet. Round eyes darker than the surrounding night stared out from her perfectly proportioned, porcelain-skinned face. She was absolutely beautiful, but something about her wasn't quite right. Though Talora saw no outward reason to be afraid of her, the newcomer's presence made her feel extremely uncomfortable.

The tall woman flashed a bright, sickeningly sweet smile. "You appear to be a bit out of sorts. Have you lost your way?" she asked, her voice soft and reassuring.

"I suppose you could say that," Talora croaked through her parched throat.

"And where are you coming from?" She didn't walk so much as glide, leaving a trail of dead, crinkled grass in her wake.

Talora squirmed as closely to the back of the bench as she could. "I'm not too sure about that part, either." She didn't know why she was talking to this strange woman. She didn't particularly want to, but her lips kept moving. Maybe it was that comforting smile. Maybe it was the feeling that unspeakable things would happen to her if she didn't reply. "I'm not really sure about anything, actually."

The woman clicked her tongue. "No idea where you're coming from and no idea where you're going. Is there anything you do know?"

Talora sat up and leaned forward, her hands clasped tightly between her knees. She stared at the ground, thinking about everything and nothing at the same time. The patch of dead grass beneath the other woman had continued spreading outward. Talora watched as the next row of plants withered and blackened, crackling as they died.

She finally replied with the one and only fact she was absolutely sure of. "Something strange is going on."

The tall woman laughed again. "Honey, you have no idea."

At that unsettling response, Talora felt a small burst of courage. "Who are you?" she asked. "What do you want with me?"

The other woman giggled softly. "You don't remember that, either? My, my, Talora! I'm not sure whether to feel sorry for you or be insulted that our time together meant so little. I'm the Witch. You and I are going to change the world."

The title seemed to fit, but Talora couldn't picture herself working together with this frightening creature. Then again, she had no means of knowing what her own life had been like, how she'd behaved, or what she'd believed in. Maybe she'd been a lot like this Witch. She banished the thought. It was far too unsettling.

"So I'm your partner?" Talora asked. "Your friend?"

The Witch smiled sweetly. "You are a means to an end. Now come along. We have much to do."

"Not until you tell me what happened to me."

"That is not relevant to our current business. Perhaps in time it will be. We really must be going."

But Talora stayed put. The Witch needed her, a fact that seemed to level the playing field. "What's in it for me?"

The Witch raised her eyebrow and smirked. "They don't get you."

"Who's 'they?'"

The smirk became a full-fledged smile. The Witch snapped her fingers and a bright flash of light illuminated the park. Through the glare, Talora could just make out about a dozen shadows ducking for cover behind the trees. Then the light was gone and the world was dark again.

"There's a reason they're keeping their distance, and it's not because you're the one they're afraid of."

Talora jumped to her feet. "Let's go."

The Witch nodded. "Don't worry. When I'm done, they'll be even more scared of you than you are of them."

— CHAPTER THREE —

Roger woke as if from a deep sleep, his thoughts and senses slow and fogged. The world around him was a swirl of color and light, like an oil painting left out in the rain. Voices assaulted his ears, pounding and insistent. Roger blinked, shook his head, and forced his mind to the surface. He immediately wished he hadn't.

"Just let me kill the stupid son of a bitch so we can move on!" bellowed a deep voice Roger would've sworn belonged to some kind of large, predatory cat. Its source was a terrifying young man seated to Roger's left. He wore bright red plate armor, and he'd shaved his head bald and his facial hair into a menacing brown goatee. That lack of hair made the tips of his pointed ears really stand out. When he noticed Roger looking at him, he gnashed his teeth and snarled. "Yes, that means you."

Roger found himself seated at the head of a long table made of luxurious wood. Its grains swirled slowly, amber and cinnamon galaxies floating gently through a chocolate universe. Roger dismissed the movement as an aftereffect of whatever Aeric had thrown in his face. Every other seat at the table was occupied.

To Roger's right, a familiar voice came to his defense. "We shall not stoop to the level of our enemies, Pike," Aeric said calmly, though a vein in his neck pulsed wildly and his face was almost as red as Pike's armor. "We practice what we preach."

The rest of the motley bunch gathered around the long table erupted, some joining Pike in calling for Roger's head, others backing up Aeric's opinion with shouts about morality and fairness. Their voices echoed throughout the largely empty chamber, off the high ceiling and the tiers of ornate seats that rose up and away from the dais on which they sat, a senate without senators. Warm light from a single globe high above lit the chamber in a soft glow.

Roger's eye, however, was inescapably drawn to the ancient, bearded man at the opposite end of the table, to the cool gray gaze he could feel dissecting him. The old man winked and snapped his fingers. Although the participants continued to gesture and move their mouths, the argument around Roger disappeared.

"It's never easy when everyone wants to be heard but no one wants to listen," the old man said slowly, his words crackling like gravel under heavy footsteps. "I'm Aldern. On behalf of the other members of the Combined Council, I welcome you to Evitankari."

Roger glanced uneasily at the aggressive battle raging around him. One old woman had climbed up on her chair to better berate a fat, well-dressed businessman seated opposite her. Pike was busy making slashing motions across his throat. Aeric slammed his fist into the table, causing the wood grains to twirl away from the impact.

Roger leaned forward toward Aldern. "I'm Roger Brooks," he said softly. "What the hell is going on?"

"No need to whisper," Aldern replied. "Just as we can't hear them, they can't hear us." To illustrate his point, the old man stood and pointed at Pike. "Pompous asshole!" he hollered angrily. Pike didn't react, and Aldern sat back down with a smirk.

"That's...um...neat." Truth be told, it was slightly disconcerting.

"Do you know why you're here, Roger?"

He tapped his fingers on the table, watching the grains scatter like leaves in a soft breeze. "No," he said matter-of-factly. "I guess you guys probably want whatever that was that powered up my shotgun. Why didn't Aeric just take it? Why did he have to bring me along?"

Aldern sighed and leaned forward. His beard pooled on the table, a tangled white nest for his craggy face. "If only it were that simple. That shotgun is very special now, but it's only special when you pull the trigger."

"Why's that?"

"Because it's your weapon. The Ether only responds to its host's owner. Like it or not, Roger Brooks, you are our new Pintiri."

Roger didn't like it, and he suspected he'd like it even less if he had any clue what Aldern was talking about. Pike's angry finger was in his face now, so he scooted his chair a few inches further away from the silently raging brute. Pike pressed the attack, spattering Roger's face with sticky spittle. "I take it that's what all the fuss is about," he said as he wiped his cheek with his sleeve.

Aldern shrugged. "Only one thing can separate the Ether from the Pintiri: the Pintiri's death. Your execution will be immediate should we decide you are unfit for duty."

A lump formed in Roger's stomach. He shifted even further away from Pike, feeling every bit the stupid son of a bitch he'd been anointed earlier. He never should've investigated the sounds in the kitchen; he should've hidden in the closet and called the cops. He should've tied his blankets together to form a rope and escaped through the bedroom window to take refuge with the neighbors. He should've loaded his weapon and shot the strange woman in the kitchen on sight. There were a million things he should've done, and as usual he hadn't thought of any of them until they'd become nothing but a useless list of past participles.

"Who are you people?" he asked, straining to be firm as his voice cracked.

"What if I told you that all of the creatures you've been taught were fictitious—things like fairies, nymphs, dryads, trolls, gnomes, demons, and imps—were all real, and that we were in charge of keeping you out of their business so that they could get on with their lives without interference?"

"I'd ask you what the hell a dryad is. Then I'd probably tell you to quit drinking," Roger replied, the words out of his mouth before he could stop them.

He moved quickly to apologize, but he was cut off by Aldern's sharp cackle. "So, I suppose if I told you that we're elves, you'd ask if I were on crack?"

Roger nodded tentatively.

"And if I told you that we choose the best of us to be the Pintiri, the greatest hero in the world— supposedly—and wielder of the most powerful magic in our arsenal, would you page the nurses to have me taken back to my padded room?"

Roger nodded again, more assured of himself this time, though he had no clue where the old elf—if he really was an elf—was going with this train of thought.

Aldern shook his head and sighed. "Typical."

Before Roger could protest, Aldern snapped his fingers again. For a brief moment the argument returned, and then it was squelched as everyone's lips slammed shut—including Roger's.

"When you've lived two hundred and fifty years, you tire of certain inefficiencies," Aldern said slowly.

Pike pulled manically at his lips, his eyes bulging out of their sockets as he struggled to speak. Aeric and the rest merely glared daggers at Aldern.

"You've all had more than your say," the old elf said. "Can we stifle it long enough to take a vote?"

The others all nodded, save Pike. He'd taken to banging his fists on the table, sending all the grains scattering to the opposite end like a herd of frightened animals.

"Good," the old elf replied. With another snap of his fingers, most of the mouths around the table lurched open and gasped for breath. Pike's and Roger's remained shut.

A vote, Roger thought hopelessly, slumping back in his seat and taking a heavy breath through his nose. *Why would any of these people vote for me?*

The voting began to Roger's right. "Mongan Aeric," Aldern said. "Do you confirm Roger Brooks as Pintiri?"

"He deserves a chance," Aeric said, flashing a nervous smile that made Roger feel a little bit better about his situation. "I confirm Roger Brooks as Pintiri."

"One for, zero against," Aldern said. "Council of Intelligence Driff, do you confirm Roger Brooks as Pintiri?"

The bookish-looking elf seated to Aeric's right pushed his spectacles up on his nose. The high collar of his black trench coat formed a wall around his thin neck. He glanced once at Roger, cold and calculating, and then he turned to Aldern. "I do not confirm Roger Brooks as Pintiri."

Roger's heart sank. Although that was only the first vote against him, he knew it wouldn't be the last.

"One for, one against. Council of Economics Granger?"

The next elf shifted uncomfortably in a chair much too small for his massive girth, his pinstriped suit straining to keep his flesh contained. Beads of sweat lined his creased forehead and trickled down his jowls. He dabbed at his face with a silk handkerchief before speaking. "As a group, humans are great for business. Individually...not as much. I do not confirm Roger Brooks as Pintiri."

"One for, two against." Aldern skipped himself, instead naming the ancient crone seated to his right, opposite Granger. "Council of Medicine Chyve?"

She wore a thick white robe of the sort Roger had only seen in bad science fiction movies shown on basic cable. A heavy ruby hung suspended on a golden hoop through each of her ears. Her smile was kindly but hard, like that of a grandmother assessing the latest exploits of a troubled but beloved grandchild.

"All life is sacred," Chyve said slowly. She paused as if daring any of the others to contradict her. Pike rolled his eyes dramatically, his lips still sealed. "I confirm Roger Brooks as Pintiri."

"Two for, two against. Council of Agriculture Piney?"

Next up was a pretty blond woman not much older than Roger's own teenage daughter. Her overalls and flannel shirt were speckled with dirt and dust. She favored Roger with a bright smile and a wink as she cast her vote. "I confirm Roger Brooks as Pintiri."

"Three for, two against. Council of War Pike?"

The large, angry elf responded with a glare, the pulsing blue vein in his red forehead threatening to burst. Beside Roger, Aeric snorted.

"Right," Aldern said, shrugging melodramatically for sarcastic effect. "Three for, three against. That leaves the Council of Sorcery."

Though Roger had done much better than he'd expected, his heart sank when he realized who must be the Council of Sorcery. He hadn't impressed Aldern with his answer about that trolls-and-gnomes nonsense. His fate was sealed—he was sure of it. His breath caught in his throat, his every muscle paralyzed as he awaited the vote that would be his end.

Aldern settled his chin in his skeletal hands and sighed. His gaze swung toward Roger conspiratorially, releasing the spell holding the human's lips shut.

"Roger, do you like pound cake?"

The entire table groaned. Pike stood, lifted his chair, and hurled it over Aldern's head and up into the seating beyond. With a violent crash, it shattered into several pieces against a railing.

Roger couldn't stand pound cake, but he knew a chance to save himself when he saw one. "I love pound cake."

The corners of Aldern's mouth curled upward into a smile. "Excellent."

The others rose to protest, but Roger didn't hear a word of it. Aldern snapped his fingers and the world shifted. What had been a long, lacquered table in an imposing senate was now the simple plastic sort in a small kitchen. The light was softer, streaming into the room between a pair of pale blue curtains hung upon the window above the stainless steel sink. A white refrigerator hummed along at Roger's left, framed by cherry cabinets and blue granite counters. The floor was blue and white tile arranged in a diamond pattern. Aldern was still Aldern, though he seemed unreasonably pleased with himself.

Roger wanted to know what in the hell had just happened, but he didn't dare ask. He took quick stock of his parts and, finding them all intact, steeled himself for whatever strangeness might be next.

"Oh dearest!" Aldern called in the general direction of the framed entry off to his left. "Do we have any pound cake?"

A feminine voice, obviously annoyed and apparently Aldern's wife, shouted back, "No, honey, we don't have any damned pound cake!"

Aldern raised one bushy white eyebrow. "Perfect."

His hands erupted in green flame as he jerked them over his head, a maelstrom of energy gathering in the space between his palms. His eyes rolled back in his head, pure white now. Roger cringed away, fully prepared to make a run for it. The old elf brought his hands together with a sharp clap, dissipating the flames. Reality above the table top shimmered and warped like heat rising off the pavement on a hot day. When things settled and Aldern's eyes rolled back into place, there was a perfectly formed pound cake in the center of the previously empty table.

Roger's jaw dropped.

"Neat, huh?" Aldern said. "Now watch this!"

Aldern reached over to open a nearby drawer and retrieved a large knife. He put it on the table beside the pound cake, then leaned back in his chair and waited expectantly. Roger was about to pick the knife up to cut the cake when the strangest thing happened: the dessert sprouted a cake-y arm, snagged the knife, cut two slices of itself, and laid the knife gently back on the table. The arm melted back into the cake as if it had never existed.

Smiling like a small child, Aldern picked up a slice and took a bite. "Bet you've never seen anything quite like that!"

Roger eyed the cake suspiciously. "That's impossible," he said, regretting the words as soon as they'd left his lips.

"No," Aldern said, stopping to swallow. "Quite the contrary. Are you familiar with the Law of Conservation of Mass and Energy?"

Roger shook his head, thinking it best to be honest.

"Energy can never be created or destroyed, and the amount of mass in an isolated system remains constant in spite of any physical or chemical changes," Aldern said. "I took a bit of mass— the air around my fingertips—mixed it with a bit of my energy, and poof! Pound cake!"

"Magic."

"Indeed. Magic can do many things, Roger, but only within the laws that govern the universe. Go ahead...try a piece. It's perfectly safe."

Roger reached across the table tentatively, nervous that the cake would snatch up that knife and make a try for his fingers. He returned the slice to his mouth safely. As far as pound cake went, it wasn't too bad. He'd had a lot worse.

"The strawberries and cream are built right in," Aldern explained happily. His mustache was flaked with yellow crumbs. "Cuts out the mess and hassle of real strawberries and cream."

Roger nodded, taking another bite. That bit was pretty convenient.

They ate in silence for a few moments. Aldern poked the cake experimentally and it flexed away from his touch. Roger could've sworn he heard it giggling.

"Unfortunately, Roger, life is not all pound cake and strawberries and cream," the old elf said sagely, swatting crumbs from his hands after finishing his slice. The cake reached for the knife again, but Aldern shook his head to dismiss its offer. "Whatever are we to do with you?"

"I'd kind of like to live. I'm sorry about what I said earlier about the fairies and the unicorns—"

"Psshhh," Aldern replied with a wave of his hand. "From a human, that's to be expected. I'm sure today has been hard to swallow."

"All but the pound cake!" Roger said, hoping he didn't sound too fake.

"Ha! You're a poor liar, Roger Brooks, and a welcome change from those rats on the Council," the old elf said with a smirk. "In most cases, that'd be enough to win my favor. But yours is a special situation. There isn't a creature in the world that can stand against the power of the Ether—assuming the Pintiri wields it properly. We elves are a strong, courageous people, but we need our Pintiri desperately. Hence the demon in your house."

Roger leaned forward, the last of his slice forgotten on the table. "There was someone else, before I met the...demon. She asked if I wanted to change the world. I found her in the kitchen. I don't know how she got there, but...she's the one who told me your Ether was in my silverware drawer."

This seemed to pique the old elf's interest. "And how did you answer her question?"

"I told her no." He wondered if he'd be better or worse off had he said yes.

Aldern shifted, apparently uncomfortable for the first time. "And yet you still might. A human Pintiri is no small thing. Tell no one else of this woman, Roger, and put her out of your mind. Some villains are not worth trifling yourself over."

The Council of Sorcery obviously knew more about that strange woman and her stranger request than he was letting on, but Roger let the matter drop. For now, he needed the elf's vote more than he needed answers.

"Tell me, Roger: if she came to you again, with the same offer, how would you respond?"

Roger flicked his gaze to the floor, pondering the possibilities. He felt that this was important, that his life hinged on his response. Aldern had already proven adept at detecting lies; he couldn't embellish too much, and he couldn't just tell the old elf what he thought he wanted to hear. And so he told the truth, crude as it was.

"I'd pick up my magic shotgun and shoot the bitch in the face."

Aldern cackled, a sound like nails on a chalkboard. In the other room, his wife guffawed. Roger blushed, searching vainly for something more intelligent to add and failing miserably. He couldn't tell if he'd saved himself or sealed his own death sentence.

When he finished laughing, Aldern wiped tears from his eyes and motioned for the pound cake to cut another piece of itself. "I do believe you could've won even Pike over with that statement," Aldern said. "I confirm Roger Brooks as Pintiri. That's four for, three against. Welcome to Evitankari, Pintiri Roger Brooks."

Roger couldn't believe it. As the weight of Aldern's words sunk in, a smile slowly spread across his face. He was going to live! "Wait," he said, suddenly nervous again. "We aren't in the—uh—senate...place. Can you do that?"

"It's called the Council Chamber," the elf replied with a friendly wink, taking the slice offered by the cake. "I'm old as dirt, I'm the senior member and thus moderator of the Combined Council, and I can make pound cake appear out of thin air. I can do whatever I want."

Of all the things Roger had seen and heard since waking up, that statement was the easiest to believe.

— CHAPTER FOUR —

Someone—most likely whoever was stalking Talora and the Witch—had shattered the bulbs in all of the park's street lamps. Where there should've been safe, reassuring pools of radiant light there was nothing but a few sharp shards of broken glass hidden in the night. Talora hadn't seen their pursuers since she and the Witch had set off, but a prickling feeling running up and down her spine told her they were still following. The park was too dark and too quiet, and there were far too many convenient places to set up an ambush.

Not that any of that bothered the Witch. She led the way confidently, ethereal in the darkness, whistling a happy tune her new charge didn't recognize. Not once did she slow or glance around. The Witch was almost daring their hidden enemies to attack.

Talora did not approve. Her gaze continually flicked from one shadow to the next. Every few steps she would peer back over her shoulder. She wished the Witch would pick up her pace.

"Relax," the Witch pleaded melodramatically. "They're aggressive, but they're not stupid. They know what will happen if they interfere with my business."

"Your business isn't what I'm worried about."

"Then stick close. If you stray from me, they won't hesitate."

Talora was careful to remain a few paces behind and beside her companion. The way the park's grass had blackened and withered beneath the Witch's feet was still fresh in her mind. Getting too close seemed like a great way to meet a quick, painful death. Still, the malice radiating from the park around them somehow seemed even more dangerous.

"What are they?" Talora asked.

The Witch hesitated for a second. "Pains in the ass."

It was Talora's turn to hesitate. "Are they yours?" It was a dangerous thing to ask, but implicitly trusting her companion could be just as fatal. The suspicion that she was being played had been bouncing around the back of her mind since they left the bench.

"Whatever could I possibly need such creatures for?"

What indeed. Talora wished she could get a straightforward answer. She didn't have the patience to try again. Secrecy was obviously a big part of whatever game the Witch was playing. Talora hated being at such a distinct disadvantage against such an obviously dangerous individual. She wondered where exactly that attitude came from. Was it her subconscious subtly tapping into memories her conscious mind couldn't reach? Had a previous, forgotten experience simply burned it into her brain? Like everything else about her situation, there was no way to know.

A stick snapped to their left. Talora gasped and scurried closer to the Witch.

"Not sure who to be more afraid of?" the Witch asked.

"Something like that."

"My, my, aren't you in a bit of a pickle!"

Talora sighed and shook her head. She couldn't imagine anything more grating than the Witch's faux innocence.

They rounded a thick stand of foliage and the edge of the park finally came into view. There was a city beyond the grass and the trees, its lights ablaze against the encroaching night. Talora was relieved to be heading for civilization. Maybe someone in the city would recognize her. Maybe someone in the city would help her.

Maybe someone in the city was waiting for her.

"Where are we going?" Talora asked.

"Before we can get to the world-changing bit, there are a few people who would like to meet you."

Talora chewed her lip, considering the Witch's answer—and, briefly, the idea of taking off on her own now that they'd made it out of the park. She dismissed that option quickly. Where would she go? How would she know friend from foe? How would she ever figure out what the hell had happened to her? For now, she was along for the ride in a speeding vehicle without windows or doors.

Talora took one final look over her shoulder as she stepped from the park's pristine lawn to the city's cracked asphalt. Where she'd expected to see a horde of shadowy creatures gazing after her there was only thick, lonely darkness. Had they ever really been there in the first place? Had the Witch tricked her somehow? Talora was really tired of not having answers for any of her questions. All the more reason to get whatever the hell they were doing over with as soon as possible.

The Witch turned right and crossed the four-lane street parallel to the park. Slick, polished storefronts trimmed in imitation gold and silver greeted them on the opposite side. No more than four or five stories tall, the squat, square buildings in this strip housed apartments and office spaces above the retail space at street level. Talora got the impression that she should've known where she was, that she'd been in the neighborhood several times before, perhaps even shopped there. She shook her head, frustrated with her inability to make any sense out of the first thing that seemed even remotely familiar.

One building, however, stood out from all the rest. The first three floors were just a boring concrete block, but atop that base the structure abruptly twisted into an organic tendril spiraling toward the sky, ending in a jagged crown of white fingers reaching up to grab the stars. Talora couldn't help thinking it looked as if the spire had somehow sprouted from the normal building. Its irregularly spaced windows were black and faceted, perhaps crystal of some sort. They reminded her of spider eyes.

"Our destination," the Witch said before the question could be asked. "That's where the movers and shakers hide from the people they're moving and shaking."

The building took up an entire block. They crossed toward it at the corner, against the light. There was no traffic, nor were there any other pedestrians.

"Where is everybody?" Talora asked.

"During the day, this area would be teeming with activity, with shoppers eagerly greasing the wheels of an economy they can't comprehend or control. But at night..." The Witch paused for dramatic effect. "...at night, this place is not for the faint of heart."

"What do you mean?"

The Witch sighed. "The most effective way to keep your business private is to scare the shit out of anyone who might come snooping around. Luckily, you and I are not so easily frightened."

"Why not?"

"Because there's nothing in that building either of us needs to be afraid of."

Talora wondered how true that was. She felt like a lamb being led to the slaughter.

The Witch stopped. "Cover one eye with your hand and look up at that building," she said, following her own instructions.

Talora did as she was told. The sight made her gasp; through one eye, the spire was gone and the building appeared the same as every other on the block, glass and concrete and normal. She switched back and forth between one and two eyes a few times, trying one side and then the other, watching the spire transform.

"This is how most people see it," the Witch explained. "But you and I...we've got both eyes open."

They rounded the corner of the building. Twenty feet ahead, a bright red awning trimmed in gold tassels spanned the concrete sidewalk above an equally bright red carpet emblazoned with a gold sunburst around a black letter T. It was the kind of entrance reserved for movie stars, or billionaires, or several dozen other people Talora hoped she was but suspected she wasn't.

A shadow stirred beneath the awning. It stepped into the light, revealing itself as a massive, hulking figure in a black and gold doorman's uniform. It was a man—or at least something that looked like a man. Pale and hairless, his skull and jaw were a little too square. Glistening yellow pupils tracked their approach from underneath his cap. Talora slowed, but the doorman's inhuman gaze didn't bother the Witch. She marched right across the red carpet and stopped in front of the massive glass and gold doors, waiting expectantly for him to do his job. He stayed where he was, motionless, and attempted to burn a pair of holes through her with his hateful yellow glare. The size difference was almost comical.

Talora lingered at the edge of the carpet, feeling nervous and neglected. She couldn't decide which was worse: that the building's guardian seemed hostile to the Witch, or that he hadn't reacted to Talora's appearance at all. Any reaction could've provided a little bit of much-needed insight into her place in the world. In a way, she guessed, maybe she had learned something: the Witch was obviously more of a threat than she was. Talora was somewhat glad she wasn't the only one afraid of the strange woman.

The Witch cleared her throat. The doorman didn't even flinch.

Talora glanced around nervously. She hadn't expected the Witch to be taking her somewhere they might not be welcome. She wondered if the doorman had somehow called for backup and was waiting for it to arrive. "Maybe we should go," she suggested. "Something about this doesn't feel right."

"The warm, heartfelt welcome, perhaps?" the Witch asked.

"Something like that."

"So why don't you ask him to get his manager?"

Talora looked over at the doorman uneasily. He still hadn't moved, and his stare was as intense as ever. "I don't think that will help."

"No, I believe not. A more direct approach is probably best. Shall I start with his fingers or his toes?"

A low, guttural growl rumbled up from the doorman's mammoth chest. His hands twisted into claws and he sprang at his tormentor, ready to rip the fragile woman limb from limb.

But he never got there. An invisible force caught him mid-stride. He was stuck there, motionless and silent. Frozen. The Witch's annoyed frown stretched into a satisfied smile. Talora moved her fingers just to make sure she could. Whatever was happening, its effects seemed to be limited to the doorman. His strange yellow eyes flicked back and forth anxiously as if trying to find a way to free themselves from the prison of his useless body. Those eyes, which mere moments before had burned with anger and aggression, had melted into wells of fear and desperation.

The glass in the building's door made a sharp popping sound. A slender crack had formed at the bottom of the pane and was slowly working its way toward the top, crackling and snapping ominously as it branched off into seemingly random directions.

"Hey, Talora," the Witch said mischievously. "Want to see something cool?"

Unsure sure how to answer, Talora kept silent. She knew this wasn't going to be pretty.

The crack reached the top of the door and the pane shattered, but the glass shards didn't fall. Like the doorman, they hovered mysteriously in the night, suspended by some unseen force—the Witch's magic, Talora assumed. The shards twinkled gently in the soft light that spilled out of the marble hallway beyond. Talora would've thought it pretty if she hadn't deduced what was coming.

The Witch turned her attention back to the doorman. She curled her lip and returned his earlier snarl. Then the razor-sharp shards of glass tore through the night and pummeled the doorman's broad back like machine gun fire. Streams of blood oozed out around the glass as his yellow eyes rolled back in his head.

Talora gasped and looked away. She didn't see the corpse hit the sidewalk, but she heard the sickening thud it made on impact, followed by her companion's eerie giggle.

"And I had such a large tip ready, too," the Witch muttered as she stepped through the remains of the door. "Come on. Show's over—for now."

But Talora stayed right where she was, eyes closed, jaw clenched. Now she knew what she was dealing with. Here was a woman with an agenda, with a means of accomplishing anything she desired, and with the selfishness to remove anyone or anything that dared attempt to hinder her. There was a damn good reason this strange woman was called the Witch. The realization made Talora want to run very far and very fast.

With flight on her mind, she glanced back the way they had come. A pair of dark shadows, aware they'd been spotted, ducked back around the corner of the building. They were still being followed.

Talora took a deep breath and headed for the door, hoping desperately that she'd made the right choice.

— CHAPTER FIVE —

The conversation had shifted back to magic, the location to Aldern's mad laboratory of a garage. Roger examined an array of crooked, mismatched shelves attached helter-skelter to the wall beside the door to Aldern's kitchen. Each shelf was packed with glass, plastic, and metal vessels of all shapes and sizes. There were carafes of pink clouds, test tubes of bubbling leather, beakers of glittering purple snow, and all manner of other containers of random stuff Roger couldn't put a name to, all coated in a thin layer of dust and occasional spiderwebs. A pair of red eyes floating in a vial of blue liquid watched him back.

"Can all of you elves make things appear out of thin air?" Roger asked.

"We all have different skills," Aldern replied, darting across the garage to a wooden workbench littered with tools Roger didn't recognize—a spring attached to an articulating handle, a giant spoon covered in rasping blades, three cross-hinged braces tipped with toothbrush bristles. "Our propensity for magic determines the courses of our lives. Elves that can make things grow become farmers. Those that can use their magic to perform great feats of strength become warriors. Some, like me, can do a bit of everything to varying degrees of success." He whipped a drawer open and began rummaging through a pile of yellowed papers, muttering unintelligibly under his breath. One page, folded in the shape of a butterfly, flitted out and up toward the white plaster ceiling.

"That explains the 'Council of Sorcery,' 'Council of War,' bit," Roger replied as he stared at what appeared to be a miniature sun in a tiny glass box. A picture of elven society had begun to form in his mind. It looked kind of like the settings in those dystopian young adult novels his daughter liked. "But what about Granger? The Council of Economics?"

Frustrated, Aldern tossed the papers over his shoulder, scattering them across the concrete floor. He swatted at the paper butterfly as it dipped down in front of his face, but it was too quick. "Numbers have a magic all their own, as do complex social systems and large masses of individuals. Many of Granger's people possess empathic abilities that aid them in their additional duties as diplomats and negotiators."

Roger nodded. A ceramic canister belched at him. "And why are you all 'Councils' and not 'Councilors?'"

"Waaaaaay back when, each Council was made up of dozens of Councilors. It's become custom to elect one person to simultaneously fill every seat on each of the individual Councils. Hence, I am in fact an entire Council unto myself."

"And Aeric? What's a Mongan?"

"Next in line to be Pintiri. The Mongan is given a seat and a full vote on the Combined Council as a means of preparing him for his future role."

"And the Pintiri?"

"A figurehead, primarily, but one whose voice typically carries significant weight because his election is the only one in which everyone has a vote regardless of caste. You get a vote in the Combined Council, but your main duty is to heroically point that weapon wherever we tell you to. Sometimes you get to lead a parade or attend a diplomatic function."

"That's a relief." Roger couldn't see himself as a big shot politician with meetings and files and constituents. "I was worried I'd have to be like the president or a judge or something like that."

"What your backwards republic might consider executive or judicial responsibilities fall upon the senior member of the Council," Aldern replied with a smile. "Me."

A pair of lips in a purple vial threw itself against the glass in an attempt to kiss Roger. He shuddered and moved on to a bookcase in the corner. Thick, ancient tomes lined the shelves, their bindings split and their covers flaking away. Some were bound in leaves, others in material that looked suspiciously like human—or maybe elven—skin. The titles were verbose and complex, and Roger couldn't make sense of them: "On the Efficacies of Transmutation," "Pyromancy vs. Geomancy: A Treatise on Elemental Defense Mechanisms," "Spontaneous Regeneration through Divination." At the end of one shelf, a crystal ball glowing with eerie purple energy served as a bookend.

"My house burned down," Roger said, his memory jogged by a title that seemed to have something to do with fire. "Someone would've called my wife. I need to let her know I'm all right." *Or about as all right as I can be while surrounded by psychopaths,* he thought.

The old elf had grabbed a net with a long handle and was using it to chase the paper butterfly across the ceiling. "Your family will be perfectly safe," he said between clenched teeth. "We're bringing them to Evitankari. They are too valuable to your enemies to leave where they are."

Despite his relief at hearing of his family's safety, Roger swallowed in a suddenly dry throat. "Enemies?" He'd never had enemies before.

"That strange woman you met, for one," Aldern replied, tossing aside his useless net. With a magical wave of his hand he sent a hammer flying at the butterfly, but the agile piece of paper dodged again. Roger sidestepped the hammer on its way back down. He cast a wary eye toward the garage door, just in case Aldern decided to bring the whole place down to catch his quarry. "But there are others," the Council of Sorcery continued. "Demons, several dozen species of fairy creatures, the few humans that know of us, and many, many others that only call Evitankari an ally when they suspect we can hear them."

"Wait...humans?"

"Aye," Aldern said. "We do our best to keep you people out of everyone's business, but there are always a persistent few who slip through the cracks. Can't dust every human that learns the truth about his or her place in the world. Ah, to Axzar with this!" He raised his left hand, fingertips splayed, and launched a blast of green lightning toward the ceiling. The paper butterfly's wings erupted in green flame, flapping pitifully as it plummeted to the concrete. The blast left a dark, butterfly-shaped burn in the otherwise white ceiling.

Roger poked the charred paper cautiously with the toe of his slipper. It occurred to him then that he was still in his pajamas and robe and probably smelled of urine. He must've looked a bit silly back in the Council Chamber. "And just what is our place in the world?"

The Council of Sorcery sighed as he stooped to pick up the black paper, taking it gingerly between his thumb and forefinger so as not to ruin it further. "Depends on who you ask," he said slowly, one eyebrow cocked. Roger could tell he was about to be judged again. "Some look at you as the foundation, the rock upon which the rest of us have built our societies. All of the manufactured goods we rely upon, all of the markets in which our money moves and grows, all of the scientific innovation that makes our lives easier—it all comes from humanity." Aldern yanked open the valve on a rusted old spigot above a square steel basin and tossed the burned note into the rushing water. "For instance, I got this sink from Home Depot—on sale!"

"It's very nice," Roger replied.

"Then there are others that look at you as just a herd of cattle: living at our whim, serving our needs, dying when we say it's your time. To them, you're just numbers that decrease costs and increase productivity and provide a soft cushion for the rest of us. It's mostly just the demons that think that way, but as in your own culture, we all have varying opinions."

Roger leaned back against the bookshelf, digesting Aldern's words. He wasn't quite sure what to make of all this. It sounded like something out of a bad conspiracy theory. Secret societies, hidden cities, demons and fairies and magic...it was nuts. Roger had always been one to believe in the things he could see and feel, reliant upon truth backed by irrefutable evidence. To think that such things had been concealed from him—and not just from *him*, but from *everybody*—was a bitter pill to swallow.

"But how do you keep yourselves hidden?" Roger asked. And then, more sharply, "*Why* do you keep yourselves hidden?"

Aldern rolled up his sleeve and reached into the sink. The paper in his fingers was whole once again, the charred bits repaired but a bit soggy. As he shook it dry, his hand glowing red with soft heat, he closed the valve to stop the water.

"The how is narii dust, a fun bit of magic powder that can be directed to block neural connections in your brain. We add a bit of it to the water supply and most of you are given a whiff at birth to proactively eliminate a few nasty truths." When Roger opened his mouth to protest, Aldern dismissed him with a wave of his hand. "Segregating a few neurons is nothing. Most of the other species prefer to kill any humans who stumble into their business. There are things you simply don't need to know, so we don't let you know them."

Roger's jaw dropped. He couldn't believe the nerve of these people. Who were they to decide what humanity could and couldn't know? That went doubly so when one considered their admitted dependence on human industry and science.

Aldern blew the last few droplets of moisture off the paper butterfly and shook it out like one might a wet bath towel. "The why...now that's trickier. To say that it's just the way things have always been done is not to tell the full truth, but it is the simplest explanation. Tell me, Roger: how would your people receive me were I to stand up in their town square and declare myself an elf, and perhaps spontaneously generate a pound cake for your leader?"

"They'd lock you up," he said timidly. "You'd be making pound cake for prison guards in white uniforms and armies of psychiatrists." He was embarrassed by the truth of it, by the ignorance and fear he knew to be hallmarks of his people. And yet another part of him couldn't get over the thought of humanity as *his people*. It was strange to think of *other people* and in doing so mean not the citizens of another nation or the faithful of another religion but another sort of intelligent being altogether. Being part of a species finally mattered more than being American, a lapsed Catholic, or a Boston Red Sox fan. It was weird.

Nodding gravely, the old elf seemed to understand. "And if, in making my appearance, I were to be attacked by a demon—a terrible, black thing hellbent on killing all those who'd come to see me—and in defeating that demon my magic leveled an entire city block?"

"They'd have your head, and they'd probably hunt the rest of you down."

"And that is why we hide ourselves. In large groups, you are reactionary and violent, easy prey for demagogues and those who would lead you astray. The world was once a complete community,

Roger, but time and time again your people proved incapable of participating in it properly."

"I don't completely believe that," Roger replied, "and it sounds like your kind is just as reactionary."

Aldern shrugged. "That is likely true. We can endlessly debate the original decision to hide ourselves from humanity, but we lost our chance to undo it generations ago. You die quickly but breed like rabbits, yet we live for centuries and may produce only two or three children. There are so many of you, yet precious few of us, and there are even fewer places that we call home."

Roger chewed on his lip. For a moment, he felt guilty; humanity, *his people*, had spread from one corner of the globe to the other, settling in any and every habitable corner. What right did they have? Who said they could have it all? Then again, it's not like they knew there were other intelligent species with whom they might need to share the planet. He knew none of what Aldern spoke of was his fault. He was just Roger Brooks, husband and father and janitor, and he was just getting by and living his life. He had more important things to worry about: namely his family and whatever was left of his home.

"But enough talk of the past and of things neither of us can change," Aldern said as he studied the restored page dangling loosely from his skeletal hand. "We've a new Pintiri, and his Council Chamber is closed to him merely because he lacks magic of his own. Luckily I've got just the thing!"

He brushed past Roger to examine the collection of strange containers, humming merrily to himself as he searched for the right one. He slid out a red vessel filled with tiny bat wings, checked the paper, slid it back in, then drew out another in which a flock of miniature sheep hung suspended like clouds in a deep green sky. "You aren't allergic to wool, are you?" the old elf asked as he once again strolled past Roger toward a heavy chest opposite the bookshelf.

"No, wool's fine," he muttered. "So, I'll be able to snap my fingers and go places, like you?"

Chuckling, Aldern flung open the top of the chest, releasing a puff of acrid gray dust. He coughed and waved it away from his face. "Very, very few people can snap their fingers and go places. The Council Chamber is one of the most secure rooms on the planet. Physically, we don't even know where it is. It could be somewhere in Evitankari, it could be on the bottom of the ocean—it could be in your basement for all we know. We Council members can 'think' ourselves there. If I'm in Evitankari and I decide I want to go to the Council Chamber, well, that's where I find myself, but only because my elven blood has been added to its complex system of wards and protections. Those of us with access can bring guests, but we can't be coming to get the Pintiri every time we need to convene." He reached into the chest, rummaged about, and retrieved an empty hourglass framed in thick, twisting oak. He moved to the workbench and the chest's lid thudded shut behind him.

"I thought you said the Pintiri possessed the greatest magic in the world," Roger said.

Aldern popped the rubber stopper off the top of the green vial and poured its contents through a one-way valve in the top of the hourglass. The green liquid congealed in the uppermost chamber but did not flow down through the narrow opening to the chamber below. Roger thought he heard a soft "baaaaaaaa-aaa!" When the vial was empty, Aldern sealed the hourglass and flipped it over. The contents of the vial, now in the bottom, began to flow upward into the top, turning into a fine pink mist as it passed between chambers.

"Different magics do different things," Aldern explained, watching the hourglass intently. "This magic will get you into the Council Chamber. The Ether will blow holes through your enemies and just about anything else—including the door to the Council Chamber, if we knew where we could find it."

Roger really couldn't believe that the elves had lost an entire senate. As he opened his mouth to say so, the last of the green mixture became pink haze. Aldern snatched up a rusted old monkey wrench and shattered the hourglass with one surprisingly violent stroke, covering the workbench with glistening crystals.

A pinky in each side of his mouth, Aldern unleashed a sharp whistle. What was left of the pound cake bounded into the garage on stubby little cake legs a few moments later, knife in hand. The cake hopped up onto the workbench and cut a slice of itself, upon which Aldern promptly sprinkled a few bits of shattered hourglass. Then he spat on the thing, his saliva turning to light blue icing when it hit. He took the final product in both hands and presented it to Roger.

"Eat," he instructed, leaning a little too close for the human's comfort, "and then we'll need a few toenail clippings to spread across the Chamber floor."

Roger took one incredulous look at the pound cake and shook his head. "There's glass and spit in that."

Aldern frowned. The earth suddenly shook. Roger stumbled and almost lost his balance as a terrible crash sounded from somewhere outside. He raised his hands defensively and took a few tentative steps away from the Council of Sorcery.

"That wasn't me," Aldern said. The ground shook again briefly, then again, and again. "Footsteps," he added softly.

It briefly occurred to Roger to ask what kind of creature takes footsteps that cause earthquakes, but he quickly realized he didn't want to know. The ghostly pallor of Aldern's face didn't help Roger's nerves.

The old elf dropped the slice of pound cake and snatched up the remote door opener from a shelf by the workbench. A quick press of the button and the motor hanging from the ceiling whirred to life. Roger's gaze was glued to the slowly rising door, his throat constricting tighter with every inch of terrifying daylight that squeezed its way inside. The door stopped halfway up and the motor unleashed a sharp whine. Aldern banged the remote against the workbench to no effect. Cursing, he hurled it across the room and raised his hands. "Fucking technology," Roger thought he heard the elf mutter as he whipped his arms forward in a gesture of obvious magical power. Metal squealed briefly on metal, then the entire garage door tore off its moorings and rocketed into the sky beyond. Aldern led Roger out into the driveway, the two of them walking gingerly as the ground continued to shake.

Aldern's little white house sat atop a steep hill on what Roger judged to be the southern outskirts of Evitankari. The elven capital was a green, rolling city with pockets of wooden buildings interspersed between lazy hills and thick forests and sprawling meadows crisscrossed with narrow brown streets. Evitankari had a rather suburban feel, organic and calm, its inhabitants living in concert with nature rather than bending it to their will. It was the kind of view Roger could've enjoyed for hours with a lawn chair and a beer—if there wasn't a very large, very ugly man spitting fire and stomping on houses halfway across the city. Aldern's garage door slammed into a stand of trees at the bottom of the hill with a loud bang.

"Holy shit!" Roger shouted, pointing. In the distance, a massive humanoid stomped angrily about a cluster of smaller buildings. "That's a giant! Am I really seeing that?"

The elf's brow scrunched in fury, his cheeks turning suddenly red. "It's not what we're seeing that I'm concerned about," he snarled. "It's what we aren't."

A snap of Aldern's fingers and a flash of light later, the pair stood atop a flat rooftop somewhere else in the city. Roger coughed against the thick smoke rising from dozens of small fires. To their right, a cottage blazed, a black wraith consumed in flame. Aldern paid it no heed, staring instead at the charred ruins across the street to their left. What looked to be the base of a tower lay burned and shattered, ringed in embers and rubble that had once been the upper floors. People cried out below, some to ask for help, others to reassure those that aid was on its way.

Aldern began to shake, his lip quivering. Roger kept his distance, unsure of what to do or say or how he was going to get off that roof. They were only four stories high, but that was still a heck of a drop. He watched the Council of Sorcery nervously. Had someone Aldern cared about been in that tower? Did it have some personal meaning to him? Roger wished he knew, and he wished he had the words to help the eccentric old elf who'd been so kind to him.

Something behind them roared. Roger flinched against the bone-rattling force of the thunderous sound and reluctantly turned to face it. Aldern had dropped them a scant few blocks from the rampaging giant. It was a terrible creature: seven stories of leather and callus, hairless and naked. He watched in terror as it slammed a six-fingered hand through the roof of a defenseless home, smashing it like a man would a fly. The giant reared back and roared, its eyes red and evil, its sharp teeth the size of Roger's car. Smoke streamed steadily from its nostrils.

"Oh hell," Roger muttered. He'd never been so scared of another living thing in his entire life. He couldn't tell what frightened him more: that such creatures actually existed, or that somehow the elves had managed to hide them from humanity.

Aldern stepped up beside Roger, his gray eyes manic. He pointed a skeletal finger at something behind and above Roger. "See that thing?" he shouted. Roger felt a familiar weight appear in his hands: his family's old shotgun. "Kill the son of a bitch!" Aldern instructed.

He didn't hesitate. The shotgun flipped up to his shoulder as if of its own accord. A squeeze of the triggers sent a pair of blue fireballs rocketing through the sky and into the giant's thick skull. The beast wobbled for a second, then a puff of blue smoke wheezed through its nose, mouth, and ears, and its head exploded in a shower of thick black blood and green gore. Roger raised the side of his bathrobe up over his head to shield himself from the disgusting shower of ichor. By his side, Aldern's fingertips glowed a deep green as he gently lowered what was left of the giant's lifeless body to a safe place in the cobblestone street.

"Well done, Roger," the Council of Sorcery said, his task complete. He took a moment to scan the carnage, sighing heavily. "Now tell me: what's strange about this attack?"

Other than the fact that it was perpetrated by a giant, an answer didn't immediately strike Roger. He stroked his chin as he examined the scene: dozens of burning homes, the ruins of the tower, elves scurrying throughout the carnage, the untouched city beyond it all. "We're in the middle of Evitankari," he suggested. "How did that giant get here without leaving a clear trail to where it came from?"

Aldern nodded sagely. "That, Pintiri, is what I'd like to know."

— CHAPTER SIX —

Any doubt in Talora's mind that the owners of the building were powerful and important evaporated the moment she stepped into the lobby. What it lacked in size it more than made up for in opulence. The white marble floor glittered under the bright lights cut into the mirrored ceiling. Waterfalls rushed down the walls on either side, illuminated here and there with green and blue and yellow hues Talora couldn't identify the source of. A donut-shaped security desk made of the same rugged black stone as the walls was the only thing between the entrance and the golden elevator at the far end of the lobby. The starburst insignia on the building's exterior was also carved into the front of that desk, this time above a single word: Tallisker. Clad in dirty rags and crusted with all manner of unidentifiable filth, Talora couldn't possibly have felt more out of place.

The Witch looked back at her and smiled. "Anyone who's ever claimed that evil doesn't pay obviously has never dealt with my associates."

Talora hesitated slightly before asking her next question. She wasn't completely sure she wanted to know the answer. "If your associates are evil, what does that make you?"

"Pissed off."

The Witch led the way around the stone donut toward the elevator. It struck Talora as odd that the security desk was empty. Glancing back over her shoulder, she found a rather frightened looking young woman peering up over the edge of the desk at them. The receptionist dove back below when she realized she'd been spotted. Talora couldn't blame her. Thus far they'd been greeted with open hostility and downright fear, neither of which made sense if the owners of the building were in business with the Witch. Something had obviously gone wrong with their relationship.

The golden elevator doors slid open slowly at their approach, revealing an interior that was a small reproduction of the lobby, complete with stone walls and another Tallisker starburst in the floor. Three lines of gold buttons to the left of the door granted access to each of the building's 100 stories. The Witch pushed the button for the top floor, the doors eased shut, and the elevator slipped soundlessly upward. Talora shifted uneasily, unsure of what to do or where to look. Though she had plenty of questions to ask the Witch or, for that matter, anyone who seemed even remotely willing to listen, she kept her mouth shut. Any answer from her present company would probably confuse and frustrate her even more.

A bell dinged softly to announce they'd reached the second floor. Talora was pretty sure she wasn't an expert on elevators, but this one seemed to be moving extremely slowly. At the rate they were traveling, it would've taken them half an hour to reach their destination, even without stopping to pick up any other passengers. That didn't seem right. Tallisker, she assumed, was fucking with them.

Bored, her eyes drifted to the mirrored ceiling. The woman staring back down at her would've been pretty, she supposed, if she didn't look like she'd spent the last month sleeping in a dumpster. Layers of dingy, tattered clothing hung from her body like late autumn leaves on a tree. She self-consciously pulled a stray strand of her long blond hair back from her dirt-streaked face. Nothing would've made her feel better than a hot shower and a change of clothes.

The bell rang again as they reached the third floor, then soon after when they reached the fourth and the fifth. The elevator was accelerating. Talora was pretty sure that elevators weren't supposed to do that—although without any memories of previous elevator rides, she wasn't sure how she knew that. Six, seven, and eight came in rapid succession. The bell chimed rapid fire, like a slot machine ringing up a jackpot. The Witch didn't look the slightest bit concerned. She stood in the corner with her eyes closed and her arms crossed tightly across her chest, softly humming a merry tune Talora didn't recognize.

Seventeen, eighteen, nineteen. The lights dimmed and flickered, casting a surreal pall upon the gold walls. Talora stumbled to the control panel and punched the buttons for twenty-two, twenty-seven, and thirty-three. The elevator blew right through all of her selections.

The bell popped and snapped at forty-five. The repetitive chime became one constant, ear-twisting squeal. The Witch's humming grew louder in response. Somehow, she'd managed to project her voice a bit above the howling speakers, as if in protest of the harsh sound.

At sixty-seven, Talora decided there was a good chance that she was going to die. She was convinced the elevator would shoot straight up through the roof of the building and never come back down. She did the only thing she could think to do: she got down on her hands and knees, curled up in the corner, closed her eyes, and covered her ears.

"Don't get too comfortable," the Witch said. "We're almost there."

Talora wanted to scream at the her. Why wasn't the Witch concerned? Why hadn't she used her terrible powers to make the elevator slow down or stop? Or was she the one behind its wild acceleration? Was she playing some sick game? Was the Witch taking perverse pleasure from Talora's terror?

The elevator finally screeched to a halt. The momentum of their ascent launched Talora six or seven feet into the air. She landed hard on the floor in an angry tangle of limbs and ragged clothing. Her shoulder ached a little, but everything appeared to be intact. Although there were plenty of things she wanted to say to the Witch about high-speed elevator rides, she held her tongue. She didn't want to prompt the strange woman to make something worse happen.

The Witch smiled down at her. "That wasn't me. When I want to mess with someone, I do it with a little more style."

Talora wasn't sure whether to be relieved or worried, but at least the bell had stopped its awful squealing. "Why haven't the doors opened yet?"

The Witch wrinkled her little nose as if she'd smelled something rancid. "Because they think they can get a reaction out of us. They want to hear you try to beat down the door and they want to see me blow a hole in it. But they'll get no such pleasure, will they?"

Talora stood and smoothed out her rags in a useless attempt to make herself presentable. She could empathize with the Witch's defiant attitude.

"Good girl," the Witch whispered. "You very well may be the beginnings of something useful."

She hoped the Witch didn't see her shiver.

The masters of the building apparently knew when they'd been beaten. The bell chimed a healthy tone and the golden doors slid open. The Witch stepped around Talora and led the way out of the elevator.

The one hundredth floor of the massive skyscraper was a small Japanese tea house, its walls made of white paper pulled taut across black lattice. Strands of red and green paper lanterns criss-crossed the ceiling between thick wooden beams. Four men in sharply pressed business suits sat on maroon cushions around a low, long table in the center of the room, each with his own cup of tea and plate of sushi. A petite geisha in white makeup and a tight red kimono waited like a statue in the far corner of the room. The four men—if they could legitimately be called men—greeted their visitors with furious scowls.

"We were just talking about you," said the man at the head of the table. The mass of wrinkles on his face betrayed him as quite a bit older than the others. While his two brown eyes tracked the Witch, the big red one in the middle of his forehead examined Talora.

The Witch clicked her tongue in disdain. "I thought my ears were burning! I'm flattered, Demson."

"Don't be," replied the man to Demson's left. He was easily the youngest at the table. Talora found him handsome despite the pair of short, sharp horns sprouting from his forehead. "You've got a lot of nerve showing up here. Why don't you tell us what happened to Trinko?" Though he spoke to the Witch, his eyes were on Talora. There was a hint of familiarity there, she thought, that both fright-ened and intrigued her.

"What happened to Trinko?" the Witch asked. "Nothing bad, I hope. Out of all your mindless lackeys, that one was definitely my favorite." She approached the head of the table slowly, coyly, almost like a young girl afraid to ask a boy to dance. Talora stuck close.

"The plan failed," the horned man replied, his soft eyes still on Talora. "And it's your fucking fault."

The Witch stopped so suddenly that Talora almost walked into her back. "If you're going to accuse me of something, get it over with," she snarled.

"Crim speaks out of turn," Demson interjected. "We merely wish to know where you were and what you were doing last night." Though he was clearly attempting to maintain the peace, the threat inherent in his tone and expression was unmistakable.

"As usual, I was up to no good," the Witch replied casually. "Now tell me what horrible fate befell poor Trinko."

"The new Pintiri killed her," explained the man to Crim's left. His skin appeared to be made out of stone.

"Aeric?" the Witch asked. "Why the hell did you send someone dumb enough to get killed by that dork?"

The stone-skinned man shook his head. "Someone else. Aeric dusted him and took him back to Evitankari before our operatives could get a closer look. But whoever he was, he knew what he was doing. Blew a hole clean through Trinko's chest."

The Witch giggled. "The man sounds quite dangerous."

"You promised us the Ether," Crim growled. "I'm sure you realize how much of a setback this is."

The Witch tapped her chin thoughtfully. "I suppose you should have sent someone qualified, rather than someone too stupid to think on her own."

"How dare you!" shouted the man across from Crim. His mouth was a cluster of razor-sharp fangs. A forked tongue flicked out between his lips before he continued. "After all we've done for you—"

"Yes, yes, the endless supply of minions has been quite nice," she replied dismissively. "I've no more need for cannon fodder. And things haven't turned out nearly as badly for you as you may think—if you would, in fact, stop being evil, raging bastards long enough to realize it."

"As always, you make absolutely no sense," Crim snarled.

"Think about it. The elves sent Aeric to recover the Ether, but someone else got to it first. Do you have any idea how much that's going to twist Evitankari's collective knickers? They'll be lucky if half the population doesn't die of an immediate aneurysm when news gets out."

"And what if the elves kill him to release the Ether again?" Crim asked with a smirk. "Maybe they already have. Whoever he is, he won't be much of a distraction if he's dead."

The Witch shook her head. "They haven't killed him yet. You know as well as I do that the Council wouldn't pick its own nose without talking about it for a few days first. Besides, our preliminary attacks will ensure that they won't have a choice. If they kill the Pintiri, it'll be another week before the Ether manifests itself again. They won't risk being without it with the threat of another attack looming in the shadows. Whoever he is, they'll have to work with him."

"Which does us no good," Demson said. "Despite what we did to Rotreego, Evitankari will still have its Pintiri."

"Evitankari will have *a* Pintiri, but not *its* Pintiri." The Witch smiled brightly. "That's an important difference. Might be I can persuade him to our cause—or at least mess with his head to the point he's completely turned around."

"That might work out," said the man with the stone skin. "If the elves think they're in control of the Ether, they'll be less likely to raise other defenses."

"Everyone has a price, eh?" Demson asked, beaming at the Witch. "That's the Tallisker spirit!"

She shook her head. "Not necessarily. But most people possess something they couldn't stand to lose."

Talora had no clue what any of the people around her were talking about. She got the impression that ignorance was probably bliss in this case, though she wondered how much longer that blessed state would last.

"As always, my dear, your perspective is as refreshing as it is informative," Demson said respectfully. Crim didn't bother to hide his grimace. "Kyoko! Tea for our guest of honor!"

The geisha bowed softly, then disappeared through a door that blended seamlessly into the wall.

Demson turned his attention to Talora. She could feel his third eye boring through her, its gaze red and penetrating. "Please, have a seat," he instructed, indicating a pair of empty cushions at the opposite end of the table. "All of this must be terribly confusing."

The Witch nodded to Talora and waved her on. She did as instructed, walking quickly and plopping herself onto the soft cushion. Finally getting off her feet again was a welcome luxury. She sat up straight and clenched her hands together in her lap, prim and proper despite her rags. Relaxing and letting her guard down around these people seemed like a bad idea. The Witch settled gracefully onto her own cushion at Talora's side.

"Tallisker thanks you for your commitment, my dear," Demson continued warmly. "Thanks to you we will finally be rid of those meddlesome elves."

Talora didn't like the sound of that. "You're welcome."

"We've all heard so much about you. Do you have a name?" asked the man with the fangs.

"Talora."

The four men cringed as if they'd been struck. Crim snarled a string of unintelligible epithets. Demson shook his head and glared at the Witch. "I warned you about playing games with us," he said calmly, like a disappointed dad.

Talora sank down into her cushion, wishing she could disappear. She liked her name even less than when she first remembered it. It seemed to have once belonged to someone infamous, someone who'd done Tallisker wrong. Had it been given to her specifically to rile up Demson and the others? Had she chosen it for herself with that in mind?

The soft sound of sliding wood punctured the awkward silence. The geisha reappeared from another hidden door. She bore two white teacups on a small silver tray.

"That name is heard so rarely nowadays," the Witch said thoughtfully. "Someone ought to carry it on, and she seemed appropriate given the circumstances."

So the Witch named me, Talora thought. In that case, there was no doubt her name was intended to evoke a strong response.

"That someone need not be one of us," snarled the man with the forked tongue. "A worse blasphemy, I've not heard." *One of us?* What the hell did that mean?

The geisha deposited a cup on the table before Talora and bowed deeply. Then she shuffled slowly to the corner of the room, stopping and turning to await further instructions with her face placid and her hands clasped primly before her. Talora saw no reason not to take advantage of their hosts' hospitality. She was a bit parched, and the tea smelled sweet and refreshing. She reached down and picked up the cup.

"Put that down." The Witch spoke so calmly and yet so forcefully that Talora couldn't help but obey. "My dear Demson, I'm disappointed that you let one of them infiltrate your ranks so deeply."

Demson glanced curiously at the geisha, then back to the Witch. "One of who?"

She smiled like she knew an interesting secret she wasn't supposed to know. "They raided your arms warehouses in Ghana and Indonesia. They've taken down three of your last four planes running cocaine out of Bogota. They set fire to your casino in Montreal and they blew up Crim's summer home in the Hamptons—"

"Minor annoyances!" Demson snapped. "The perpetrators of which lack both the means and the intelligence to infiltrate this circle."

The Witch raised one thin eyebrow. "Sure about that?"

A small flame erupted from between the floorboards in front of the geisha. It split in two and traced a circle around the surprised woman's feet. She squeaked pathetically, then asked Demson something in Japanese.

"Don't worry, my dear," he responded. "She wouldn't dare harm you here."

"I take it no one's informed you that you need a new doorman?" the Witch asked playfully. "Oh, and by the way, he was one of them, too."

The flames leapt toward the ceiling with a sharp whoosh, but they still didn't touch the geisha. Her features began to soften like they were made of putty and her white skin soon became reflective silver.

"What—what is this?" Demson asked, incredulous. "One of your tricks, Witch?"

The geisha cut off the Witch's response in a deep, terrible voice. "We know what you are planning, and we will see to it that you don't succeed. You and all those who stand with you shall die horrible deaths at our hands."

The Witch rolled her eyes and mimicked a speaking mouth with one hand. "Blah-blah-blah, doom and gloom and empty threats, blah-blah-blah."

And then the circle of flame collapsed in on the thing that had once been a geisha, closing around her like fingers clenching into a fist. The silver humanoid screamed once and then it was no more, just a puddle of silver goo seeping away from the dying fire like mercury escaping a thermometer. Talora and the four Tallisker men stared at it in shock.

The Witch stood up and clapped her hands merrily. "Our work here is done. See you at Jackson's retirement party next week! I hear there's going to be cake."

Before Demson could reply, the world around Talora twisted and melted. Only the Witch remained solid and firm, rolling her eyes and sticking her tongue out at the blob that only moments ago had been a demonic businessman. When reality thickened again,

Talora and the Witch were outside on the sidewalk opposite the terrible tower.

"Fucking idiots," the Witch snarled.

"What was that all about?" Talora asked, her head spinning.

"Just peeling back a few layers," the Witch replied as she took Talora's arm and led her away. "We want those Tallisker fucks good and riled up!" *Of course we do,* Talora thought as she stumbled to keep pace. *What a great idea...*

— CHAPTER SEVEN —

Roger, we should move you somewhere safe until we've got a better understanding of what's happened here," Council of Sorcery Aldern said sadly.

Part of Roger thought that was a great idea, but he also sensed an opportunity to make a great first impression. Not that his altruism was completely opportunistic; he'd always entertained thoughts of pulling through in tough situations, although he'd rarely faced anything more threatening than a clogged toilet or a teenaged daughter who'd broken curfew. "There's a lot of people down there who need help," he said. "Isn't the Pintiri supposed to be some kind of hero? Take me with you."

Aldern arched an eyebrow in surprise or perhaps admiration. He didn't waste time arguing. A quick snap of his fingers teleported them down to the street beside Mongan Aeric and Council of Medicine Chyve. The Council of Sorcery strolled purposefully into the smoldering ruins of the fallen tower's base.

Aeric clapped a strong, reassuring hand on Roger's shoulder to stop him from following. The elf jerked his head toward a pile of rubble on the other side of the cobblestone street, a trail of shattered blue crystal the length of a football field. The chunks that hadn't been flattened or shattered or melted were eighty feet tall and probably the same in width. The tower's base—into which Aldern had just disappeared—was two stories of slag.

"That was the Kralak, the Sorcerer's Tower," Aeric explained. "The oldest and grandest building in Evitankari, where our strongest magic users work and learn, where our greatest magical knowledge is cataloged and studied. On any given day, thousands of Aldern's constituency are inside. His son practically lived there." He didn't need to say more.

The owner of a nearby home the giant hadn't touched loaned Roger work boots, a T-shirt, and a pair of jeans two sizes too big. He tied his shotgun to his hip with the cloth belt of his robe and joined Aeric in a line of elves passing buckets of water across the street to a burning warehouse.

"Normally the sorcerers would put the fires out," the Mongan explained sadly as he took a bucket from Roger. "We've never needed hydrants or fire trucks."

Men, women, and children wearing white shifts similar to Chyve's swarmed here and there, aiding the injured and collecting the dead. Roger watched in awe as one little girl bent over a muscular man lying in a pool of blood, bleeding out from a ragged slash in his chest. The girl's brow scrunched in concentration as she placed her hands on either side of the wound. Blue-white energy coursed up and down her arms. The wound made a sickening slurp as it sealed itself, the skin clean and only lightly scarred. The man groaned and sat up slowly, blinking the light out of his wet eyes. When the girl stood, Roger thought he saw a few new strands of gray in her bright red hair.

In the end, the elves couldn't save the burning house. It collapsed with a heartrending crash. Flames and smoke leapt high in defiant victory. The owner, a lean man a few spots in line behind Roger, fell to his knees and sobbed.

Aeric took charge, leading the work crew to the remains of the Sorcerer's Tower. They found Aldern hard at work, lifting chunks of crystal with a sweep of his hand, extinguishing fires with only his breath. The man looked like he was striding through hell, his white beard black with soot and his eyes unfocused. No one bothered him. He freed survivors and corpses alike from the rubble, and the others moved them to safety or to the homes in which Chyve's people were storing the dead.

Few people spoke, but Roger caught bits and pieces of quiet conversation as he took his turn dousing the flames.

"Fucking thing just kind of appeared," one man in a farmer's coveralls told a rather official-looking woman in all black. "In the alley, over there. It walked right through a block of houses to get to the Kralak. A blast of fire breath, a few swings of its terrible fists..."

"What's with the human?" one healer asked another, nodding suspiciously in Roger's direction as he and Aeric helped a grateful man out from beneath a pile of stone and wood.

"Lucik says she saw him take down the giant with that gun," the other healer replied. "Says that's the new Pintiri."

"A human? Why didn't they just kill him so someone who deserves the Ether can retrieve it?"

After that, Roger ignored the chatter and focused on his work. Everyone he and Aeric found was still alive, some just barely so, but for that he was glad. The others weren't so lucky, and soon wooden carts drawn by powerful six-legged horses were removing shrouded corpses by the dozen.

As the sun set in the distance, the Combined Council held an impromptu meeting in the backyard of a ruined home. The green grass was pocked with black scars and fallen brick from the flattened house. All those gathered were covered in blood and grime, save Granger, who looked as if he hadn't lifted a finger to help. Pike sat atop a picnic table, sharpening his broadsword with a whetstone and glaring at the Council of Economics. No one suggested relocating to the Council Chamber; they wanted to be on the ground, in the midst of it all, where they could still feel the power of the open wound ripped through the heart of their city.

"Driff," Aldern croaked, the word a struggle. He lay in a patch of green grass, gazing up at the twilight. "What happened?"

The Council of Intelligence pushed his spectacles up on his soot-blackened nose. "*Continens giganticus*. A bottle giant." He pulled the bottom of a shattered red bottle from a pocket in his coat. "Left in a dumpster one block from the Kralak. Wired to crack at precisely 2:30 this afternoon."

"Wait," said Council of Agriculture Piney. "That monster came out of that tiny bottle?" Roger was glad he wasn't the only one who didn't believe it.

Driff nodded. "All it takes is the correct ingredients combined in the proper proportions. The mixture congeals when exposed to air, creating a biological lattice of sorts used by the magic inside to create the giant. A tiny charge shattered the bottle and triggered the reaction."

"Is there a reason it headed straight for the Sorcerer's Tower?" Granger asked, chewing on a fingernail.

"*Continens giganticus* has a very keen sense of smell," Driff explained. "And it hates the smell of magic."

"Magic smells?" Roger asked, incredulous.

"Like chicken soup," Pike growled. "Can we kill him now?"

All eyes turned to Aldern. "I've confirmed Roger Brooks as Pintiri," he said firmly.

The Council members reacted exactly how Roger expected. Those who voted for him nodded or smiled. Granger kicked the grass and wandered toward the next yard, grumbling to himself. Driff didn't seem to care.

But Pike leapt to his feet, the whetstone forgotten. "You did what?" he bellowed, waving his broadsword like a deadly baton. "Aldern, he's fucking human!"

"Roger Brooks killed a giant today,"

Aeric said smugly, "And what did you do today, Pike? Oh, that's right! The giant he killed kicked you in the face and buried you under a building."

In the waning light, Pike turned a shade of purple usually reserved for grape juice. "Who the hell asked you?"

"Save the schoolyard bullshit for later, boys," Aldern snapped, a tinge of sadness creeping into his voice. "Chyve...what's the count?"

The Council of Medicine sighed as her soft gaze drifted down to the grass at her feet. "Of the three thousand, four hundred and twenty-two in the Kralak at the time of the attack, two thousand, seven hundred and eight did not make it."

Roger's heart sank. Aldern closed his eyes and pursed his lips.

"Another two hundred and eighteen died elsewhere. The giant also destroyed fifteen homes, three warehouses, and a playground."

A heavy silence hung over the Combined Council. Even Pike and Driff seemed depressed. Roger shuffled his feet and wished he had something worthwhile to say.

"Whoever planted this thing had inside knowledge of the activities inside the Kralak," Driff said. "Most senior staff were on the top floors, working together on a massive spell designed to remove all the moss from Evitankari's cobblestones. The Kralak never stood a chance."

"Driff, you will find the parties responsible," Aldern said softly. "Someone see the Pintiri home." The old elf disappeared with a snap of his fingers, leaving nothing behind but a slender, Aldern-shaped patch of flattened grass.

"Well, that's that," Pike said merrily, heading for Roger nonchalantly. "Let me show you the way, bud."

Aeric stepped in between the two. "I don't think so. Let's go, Roger."

They left the Combined Council behind, striding through the burnt-out ruins of the house to reach the cobblestone street beyond. Great iron streetlights gave the night a cool blue glow, their thick bulbs glowing with sky-colored gas. Dust and dirt and all manner of debris and bodily fluids still covered the cobblestones.

"How much longer do I have to worry about that Pike asshole?" Roger asked.

Aeric smiled. "Kill three or four more giants and he might come around. He's never going to like you, but he's not stupid enough to try anything extreme."

Roger's hand drifted to the shotgun at his hip. He wasn't so sure of that.

They walked without speaking, both men physically and mentally drained by the day's events. Roger felt proud of the way he'd handled himself; he'd felled a giant, after all, and then he'd worked himself to exhaustion aiding its victims—but in spite of everything he'd done, Evitankari had still lost thousands of lives. His sense of accomplishment quickly felt embarrassing and selfish.

Beyond the disaster area, Evitankari was a beautiful city. The cobblestones were clean and straight, sans the blue-green moss sprouting here and there. The land itself rose and fell in gentle, undulating slopes that added character to the city without making travel too difficult. Homes and businesses were simple buildings made of wood or stone, some seemingly carved out of a single boulder or a great tree. All were decorated with blossoming flowers or crawling ivy. Not one residence showed any signs of neglect. Warm light spilled out from the windows. Families were staying in tonight, mourning the day's losses and consoling each other. The night sky was surprisingly clear here, even under the strange streetlights, a sparkling blanket of stars unlike any Roger had ever seen. He didn't recognize any of the constellations.

"We're in the southern hemisphere," he said.

"South Africa, to be exact," Aeric replied. "Not far from the Atlantic. We regulate the temperature ourselves to keep things more comfortable than they would be otherwise."

They left the residential area, cresting a forested rise green with oak and elm and a few other deciduous trees Roger couldn't name. Low-hanging branches twisted into shapes reminiscent of benches or chairs cushioned with soft brown moss. Flowers were everywhere, all different colors and shapes and sizes, some closed for the evening, others open to drink the moonlight.

His family would like it here, he thought. He was sorry that they were about to be dragged into all of his strange troubles, Samantha uprooted from college and Ricky from fourth grade. But his children would be ecstatic to see him, especially if news of the fire had reached them, and they'd be so proud when he told them about how he killed that giant. He wasn't so sure about Virginia; they hadn't parted under the best of circumstances. Maybe all he and his wife needed was a change of scenery, something to shake up the simple suburban life she'd come to look at as routine and boring. Maybe Evitankari could be the second chance he so desperately needed.

"Aldern said you're trying to find my family and bring them here," Roger said tentatively. "How's that going?"

"Best that you trust us to do our jobs and focus on learning yours," Aeric replied in a manner that made Roger feel like a small child being lectured by his mother. "The Pintiri exists to serve the greater good, not himself. You'd do best to remember that."

Roger bit his tongue. Apparently his new Pintiri gig came with a great big helping of stereotypical action hero morality and responsibility. He hoped the benefits package also included a chance to win back his wife and blow up something cool. Being a smartass made it easier to cope with the mental and physical exhaustion threatening to knock him out and leave him right there in the road.

Aeric delivered him to a sprawling brick mansion set atop a hill ringed with thick pines on the outskirts of town. It reminded Roger a bit of the White House, its round center framed in twisting columns, one square wing to either side. The Mongan stopped and shook his hand at the top of the steps to the front porch.

"You did well today, Roger," he said. "But I'm afraid this was just the beginning. Be sure to get a good night's sleep."

The door opened at Roger's touch and he stumbled, exhausted, into the expansive foyer. The center of the mansion was a single round room, a staircase winding up either side to a balcony above. It was all dark wood and red brick, ancient and earthy and beautiful. To his right, a large opening led to a plush sitting room with several fur-lined couches and the biggest flat-screen television he'd ever seen. To his left was an exquisite dining room with a long, lacquered table under a series of heart-shaped chandeliers, each trimmed in gems of a different color: emeralds, rubies, amethysts.

It was through this door that a short, bent old woman waddled up to Roger. She was about half his height, twice his width, and probably three times his age. Blue-gray hair stuck out in tufts from under her red bonnet. She wore a thick brown apron over a simple blue dress.

"It's true, then," she rasped, sneering at Roger through crooked, yellow teeth. "A human Pintiri."

Roger was too tired for whatever this was, but he knew better than to be impolite. "Hi. I'm Roger Brooks. Nice to meet you."

She ignored the hand he offered. "I'm Tam. I've served my people as steward of Merrowood for eighty years." Her withered old fingers untied her apron and let it fall to the floor. "I quit."

Roger watched her waddle out through the front door, unable to find the words to protest. He wasn't just a human; he was the Pintiri, he'd killed a giant, and he'd rescued strangers—*Tam's people*—from the rubble of a fallen tower. That woman had been caretaker here for more than twice as long as Roger had been alive, a fact that spoke to a strong dedication to the job and probably a lot of love, yet she'd thrown it all away simply because her new master didn't have pointy ears. He'd never been on the receiving end of bigotry before. It made his stomach churn and his heart ache. No matter what he did, he realized, there were people living in Evitankari who would never accept him—or his family, for that matter, a thought altogether more frightening.

He staggered into the living room and threw himself onto one of the couches. Sleep claimed him immediately. His worries, he thought as he passed out, would still be there in the morning.

— CHAPTER EIGHT —

That night Talora dreamed of Crim. She was alone on a small island of sand in the middle of an angry, roiling ocean. Hungry tides crashed down all around her, eating away at her precarious perch. Heavy rain and frigid wind hammered her from a black sky. She couldn't tell if the booming echoes in the distance were thunderclaps or tremendous waves collapsing back into the sea. The occasional blast of lightning lit up the night like a strobe, revealing the twisted forms of huge, terrible beasts looming just over the horizon. Yet she wasn't afraid. She stood stoically, defiantly, daring the sea to swallow her and drag her away to the dark things. She caught a mouthful of rain and spat it into the storm.

The clouds directly above her parted, wrapping Talora in a warm spotlight that seemed to deflect the wind and rain. Crim appeared, falling slowly headfirst out of the sun, an angel descending from the heavens to save the last woman on earth. His warm smile set her stomach aflutter. She reached up to him expectantly, but he avoided her outstretched hand and touched down on the sand beside her. His smile slowly twisted into an evil sneer. Before she could react, he shoved her bodily into the cold sea and she was lost.

Crim's hard blue eyes were the first thing Talora saw when she woke up. He was seated beside her on the bed, dapper in his black suit, her limp hand held softly between his own. A shiny black walking stick topped with a glittering red stone rested across his lap. She pulled away and scrambled back up against the headboard like a frightened animal.

Crim sighed. "I suppose that's to be expected," he said sadly. "I don't make the best first impression." He rubbed one of his horns for emphasis.

Talora suddenly remembered that her wispy nightgown left little to the imagination. She snatched the blankets and pulled them up over her chest. "What do you want? How did you find us?"

She and the Witch had left the city as quickly as their feet could've taken them, weaving their way between the skyscrapers until the concrete and steel gave way to vinyl and clapboard. The Witch, it turned out, made her home in a quaint little cottage in a suburban neighborhood bursting with other quaint little cottages. Two stories of peace, Talora's frightening companion had called it, complete with a perfect lawn and quite the impressive row of roses. The orderly interior was trimmed with old bric-a-brac and Victorian furniture. And the neighbors, the Witch claimed, were positively delightful.

"You really don't remember, do you?" Crim asked. "This *will* take some getting used to." He shook his head. "You and I and the Witch have been in cahoots for quite a while now. Shh, don't tell Demson. He thinks we hate each other. She's playing him like a fiddle."

What in the hell had Talora—or, more accurately, the woman who had become Talora—gotten herself into? Her former self's association with these people had terrible implications. Or was she being played? Were Crim and the Witch working together to deceive her? She had no means of knowing, save to wring them for as much information as possible and hope to catch them in a contradiction. Maybe she could learn something more about what they were planning for her.

"Who am I?" she asked. "What am I?"

Before Crim could respond, the door to the tiny bedroom opened to admit the Witch. "You are Talora, and you are the hammer that's going to obliterate the glass ceiling under which we all live," she said with a crooked smile. "You should be very proud."

"That's not what I asked."

"True, but that's all we can tell you," Crim responded gently. "Your new...frame of mind...will take a while to settle in."

"We've found that immediately refreshing the subject's history causes a bit of a disconnect," the Witch added. "It drives the person quite insane."

"How do you know that?" Talora asked skeptically.

"You're our fourth try," the Witch said with a satisfied smirk, "*and* you were the one who figured it out."

Somehow, Talora was not surprised. "So, what exactly did you—*we*—do to me?"

The Witch sauntered closer, a hungry predator stalking its prey. "Have you ever tried to fit a square peg in a round hole? It's a lot easier to do if you shave off a few of those nasty corners."

She considered this for a moment, working her lower lip. "Am I the peg or the hole?"

A cacophony of wailing sirens and squealing tires cut off the Witch's response. Crim swung himself off the bed and peered between the curtains shrouding the room's one small window. "Twelve officers. Small arms. Oh...and they've ruined your lawn."

"This is the Detroit P.D.!" boomed a megaphone-amplified voice. "We have you surrounded. You have one minute to come out peacefully."

"Deal with them," the Witch said with an annoyed flick of her wrist.

Crim hesitated. "What if they're...you know..."

The Witch sighed and stomped haughtily to the window, savagely yanking the curtains open. "They're the real thing," she said. "I'm sure the shifters sent them. They think they're sooooooo tricky."

"We know you're in there!" the megaphone boomed. The Witch rolled her eyes.

"Fine," Crim spat. He tipped his walking stick to Talora as he left the room. "Till we meet again, my love."

The Witch slammed the door behind him. "I'll never understand what you saw in that asshole."

Talora shrugged. "Beats me." She turned her attention to the window, but she couldn't quite see what was going on out there.

"Go ahead, take a look. They won't shoot you."

She wrapped the sheets around herself like a robe and did as the Witch suggested. Below, Crim strode nonchalantly down the three porch steps, twirling his cane like he hadn't the slightest care in the world. Officers tensed behind their makeshift automotive barriers, pistols ready.

"You realize, of course, that they're merely a distraction," the Witch purred.

Talora didn't reply. Her attention was glued to Crim and the meter-long blade he drew from the sheath of his walking stick. He raised the weapon to his foes in a sharp salute, then he took a fencer's defensive stance with his feet spread wide and his free hand behind his back.

A harsh crash echoed from somewhere downstairs, as if adding an exclamation point to the Witch's statement. One, two, three sets of heavy footsteps tore into the house. "The real threat, the ones who are not human, the ones who...you know...think they can flank me and steal away with you."

An officer using the door of his cruiser as cover fired at Crim. With a quick flick of his blade, the man with the horns redirected the bullet back into the officer's skull.

"They are afraid of you, Talora. Petrified. They will do anything to possess you, but you can stop them."

The rest of the officers opened fire on Crim, their weapons cracking like thunder. Crim spun and pirouetted and dove through the hail of bullets, a fragile dancer amidst their destruction, twirling close to the nearest officer and gingerly beheading him as if he were cutting a flower from its stem. Somewhere in the back of Talora's mind, a tiny voice told her that no one was supposed to move that fast.

Inside the house, three more sets of boots joined their brethren. They'd made their way through the small kitchen and into the living room.

"They're coming for you, Talora," the Witch hissed, "and you will stop them—because I won't."

Talora gasped and whirled on the Witch, but the strange woman was gone. Her mind flashed back to the terrible silver thing in Crim's building. How was she supposed to deal with something like that?

"Reach down deep," the Witch's voice continued, though Talora couldn't pinpoint its source in the room. "Find the darkness and ignite it."

Talora had no idea what the Witch was talking about, but she took a deep breath and tried to concentrate. What other choice did she have? She could sense that she was being tested, and if the Witch were to be believed, probably with instructions she herself had left behind. Talora closed her eyes and concentrated on searching her mind. She felt nothing: no darkness, no light, nothing other than her experiences since she'd woken up on the park bench and the empty knowledge that helped her speak and walk and look out windows and worry about what a bunch of shape-shifters might be capable of doing to her. If only she had some clue as to who or what she was, maybe she could find what the Witch wanted—if it was even there in the first place.

The bedroom door swung open seemingly of its own volition. "She's up here, fellas!" the Witch's disembodied voice shouted. "And wipe your damn boots! I don't need your dirty fucking footprints all over my hallway!"

The intruders changed direction, heading back the way they came and to the house's back stairwell. The rickety old steps creaked and cracked in time with Talora's racing heart.

"Come now, Talora!" the Witch continued. "We won't be able to outmaneuver that silly Demson if you can't perform this simple little trick."

"You couldn't have picked a worse time for a test," Talora growled, fighting to still her nerves. What if the Witch was wrong; what if the darkness wasn't there? What if whatever she'd done to herself hadn't worked properly? What if the Witch was full of shit, tricking her into remaining there in that bedroom, utterly defenseless. What if—

Before she had time to finish her next thought, a man in black body armor and thick goggles appeared in the doorway, rifle at the ready. The heavy dart he fired caught Talora above her left breast, knocking her backward off her feet. The room around her spun and twisted, and then all was black.

— CHAPTER NINE —

The cloaked figure stopped at the edge of the tree line, inspecting the sleepy little town in the warm glow of a waxing crescent moon. It was like something from a postcard: nine white stone buildings with small windows, thatched roofs sandwiched between a lush deciduous forest, and a towering gray peak. Gardens, picket fences, picnic tables, and a few covered wells. One dirt road in, one dirt road out. The perfect place to hide from the world.

The figure moved quickly across the fresh snow without leaving a trail, as many of his kind could, and pressed himself against the back wall of a small cottage. Here, away from the hustle and bustle and pervasive white noise of a larger settlement, he could hear it all: the snoring couple on the opposite side of that wall, the man talking in his sleep in the next house, even the old woman across the street who farted every time she rolled over. Most importantly, he could hear the local barkeep wiping down the bar. He darted around the corner and onto the dirt path that served as the town's main and only street, still not leaving a trail. A frontal approach would do; the town was asleep, his quarry distracted by work.

He reached the front door of the pub without incident. Above, a rickety wooden sign shaped like the horned head of a mountain goat proclaimed that the Ram's Mistress had the best ale in Galworth. Inside, the barkeep had moved on to rearranging bottles on the shelf behind the bar.

The dark figure reached into his pocket and retrieved a key with a slender handle and a thick bulbous head. It slid easily into the simple lock, adjusting itself to the required shape. The door opened with a soft, satisfying click.

And the man found himself staring into the six revolving barrels of an M134 minigun.

"Fucking hell, Lep," he said angrily. "Glad to see you too."

The weapon's dangerous end swung away, replaced by a warm, smiling face. Lep looked like a bulldog happy to see its master. "Just like to keep you on your toes, Pikey. Come on in."

The big elf followed the even bigger elf inside and locked the door behind him. The Mistress was a true hole-in-the-wall, fifteen feet wide by ten feet deep. Lep's short hair brushed the ancient black beams as he headed behind the bar and stowed the minigun in a secret compartment in the floor.

Pike strode past the Mistress's only booth and took the middle stool at the bar. "Place looks good, Lep," he said, pulling back his cloak's hood as he sat. "Killin' business must be booming."

Lep winked at the Council of War and lit two used candles. The firelight flickered playfully across the dark wood that everything in the Mistress was made of. "I'm into quality now, Pikey, not quantity. One or two big hits a year. Chas and I are the best, and those what needs to know it knows it."

Pike reached down into the well, pulled up a bottle of whiskey, and popped the top off with his thumb. "How is Chastity these days?" he asked, taking a long swig.

"Just as full of piss and vinegar as always," Lep's wife said as she entered from the back room. She wore a pink bathrobe and slippers shaped like happy white rabbits. Chas took a seat beside Pike and punched him playfully in the arm. "You never visit anymore, big guy. Which name on Evitankari's shit list do you need us to erase this time?"

"Officially, I'm not here."

"We know how it works, Pike," Lep snorted. He handed Chas the bar rag and she proceeded to rub it over her pale face and through her bright red hair. "You didn't come to us, you didn't tell us who and when, you would never have anything to do with something as vile as assassination, and that guy that shows up dead in his hotel room, looking a bit like bloody Swiss cheese—well, no one will know whose fault that was, and high-and-mighty-and-gosh-darn-wonderful Evitankari certainly won't be suspected."

Chas tossed the rag aside and smiled at Pike through a set of pointy teeth. Her soft white skin was gone, replaced by blue and gold scales, and a set of twirling horns sprouted from her skull in place of her bright red hair. "This ain't our first time 'round the block, hon."

"I'm not here on elven business," Pike spat.

"Then you're taking one hell of a risk leaving the city in the dead of night, considering what happened there today," Lep replied. "I hear the Council's a bit miffed that someone knocked over their tower."

"The Council's running around with their heads up their asses, as always. They aren't going to find anything." Pike took another long hit from the whiskey, swirling it in his mouth for a moment to savor the burn.

"A few well-placed explosives might fix that," Chas said. "The heads-up-their-asses problem, not the lack of finding anything. Just say the word."

Lep leaned forward, playing anxiously with the pointy tip of his ear—a habit he'd had for as long as Pike could remember, back to their days growing up a few houses apart. "If there's something there, chances are they're too dumb to find it."

"There's nothing there, Lep," Pike said. "It was...her."

"Her?"

Chas whacked Lep in the arm. "You know. Her." She stood up, straightening her robe. "I love ya, Pikey, but you're insufferable when you get stuck on that bitch." She stomped to the back room and shut the door behind her.

Lep feigned sadness. "Women. They just don't know what they can do to a man's heart. Makes us do strange, ridiculous, stupid, stupid things," he said with a glance toward the closed door.

"I'm serious, asshole. There hasn't been an incident like this on elven soil since Axzar breached our walls three thousand years ago. We bend over fucking backwards to keep everybody happy. She's the only one with the motive and the resources."

"Bottle giant pieces 'n parts are contraband, but they ain't hard to find if ya knows where to look."

"There's more to it than that, you big fucker." He paused, wondering how much he should give away. Lep was his friend, but any allegiance he once professed to Evitankari had long since been blown to a million tiny pieces. He'd sell out the elves in a heartbeat—but this was one secret the elves wouldn't be able to keep for long anyway. "Shitwad didn't come back Pintiri. He came back with a human who'd somehow wound up in possession of the Ether."

The other elf's jaw dropped, his jowls quivering. "Well now. That's a fine howdy-do. And the human?"

"About what you'd expect."

Lep switched to the tip of his other ear, frowning. "Sounds to me like someone's aiming for Evitankari's kneecaps."

Pike nodded and drained the rest of the bottle. "No shit. And we're just going to stand there and take it."

Lep blanched. "You idiots are keeping the human around?"

Pike angrily hurled the empty bottle across the room. Lep caught it telepathically before it could hit the wall and shatter, lowering it gently to the floor. "Aldern gave us the script a few minutes before the poor bastard woke up. We're playing dumb for now, trying to draw her out."

His friend raised his eyebrows and scratched his chin. Pike had seen that motion countless times. It meant Lep thought the Council's plan was such an obviously terrible idea that there was no reason to waste words explaining just how bad it was. "If your little honeydew is involved, she's just the tip of the iceberg."

"How's that?"

"Well, see, the Witch isn't exactly the most popular girl at school. She has a habit of pissing people off. Usually there's a few prices on her head, least until she gets around to taking care of the buyers. Ain't been a new one in six months. Someone's protecting her, Pikey. Someone with a lot of stroke."

The Council of War took a deep breath. Evitankari and the powers-that-be had maintained a tense truce for the last few centuries; had someone finally decided that the elves were too dangerous to keep in their back pocket?

"Leave the bastards," Lep said so firmly it may as well have been a demand. Something sad had crept into the big elf's dark eyes. "They deserve whatever they get. Chas and I can get enough business for three. If you've got to work for Tallisker, best to at least be aboveboard about it."

Pike shook his head. They'd had this conversation a hundred times since Lep lost his job as Council of Intelligence to that upstart Driff, and he always ended it the same way. "You know I can't do that."

"Right. I know. Do me a favor, will ya, Pikey?" Lep said sadly. "We all know the Council has kept one finger out of its collective ass and over the button. Whatever you do, don't let them push it."

Pike glanced at the door to the back room. He could hear Chastity snoring, sound asleep.

"It won't come to that."

"Good," the big barkeep said, his smile forced. "Because Chas'd slaughter both of us."

— CHAPTER TEN —

The dining room was awash with that post-Christmas morning glow, soft and warm and happy. From his seat at the head of the table, Roger could smell the turkey Virginia was plating in the kitchen. The table was already piled high with turnips, potatoes, green beans, fresh rolls, and a gravy boat. He took a sweet swig of rich eggnog from one of Virginia's fancy Christmas mugs, green glass with a smiling red snowman and a pair of jingling bells tied to the handle. To his left, Ricky pounded away at a handheld video game, his blue eyes peering out through his unruly blond mop in strict concentration. To his right, Samantha was already a quarter of the way through a new novel with a half-clothed vampire on the cover that he really hadn't wanted to buy but which Virginia had insisted was all right (and probably intended to borrow later). Neither of his children looked back at him, but he didn't mind. It was enough that they were together and enjoying the things they loved. Roger took another long drink of nog, letting the rum he'd snuck into it warm his stomach to match his heart.

"Turkey!" Virginia chirped as she hauled the steaming bird into the room on the silver platter she'd inherited from her mother. She only took it out for Christmas. As always, she slid the bird in front of Roger and handed him the big carving knife. The kids smiled at him and put away their presents, licking their lips. Roger closed his eyes and took one more taste of his drink, wishing this moment could last forever.

When he opened his eyes again, the room was in flames. Fire raced up the walls and across the ceiling, lapping hungrily for the family trapped inside. Roger's children didn't seem to notice the danger; they continued to stare at him intently, waiting, their suddenly pointy ears quivering in anticipation.

"Go ahead, Roger," cooed his wife, her blonde hair now black, her blue eyes gone brown and dark and brooding. "Dive right in."

Roger's fear melted away as he hefted the knife and leaned forward—if no one else was worried, why should he be—and then he was falling through the turkey and the platter and the table...

He landed hard on the floor, blinking up at the ceiling and the furry beige couch he'd rolled right off of. The shotgun he'd snuggled up with teetered on the edge of the couch, once, twice—and then it plummeted into his stomach. He gasped and rolled to his left and banged his forehead on the leg of the coffee table.

"Good one, Pintiri," he growled between clenched teeth as the room swirled back into place around him. Thunder pulsed through the knot in his brow and the bruise on his gut.

He groaned at the sound of the doorbell. Yesterday had been a big enough shock to his system, what with the magic and the suicidal dessert and the giant and the threat of execution. Couldn't the damn elves give him a day to recover? The bell rang three more times, a cheery chime that grated on his nerves. "Come out, come out!" it seemed to say. "We've got a walking cheesecake in need of a chess partner, and Pike wants to give you a shave with his new battleaxe..."

One swift kick blew the door out of the jamb. "Roger?" Aeric called hesitantly. He stalked slowly inside Merrowood, knives drawn and ready, a predatory bird on the hunt. The previous day's black fatigues had been exchanged for a sharp-looking blue and red uniform with gold lapels. His crew cut glistened with gel.

Of all the elves that could've walked through his door, Roger supposed Aeric was the least worrisome. "In here," he replied half-heartedly.

The Mongan rushed to Roger's side, sheathing one blade on each hip and taking Roger's head in his hands to examine the bruise above his eye. "Pintiri, is everything all right? We couldn't get a hold of Tam this morning."

"She quit," Roger said. "And I fell off the couch."

"She quit?" the elf repeated, his brow furrowed. "Why? She's served Merrowood for eighty years."

"So she told me," Roger groaned as he sat up, brushing Aeric's hands away from his face. "I don't think she would've voted for me yesterday."

The elf sighed. "Well, come on. We've got to make you presentable. The funeral service for yesterday's casualties starts in an hour. It'll do Evitankari good to see their new Pintiri."

He led Roger into the foyer and up the gently curving stairs, then right into the second floor of the building's south wing, above the living room. A towering pair of wooden doors inlaid with gold scrollwork opened into an expansive master suite: a bedroom with an attached bath and a walk-in closet the size of Roger's living room at home. The white shag carpet was soft and warm between his toes. The canopied bed to the right of the door was bigger than any he'd ever seen, perhaps three times wider and twice as long as a typical king-sized mattress. Crimson fabric hung seductively from high posts above red and white sheets and two dozen plush white pillows.

"The former Pintiri was...ah...a bit of a romantic," Aeric explained when he saw Roger gawking.

The wall opposite the bed was covered with framed pictures of Evitankari: gently rolling hills, a few parks and fields, cobbled streets crisscrossing between important-looking buildings. The scenes moved, alive with wind rustling the trees and grass, with soft clouds floating through the bright morning sky, with people going about their business—some stopping to chat, others trading in the market or drilling with sword and shield or other weapons Roger didn't recognize. Sadly, one showed the still-smoking ruins of the Kralak. Roger realized that the Pintiri could keep an eye on the entire city from there. He wondered which members of the Combined Council had a similar look into Merrowood.

"You look like hell," Aeric said suddenly. "Take a shower, but be quick about it. I'll lay out your uniform."

The bathroom was white and pristine, trimmed in wide tile with light blue grout. Roger was surprised to find the gold spouts in the porcelain sink were motion-activated, though he couldn't tell if it was via magic or machine. He stripped down quickly and left his clothes in a heap atop the toilet.

After playing with the bidet for a few minutes, he stepped into the shower. The water started on its own. It was scalding hot, and Roger covered his sensitive bits and looked around in panic for valves or controls that didn't seem to be there. But then the water adjusted on its own. He found that when he wanted it warmer, it got warmer; when he wanted it colder, it got colder. A spigot in the wall spat a blob of shampoo into his hand when he thought of washing his hair. *Damn elves and their magic,* he thought as he lathered up, enjoying the warmth and the water. He wondered what other thoughts the shower was reading and possibly recording or transmitting. Try as he might, he couldn't convince it to make breakfast or get him a beer.

He knew his children were going to love all this. Virginia would be skeptical, but Ricky and Samantha were going to eat it all up. Even though all the magic in Evitankari made Roger a bit nervous, he couldn't wait to show it off. Maybe he could light a campfire with his magic shotgun and then they could sit around it and roast marshmallows like they'd done in the backyard on so many warm summer nights, except with invisible sticks and one of Aldern's pound cakes trained to tell them ghost stories.

He toweled off and threw his dirty clothes back on in case Aeric was still around, but the bedroom was empty and the double doors were closed. A uniform similar to Aeric's was waiting for him on the bed, though this one also included a long black cape and a flame in a circle of oak leaves sewn in gold thread above the left breast. Roger was ecstatic to find a fresh pair of boxer shorts and clean black socks underneath.

At first the clothes all seemed too big. He pulled on the shirt and closed each of its buttons, but it hung off his frame like a billowing curtain on a rod. *Like Ricky when he tries to wear my clothes*, Roger thought. But then the shirt began to shrink, slowly and silently, and soon the fit was perfect. The pants, socks, and shoes all adjusted themselves in a similar fashion. The cape was too short and grew a few inches to compensate.

Dressed, Roger stopped to admire himself in the floor-length mirror in the corner. The uniform looked rather regal, he thought, like a militant king come to address his loyal subjects. He'd been skeptical of the cape and it felt awkward on his shoulders, but he really liked the way it looked. He swept it back and forth around the shotgun holstered at his hip, a gunslinger parting his jacket to show off his six-gun.

He met Aeric on the landing. "You definitely look the part, Pintiri, but be careful with that smile. You killed a giant and the uniform is nice, but thousands of good people lost their lives yesterday."

That brought Roger back to earth, which made him a bit angry. Aeric was right, but that didn't mean the elf had to ruin his fun so soon.

They made the trek through Evitankari quickly and quietly, heading in what Roger judged to be a general northwestern direction. Their route took them around the populated areas, over wooded hills and through gently rolling glens. Strangely, they didn't pass any other pedestrians. The vegetation grew denser, and soon the thick old oaks were crowding the suddenly narrow road, their heavy branches forming a green canopy that let only fingers of sunlight through. The result was an ethereal, almost spooky tunnel of green leaves and mossy brown cobblestones that Roger found strangely beautiful.

The tunnel ended at a towering wrought iron gate set in a pair of red brick towers. The view through the wide open gate was like something out of a fairytale; the thick wood abruptly gave way to an immaculate park bathed in the warm sun. The cobblestones became fine red sand that crunched softly beneath their boots. In the distance, a tremendous willow with dark green leaves watched over the park from a tiny island in the center of a small blue pond. All of Evitankari stood along the opposite shore, thousands upon thousands of people gathered to pay their respects to those who'd fallen the previous day.

"Welcome to Willowglen," Aeric said softly, reverently, a bit like a proud father. "This is where we lay our dead to rest."

"It's...very pretty," was all Roger could manage. The park was, in fact, beautiful. The perfectly manicured grass was speckled with rainbows of short flowers. Not a single blade or blossom showed the slightest sign of wilt. Here and there a wispy maple or birch created a small shaded area, but the stately willow lorded over them all. Willowglen possessed the kind of beauty that seemed too organized to be natural but too wild to be man-made, but what really caught Roger's tongue were the thousands of elves staring at him as Aeric led the way around the pristine blue pond. He had always thought of the metaphorical weight on one's shoulders as just the whiny complaint of a whiny complainer, but there in Willowglen he found the metaphor apt and real. The opinions and expectations of the elves dissecting his every step were a knot in his muscles, an ache in his bones, a tremor in his heart. Quick whispers and muted discussions combined to form a dull, oppressive roar. He kept his eyes on his boots.

He and Aeric joined the other members of the Combined Council on the far shore, their backs to the pond and the great willow as they gazed out upon the citizenry of Evitankari. Each wore a blue and red uniform similar to Roger's and Aeric's, with a different symbol representing his or her constituency: a saber for War, a red cross for Medicine, a star for Sorcery, an ear of corn for Agriculture, a coin for Economics, an open book for Intelligence. Chyve greeted them with a solemn nod and Piney reached out to squeeze Roger's hand.

He examined the crowd, which had divided itself on either side of a narrow, grassy path. It struck him how easy it was to determine which elves belonged to which Council member: the farmers wore flannel or denim, the businessmen finely starched suits, the medics heavy white robes. Though there were a few mixed families, most of the castes stood with their own kind. The intelligence community was gathered in a thick knot to his left, the soldiers in their crisp uniforms way off to the right. Roger wondered if this was tradition or some sort of class divide or a mixture of the two. He realized then just how much he still had to learn about the elves and their culture.

Council of Sorcery Aldern stepped forward, his uniform half-hidden under a billowing black cloak. He looked even older than he had the day before, his bright eyes subdued by dark circles. The soft murmuring and discussion wafting up from the crowd ended immediately.

"Elves. Countrymen. Friends." Aldern's mouth moved only slightly, but his voice boomed as if amplified by a stadium's sound system. "The horrors that befell Evitankari not twenty-four hours past will not soon be forgotten, nor will our memories of those who fell so suddenly in defense of our great city. Each is a hero in his or her own right, a light extinguished in our eyes but not in our hearts. The villains behind yesterday's heinous attack will suffer our justice, but first we lay our beloved companions to rest."

The Council of Sorcery stood stoically as the first casket appeared, borne on the shoulders of two muscular elves—soldiers, judging by their uniforms and the ceremonial sabers at their hips. The casket was a simple, somber box made of red wood thick with swirling grain and draped with a green cloth adorned with a single white "E." Roger watched in reverence, still feeling out of place, as the fallen elf was carried up the narrow path in the center of the crowd.

"Kluthat." Aldern's voice cracked with grief as he spoke the deceased's name. "Long before he was named Archmage of Geomancy—best with granite I've ever seen—he and I memorized spells together in wizard's school. I'll never forget the time he tried to heal the pimples on Harq's nose and accidentally turned him into a frog."

When the casket reached the shore of the pond, the pall bearers tapped its sides once and then lowered it into the water. It floated for a moment, a wooden island in a sea of bright blue, and then the pond claimed it, pulling it down hungrily. Though the water was clear and clean, Roger lost sight of the casket the instant it submerged.

And so it went. A pair of burly soldiers carried one of the fallen elves through the crowd, Aldern recited a reminiscence of the deceased, and then the casket disappeared into the pond. The ritual continued rapid fire, every ten seconds or so, leaving neither Aldern nor the crowd time to take a breath. Those the Council of Sorcery didn't know personally were instead saluted via reputation or hearsay, but not a single eulogy rang false. The ancient elf did it all without note card or prompt, either by memory or sorcery, and Roger found himself wildly impressed with Aldern's knowledge and poise. His voice mostly held steady, the set of his jaw strong and defiant.

Roger watched quietly, fighting the urge to fidget. He'd never been good at standing or sitting still for long. The heartfelt memories with which Aldern dispatched each coffin made Roger even more uncomfortable. These were not his people; he felt like a trespasser, or perhaps a voyeur. The previous day's tragedy was Evitankari's, not Roger's. He was merely an accessory, an official come to show an officially distraught official face. Still, he found it a truly sad occasion, one he could hardly bear to watch. He felt heartbroken and angry and afraid all at once, and he genuinely hoped the elves could find whoever was responsible for the bottle giant's attack.

He did his best to control his emotions, to look somber and appreciative and dignified like his fellow Council members. Aeric stood rigid, his hands clasped at his belt but his eyes shined hotter with each name Aldern announced. Tears streamed down Piney's face, but she didn't once sob, and Chyve held her hand for support. Pike stood off to the side, glaring at the horizon as if daring someone else to try to harm Evitankari. Only Granger seemed disinterested, occasionally rolling his eyes or huffing his disapproval of a particular fallen elf.

Several hundred names later, Roger realized that something about this scene wasn't right. Something was missing, something he'd always taken for granted. He quickly scanned the crowd, searching, thinking. And then he had it: there were no cameras, no microphones, no reporters, no vans heavy with antennas and satellite dishes. No one streaming the despair into remote and impersonal screens, no one seeking to make an advertising buck off the terrible spectacle. Everyone that cared was there in Willowglen, in the flesh, and those who might otherwise had only paid lip service or watched just for kicks had no means of participating. The elves, it seemed, treated their tragedies with dignity and respect.

The funeral lasted well into the afternoon. Roger wished he were anywhere else. Hearing that nearly three thousand people had died was one thing; numbers, after all, were cold and inhuman and tolerable. Actually watching that number laid to rest, one by one, each named and memorialized and mourned, was altogether heartbreaking.

Roger's mind drifted to the pond itself. Despite the huge number of elves it had swallowed, its waters hadn't risen. He squinted into the impossibly blue water, trying in vain to spot the heap of caskets he knew must be piling up on its bottom, but he saw nothing. The blue seemed to go on forever. Either the pond was impossibly deep, or there was magic at work once again.

When the final casket sank and disappeared, Roger's feet and legs and back were screaming for a rest. Old Chyve and fat Granger had both sat down in the grass, the former with her head heavy in her hands, the latter pecking aimlessly at his smart phone. Every so often one of the other members of the Council had tried to correct Granger's behavior with an angry look or a tap on the shoulder, but he didn't seem to care. The powerful empathic skills Aldern had called common of Granger's constituency apparently weren't a part of the Council of Economics's repertoire.

"The waters of the Origina have taken our loved ones so that the great Evertree might blossom in their memory. They shall never be forgotten."

"They shall never be forgotten," the crowd repeated solemnly. Roger mouthed the words after the fact.

Aldern took one last sad look at the Origina and teleported himself away with a snap of his fingers. The crowd began to disperse, heading around the pond in twos and threes or meandering off toward what Roger assumed to be a second exit on the other side of the park. A pair of small children, a brother and sister in the whites of Chyve's healers, waved timidly at Roger as their distraught mother lead them past. He smiled back, but the harsh sneers from a pair of farmers quickly squelched the moment.

"Never mind them," Council of Agriculture Piney said soothingly as she wrapped herself around his arm and pressed her head to his shoulder. "Ignorant bigots. They've never bothered to leave Evitankari, so their opinions of humanity are built on the prejudice of others rather than any firsthand experience."

Piney was warm and comfortable and smelled like lavender. She wore no makeup, her face trimmed instead with sorrow and stress and not enough sleep. The urge to protect her made Roger uncomfortable. "And...uh...you?" he stammered.

"Me?" she said coyly—well, as coyly as she could between sniffles. "Have I left the city? My work on the Council occasionally takes me elsewhere, but rarely does it put me among humanity. Still, you and I might have more in common than you think. We farmers have few friends on the Council; we feed the people and we keep the city green, and they treat us like the very dirt we tend. Like a 'redthroat,' I think your people call it."

"Redneck."

"Redneck." She tried the word on, sniffled again, and launched back into her explanation. "Our worth is measured not in the money we make or the enemies we kill or the information we gather. There is no such thing for us as exceeding expectations. We feed the masses and keep the parks and streets clean—and we do a damn good job. It's funny the things we take for granted. Like your people: without humanity to prop us all up, well, we wouldn't have come as far as we have. And so, I figure someone like you might understand my people and me better than the meatheads they keep handing the Ether to."

Roger wasn't sure whether to be flattered or offended. *You're nothing, just like me, so let's be friends!* The cynicism surprised him.

How had life in Evitankari made him so defensive in such a short time? He didn't like it.

"Well, thanks for the vote," he said with a smile that he hoped looked less forced than it felt. "I won't forget it. If you'll excuse me, I have to find Aeric." He wanted to ask the Mongan when his children would be arriving.

Piney gave his arm a firm squeeze and smiled back up at him. "Aeric can wait. There's someone else that needs to talk to you."

"I'm sorry, I really need to find out when my family's going to arrive—"

Piney's gaze darkened. "This is not someone you keep waiting."

He flinched, taken aback. "Who?"

Piney nodded over her shoulder, at the pond and the island behind them. "The Evertree," she said slyly. "My people tend the fields and the streets, but Willowglen is mainly my responsibility."

A tiny wooden boat, its prow tipped with a leaping trout, floated slowly across the Origina toward the bank where they stood. On the island, the massive willow's long, drooping branches rustled as if in a breeze, though Roger felt no wind and saw no waves rippling in the water.

Pike interjected himself into the conversation then. "Let the Pintiri go. I'll do it. This isn't something a fucking human should be involved in anyway. The things the Evertree can tell us about the attack on the Kralak are too important to trust him with."

Roger hadn't noticed the Council of War lingering. He didn't like the thought of that asshole being able to sneak up on him so easily. Still, he'd be more than happy to send Pike to talk to the tree, and he really couldn't argue with the elf's logic.

Piney put one hand on her hip and scoffed. "You're not invited. The Evertree will speak with Roger Brooks and Roger Brooks only."

A million questions came to mind. *Why does the tree want to talk to me specifically? How do I talk to a tree in the first place? Where did the* boat come from? *How could it possibly know anything about the giant that brought down the Kralak?* He let Piney escort him to the little boat, his questions left unasked. Best to get on with it so he could track down Aeric and inquire after Virginia and the kids. Pike stomped away, shaking his head and muttering under his breath.

The boat appeared rather fragile, and Roger worried it would sink beneath his weight. Dozens of thin, brownish-red branches intertwined to form a thin keel and gunwales. The figurehead on the prow was a wooden fish leaping up from the front of the boat, its fins spread wide almost like wings. Its blue eyes swiveled to watch him as he tentatively lowered himself into the vessel. Its bottom was surprisingly soft, though he didn't have much room to maneuver. He expected Piney to give the boat a little shove to set it in motion, but she just waved as it began to move on its own accord, slowly and surely. It executed a quick turn so that the bow faced the island, and then Roger was off to chat with the Evertree.

— CHAPTER ELEVEN —

Talora woke with a gasp, biting back a scream and arching her back against the fire racing through her nerves. Metal restraints at her wrists and ankles kept her from spasming far. She shut her eyes tight against the harsh light warming her face from above. She was on her back, on something hard and cold.

The pain subsided, leaving behind a dull throb in her chest where the dart had struck her. Acknowledging that ache brought it all crashing back—the Witch, Crim, the soldiers coming for her, the void in her mind where her life should've been. She struggled anew, flailing against her bonds, but nothing gave. The long needle that had been left in her arm fell out and clattered to the hard floor.

"Oh, sorry about that," said a warm, feminine voice.

The light and heat were suddenly taken away. Talora slowly opened one blurry eye, then the other, breathing deeply as she fought a wave of nausea. She found herself on a table in the middle of a long, narrow room. An operating table, she thought nervously, judging from the sterile white all around her and the tray of sharp instruments on a table to her left, but the gorgeous blonde woman in the skimpy red dress adjusting the pivoting dentist's lamp by Talora's feet didn't seem to fit.

"How you feelin', deary?" she asked.

"I'm getting a bit tired of waking up in strange places around even stranger people," she croaked.

The woman killed the lamp, leaving the room illuminated by the long fluorescents in the white ceiling. She put her hands on her hips and shook her head. "Well, that won't do."

The woman's features softened and melted. Her arms, legs, and head were absorbed into the fleshy blob that had been her torso. Even her clothing sank into the mass of pink, distorted flesh. Her eyes stared back at Talora from roughly where her chest should've been, one floating lazily above the other, and her upside-down mouth smiled viciously off to one side. Blond hair sprouted here and there like tufts of tainted grass. Talora gagged, fighting back against the bile rising in her throat. Then suddenly the glob turned quicksilver, glistening like molten metal in the fluorescent light. Thin tendrils sprouted out to form arms and fingers as its bottom half split into a pair of legs. It grew a head and its middle plumped out to form a thick gut. Patches of color blossomed across its body like flowers: gray hair, light skin, pink lips, thick brown glasses, and a white lab coat over black trousers. It opened its eyes and sighed.

"Is this more what you expected?" the dumpy little scientist asked in a squeaky voice, his jowls quivering. "Personally, I think you ladies have a lot more fun."

Talora thought back to the night in Tallisker's office, to the geisha the Witch had melted into a puddle of silver slime. These people—these things—could be whoever and whatever they wanted. But why were they so interested in her?

"Neat trick," she replied as the scientist plucked a pair of scissors from the tray of tools. "Must be a real hoot at parties."

She cringed as the scientist took her hand. His touch was warm, surprisingly real. She was relieved when all he cut off was her thumbnail. He briefly examined the little bit of nail, then he tossed it in his mouth and swallowed it. "Not bad," he squeaked. Then he began to melt again, his features once more degenerating into a disgusting glob of pieces and parts. This time Talora couldn't help it; she turned her head and retched, vomiting all over the side of the table and onto the floor. She wanted to close her eyes, but she knew better. She needed to learn as much as she could, and she needed to find a means of escape.

This time, when the glob turned silver, it vibrated as if it were being electrocuted and unleashed a keening wail that made Talora wince. When it put itself back in order, it was once again as the pudgy little scientist. "Well, that was exciting," he said, once again taking up the scissors. "I didn't think it was possible."

"Was it something you ate?" Talora spat.

He rolled his eyes and snipped away a lock of her hair, which he promptly swallowed. "Tastes like strawberries. What's your shampoo?"

"I'll give you all the beauty tips you want if you tell me who you're working for," she said. An obvious possibility sprung to mind, given that these people seemed to be Tallisker's enemies. "The elves?"

"We don't work for anyone, honey. Not anymore." He tried to shift again, with the same results. He stared at her for a moment, tapping his finger against his chin. "Ah ha!" he shouted happily. "It should've been obvious from the start!" He retrieved a hacksaw from the table and began sawing through one of the points on her left antler, whistling as he worked.

Talora smiled wickedly. "There will never be another like me," she goaded. "I'm one of a kind."

"Exactly our problem," the scientist said as his chosen bit of antler came free. He set it down beside his tools and began pounding it into a pulp with a steel hammer.

"Why don't you let me off this table so I can show you how it's done?" she growled. She was a bit surprised by her own resolve.

Was it a product of whatever had been done to her? Was it some part of her personality that had survived the process?

He gathered the tiny fragments of antler in his palm, carefully sweeping up every last shard. "Because I don't think you know," he said matter-of-factly. He tossed the antler dust down his gullet, then swiped one finger through the vomit on the side of the table. "Just in case," he said as he licked it clean.

Melt. Shimmer. Struggle. Wail. Talora heaved, but her stomach was empty. When the scientist reformed, he stomped one foot angrily and turned to ponder the tools on the table, muttering under his breath. Talora knew she had to do something quickly before he started hacking off more important pieces. She didn't think she could talk her way out of this, and she knew she wasn't strong enough to break through the manacles at her hands and feet. That left one option, one that had already failed her back in the Witch's home. She took a deep breath and reached within herself, combing the empty corridors of her mind for the darkness the Witch had claimed would save her.

The scientist whirled, playfully slashing the air above her face with a wicked-looking cleaver. "Before they came to understand the miracle of genetics, my ancestors believed that the only way to steal someone's form was by devouring her heart. Perhaps they were right."

Talora closed her eyes and took a deep breath, fighting the panic rising in her gut. She redoubled her efforts, searching and reaching and pulling for anything dark. But there was nothing; nothing dark, nothing light, nothing other than her experiences since waking up on that bench. Just nothing.

And then it hit her. As she felt the cleaver parting the fabric and skin above her breastbone, Talora laughed. She took firm hold of the nothing, letting the surprisingly hot darkness wash over and through her, and then she opened her eyes and hurled it toward the scientist. Flame leapt from her hands as if expelled from a jet engine, launching the shifter and his blade across the room. He landed in a heap, silver splotches blooming over his skin and clothes where she'd burned him. She called the nothing again, covering him in a steady stream of crackling flame. He dissolved into a screaming, struggling blob of quicksilver, fighting to retain form against the intense heat. Talora could feel the liquid metal of the manacles streaming down her hands, but it didn't burn her.

She kept the fire trained on the little puddle of quicksilver that had been her tormentor for a few minutes more, just in case. Then she melted the bonds at her feet and swung herself off the table. She pressed a hand to her chest, testing her wound. He'd gotten through to her breastbone, but she wasn't bleeding too badly. *You can burn me this time*, she thought at the darkness. With a deep breath and a sharp scream, she cauterized the wound.

There didn't seem to be a door or a hatch or an exit of any sort in the solid white walls, but Talora didn't care. She concentrated and pooled a blast of fire in her hands, a little meteor born of her empty mind, and she hurled it into the nearest wall. Sunlight streamed in through the ragged hole.

This, she thought, *feels damn good*. But it might also mean that Crim and the Witch had been telling the truth. She banished the thought for later consideration.

Talora climbed out onto the cracked asphalt of a deserted parking lot surrounded by a rusty chain link fence. She spun around to examine her prison, which turned out to be a long white trailer devoid of windows or doors. Just for kicks, she set it ablaze. If there were any more of those things around, this would get their attention—and then she'd deal with them.

A sharp whistle from her right caught her attention. The Witch was seated atop a pile of old wooden pallets, flying a kite shaped like a cartoon cat. She waved and smiled.

Talora pointed up at the kite and lit it on fire. "I don't need you anymore," she snarled. "Fat lot of good you did me anyway. I can take care of myself."

The Witch sadly watched the ashes of her kite falling around her like snowflakes. She tried to catch one with her tongue. "Is that so?"

Her nonchalance pushed Talora over the edge. The fire flared around her hands, begging to be set free. "Yeah, sure, you helped me find this...this..."

"Magic."

"This magic." Somehow, that didn't sound as strange as she thought it should have. "But you could've worked *with me* rather than leaving me to find it as part of some sadistic test."

The Witch straightened and crossed her legs. "You've no one to be angry with but yourself. That was your idea. Extreme conditions to bring about extreme results, or some such. I have to be honest—the science part of our little scheme always bored me."

She could feel the fire pulling at her consciousness, roaring through the emptiness in her mind, and she couldn't fight it any longer. The flames leapt from her hands in a tremendous blast, blowing away a section of metal fence to her right. The Witch whistled, clearly impressed. Talora stomped away without another word.

"But where, oh where, will you go, Talora?" the Witch called after her, feigning concern. As she stepped through the flaming rubble toward the city looming in the distance, Talora wondered the same.

— CHAPTER TWELVE —

The little boat gently ran itself aground on the sandy shore of Evertree's island. The fish on the prow once again swiveled one big eye to watch Roger clamber out. He groaned and cursed his knees as his aching joints popped back into more comfortable positions. He took a few steps forward and stretched. When he looked back, the boat was gone.

Piney waved at him happily from the far shore, oblivious to the crowd streaming out of Willowglen behind her. She struck him as one of those women who never stopped trying to be cute. Samantha was going to hate the Council of Agriculture.

Roger parted the willow's drooping branches like a pair of curtains. They shivered softly as if they'd been tickled. Although little sunlight punctured the dense tangle of wispy boughs, the area under the Evertree's canopy was anything but dark. Half a dozen fireflies the size of small birds wafted lazily through the branches, each a different color of the rainbow. The colors mixed and mingled and danced among themselves, painting the grass in patches of deep red and bright yellow, the leaves above purple and blue. An orange firefly wafted down to land lightly on Roger's shoulder. Its light went out, and Roger was surprised to find that it was actually a little winged man in a tiny black track suit, his dark hair pulled back in a snarl of dreadlocks.

"You're not a firefly," Roger stammered. "You're a pixie!"

The little man rolled his dark eyes and twitched his gossamer wings. "You're not a human," he replied. "You're a dumbass!"

The orange light flared back to life, concealing the pixie's form once again, and it flitted back into the canopy. The other pixies chittered with laughter.

A knot in the tree's thick brown trunk rolled and twisted, creaking and crunching like a paper bag. The bark settled into the face of a kindly old man with heavy brows and a bulbous, crooked nose. The wide smile beneath was black and toothless.

"Welcome to Willowglen, Pintiri Roger Brooks," the Evertree croaked, its voice deep and slow. "I apologize for the behavior of my stewards. They work hard, but their manners could be better."

Roger nodded and took a step forward. Compared to some of the other things he'd seen lately, a talking tree wasn't all that surprising or frightening. "I'm getting kind of used to it," he replied.

"That, I am truly sad to hear." The tree's face crinkled into a caricature of a frown. "For all the good Evitankari does, there are often times when the elves are little better than those they've sworn to fight."

"I'm still not sure I understand all of that," Roger said, scratching his head. "But I'm learning," he added hastily. He wanted to get this over with as soon as he could. The thought of sitting through yet another lecture about the true nature of the world and human-ity's place in it made him want to risk a swim through the creepy waters of the Origina.

"That's the spirit!" the Evertree boomed, its face friendly once more. "But unfortunately, Pintiri, I fear you've no choice but to learn very quickly. Yesterday's events portend a most troublesome future."

The purple pixie's light flickered and the little creature sighed. Roger agreed, but he wasn't sure how to express it. He rolled his shoulders and took a deep breath, watching the pixies zip through the canopy. This, he thought, Samantha would probably like.

"I've summoned you not just for introductions but because you may be the only member of the Council I can trust," the tree continued. "We've a traitor in our midst, Pintiri, and that traitor may have infiltrated our most powerful institution."

"The Council?" The possibilities streamed through Roger's mind. *Not Aldern, surely, or Aeric, or Piney or Chyve. But Pike...or that shady Driff character...or Granger, aloof and distant. Or maybe it is Aldern or Aeric or Piney or Chyve, and he or she is just really good at playing the game.* A shiver ran down his spine. A member of the Council was working for the enemy. He doubted he'd know who until the knife was firmly in his back.

The Evertree nodded, as much as a face in a tree trunk can. "Place your hand on my bark, Pintiri, and I'll show you all I know."

Roger reached out and gingerly pressed two fingers to the rough bark beside the Evertree's nose. The tree was surprisingly warm, almost hot. The heat rushed into Roger's hand, up his arm, and through the rest of his body. He tried to jerk away...

...and suddenly he was elsewhere, strolling casually down a cobblestone street lined with square brick buildings. His name was Kacen, and he walked arm in arm with his wife, Trisly, a pretty young blonde in the white robes of one of Chyve's healers. They were heading out of the city proper, picnic basket in hand, for a bit of lunch in the parks beyond Willowglen.

"Granger's been called to an emergency meeting of the Council," he found himself explaining in a voice crisper and more precise than his own. His stride felt off, shorter and quicker, his footfalls lighter. His pinstriped business suit was tight and constricting, but he'd loosened his tie to let the cool air swirl into his collar. "Something big is happening. He won't miss me for a few hours."

Trisly smiled up at him, brushing a strand of curly blonde hair out of her face. "Something big, huh? Pike probably caught more gnomes settling in the sewers."

He laughed. "Or Piney's convinced that some sinister force is limiting barley production again. Sometimes I think the Council blows everything out of proportion just so they have something to do."

She gave his arm a squeeze. "Keep playing your cards right and you might get to join the fun someday."

They passed other elves going about their business, most in casual dress that betrayed no hint of their caste or social standing. *They're nobody*, Kacen thought. *They're low on their respective totem poles and they don't want anyone to know.*

He glanced up at the Kralak, a solid block of blue crystal that pierced the sky like a dagger. His vision was hazy, like he was looking through a dirty lens. "Council of Economics Kacen does have a nice ring to it," he said. "And once I'm rid of Granger, I'll build my people a tower even grander than Aldern's..."

A woman collided with them, screaming and pointing at something behind her. Kacen followed her finger to the alley from which she'd burst. A fleshy red blob oozed out through the lid of a dumpster, pulsing and throbbing. It was easily the most disgusting thing he'd ever seen.

"What in the name of Axzar is that?" he asked.

Trisly clutched him tighter. "Whatever it is, it's getting bigger."

The blob had sprouted legs and stubby little arms, and now it was as tall as the surrounding homes, each two stories high. A bubbling mass sprouted upward to become a massive head. Shapeless flesh congealed into hard muscles and coarse hair. A mouth tore open in the half-formed head, shrieking in terrible pain.

The streets around them erupted in chaos. Those who couldn't fight huddled together in frightened groups or ran off screaming.

A pair of soldiers in plainclothes, pistols in hand, shouted for the crowd to get out of their way. A young sorcerer in a black sweatshirt launched a weak bolt of lightning at the thing, but the energy dispersed across it and seemed to make it grow even faster. The bottle giant's left eye appeared first, sprouting like some vile flower, followed quickly by its right. A thin layer of disgusting ooze crackled and spat as it solidified into coarse green skin. Finally complete, the creature thrust its tremendous fists skyward and roared in triumph.

Kacen's jaw dropped and he fumbled in his pockets for his phone. He had to get a hold of Granger. Trisly was gone; he hadn't seen her leave. Frantic, he scanned the scene for his wife but saw no sign of her in the chaos. She'd taken off without him.

The Sorcerer's Tower came down with a sharp crack, and Kacen couldn't get out of the way...

...and then Roger was in a loading dock, surrounded by crates and packages of all sizes stacked not more than ten high and twelve deep. The idiots that worked for him sometimes piled up way too many, and then he—no, she—would have to track them down and berate them for being idiots and maybe dock their pay, depending on how benevolent she was feeling at the time.

"...I told you, Greven, I can't let that shit into the city. Unicorn placenta is not allowed without special dispensation!"

Shellae felt her jowls quivering as she howled at the traveling merchant. The rough nylon of her black uniform chafed at the folds in her ample stomach. If only she didn't have to put in so much overtime correcting the mistakes of her subordinates, maybe she could get to the gym and lose a few pounds. And find a husband. Or at least make friends with someone other than her cat.

Greven's long white fingers dug furiously through the mess of torn and wrinkled papers in his ancient briefcase. The skeletal old man was the best finder in Evitankari. It was Greven's job to track down and acquire items of rare or dangerous repute for elven buyers. It was Shellae's job to make sure that the things he and his clients tried to bring into the city were legal and recorded. "One moment," Greven hissed. He smelled like humans, she thought: warm and humid, like an overgrown swamp in heat. She was glad her job kept her in Evitankari, where all good elves belonged.

"Ah, here it is!" He thrust a thick sheaf of white pages in her face. She snatched it away for a closer examination. All the seals and codes were there, the credentials a Council member used when he or she wished to exert power anonymously. She fitted a square lens to her eye and held the last page up to her face. Through the purple glass, the paper burned with blue flames. These were legit.

"Fine," Shellae snarled as she tossed the papers at Greven's feet. "But I want that shit through my gate quick as a pixie. The hell do they want with it, anyway?"

Greven shrugged and bent down to retrieve his documentation. "It doesn't have many uses, but none of them are good..."

...and then Roger was back in Willowglen, himself once more. He stumbled away from the Evertree in shock and fell flat on his ass. He stayed seated, propped up with his arms, and stared at the grass as he waited for his heart rate to return to normal. The red pixie zipped down to check on him, circling his head and humming to itself. He understood then the significance of the elven funeral ceremony. When the elves decreed the deceased to be "gone, but never forgotten," they meant it. Kacen and Shellae were dead, but they lived forever here in Willowglen.

"I take it one of the few uses for unicorn placenta," Roger paused, amazed he was speaking seriously about such a thing, "is growing a bottle giant."

The Evertree nodded. Up in the canopy, the orange pixie muttered, "No shit."

"I can't find the culprit on my own," Roger said. "I'm not sure I could even find my way back to Merrowood by myself."

"Then you'll have to choose your allies wisely," the Evertree replied.

Roger rose and dusted himself off, resisting the urge to swat at the red pixie that still hovered around his brow. He raised a hand to shield his eyes from its harsh glow. "How did the previous Pintiri die?" he asked, suddenly suspicious of his place in recent events.

"We don't know. Rotreego's body has yet to be recovered."

He'd suspected as much. Someone—and he had a pretty good idea who—was setting him up to fail and bring Evitankari down with him. But how had she compromised the Combined Council? None of the elven leaders struck him as easily manipulated. He was in way over his head, and it was starting to give him a migraine.

Behind him, the little boat ground ashore with a loud scrape. He took that to be his dismissal and turned to go.

"Roger," the Evertree called after him. "Since you're short a steward, why don't you take one of mine? Walinda seems to have taken a liking to you."

The red pixie tried to land on his shoulder but slid right off with a tiny screech. Roger bent forward and caught the little creature in his hands. The pixie put its light out, revealing a young girl in a modest black dress. She reached up to straighten the tiny black hat that rested perilously atop an impressive mop of red hair. "Thanks!" she chirped at him in a scratchy little voice. "And, uh, pleased to meet you!"

Her light flared back to life and she zipped into his breast pocket. Roger wondered just how a pixie was going to take care of Merrowood for him, but he was grateful for the help. "Thank you," he said with a short bow.

The tree smiled. "Remember, Pintiri: trust is a precious thing, and it should not be given away lightly."

— CHAPTER THIRTEEN —

The dirt and gravel and scrub surrounding the decrepit industrial park quickly gave way to a forest of thick pine. Talora avoided the cracked, narrow road leading in the general direction of Detroit, choosing instead to walk parallel to it while using the woods for cover. The going was slow; barefoot, Talora carefully picked her way across the uneven ground. Where there wasn't a sharp rock, there was a downed limb; where there wasn't a downed limb, there were thorns or pine needles or insects. Recent rain made it all slippery or sticky or just plain disgusting. Low-hanging branches and scraggly bushes scratched her skin and tore at her flimsy nightgown. Every few yards she'd glance longingly at the road, at the clear, dry path to the city, but she knew better than to chance it. She wondered briefly if she would've been better off with the Witch but dismissed the thought almost as quickly as it came.

A caravan of automobiles rumbled past half an hour after she started. She ducked behind a bent old pine, peering around its side and through the thick brush at the four black SUVs. Tinted windows hid their occupants, but she knew who was inside. The shifter cavalry was on its way.

Talora sat down with her back against the tree, fully hidden from the road. Her feet were dirty, wet, and caked with leaves and mud and other outdoorsy shit. She really hated the fucking woods. Was that feeling something new, or was it some vestige of her previous life that had survived whatever had been done to her? Not knowing anything about anything was getting really frustrating.

A thunderous explosion echoed from the general direction of the industrial park from which she'd escaped. She looked back and found a thick plume of black smoke billowing above the treetops. The Witch and the shifters must've crossed paths. She didn't much care which side had won. In fact, she hoped they'd both lost.

"No way they got the better of that crazy-ass Witch," she muttered under her breath. Talking to herself soothed her nerves. "Damn forest is too fucking quiet."

Talora stood and brushed herself off, though doing so only further ground the mud into her nightgown. She still wasn't sure exactly what she was going to do when she reached the city, but finding something better to wear sounded like a great start. The weather was pleasantly warm, but it was bound to get colder at night and she'd be downright miserable if she got caught in the rain.

She started off again, veering a bit further from the road and into the thicker brush. How many ways were there into and out of the industrial park? She had to assume that her enemies knew what they were doing, that they'd try to cover any and all escape routes. But how would she know if she encountered a shifter? She'd have to avoid *everyone*, but she knew she couldn't live that way forever. The Witch seemed able to pick out the doppelgangers; she'd done so at the tower and back at her house. Maybe Talora could figure out how she did it.

"If push comes to shove, I've got the fire and I'm ready to use it." Or so she kept muttering to herself every few minutes. What if she roasted someone that wasn't a fake? She didn't want to think about it.

The sun set a few hours later. The forest still gave no sign of becoming civilization. She stopped against a glacial boulder to catch her breath. Waning light leaked through the canopy, softening the gloom just enough so she could see. It wouldn't be long before the woods were pitch black.

"Luckily, I've got a built-in torch," she gasped. "Right. Which will give me away to anyone within a mile."

Somewhere close by, running water burbled across rock like a siren's song. Talora licked her parched lips. She needed to keep moving, but a quick drink wouldn't hurt. She followed the sweet sound, heading away from the road and deeper into the foreboding forest.

After a few moments, the wood seemed to close around her, the space between trees tightening. Skylights in the canopy became few and far between, and the setting sun couldn't penetrate the thick foliage. Talora wondered if she should turn back, but when she looked over her shoulder she found the path she had traveled filled in with thick trees and impenetrable tangles of brush. Danger prickled the back of her neck, but she was tired and dehydrated, she thought, and a drink would do her good. She soldiered on, at places turning sideways to squeeze between trees and bushes. The sound of running water grew louder with every step she took.

Talora stepped between a pair of gnarled, twisting oaks and into a courtyard of sorts, an open space ringed at her back and sides by the forest and in front of her by a massive wall of red thorns. Branches from the forest's edge reached over and above like the roof of a tent, blocking almost all of the quickly fading sunshine. When she looked back the way she'd come, the trees seemed to have edged closer, as if herding her forward toward the imposing fortification.

"A trick of the light," she muttered to herself, though she didn't believe it. "Let's brighten the place up."

She summoned the fire, lighting the tip of one finger like a candle. The urge to unleash the magic, to let the darkness flow through and out of her to destroy the obstacles in her path, was almost overwhelming. She took a deep breath, sweat beading on her brow, and stepped forward to examine the wall of thorns. The light from her flame flickered across the twisting mass of vines like a ballerina twirling across a stage. If this was one plant, it truly was one heck of a plant; not even the faintest hint of light penetrated from the other side. The water was a steady trickle now, echoing forth from just beyond the barrier. She walked up and down the wall but couldn't find a way through. The trees seemed to be pressing even closer, threatening to crush her against the sharp thorns.

A soft gust of cool air caressed her right side, drawing her attention. The leaves above rustled as another breeze wafted past, parting a section of the canopy so that a thin tendril of pink sunset could pierce through to trace a jagged line across the forest floor, like the trail of a drunkard who could only move at sharp angles. Talora followed the line with her eyes, tracing it from her feet, out toward the encroaching trees, back toward the thorn bush, back toward the trees, then finally along a sharp spike that lead to a shadowy gap in the thorn bush that hadn't been there moments ago.

She rolled her eyes and sighed. Someone was stringing her along, and she was pretty sure she knew who. "Fucking Witch," she muttered. The trees behind her creaked ominously in response, a sound like snapping bone. "All right, I'm going."

Talora stomped up to the gap angrily, stopping to peer down the narrow corridor. The wall of thorns was a lot thicker than she expected; the path stretched forward for what seemed like forever, lit by a small pinprick of sunlight at the far end. There wouldn't be much head room underneath the thorny canopy. She didn't like it, and the fire flared angrily in her hands. Still, where else was she to go? She strode slowly, purposefully into the treacherous corridor, keeping her hands close to her sides and concentrating on walking straight.

Several yards in, she spun to face a sudden stream of snaps and pops. The corridor behind her—the way out—had grown over with branches. Burning her way out seemed dangerous. There was no turning back now.

"Idiot," she swore under her breath. The crackling and crunching continued, and to her horror Talora noticed that the tangled branches of the walls and ceiling were steadily growing to fill the corridor behind her. And that growth was gaining speed.

She turned and ran, moving as fast as her bare feet could take her. The ground here was solidly packed dirt, hard and unforgiving, but at least the path was clear of any forest detritus she might trip over. The *crunch-crunch-crunch* of expanding vegetation drowned out her own heavy breathing and racing heartbeat. Every stride jolted her feet and ankles. The rough burn in her chest ached with every ragged, hurried breath.

Three quarters of the way through, her right toe hooked her left heel and sent her careening into the wall of thorns to her left. She shrieked as the sharp teeth raked her arm and leg, but she pushed onward toward the blazing ball of pink and red sunset that was the exit. "I hate the fucking woods!" she growled as she hurled herself through the gap. She landed in a patch of soft, moist grass, her feet aching, her arm throbbing, and her chest burning. She looked back just in time to watch the thick thorn bush seal itself up with a rather ominous slurp.

Talora rolled onto her back and sprawled out on the grass, laughing to herself. That damn Witch had put a hell of a scare into her this time. She gazed up at a thread of paper-thin clouds clinging desperately to the remaining sunset, thinking how silly she'd been. That bush wouldn't have killed her; it was all a game, a test, an I-told-you-bad-things-would-happen-if-you-didn't-stick-with-me. She should've seen it coming from a mile away. Never again.

She rolled to her knees, taking stock of her surroundings. The path had delivered her to a pristine meadow speckled with gray and blue pines thick with age, many as big around as she was tall. Lush green grass surrounded a great cauldron of black stone, a pool almost too perfect to be natural but too beautiful to have been forged by man. On one side a twisting pillar sprung up from the ground. Water trickled out of a crack in its side and then cascaded back down the slick stone to the pool below.

Most importantly, there was no Witch, no demons, and no one who could've been a shifter. Talora was alone in that meadow, and yet she couldn't help feeling like she was being watched.

"I came for a drink," she mumbled. "After all that, I'm getting one."

She rose and moved cautiously toward the pool. The grass was warm and strangely firm beneath her feet, as if it were trying to cushion her stride and soothe her aching feet and legs. There were no dead leaves here, no fallen branches or sticks to trip over, no rocks to scrape her skin and rattle her bones. Talora almost would've sworn she was inside if her eyes hadn't told her otherwise. The place had one heck of a landscaper.

She climbed up onto the smooth lip of the basin, using the extra few feet of height to once again scan the meadow for signs of surveillance. If someone was watching her, that someone was very, very good at remaining hidden. "I know you're here!" she called out. Nothing stirred. Nothing moved. The only response was the distant echo of her own voice.

Talora sank to her knees and craned her face over the rocky edge, even though she was pretty sure the Witch was going to sneak up from behind, shove her in, and then laugh about it like a little girl.

The water was cooler and crisper than any water had a right to be. She drank deeply, surprised by her own thirst. When she pulled her head back up, there was a figure standing on the opposite side of the basin—just as she'd expected. The fire exploded to life in her hands, and with it came that addictive feeling of power and aggression.

"You'll not need that here," the bent old man croaked, his voice like a soft breeze rustling through the forest canopy. The head atop his neck did the talking; the identical head hanging lazily from his left shoulder just stared at her with its gentle black eyes. It was as if someone had tried to cleave the man in two, from his shoulder to his sternum, only to have caused the split half to regenerate the features it was missing. Where there should've been a terrible scar there was instead a crust of black asphalt. He leaned heavily on the gnarled cane in his right hand, his left hanging uselessly at his side. Nude and unashamed, soft green grass sprouted from his weathered brown skin wherever there should've been hair.

Talora tried hard to keep her gaze from drifting downward—not to his manhood, but to his eerily fascinating second head. She kept the fire in her hands alive. "That bush tried to eat me."

The head at his side snorted. "Eat you? 'That bush,' as you refer so callously to the being that just saved your life, was the only thing that kept the shifters from jumping you."

The top head nodded. "The situation called for a measure of haste."

"It wouldn't have had she bothered to cover her trail," the head at his side spat angrily. "Piss-poor escape attempt if you ask me."

The top head rolled its eyes. "Please forgive my other half," he said graciously. "He's still a bit young and impetuous."

"And my other half is senile and out of touch," growled the side head. "Don't feel like you have to humor him."

Talora's gaze flicked from one head to the other as they continued to argue. The effect was a bit dizzying. *Why,* she wondered, *do I never find myself stuck with someone normal?*

"All flames burn some sort of fuel," the top head said mysteriously. "What do yours consume?"

"Hold on a second," she snapped, chopping one fiery hand sideways through the air. "Who the hell are you...guys?"

"Polite, isn't she?" complained the side head.

The strange old man straightened as much as his crooked form would allow, puffing what was left of his chest out with pride. His partially severed side wobbled a bit in response. "I am Pym, King of the Forest!" the top head declared. "Pleased to make your acquaintance, miss..."

"No!" bellowed the side head. "I am Pym, King of the Forest! Get the hell out, you ungrateful wench!"

Talora wasn't sure how much information she could safely divulge; even her name may have been too much. She didn't detect any malice from this odd creature, at least not from the part of him that seemed to be in control, and she couldn't imagine the doppelgangers going to such ridiculous lengths to fool her—although she had to allow that the Witch might. There had to be other forces at work in the world, though, besides those to which she'd been recently exposed, with their own agendas and goals, and there was no telling how they'd react to whatever it was that she had done to herself.

There was only one way to find out. "My name is Talora," she said hesitantly.

"Bull pucky," the side head snarled.

"An old name," Pym replied thoughtfully, "and one that's not been used in quite some time. Forbidden, in many circles."

That explained why the Witch's associates had reacted with such venom toward the word. "Why is it forbidden?"

"To some, your name is a curse. Others leave it be out of reverence, out of gratitude." Pym's face suddenly saddened. "As for why...I remember not."

"There's a surprise," muttered the second head.

Her gaze drifted back to the creature's side. "Are you, um, having a child?" she asked.

The look with which the king fixed her made her feel inexplicably stupid—doubly so, since the second head was eyeing her the same way. "The humans are cutting a road through my woods. The new forest they are creating will need a king." The second head smiled arrogantly.

"You don't mind that they're splitting you in half?" Talora asked.

"It is the way of things. I was king of a much larger forest, a long time ago, one that spread from sea to sea. Before the people. Before the roads."

"Times change, old fart," said the other head.

"That they do, you little twit," Pym replied. He took a few steps closer, following the rim of the basin. His split side jiggled as he moved, popping away a few bits of asphalt. "And that they will. Those most likely to cause these changes are interested in you, Talora."

That was it, then. Here was just another in a long line of people looking to use her for his own ends. "And your interest?" she asked darkly.

"I am but a humble caretaker curious about the confused girl who's led so many troublesome individuals into his woods. Please, extinguish your flames."

She considered Pym for a moment, pondering again how much information he could be trusted with. Then again, she hadn't much information to give. She let the fire in her hands die. "Confused isn't the half of it. I woke up yesterday in a park in downtown Detroit with no memory of my past or how I got there. I don't know why everybody thinks I'm so special."

Pym had continued his trek around the rim of the pool as she spoke. Now, he was a mere quarter turn away. "The King of the Forest knows the souls of all creatures. I may be able to offer some assistance, if you'll allow it."

Talora looked back down into the clear water, locking eyes with the blond, antlered stranger staring back at her. The questions that had been bothering her since she'd woken up on that park bench streamed through her mind once again. *Who am I? Why can't I remember anything? What happened to me?* But what if Pym didn't like whatever it was he found? If he could fill in even the smallest blank it would be worth the risk.

"Do it," she said.

The King of the Forest completed his journey around the basin and took Talora's hand in his own. Pym's solid, bony grip was warm and somehow reassuring. He smelled like rich earth, like fresh, fertile ground. Talora felt the hair on her arm rise as something akin to static electricity flowed from the King of the Forest and into her body.

"Don't be afraid," he cooed. White pupils opened in his all-black eyes like blossoming lilies. "The truth is in there, but it's buried deep..."

A strong breeze kicked up from the east, whipping Talora's hair across her face. Both of Pym's heads began to hum, their lips quivering as they unleashed a piercing buzz like a million angry bees. The pool suddenly boiled beside them, giant bubbles bursting to expel jets of steam angrily into the sky. A cacophony of scents assaulted Talora's nose: warm soil, decaying plant matter, blooming flowers, blood. She could feel a thin tendril of something snaking through her mind, winding and weaving through the dark emptiness as it searched wildly for something she feared it would never find.

And then suddenly she felt Pym grasp at something, at a dark form she never would've discerned from the black background of her consciousness, and then the King of the Forest started to pull. A flash of white burst behind Talora's eyes and every muscle in her body screamed.

When the world came back, she found herself lying on the hard stone of the basin's edge, looking up at the King of the Forest. He seemed puzzled and a bit troubled. The meadow was peaceful again, the pool calm.

"He has no idea," the side head said mockingly.

Pym offered Talora a hand up, but she rose on her own. "All that, and you don't know?"

"I know what you are," he replied. "But I don't know *what* you are."

He waved his hand toward the grass at their feet, beckoning an army of sprouts up from the earth. Buds formed at their tips and then blossomed into bright blue roses. The flowers spelled a word which Talora read out loud. "Serat." She had hoped that saying it would make it stick, give it some meaning, make it her own, but the sounds meant nothing to her. Was it a species? A title? A name? A rank?

"Every forest needs its king," Pym said softly, "and a king cannot rule without knowledge. When I divide, I bestow a bit of knowledge upon my progeny. Most things I learn again in due time. But this term—it must be very old, very rare. Something that's no longer part of our world."

Talora sighed. "It's more than I had before, I guess."

"We must learn to walk before we learn to run, Serat," the king said. "Stay in my meadow tonight. I will keep the shifters at bay."

"What are they?" she asked. "Why are they so interested in me?"

"I know not. This is the first time they've entered my woods. Do not worry about them, my dear. You need your rest."

She shook her head. The King of the Forest had been kind and helpful, but she couldn't help wanting to leave him as soon as she could, especially after his little display of power. "Thank you, Pym, but I really should be going."

He smiled, waving one hand slowly across her eyes. "Sleep, my dear. While you can."

And though she fought it, she did.

— CHAPTER FOURTEEN —

The Evertree's boat ran itself aground beside Piney, who'd taken a seat on the shore. Disembarking, Roger watched as a green sprout poked up through the mud beneath her hand, twisting and unfurling a thin stem and broad little leaves. She smiled up at him and wriggled her fingers. A bud at the top of the stem bloomed into a bright purple blossom.

"Neat trick," Roger said warily. He couldn't help wondering about her intentions. She was so sweet, so innocent, so perky—was it all an act? Was there a lying, scheming, manipulative traitor under that warm veneer?

"One's not so hard," she said happily. "I'm a real hit at parties."

He offered his hand and she took it. Her palm was soft and warm but a little dirty. Roger had been looking for some sweat or clamminess or hesitation, anything that might betray any evil intentions. She giggled as he pulled her to her feet.

He let go, but she didn't. "Need someone to show you back to Merrowood?" she asked.

Unfortunately, as he'd told the Evertree, he did. "If you don't mind, I'd appreciate it," he said shyly, pulling his hand away.

"My pleasure. Follow me, Pintiri."

The crowd in Willowglen had mostly dispersed, though a few knots of conversation still lingered here and there. Roger could feel their judging stares as he and the Council of Agriculture casually wound their way around the Origina toward the far gate. Along the way they passed Tam, his former steward. She wrinkled her nose at them and spat, much to the cackling delight of the two other crones standing by her side. Walinda craned her head out of his pocket, stuck out her tongue to give Tam a tiny raspberry, and then ducked back inside.

"Did you make a friend?" Piney asked, craning her neck to try for a closer look at the pixie. He could feel Walinda shifting angrily in his pocket, but she didn't come back out.

"Merrowood needs a new steward," Roger replied. "The Evertree offered Walinda's services."

"The Evertree is nothing if not generous," Piney chirped. In the waning light, her pale skin seemed to glow. The sun was setting in the distance, burning the thin clouds orange and pink. "The pixies are here to learn the ways of the wood from us. They'll take what they learn back to Talvayne so they can tend the forests there. We host a new group every year."

Roger wasn't all that interested in the details of the pixie foreign exchange program. "Have you seen Aeric?" he asked. "I was hoping to ask him if he'd heard anything about my family."

"I'm sure they're in good hands!" Piney said, perhaps a little too emphatically. "Aeric's the best."

"He's been a good friend. Very supportive."

"That's his main responsibility," she explained. Roger was reminded of his daughter when she was ten years younger, when she'd come home from school and happily recite something complex or interesting she'd learned that day. "The Mongan serves as the Pintiri's right hand, both in combat and in government. The two are supposed to function as a single unit—but it doesn't always work out that way. The Mongan is next in line to be Pintiri, after all, and sometimes that breeds contempt."

Next in line to be Pintiri. That seemed like a possible motive for a traitor, but Roger couldn't make the pieces fit. Aeric could've killed him in his own yard, in the glow of his burning home, and no one would've been the wiser. The Mongan also could've slit Roger's throat when they were alone in Merrowood that very morning. Aeric seemed an honorable sort, so maybe he simply didn't have the stomach for murder. But if that were the case, he could've just voted against Roger with Pike, Driff, and Granger. Unless keeping Roger as Pintiri served some greater purpose...

He sighed deeply. When they got back to Merrowood, his first task for Walinda would be to track down some aspirin and a six-pack of beer.

"Something wrong, Pintiri?" Piney asked.

Roger flashed her a grin. "Just feeling a bit overwhelmed by all the things I don't know."

She reached up to give his shoulder a soft rub. "Evitankari's a lot to swallow, even for those of us who've spent our entire lives here. There are so many rules and regulations and traditions that sometimes I think it's a wonder anyone can accomplish anything."

Roger blinked against the glare as they stepped out from under the wooded canopy that covered the road outside Willowglen. The city was a wash of orange and red where the setting sun hit, purple and blue where the warm light had been stolen from the city's gentle valleys by its rolling hills. Piney casually slipped her arm around his. He had to admit, the view was quite romantic. Shrugging away from her was hard, but he did it anyway. His marriage wasn't officially over, after all, and he still held out hope that Virginia would give him a second chance when she arrived in Evitankari. It was a fresh start, a new beginning, a spark to relight their fire, a literal chance at putting some magic in their relationship—any number of corny phrases and terrible metaphors he thought he might find described in certain magazines or on a few talk shows. Getting too close to Piney could ruin that, but he couldn't just throw her away. If the Council of Agriculture was the traitor, she might slip if she thought she had him under control; if not, well, Piney was one of the few welcoming people he'd met in Evitankari, a rare elf who didn't hold his race against him. He needed to make friends just as desperately as he needed to identify his enemies. He was relieved to see Piney simply shrug and smile at the rejection.

They rounded the corner and dipped down into a shallow bowl. Piney rambled on about her childhood, about being an agricultural prodigy, about how shocked she was to learn she'd been elected Council even though she hadn't mounted any sort of proper campaign. Roger was content to let her go, to nod in situations that seemed to call for it and to offer a "yeah" or a "go on" when more was required. This was probably the closest thing he'd have to peace for a long while. He decided to savor it.

An ominous shadow darkened the slope ahead like a skeletal finger pointing death their way. Roger slowed, tracing its source to a ragged man staring down at them from atop the hill. The fiery light of the sunset at the man's back blurred his features so that he looked like a figure in an abstract painting.

"Get down!" Piney shouted as she threw Roger to the ground and covered him with her body. A bright red fireball tore through the place they'd been standing, colliding with the grass beyond the road and setting it aflame. Roger landed hard on his shoulder and the side of his head, setting the world spinning. In his pocket, Walinda shrieked and beat her little hands against him. He groped for the shotgun at his hip, but he couldn't free the weapon from its holster.

"Roll!" the Council of Agriculture cried, and together they tumbled away from a follow-up blast. Roger could feel the heat on his arm and the smell of sulfur burned his nostrils. Walinda squealed again, fluttering manically, but she was trapped in the fabric of his uniform. He looked up at the hill to find the figure descending, a wraith cloaked in the black robes of Aldern's sorcerers. Their attacker was a tall young man, his dark hair and clothing unkempt and his eyes bloodshot. He would've been handsome if he hadn't been such a wreck. The sneer on his face was absolute death.

"It's not fair!" he snapped, tossing a flame up and down in his right hand like a child might a baseball. "They're taking my boy, but they're keeping *you* around? I'll free that Ether, you son of a bitch, and I'll give it to Evon so they won't send him away."

He took firm hold of the flame, which exploded to twice its previous size with a flare and a whoosh, and he reared back to throw. Roger cringed and Piney pressed herself tightly against him, prepared to shield his body with her own even though the next shot would easily tear through them both. The man was too close; there was no way he'd miss again, and Roger knew he had no time to draw his own weapon and defend himself. His mind flashed to his family, to his last argument with Virginia, to Ricky's confused face as he waved good-bye from the backseat of the departing car, to the last time he'd drunkenly called Samantha at three in the morning and she hung up in an annoyed huff.

A gunshot suddenly rang out and the left side of the man's head exploded in a geyser of blood and bone and flesh. The fireball in his hand died as he fell backward to the cobblestones, a ruined, contorted sack of meat that had mere heartbeats ago been a very alive, very dangerous elf.

Roger pushed Piney aside and leapt to his feet, his heart in his throat and his shotgun in his hand. He scanned the patch of woods to the left of where the man had fallen, but he couldn't find the shooter.

"Hello out there!" he called. "Thanks for the assist!"

Driff melted into view, not out of the trees so much as out of the very shadows. A silver six-gun with a long barrel hung from his hand, smoking. He pushed his spectacles up on his nose. "You're welcome, Pintiri."

Piney sprang to her feet, her fists balled in anger. "You were following us that whole time, weren't you?"

"Guilty," the Council of Intelligence replied nonchalantly. He didn't waste his breath making excuses or trying to justify his actions. "Anyone injured?"

"You saw it all from your damn shadows. You tell us!" Piney snapped.

Roger heard Walinda giggling and pried open his pocket for a look. She waved a tiny hand in response. "I'll live," she sang up at him. "Working for you is already much more fun than spending all day with that tree!" He smiled at her nervously and closed his pocket.

They gathered around the fallen elf. Roger trembled from head to toe. He'd never seen a man killed in cold blood before, and he hoped he'd never have to again. Driff looked down at the sorcerer and sighed. Piney gave the corpse a swift kick in the ribs.

"To Axzar with him," she spat. "Trash like this doesn't deserve eternity in the Origina."

Driff's eyes narrowed and his voice turned to ice. "He had his reasons, as you well know."

Roger was incredulous. "He had his reasons?" He wondered suddenly about Driff's loyalties, even though the man had just saved his life. His knuckles turned white around his shotgun. "What might those be?"

The Council of Intelligence stowed his six-shooter somewhere in the depths of his overcoat. "I'll show you. Tomorrow."

Piney gasped. "But Aldern said—"

"The Pintiri needs to see this," Driff replied firmly. Piney was too stunned to protest. "Show starts at ten. I'll pick you up at

Merrowood at nine thirty." And then the mysterious Council of Intelligence melted back into the shadows as quickly as he'd appeared.

The implications of that short exchange weren't lost on Roger. "Got something to tell me?"

"Yeah," Piney said sadly. She kicked the corpse again. "Driff's an asshole."

— CHAPTER FIFTEEN —

This time Talora woke on her back in a wooden swing, staring up at plastic-wrapped chains, a red and white crossbar, and the soft clouds and blue sky beyond.

"This really needs to stop," she muttered, shaking away the cobwebs. She grasped the chains with both hands and pulled herself up into a sitting position. The outlying pines of the forest loomed ominously to her left, rustling in a soft breeze as if acknowledging her attention. She rolled her eyes and sighed.

"What the hell are you doin' in my backyard?" boomed a deep, gravelly voice from Talora's right. The speaker was the ugliest... thing...she'd ever seen, a hulking blue monstrosity with beady black eyes and a mouthful of thick, crooked molars in a jowled face. Scraggly white hair cascaded down from atop its head and out of its bulbous ears and sprouted from its long, muscular arms. It—she, Talora guessed, judging from its figure and the pink floral print dress it wore—glared down from her perch atop a weather-beaten deck attached to a blue, ranch-style house. When Talora hesitated, the terrifying woman crossed her arms and scowled. "Come on, out with it! I got cookies in the oven and I swear I'll whoop your ass from here to Cleveland if they burn 'cause I'm out here yappin' at you!"

Talora considered calling the magic, but this new creature's rugged skin looked suspiciously fireproof. "I...um...I was just passing through," she stammered. "Sorry to bother you." She stood and searched for an exit. The small backyard was flanked on both sides by white picket fences tall enough to hide the neighboring homes. She really didn't want to go back into the forest. The only way out, without burning down the fence and pissing this woman off even more, would be through the house.

"Nobody that gets dumped in that swing is ever 'just passing through,'" the woman replied. "Why dontcha come up here where I can take a closer look at that thing on your wrist, hmmmm?"

"What do you mean..." Talora started, trailing off when she noticed the bracelet around her left wrist. Thin as a piece of dental floss, it appeared to be made—or grown—of reddish wood with a dark, streaky grain that shimmered when it hit the sunlight just so. It wouldn't move no matter how she tugged at it. "I have no idea where this came from."

The woman sighed and her shoulders sagged. Her hard features softened perhaps as much as they could—which still left her looking like an angry bulldog. "Lord Trelog damn him, he always leaves out the important bits," she grumbled. "If he's gonna go on droppin' every stray he finds in my lap, least he can do is leave 'em a note. Come on up here, child, and let ol' Jehia fill in what Pym forgot to mention."

Talora slipped off the swing and onto her feet. The hair on the back of her neck stood up straight, her danger sense crackling. "Just what did that crazy old fart forget to tell me?"

Jehia's hearty laugh was a mix of thunder and squealing brakes. "Most people hear 'bout the King o' the Forest and assume he's some wise, thoughtful sage like in the movies and the story books. Only those who've met him know how batshit insane ol' Pym really is, though I suppose I'll be doing damn well for myself if I've got it that good when I'm his age. Now c'mere and let's see what his little trinket can tell us."

What choice did Talora have? She approached slowly, trying to look confident, to dissuade Jehia from anything malicious she may have been plotting. It wasn't until she climbed the three rickety stairs to the deck proper that she realized what she was dealing with. Jehia was a good eight feet tall and at least twice her weight. The woman took firm hold of Talora's hand and jerked it up toward her face, twisting and turning it slowly so she could watch the early morning light dance across the grain.

"This bracelet marks you as a friend of the King of the Forest," Jehia explained. Up close her breath was putrid, like an entire henhouse of rotting eggs. "There are many, many Pyms, and he can't have one of his compatriots insulting someone who's earned the confidence of another, hmm? But there's more here. For those of us what knows how to read 'em, Pym's bracelets can tell a bit about our relationship to the wearer—and sometimes he includes special messages for certain folks." Her eyes narrowed as she studied the grain. "Danger," she growled. "Mystery. Flammable: handle with care. Well, ain't that a kick in the pants."

A little peanut of a girl darted out through the sliding glass door behind Jehia and onto the deck, her blonde hair a tangle atop her tiny head. She wrapped herself around Jehia's leg and nuzzled her cherubic face against the big woman's calf. "Cookie time?"

"Almost, deary," Jehia said, patting the girl on the head. "Head back inside and watch Big Bird like a good girl."

"Yay!" the child chirped, disappearing back inside the house just as quickly as she'd emerged.

Talora watched her go, suddenly saddened. "I'm being hunted," was all she could manage.

Jehia nodded. "Shifters and probably worse, the bracelet says. Curse him! He knows I sit for the Grant family on Thursdays." She tapped her chin thoughtfully. "Or maybe that's the point."

"I should go," Talora said awkwardly. She felt like she'd been branded, like the slender line across her wrist was a scarlet letter marking her as someone to fear...or worse. Why would Pym do such a thing?

"No," Jehia said softly, as if trying to convince herself. She rubbed at something hidden under the sleeve of her dress, something at her wrist. "No. The King o' the Forest, crazy as he may be, left you here 'cause you need help. Jehia helps."

The harsh buzz of the oven timer cut through the awkward silence that ensued, soon accompanied by the elated shrieks of several small children. Both women smiled.

"Thank you, Jehia," Talora said. "I'll make it quick."

"And if you don't, we'll give 'em hell," the other woman replied with an evil smile. "One thing before we go inside. Tell me the truth, now: do I look like a troll to you?"

Talora gasped. "Um, no," she stuttered helplessly. "You're very beautiful."

"Ha!" Jehia cackled. She reached down the top of her dress and withdrew a tiny purple stone that hung from a slender silver chain around her neck. "'Fools all manner of magi' my ass. Think I'll get my money back. Just...don't tell the children. This thing's good enough to trick most folks in these parts, and I don't want 'em breathin' anymore o' that damn dust than they have to."

Though she had no idea what Jehia was talking about, Talora crossed her heart and smiled. "Promise."

"Come on in, then," the troll said, smiling. "We'll get you fed, we'll get you dressed, and we'll get you on your way."

Talora followed Jehia through the sliding door and into a wide, open room. Beyond a long dining room table to her left, a set of cherry cabinets framed a large farmhouse sink and matching white appliances. Ahead of her, a long green sectional wrapped itself around a plush blue rug, forming a living room of sorts focused around a big old television in a wooden hutch. It was on that rug that the children lounged around a mound of coloring books and crayons—a boy and two girls, none of them more than seven years old. The boy and the oldest girl had the same curly brown hair and piercing blue eyes.

Jehia made a beeline for the stove and silenced the buzzer. "Now, go wash up, all of you," she commanded, although not without a touch of warmth. "Can't have crayon fingers when it's cookie time. And Jacob, no splashin' your sisters!"

"Yes, Auntie!" the three squealed. They leapt to their feet and disappeared down the hallway to Talora's right.

The oven door fell open with a loud creak. Jehia didn't bother with a mitt; she reached right inside, pulled out a baking tray covered with golden brown chocolate chip cookies, and deposited the tray atop the oven. She used a thin plastic spatula to carefully move each cookie to a cooling rack on the counter. Talora had to admit that the rich aroma of those cookies was probably the best smell she could remember.

"In case you couldn't guess, we're not kin," Jehia explained as she worked. "I've been Auntie to the kids in this neighborhood since...well, since your grandmama's grandmama was in diapers, I'd wager."

"How is that possible?" Talora asked, scanning the room for threats.

"A new concealment crystal every few years. Some new décor. Not that hard, really. You humans are so quick to forget."

Some of us more so than others, Talora thought.

There came a screech from the hallway the children had disappeared down. Jehia put her hands on her hips and smiled. "Jacob!"

"Sorry!" came the contrite reply. Talora snickered.

"Do you have any children of your own?" Jehia asked. She'd finished transferring the cookies to the cooling rack and had moved on to dusting them with powdered sugar from a metal shaker.

Talora hesitated, surprised that the troll had called her by a name she hadn't given, then decided it must've also been encoded on Pym's bracelet. The realization made her uncomfortable, especially considering what he'd said about her name being taboo among certain people. "I don't know."

"Ahhh, an amnesiac. Or someone who was dusted out o' her gourd. Pym's favorite kind of stray."

"Dusted?"

Jehia clicked her tongue. "Golly, you got it *bad*. The dust locks away unwanted memories—usually the kind other people don't want you to have. Keeps the humans from mixing with the rest of us and causing all kinds o' trouble."

Talora bit her lip, thinking. She was the one responsible for her own condition, if the Witch could be believed. What had she wanted to hide from herself? What horrible thing had she wanted to forget badly enough to blast her entire life out of her skull? The possibility that she might be better off not knowing about her past had never entered her mind.

"The rest of us?"

The troll waved her free hand about her face. "Us. People like me. People like Pym. People like nothing you've ever imagined. And now, people like you."

"And the humans are fine with this arrangement?"

"Truth be told, most never get much of a choice," Jehia said with a heavy sigh. "They're better off, or so says those in charge. Seems like a load o' bull to me."

The children came streaming back into the kitchen to swarm around their Auntie and leer hungrily at the cookies cooling on the counter. Jehia smiled at Talora once more and turned her attention to the little ones. "Everybody show me your hands." They raised their little hands high so she could inspect each in turn. Satisfied, she nodded and winked. "Have at it, dearies."

They descended upon the rack of warm cookies like vultures, shrieking and grasping wildly for the choicest morsels. When Talora reached out to take a cookie for herself, Jehia swatted her hand away. "Not until you wash up and put on something respectable," the troll said primly. "You smell like a barn."

Talora nodded, then blushed. She'd forgotten that the nightgown she wore was barely more than a wisp of shredded, filthy cloth. Little Jacob was staring up at her with saucer-sized eyes.

"Thanks, Auntie," she said as she brushed past the children on her way to the bathroom.

"There's extra towels in the linen closet by the door. Stay out of the red shampoo unless you want all of your hair falling out."

Modest and narrow, the bathroom was decorated with blue and yellow pastels and plain white tile. A single frosted window opposite the door let in a bit of sunshine. Talora found a fluffy white towel in the tiny linen closet and turned to face herself in the mirror above the pedestal sink. She had hoped that the grimy, disheveled woman staring back would seem somehow more familiar, but if anything, her own reflection was even more foreign than it had been in that elevator with the Witch. She had a name and a title of some sort, but none of it felt like it fit.

"Serat," she whispered to the woman in the mirror. Saying it out loud like that made her feel awkward.

Talora reached around the yellow shower curtain and cranked the hot water. She slipped out of the nightgown, gingerly pulling it around her antlers. Although she felt a bit silly about folding the ruined garment and placing it atop the toilet seat, it was her only possession and she wanted to take care of it. The thought made her sad.

She didn't climb into the shower until steam poured out over the curtain. The hot water was fantastic. Dirt and muck sloughed off her like a dead skin from a shedding snake, temporarily taking her concerns with it. Showers, she decided, had not been built with antlers in mind; she had to keep her head at a very precise angle so as not to painfully jar one of them against the wall. The warmth loosened her muscles and settled her nerves—at least until the soap and hot water found her ruined feet. She stepped away and sat down on the far side of the shower, letting the water rush down her back. For the first time Talora could remember, she truly felt safe. No Witch, no demons, no shifters, no crazy woodland royalty. Sure, there was a big, ugly troll, but Jehia was a big, ugly troll with a heart.

She raised her wrist to take another look at Pym's band. Glistening water beaded across the thin wood. It had assisted her with Jehia, she knew, but she couldn't help worrying that it would betray her to the wrong people. She summoned the fire, watching the steam rise from her fingertips. Though flames danced around it, the bracelet didn't catch.

Then she remembered something Pym had asked her. *All flames burn something. What fuels yours?* Suddenly overcome with worry, she let the fire die. She stood, killed the water, and clambered out to towel herself off.

Sometime during her soak, the nightgown had been replaced with a blue dress, modest but pretty, and a simple set of cotton underwear. She gladly put it all on, happy with the way she looked in the mirror, and then she blow-dried her hair—another task that seemed like it would've been much easier if she hadn't had foot-long antlers sticking out of her head. She looked good, she thought. Normal. Untroubled. Like someone no one would pay unnecessary attention to, if only she could get rid of the damn antlers. Maybe Jehia had a saw she could borrow.

The little blonde girl waiting for Talora in the hallway stared up at her as if she was anything but normal. "You're empty," she said sadly, her two hands wrapped around a cookie as big as her face. She looked guilty, like she'd opened something she shouldn't have.

Talora was taken aback, her illusion shattered. To hear it put so plainly by this little girl was flat out jarring. "Something like that."

"You used it alllllllll up," the child continued, braver now, proud of her assessment. "I felt you using it in there."

Talora looked back at the bathroom door. The fire. Could this seemingly normal child somehow sense the use of magic? "You're a very smart girl," Talora said soothingly, trying to mask her unease with what she hoped was a warm smile. "What else can you tell me?"

"That's it!" The girl shrugged, took a big bite of her cookie, and scampered back to the living room.

Jehia appeared around the bend, holding a small tray of cookies and a big glass of milk. "Let's chat out front."

Engrossed in a loud, brightly colored cartoon and a pile of freshly baked treats, the children didn't even notice the two adults exiting through the front door. Talora thought about calling the fire to see if it would catch the little blonde girl's attention and then decided against it. Jehia had been very helpful, but there was no telling how the big troll would take to a magic fire being lit in her living room, right behind her back.

The thin white decking of the front porch groaned at Jehia's weight but didn't seem to notice Talora's. They sat on a long white bench built against the baby blue siding, the steaming plate of cookies between them. The neighborhood beyond was quiet, serene, almost worthy of the front of a postcard. But the roads and sidewalks were weathered and cracked. Small suburban houses listed to one side or were in dire need of a painter's attention, many of them in imminent danger of being swallowed whole by their untamed lawns. Plywood covered the windows of one heavily graffitied home down the block.

"Place ain't what it used to be," Jehia said with a heavy sigh, "but home's home."

Talora fought back her sudden, surprising jealousy by grabbing a cookie and taking a big, greedy bite. It was the best thing she'd ever tasted. She couldn't describe why, but that sweet, chocolate taste brought her back to a childhood she couldn't remember. It wasn't that it evoked people or places, but feelings—warmth and security and contentment. She understood then exactly why the King of the Forest trusted Jehia with his runaways. She couldn't imagine a person more hospitable, more nurturing, or better equipped to get someone rested and relaxed and ready to get back to life.

"You're amazing, Jehia," she said between bites. "I can't thank you enough."

"Pass it on, dear," the troll replied, all modesty. "Did little Rachel tell you anything helpful?"

Talora paused to consider the question. "Yes and no. Can the other children do that too?"

Jehia shook her head sadly. "No, Rach is a rare breed, the product of an elf and a human. Got no magic of their own, but they're extremely sensitive to the magic of others."

Magic. There was that word again. The thought that she was somehow magical made Talora uncomfortable, and yet in a way it also felt right. It felt good to have power, to have a fighting chance against anyone or anything that might want to harm her. It made her different, and she liked it.

"The children," she said, reaching up to touch her left antler. "Will you have to dust them? Or anyone that walks past?"

The troll chuckled, a sound like rocks tumbling down a hill. "I don't think so. Adults never believe the fantastic stories of children. They'll tell their parents about you, and their parents will shrug and play along and not believe a word that comes out of their precious little mouths. As for the neighbors..." She pointed up at a complex rune carved into the ceiling that pulsed faintly with red light. "That ward makes sure they won't see nothing I don't want 'em to, unless they've got the sight."

Talora nodded. The world was starting to make a little more sense, for all its seeming lunacy. "So, what do I do next? I don't want to be a burden on you, but I'm not sure where I should be going or what I should be doing."

Before Jehia could respond, a sleek black sports car with tinted windows roared around the corner and came to a screeching halt right in front of the house. The door swung open and a thin, dashing man in a sharp black suit climbed gracefully out. His horns glinted softly in the sunlight, polished to a sheen that matched that of his shoes. He carried a black walking stick topped with a red jewel.

"Talora!" he called. "We've been looking everywhere for you!"

Talora could feel Jehia tense beside her, but the troll stayed still, waiting for her to make the first move. The man seemed familiar, but she couldn't quite place him.

"Come now, love," he said, continuing to stroll casually toward the house. "Say your thank yous and get in the car."

When his wingtip hit the first step, Jehia leapt to her feet. "That's close enough, demon!"

Demon. That was it; Talora had met him that first night with the Witch, in that terrible boardroom atop the white tower. He was one of the Witch's associates. Talora couldn't recall his name. Her memories of the man were a ragged, disconnected mess. How had that happened? She struggled to sort through it all.

"You are in no position to dictate to me, troll," he said sweetly, smiling like a used car salesman. "One phone call and this whole neighborhood never existed."

Jehia snorted. "Need to get some new damn wards," she muttered.

And then Talora settled on a particularly powerful memory: a vision of this demon on the lawn of a quaint home in a nice neighborhood, surrounded by police cars and armed officers—massacring them all. He was a killer, plain and simple, and he'd come to collect her and drag her kicking and screaming back to his tower. What would he do to Jehia and the children? Talora couldn't let anything happen to them.

The fire came almost of its own accord, blossoming with a sharp crack. She raised her flaming left hand to her face and glowered over it at the demon. Both he and Jehia took a step back.

"Hold on," the demon said, raising his hands. "Let's not do anything hasty. It's me. It's Cr—"

She didn't let him finish. The fire snapped from her hand like a whip, wrapping itself around him and lifting him into the air. She'd only meant to knock him away, but the exhilaration of using the magic took over. His suit and hair caught first, flaking away in small bits of fabric and ash. Then his skin split, the wounds cauterizing instantly and then splitting and sealing again and again and again. She didn't stop the fire until he stopped screaming, and even then, the wave of euphoria that came with using the magic was almost too much to bear. The blackened husk of the demon's body hit the pavement with a sickening thud.

"That," Jehia said, her voice quivering with fear, "was some trick."

A soft whimper drew Talora's attention back toward the house. Three very distraught children were staring out the window, their saucer eyes caked with tears. Talora's heart dropped, wiping away the rush that came with using the magic.

"I'll get the dust," Jehia said sternly. "You get the hell out of here."

Talora nodded and scampered down the steps, her lip quivering as she stepped over the smoldering corpse. She climbed into the car and slammed the door behind her. The demon had left his keys in the ignition and the engine running. Talora gripped the steering wheel so hard her knuckles turned white. Although she wanted nothing more than to collapse in a sobbing heap, she refused to let her emotions get the better of her. She knew this wouldn't be the last time she'd have to defend herself. Best to get used to it now. Shedding tears for a demon would be a waste anyway.

Talora threw the vehicle into gear and sped away, unsure of where she was going or what she was going to do when she got there. All that mattered was putting distance between herself and her pursuers—and the friends she'd lost because of what she'd just done.

— CHAPTER SIXTEEN —

Roger didn't sleep well that evening. Upon returning to Merrowood, he'd said his weary good nights to Piney and Walinda and trudged upstairs to the massive fourposter bed. Unconsciousness took him quickly, but it did so only to torment him. Dreams took him to the Council Chambers, accompanied by the other members of Evitankari's government, and one by one each transformed into a depraved man in a black robe, a ragged hole where the side of his head should've been. Sometimes Roger was back in his own home with Virginia at his side, watching his children open their Christmas presents as the house burned around them. Reliving the Evertree's memory of Kacen, he frantically searched for his phone while the top floor of the Kralak plummeted his way. Roger would wake from one grisly nightmare, try in vain to convince himself to relax, and fall back asleep to yet another terrible vision.

Early in the morning he finally gave up trying to sleep and turned his attention to the pictures on the wall. The sun was peeking out over the horizon and most of Evitankari was still asleep. He paused for a moment over the ruins of the Kralak. All of the debris was gone and its foundation had been torn from the earth, leaving a rather ominous crater shrouded in a cloying haze. Out of respect, he removed that one from the wall and stowed it in the nightstand. The others were less unsettling. He watched as merchandise and livestock moved through the cavernous customs house, measured and weighed and taxed where applicable. Willowglen was calm and serene and beautiful. Roger had a hearty laugh at the sight of Pike rushing out of his house in a fuzzy robe and slippers to cuss out the paper boy who'd put the day's news through his front window. Merchants arranged their wares in breezy tents packed almost on top of each other in an open-air market. A host of elves buzzed about a town square dominated by the towering statue of an armored man clutching a huge sword, sweeping the cobblestones and hanging flowers from a dais at the statue's feet.

Evitankari looked a lot like the cities and towns Roger was used to, only prettier. Were it not for the magic and the intrigue and the elves and the never-ending threat of a gruesome demise, Evitankari might have been a fantastic place to live. Roger shook his head, killed the light, and curled back up on top of the sheets. How had things become so complicated so quickly? Three days ago, he'd been cleaning toilets, his biggest decision coming down to a choice between Chinese takeout and a few hours at the pub. He'd had his worries, sure, about Virginia and Samantha and Ricky and the ever-tightening budget at the school, but they all paled to what he was feeling now.

He finally managed to get a bit of rest, but it was not to last. Walinda burst into the room, her harsh red glow warming his eyelids. Roger cracked one eye to watch, annoyed. The pixie stopped at the foot of the bed and gave a sing-song little whistle. The heavy curtains over the windows sprang open, removing Roger's only defense against the intrusive morning. He closed his eye and groaned.

"Wake up! Wake up! Wake up!" Walinda chirped. The gentle breeze from her wings ruffled the hair on his forehead. "The Council of Intelligence will be here in an hour!"

"So let me sleep another thirty minutes," he mumbled into his pillow through a mouthful of drool.

"Hrmph!"

Something pattered across his cheek, up to his temple, back down the side of his face to his chin, then to his lips and his nose. When Roger realized what it was, he couldn't believe it. "Okay! Okay! Just stop kicking me in the face!" He sat up and rubbed the sleep from his eyes, stifling a yawn.

The pixie's red light faded as she landed on the bedspread between his feet. Walinda had traded her black dress in for a blue maid's uniform, a short skirt with a white apron and black leggings. Her fiery red hair was pinned up behind her head in a bun. Roger found himself strangely attracted to the cute little woman. He wasn't sure what to make of that.

"Stop gawking at me and get up!" she snapped, her hands balled on her narrow hips. "You're never going to be late for *anything* while I'm around, that's for sure, and you'll never leave my house without a shower and a good breakfast! Go get washed up while I find you something decent to wear—and be quick about it or your eggs'll be colder than a gnome's toes in August!"

"A...a...what?"

The curtains and the canopy over the bed rustled, and the drawers in the nightstand whipped open and slammed shut. A strange quake shook the pictures on the far wall, knocking them all askew. Walinda's bright eyes flared black and her voice turned deeper and angrier than even Pike's. "DON'T MAKE ME SAY IT AGAIN."

Roger bolted off the bed, stumbled over the threshold into the bathroom, and slammed the door behind him. "I live with a fucking poltergeist," he muttered under his breath, his hands quivering.

The sound of Walinda's cheerful humming on the other side of the horribly thin door made his skin crawl. He undressed quickly and leapt into the shower, thankful that the rushing water drowned her out. Midway through washing his hair, he burst into a fit of self-conscious laughter. The supposedly high-and-mighty Pintiri, hero of the elven nation, had run in fear from a seven-inch tall woman with a sassy attitude and a bit of telekinesis. He hoped she wouldn't tell anyone.

Showered and dried and wrapped in a fluffy towel, Roger cracked the door open very slowly and peered out into the bedroom. Walinda was nowhere to be seen and the door to the hallway was shut tight. He gave himself one last rub-down with the towel and quickly changed into the outfit his steward had left on the bed: black jeans, black shirt, black boots, and a black leather jacket with a white stripe down each arm. His shotgun hung at his hip in a holster on his belt as it had the day before. He liked having it there; its weight was a comforting reminder that he wasn't as powerless as he had so often felt since arriving in Evitankari.

He left the bedroom timidly, his hand drifting to the stock of his shotgun as he crept down the stairs to the first floor. Walinda's cheerful humming drifted up from the dining room, echoing softly against the foyer's high ceiling. Roger took a deep breath and entered the room. Only the place at the head of the long table was set. A simple white plate piled high with scrambled eggs, bacon, sausage, and hash browns waited for him beside a bowl of fruit salad and a heavy mug of steaming coffee. Walinda sat atop the back of the chair, her legs dangling like a child's. "Breakfast is served!" she chirped. "Eat up. You've got a big day ahead of you."

Roger's stomach growled as he quickly crossed the dining room and took his seat. Walinda flared red and took off, zipping into the kitchen off to his left. He wasted no time diving into his meal. It felt like forever since he'd filled his stomach. The eggs were soft but firm, the sausage sweet and savory, the bacon crunchy and smoky. Breakfast was perfect.

But the potatoes were the best part. "These hash browns are great, Walinda!" Roger called out after wetting his whistle with a swig of coffee. He hoped a bit of flattery would keep his steward happy—and keep her from pelting him with silverware or bringing the chandelier down on his head. "There's something different in them. What is it?"

The little red light dashed back into the dining room and stopped beside the chandelier. "I'm glad you like your meal, Pintiri, especially those potatoes. I couldn't remember if human physiology could handle troll's milk."

Roger gagged around the bite of potato in his mouth. He could feel the blood draining from his face, turning him a pasty, sickly white as he fought against the bile rising in his throat.

Walinda cackled down at him, her flight suddenly unsteady and ragged. "You're too easy, Pintiri! That's just a bit of nutmeg!"

And then she zoomed back into the kitchen, leaving Roger speechless and a bit humiliated again. He wondered if she had been like this with the Evertree. Maybe that was why the old willow had been so willing to give her away.

The doorbell chimed as Roger finished his last bite of sausage. Walinda zipped by to answer it. "Pintiri, may I present Council of Intelligence Driff," she announced as she led the elf into the dining room. Driff followed casually, his eyes flickering across every corner of the room before they finally settled on Roger.

"Good morning, Pintiri," the elf said coolly. There was an icy calm to the man, an alertness to his situation that made Roger uncomfortable. Driff's business-like execution of yesterday's attacker didn't help Roger's nerves. "Are you prepared for today's festivities?"

"Not really." Roger sipped his coffee anxiously. "What exactly are you dragging me into?"

"One of Evitankari's oldest and most storied rituals. It's kept the city safe and the elven people strong for many millennia." His tone had changed ever so slightly. Was that sarcasm?

"I'm looking forward to it," Roger replied. "There's so much to learn about your people."

Driff nodded, his expression and body language completely unreadable. The mysterious Council of Intelligence obviously wasn't one for polite small talk.

Roger wiped his mouth with his napkin and stood. "Thanks again for breakfast, Walinda. I, uh, I'll see you later." He wasn't sure how else to dismiss his steward. Anything more formal would've sounded wrong.

Roger and Driff stepped out of Merrowood and into a gray, overcast morning. Storm clouds gathered on the horizon, big puffy bundles of rain and thunder. Roger zipped his jacket against the cool breeze wafting in from the northeast.

"Appropriate weather," Driff said, gazing up at the ominous sky.

"Just what kind of ritual is this?" Roger asked, burying his hands in the pockets of his jeans. He wished Walinda had provided a hat. "And what does it have to do with what happened yesterday?"

"You'll see soon enough," the elf replied as he stepped off the porch and strode quickly down the path to the road. Roger hurried to catch up.

Driff charted a course toward the heart of Evitankari, opposite the way Aeric had taken him to Willowglen. The Council of Intelligence made no effort to engage Roger in conversation. He kept his eyes forward and his pace steady. It was like he was in a trance, Roger thought, like his consciousness was somewhere else entirely. He found himself wondering about Driff's sanity. There were too many shadows on this particular road, too many convenient places in which Driff could fade away, circle around Roger, and put a bullet in the back of his head.

Stop being so paranoid, dummy. If he wanted you dead, he wouldn't have saved your life. Roger couldn't take the silence anymore. "I wanted to thank you again for yesterday, Driff. I don't know what we would've done if you hadn't stepped in."

"You would've died a horrible, fiery death," Driff said matter-of-factly, his eyes still distant.

Coming from anyone else, there would've been no doubt that statement was a joke. Coming from Driff...Roger wasn't so sure. He forced himself to laugh anyway. "You're not going to follow me everywhere I go, are you?"

The elf shrugged. "It's my job to know what's happening in Evitankari. It's also my job to disseminate word of such happenings among the appropriate parties. Hence today's excursion."

So, you're basically the town gossip, Roger thought. He wondered which nosy elves needed to know what the Pintiri was up to. He suddenly felt very self-conscious about having walked out of Willowglen with Piney.

"Have you heard anything about my family?" Roger asked hesitantly. He wasn't completely comfortable bringing them up around Driff.

"The extraction's in progress," the Council of Intelligence replied. "It's not a simple grab. Your name spread quickly and certain unsavory characters are looking for your wife and children. We've taken your family into our custody. They're likely in no immediate danger, but all of the obvious routes away from the safe house in which we've stashed them are under heavy surveillance. We've got a bit of a bait-and-switch in the works. They'll be here in a day, maybe two."

Driff's answer left Roger both reassured and concerned. Despite Aldern's warning, he hadn't expected his family to become a target this soon. He'd barely been in Evitankari for two days. But Driff's response was also the most direct answer Roger had received to any question he'd asked of the elves, and the Council of Intelligence seemed like he knew his stuff. Roger wasn't happy about it, but he had no choice but to trust the elves to get the job done.

The rain came then, hard and almost horizontal. Roger cringed, trying to force as much of himself into his jacket as possible. He watched the lightning playing off in the distance, counting the seconds before the thunder. *One one thousand, two one thousand, three.* Driff didn't seem to care, though occasionally he'd wipe the moisture off his spectacles with a soft black cloth stowed in the pocket of his overcoat.

Their destination, a neighborhood on the northern edge of the city, seemed older than the others he'd seen. Bent, cracked cobblestones jutted up from the street at jaunty angles. Here, the elves had built with a different material, a brick the color of sandstone that had pitted and chipped over time. Windows were slim panes of glass, doors single flat pieces of steel. Nothing was trimmed, detailed, or decorated, though narrow gardens of bright flowers bloomed between the buildings and the streets. Torrents of rain streamed off the steeply pitched tin roofs, creating drier tunnels of a sort against the sides of the buildings. The few elves they encountered squeezed past with nods or smiles—the vast majority of them directed at the Council of Intelligence—though the passersby were all as dour as the day.

"This is Old Ev," Driff explained, his voice raised over the pounding waterfalls and the sharp patter of rain on the metal roofs. "We first settled here, before we raised the city wall and cast the directional wards. These homes were built for defense."

Roger noted the sharp angles on either side of the windows. The shape would've allowed a bowman or a gunner to fire at a wide view without exposing himself to counter fire. The foundations, he saw, were granite and mortar painted with black pitch—flame retardant, he guessed. No attacker could've possibly found any purchase on the steep roofs, though he noticed a few hatches through which the inhabitants could send hot oil cascading down the incline. Roger was glad to see all the time he spent watching historical documentaries finally paying off.

"What's a directional ward?" he shouted back over the rain and thunder.

"Very, very powerful magic. Those who know what they're looking for are allowed access to a strict path that funnels them directly to our main gate. If you're heading our way and you don't know we're here, the wards will force you to turn around and walk in the opposite direction without you even realizing it."

The narrow street they traveled emptied into a sprawling plaza. A perfect hexagon, a good three hundred paces from one side to the other, each of its six corners connected to another avenue. Cobblestones gave way to ancient red brick worn smooth and round by millennia of weather and traffic. The bricks spiraled around and around to the white and red marble dais in the center and the towering monument it supported. A stone warrior loomed above Old Ev, carved from a single rock as black as night. The man wore thick plate armor inlaid with swirling designs. His left hand clutched a round shield, his right a tremendous longsword. Strangely, he wasn't an elf; his ears were round.

"Tash Square," Driff said.

"Oh," Roger replied. He pointed up at the statue, recognizing it from his time examining the pictures on his bedroom wall. "Is that Tash?"

Driff shook his head. "Long story. Better left for another time."

The Combined Council had gathered at the statue's feet beside a three-foot tall pillar that seemed cut of the same chunk of marble as the dais from which it sprouted. Small groups of elves gathered around in tight knots of no more than three or four, many clustered together beneath broad umbrellas. No one looked particularly excited to be there.

Aldern stepped forward from the gaggle of elves to welcome Roger. He carried no umbrella and he wore no jacket over his thick robes. The rain parted around the fragile old elf as if he were generating some sort of hydrophobic field. Roger had no doubt that he was actually doing just that.

"Good of you to join us, Pintiri," Aldern said gravely. "I fear we may bury your good spirits beneath all of our solemn rituals."

Driff ignored the old elf, strolling casually to the statue's far leg where he stood separate from the other members of the Council. Roger let him go. "Evitankari can't be all doom and gloom," he said. "Besides, if I'm going to do my job, I should participate in everything I can." Not that he particularly wanted to be Pintiri, but he assumed he'd live a lot longer if he served well.

The Council of Sorcery nodded and turned back toward the dais. Roger followed, searching for some clue as to what Driff had gotten him into. Someone in the crowd was sobbing, but none of those gathered would meet his gaze. Piney nodded at him and wandered over toward Driff.

Roger and Aldern stopped before a small boy in a bright yellow raincoat standing beside the pedestal, his face streaked with tears and his brown hair matted down and sopping with rain. Chyve stood to his left, a reassuring hand on his shoulder. Pike was to his right, looking none too happy. The little boy looked up at Roger and sniffled. He was a little peanut of an elf, no more than eleven or twelve.

Aldern groaned as he lowered himself to one knee at the boy's side. "All right, Evon. This is it. Your last chance. Show me something, son."

The name took Roger aback. This was the Evon to whom his attacker had wanted to give the Ether. But what did the Ether have to do with this strange gathering? And why had it mattered enough that the sorcerer—who had to be the boy's father—was willing to kill to get it?

Little Evon took a deep breath, balled his fists, and closed his eyes and mouth tight. His cheeks and shoulders quivered with effort as he put his all into whatever Aldern wanted him to do. Roger had no clue what the Council of Sorcery expected of the boy, but he was strangely impressed by how hard he was trying.

Evon's breath came out in a ragged gasp about a minute later and his entire body seemed to slump. Beside him, Chyve shook her head and looked to Aldern. Granger, disinterested as always, yawned and checked the gaudy gold watch around his wrist.

"You gave it all you've got, son," the Council of Sorcery said solemnly. The compliment rang a bit hollow. "Most just give up."

Aeric shouldered past the others to stand beside Roger, carrying a little black pouch tied tight with a leather band. He opened it up to reveal its contents: a fine silver powder that sparkled even in the darkness of the storm. "The next part is usually the Pintiri's job, though the task falls to the Mongan if the Pintiri is indisposed," he explained. "No one will think ill of you if you refuse."

Roger eyed the powder, realization dawning. "That's the dust you mentioned. The stuff that knocked me out, that you said can erase memories."

Aeric nodded. "Narii dust. It only takes a pinch. Sprinkle it around his nose. When his eyes go white, tell him to forget."

Everyone's attention was on Roger and he knew it. If he were going to survive, he needed to win over as much of Evitankari as he could. Aeric was giving him a chance to do just that.

He reached into the bag and withdrew a pinch of the dust. The soft, round grains radiated a surprising warmth. Evon kept his gaze downcast, but he couldn't help inhaling the dust Roger let fall just above the tip of his nose. The boy's head jerked, his green eyes rolling back into his head to reveal their white undersides. Evon stood stiff as a board, awaiting a command.

"Forget," Roger croaked, his voice cracking. "Forget it all."

Evon's small frame spasmed once and then he was still again. As his eyes rolled back into place, Aldern took his little hand and pressed it to the top of the marble pedestal. A flash of light cut through the gloom, and then Evon was gone.

It would be better for the boy this way, Roger thought. No more pressure to be something he couldn't be. No memories of his fallen father. A fresh start.

"Congratulations, Pintiri," Driff called from his spot beside the statue's far leg. "You've just exiled your first shala'ni."

— CHAPTER SEVENTEEN —

The needle had been on empty for the last five miles. Talora grudgingly pulled off the highway and into a service plaza—the last for twenty miles, if the signs were to be believed. With the skyscrapers of Detroit mere smudges in her rearview mirror, she didn't doubt it. The thought of stopping for any reason troubled her, but she was far enough from the city—she hoped—that the risk of discovery was minimal. She rolled the car to a halt beside one of the four pumps and killed the engine. There were other vehicles parked in the lot on the other side of the big white building, but she was alone at the pumps.

She leaned across the dash and flipped open the glove compartment, rummaging through the papers and trash in search of a few dollars for gas. Her fingers closed on something cold and metallic: a locket, a little gold heart on the end of a thin gold chain. Not the kind of thing she expected a demon to keep in his vehicle. Curious, she popped it open with her thumb and found a familiar face staring back at her. The picture in the locket was of Talora, sans antlers, leaning her head against the chest of the demon she'd immolated from Jehia's front porch.

Time seemed to stop. What the hell was this? Why had she taken pictures with that monster? Why did she look so happy? She was confused and angry and frustrated that she couldn't answer any of the questions streaming through her empty mind. It was obviously a woman's locket; it would've been hers, not his. She'd just killed someone important to her in her previous life, someone who, in hindsight, didn't seem to have meant her any real harm. Someone guilty by association.

"I don't have time for this shit," Talora growled as tears streamed down her face. Despite the complications the locket implied, it was the only link she had to her previous life. The dress Jehia had given her didn't have pockets, so she begrudgingly put it on. It felt like an eighty-pound weight dangling from her neck.

Crim hadn't left any cash or credit cards in his vehicle. The handful of quarters in the cup holder wouldn't buy more than a half gallon of fuel. As Talora cleaned up her face with a handful of napkins, she realized she'd have to steal a tank of gas and immediately get back on the road. Her empty stomach growled; she'd hoped to grab something to eat here, too, but she didn't think she was savvy enough to rob the rest stop's convenience store without getting caught. The magic could certainly get her out of any sticky situation, but its use could also give away that she'd been here. How many antlered women could burn down a rest stop just to steal a few sandwiches? Best to ignore her hunger and move on quickly.

Talora climbed out of the sports car and into a bright, sunny afternoon. Traffic streamed steadily down the highway on the other side of the rest stop's small patch of yellow grass. Talora couldn't make out any faces in the passing vehicles; she hoped that meant the motorists couldn't see her antlers well, either. She removed the gas cap, pushed the nozzle into the receptacle, and squeezed the trigger. The digital numbers on the cracked screen counted upwards at an unbearably slow rate. Relying on fire as her only defense in the middle of a gas station, she realized, would be a dangerous proposition.

The main building's automatic doors slid open to allow a heavyset trucker in a matching camouflage cap and sweatshirt to exit. He spat, pulled up his sagging sweatpants, and headed for Talora. She watched him out of the corner of her eye, hoping he'd go away if she didn't pay any attention to him. He didn't.

"Afternoon, miss," he drawled cheerily, tipping his cap. "Mighty fine set of antlers you got there."

Obviously, he wasn't the type to take a subtle hint. Bitchy it was, then. "Awww shucks, I bet you say that to all the girls. Get lost."

That elicited a smile. "You she-demons are always so prickly. It's kind of hot."

She released her hold on the pump for a moment and let the fire flare and die in her hands. "It can get a lot hotter." When the flames dissipated, she squeezed the pump's trigger angrily and willed it to fill the car's tank faster.

"Cool trick. You showed me yours, so let me show you mine." He unzipped his sweatshirt and yanked it open, revealing his bare torso. His chest was gone, replaced with a clear glass orb through which Talora could see the back of his sweatshirt. A pixie lounged on a small recliner inside the orb. The little creature smiled up at her and waved. "Beats flapping my little wings to get everywhere." The man's mouth moved to match the pixie's. "And it keeps the humans from getting nervous. Do you know how hard it is to go to the bank or do some grocery shopping when you're a fucking pixie?"

"Can't say I do, or that I particularly care. Just tell me what the fuck you want so I can tell you where you can stick it."

"Ooooooh, saucy!" He zipped his sweatshirt back up. "Obviously you're new at this whole demon thing, given that you look relatively human. Judging from how nervous and alert you are, I'm assuming you stole that car and you have no money with which to pay for the gas you're pumping into it. You're frightened and confused, and you don't know where you're going, just that you're going as far as you can as fast as you can. How am I doing so far?"

She didn't answer. The numbers on the pump crawled inexorably higher.

"There's always a bit of profit to be made from your type. Not in selling you out—no-no-no—but in helping you find your way. If you don't, I'm down the cost of a tank of gas and a cheap lunch. But if you do...well, you can never be on the good side of too many demons."

The trucker's talk of food set Talora's stomach in motion. She wished she could believe him, if only because he'd come right out and told her his intentions. That was more than the Witch or Crim or Tallisker or even the King of the Forest had done, but it wasn't reason enough to trust him. She accepted his offer with a simple nod, ready to call forth the fire at the smallest provocation. Crim and the shifter had fallen to her magic quickly enough; surely a pixie wouldn't stand a chance, either.

"I go by Cletus," he said, offering his hand.

She ignored it. "Laura." It wasn't the most inventive alias, but it was better than giving him the name by which Tallisker and the Witch and presumably the shifters knew her. The tank full, she hung the hose back on the pump and replaced the gas cap. "Lead the way."

They walked side by side through the automatic doors and into a long white hallway ending in an expansive food court. An open entrance to their left led to a convenience store and the counter where shoppers paid for gas. Cletus pulled his battered brown wallet out of his back pocket, removed a ten-dollar bill, and offered the money to Talora.

"You head on into the food court and get yourself something to eat. I'll take care of the gas and find you."

Talora took the cash and they parted ways. She was content to let Cletus pay for her gas and her lunch, but she didn't intend to let him find her again. The food court would certainly have a back door or a fire exit through which she could escape. She appreciated the pixie's charity, but she wasn't about to give him the opportunity to screw her over.

The food court was a tall, round space ringed with various counters. Most of the cheap metal tables were empty, save for a few scattered families and a group of truckers drinking coffee by the windows on the opposite side of the room. Every eye tracked Talora as she headed for the pizza place. She made a mental note about the fire exit between the Chinese joint and the burger dump opposite her destination. "Two slices of pepperoni and a large lemonade to go, please," she said to the pimply-faced teenage girl behind the counter. The girl looked up at her antlers, shrugged, and sauntered away to fill Talora's order.

As she waited, Talora watched the small television behind the register, which was tuned to an emergency news report. A pretty older woman in a blue suit read the teleprompter in a soft, steady cadence. "...authorities are now offering a cash reward for information leading to the apprehension of a woman wanted in connection with this morning's terrorist attack on downtown Detroit."

The screen shifted to an image of Talora, sans antlers, seated at a picnic table before a heaping pile of barbecued ribs with a big smile on her face. Her jaw dropped.

"The unnamed woman is described as between five-foot-eight and five-foot-ten, approximately 140 pounds. She may be using the alias 'Talora.' She should be considered armed and extremely dangerous."

"Fucking Witch," Talora growled. She didn't know how that crazy bitch had done it, but there was no doubt that the Witch was behind the report—and probably whatever terrorist attack the anchor had mentioned. Suddenly, Talora wasn't hungry anymore.

As she turned to flee, something heavy struck her in the temple. Her vision blurred as she fell and she was out before she hit the floor.

— CHAPTER EIGHTEEN —

His name was Barso and he was fully prepared to die. It was an odd sensation, Roger thought from afar, to feel his own mortality reduced to little more than waiting for the bus. The Evertree solidified the scene around him and Roger's concerns were lost to the wind. He was calm and proud and ready to give his life for his people.

Barso craned his head to look over his fellow soldiers, each equipped with the same bronze shield and spear he carried. They were a ragged, desperate looking host, perhaps a thousand strong, men and women who'd volunteered for a mission sure to go down in the annals of history. They had been given but one order: die slowly to buy time for the sorcerers back in Evitankari.

Although Barso was ready to die, he still wanted to have a little fun before the final curtain came down. "Hey Sturbeck," he growled to the man beside him. "Any clue what those damn magicians are up to?"

Fat old Sturbeck took a long drag from his bulbous, twisting pipe and exhaled a stream of blue smoke in the shape of a topless woman with huge breasts. "Oh, something real useful, I wager. I hear it's a potion what'll give ol' Axzar his hair back, make him turn around and go home and forget the whole thing."

A tall, slender woman in mail two sizes too big punched Sturbeck in the shoulder. Her blue eyes flashed with anger under a tight blonde braid. "Sturbeck son of Yant, you take that back! You know damn well that's not what they're working on!"

"I know, I know," the large man replied with a chuckle. His ample belly spilled out under his rusted old mail and it jiggled merrily as he laughed. "Your Durtzen's brew is going to save us all!"

Barso knew Stenna's temper was always good for a little amusement. She was his little sister, after all, and he had certain brotherly responsibilities to fulfill, impending doom or no. "How could he not, what with those gorgeous eyes and that bright smile and that perfect skin?" he said in a terrible approximation of a feminine voice, mocking the way Stenna had first described her then-future husband to him so long ago.

She jabbed Barso's boot with the hard bottom of her spear, but Sturbeck cut her off before she could unleash whatever tirade she'd prepared. "Might be better for us all if he just gave the dark lord those pretty golden locks o' his. Save the trouble of making a potion."

That bought him a tremendous slap from Stenna's shield that rang across the camp like a gong and knocked the big man onto his back. "I'll have you know my Durtzen is the greatest wizard since Allemania herself!"

Sturbeck belched as he sat up and adjusted his helmet. "An' a magicless wench like yerself would be an authority on wizards, eh?"

Barso had seen that tightening in his sister's jaw often enough to know it was time to step in. "All right, all right! We were just having a little fun. If we didn't trust Durtzen and the magicians, none of us would be laying our lives down to protect them."

"Speak for yourself!" Sturbeck slurred. "Some'ody's gonna write a song 'bout this and ol' Sturbeck's gonna be in it!" He exhaled a stream of smoky blue notes that wafted away on the breeze. "Like as not the one writing it'll be the same demon what takes your dearly beloved's head," he added with a shrug.

When Stenna pointed her spear at Sturbeck's throat, Barso took her arm and led her away. "Don't listen to that fat fool," he muttered. "Soldiers like us have more courage than sense."

"True enough," she said. "Anyone with any sense wouldn't be here."

"What's that make you?" he asked playfully.

"Just another fool in love," she replied. "Hiding in Evitankari wasn't going to do Durtzen any good."

"So, you figured he'd work harder and faster if you put yourself on the front?"

She brushed a stray lock of golden hair back behind her right ear. That strand had always possessed a mind of its own. "Something like that," she said.

They stopped to warm themselves beside a cooking fire. Thick brown gruel burbled menacingly in a battered cauldron suspended from a rickety tripod above the crackling flames. It looked to have the same consistency as the mud in which they stood—for all Barso could tell, it *was* the mud in which they stood, perhaps with a pinch of salt and pepper. The chef, a greasy weasel of a man in black rags, offered them a bowl. "Last meal?"

Stenna covered her mouth and turned away. "No thanks. Don't think I'd enjoy my last trip to the latrine," Barso answered. His sister giggled.

The crowd gathered around the fire looked more like a family reunion than an army. There were a few soldiers, hardened and ready like only veteran warriors can be, but there were many more women and youngsters than Barso would've liked, farmers and merchants and healers. They were used to being safe and comfortable in Evitankari, protected by towering walls and powerful wards and men and women better equipped to deal with evil. It showed in their furtive glances, in their pacing, in the sad notes washing over them from a fiddler in a nearby tent. Many he recognized as having no magic of their own, like his sister, which made them useless to the mages toiling away back in the city.

Good for them, he thought, giving Stenna's arm an affectionate squeeze. *Better to die standing up with a blade in hand than cowering under the bed, waiting for the enemy to take your city.*

And die they would, he had no doubt. Axzar's hordes had smashed the elven army three times already. This inexperienced group couldn't hope to be more than a thorn in the Devourer's side, an afternoon's bloody diversion. But if the sorcerers spoke true, that was all Evitankari needed.

A war horn sounded off to the west, followed by another as the signal was repeated through the elven line. The civilian volunteers leapt to their feet, flitting here and there like a gaggle of geese disturbed by a passing boat. The soldiers rose calmly, checked their equipment, and headed for the front. Barso and Stenna exchanged a sad look and followed.

The elves formed a ragged line at the crest of a tall hill overlooking a gentle valley. On the opposite side of the swath of lush green was a dark forest speckled with wildfire and cloaked in smoke. As Barso and Stenna took their places, a ragged gasp rose up from the elves. Demons poured forth from the woods, a snarling mass of teeth and weapons and ruined humanity. Their terrible drums boomed in the distance, accompanied by the tremendous roars and blood-curdling screams of Axzar's worst.

"It's been fun, Barso," Stenna whispered.

"It's been all right," he replied with a lopsided grin. "You could've married someone that wasn't a self-serving prick."

She laughed. "And you could've refrained from breaking his nose the first time you met him."

"Someone had to make the pretty little thing look a bit manlier."

The drums crashed one final time, stopping the horde halfway across the valley. Barso could feel the tension in those around him; the enemy was so numerous, so deranged, so dark. Someone nearby sobbed uncontrollably. The air suddenly reeked of piss and vomit. He was glad he hadn't tried the soup.

"What are they up to?" asked one grizzled soldier with a giant battle axe. "Fuckers usually just charge."

"Maybe Axzar had to take a leak!" Sturbeck suggested to a round of nervous laughter.

That laughter came to an immediate end when a towering rider emerged from the demon ranks. He was huge, easily twice the size of any of the elves, and he was covered in thick black armor that appeared somehow aglow. The top of his grisly death's head helmet had been sheared off to reveal the black flame that burned perpetually from his ruined scalp. The black destrier beneath him pawed the ground and snorted, angry that his rider had chosen not to charge the elven ranks.

"There he is," came the voice of General Armont from behind them. "The Devourer. The scourge of Alexetta and Hardinia. In Prelane and Caston, he promised the men he'd spare the women and children if they all fell on their swords, then he fed their families to his hellhounds as the dying men watched. He built a bridge to Arlon with the bones of the dwarves of Westerlen. The bald son of a bitch sank Atlantis with naught but an evil roar. That's Axzar, men, and that evil motherfucker is the only thing keeping those vile creatures working together. We don't have to stop the horde; all we have to do is lop off its head!"

"Sounds like a heckuva guy," Barso said to his sister.

Stenna nodded, visibly pale and breathing heavily. "You think it's true? Think they'll all just go their separate ways without Axzar?"

Barso stroked the stubble on his chin. "Demons have always been around, sis, but they were never organized before Axzar showed up. It's the best chance we've got."

His sister suddenly dropped her spear and flung her helmet to the mud, clutching her head tightly in her hands as if something or someone were trying to pull it off. Barso dropped his own weapon and took her in his arms.

"Stenna? Stenna! What's wrong?"

She struggled against him, writhing in agony. "He's...he's in my head..."

A keening wail erupted through Stenna's clenched teeth. Barso thought he heard her soul going with it. She had never been stronger than her brother, but she threw him aside almost effortlessly. When Barso looked back up at his sister, her eyes had gone completely white and had begun leaking blood.

With an unearthly howl, Stenna yanked Sturbeck's blade from its sheath and shoved it through the unarmored gap under his arm. The big man wobbled once, spitting up blood, then collapsed into the mud. Stenna leapt on the surprised man beside him and began to tear at his face with her fingernails.

Chaos shattered the elven line as similar scenes erupted elsewhere. Ghastly battle cries joined the clash of steel and Stenna's own wild screams. Barso leapt to his feet and pulled her off her blood-soaked victim, flinging her aside. The soldier she'd mauled stared up at him with dead, shocked eyes, just as surprised as Barso that his sister had ripped out his throat.

"Stenna!" he screamed, desperate now. "Whatever it is, fight it!"

She glared at him, her head tilted at an odd angle as she took his measure. Blood caked her face and hands, making those all-white eyes all the more eerie.

"It's me! It's Barso! Do it for me!"

Her body jerked once, a puppet on twisted strings.

"Do it for Durtzen! Stenna, he's counting on you!"

She shuddered again, but this time she screamed and charged. Barso loved her, but he couldn't deny what he had to do. He leaned in under her thrashing nails and jacked her jaw with a sharp uppercut. Stenna fell like a sack of grain, knocked out.

To his left, he saw a trio of soldiers facing off against another white-eyed elf. The possessed man watched them circle like an animal searching for a way out of its cage. One went for his legs and instead got the business end of a short sword. But that was all his companions needed; they closed around the wild man like a vise, stabbing and pummeling and weighing him down.

That was Hinger. And that one over there was Yarly. And just like my sister, neither of them...

"General Armont!" he shouted. "General Armont! None of them have any magic! They're all shala'ni!"

"You're sure, boy?" Barso whirled to find Armont behind him, his armor and his broadsword bloodied. The huge old warrior was almost as imposing as Axzar in his full red plate. His long white mustachios quivered as he spoke. "Positive?"

"I am, sir," he replied, straightening. "The one at my feet is my sister. That one over there was my neighbor, and the one with the axe in his skull was the bartender at our favorite pub." The general nodded, considering. His reply was squelched by a blood-curdling roar from the floor of the valley.

"They come!" shouted a man on the line.

Armont frowned. "Important information, boy. Take it back to Evitankari. There are still many shala'ni tending to the sorcerers. If Axzar turns them, they will destroy the city from within. Our sacrifice will have been in vain."

Barso nodded and started away from the lines, fueled with a new purpose. The general was right: those born without magic, the shala'ni, would be like a powder keg rigged to explode. There were many more back in Evitankari than there were on the front. He had to get word back to the Council. The shala'ni would have to be sent elsewhere, for their own safety as well as that of their fellows.

Stenna.

Barso turned, intending to ask the general to take care of his sister. But Armont already had. Barso's heart broke when he saw the big man pulling his sword up out of her throat.

"Go!" the general snarled.

He wiped away the tears and ran.

And then Roger was back in Willowglen, gingerly pulling his hand away from the Evertree's trunk. The pain of Barso's loss still twisted his gut and dulled his senses.

"The elves are a people shaped by difficult decisions," the willow said sadly, its features solemn. "They make the choices they make not only to ensure their own survival but to ensure the continuation of all life on this planet."

What he'd seen had left Roger in shock. The battlefield, Axzar, the demons, the sudden insanity and cruel death of his sister... it was too much to process. And he felt dirty, like some sort of time-traveling Peeping Tom. What had happened to Barso was something profoundly personal, and the Evertree had served it up to Roger without hesitation. Could there possibly exist a greater violation of privacy? The wound of having watched his sister die ached badly even though he knew it wasn't real. Roger wondered what Barso would think of the intrusion into his life.

"I don't know," Roger replied, more so because he felt he was expected to rather than because he actually had something to say. "It still doesn't feel right."

"Few will tell you that it is right," the Evertree said. "Fewer still will tell you it isn't necessary."

"But where do they go? They touch that rock and they just... disappear."

"The exiled shala'ni are teleported to a remote island in the Pacific where they are welcomed into a well-equipped community of other elves without the use of magic."

"So, what, they're sent to Club Med? Are they well taken care of? Do they have food and water and medicine and the things they need to live comfortably? Does the Council ever check up on them, or are they swept under the rug?"

"Your questions would best be answered by one who has been there."

Roger shrugged and reached one hand toward the big willow's trunk. He stopped when the Evertree shook its face.

"From a real live person this time," the tree said. "There's one on the far shore, waiting for you."

He nodded, somewhat relieved. He'd come to the Evertree to find out about the shala'ni because he thought of it as the only being in Evitankari he could trust. He'd dismissed the notion that it had its own agenda, that it was somehow tailoring the things it showed him to push him in a particular direction. It existed for one purpose and one purpose only, he figured, and that purpose was to give people whatever information they needed. But the idea of stepping into another's memories still made him nervous, as did the way in which the tree absorbed those memories.

Roger said his goodbyes to the Evertree and its pixie attendants and climbed into the little boat. He looked over the side as it launched, searching for signs of life or afterlife in the clear blue water. What would happen if the boat capsized and he fell in? He decided he didn't want to know.

The boat ran itself aground on the opposite shore and Roger climbed out. Willowglen's grass, still wet from the morning's storm, glistened a particularly bright green in the waning sun. Despite what the Evertree had said, it didn't seem as if anyone was there—which told him exactly who had been waiting for him.

"Afternoon, Driff."

The Council of Intelligence melted into view in the shadow of a nearby tree. His coat and hair were soaked, but he didn't seem to care. "Afternoon, Pintiri. I trust you've had an enlightening day?"

His nonchalance made Roger's blood boil. "What happens to those children you exile, Driff?" he blurted. "The Evertree says you've been to wherever they go. Checking up on them, to make sure they don't escape?"

Driff sighed. "The Council thought I was shala'ni."

"The Council—what?"

The elf removed his glasses, wiped them off with the cuff of his coat, and put them back on. "My twelfth birthday came and went and I still had not produced a single speck of magic. I tried to outsmart Aldern with a card trick I learned from a book. Stupid idea. So, they marched me to the square in Old Ev, stood me up there in front of my family, and gave me one last chance. I failed. They dusted me, and then they pressed my hand to the pedestal. The next thing I knew, I was standing beside a big rock on a white sandy beach, the sun beating down from on high, watching dumbly as a group of elves in simple clothes approached to welcome me to their community and wondering how it was that I had popped into existence all of a sudden." He paused, scratching his chin. "Or so I'm told. I only remember that last bit."

Roger grasped uselessly for words, completely dumbfounded. Driff's admission added a whole new level of depth to the day's events—and to the Council of Intelligence himself. "That's...that's terrible," was the best he could manage.

"Oh, it wasn't so bad," Driff replied with a small smile. "I didn't remember that my people had kicked me out, after all. And the weather was nice—Evitankari was kind enough to set up a ward that keeps the big storms away—and there was a lot less drama than there is here. On Poa, your worth is measured in simple terms: your work ethic, your manners, your willingness to help others in the community. The shala'ni have to work together if they want to survive. In that regard, Evitankari could learn a lot from Poa."

"Discovering your magic must've been a bit of a shock."

"That's putting it mildly. My adoptive family lived right next door to Granal, a crotchety old woman nonetheless known as the best baker on Poa. I snuck into her kitchen one afternoon looking for something sweet. When I heard Granal coming, I realized I was trapped. I hid under the table, hoping desperately that she wouldn't see me. That's when the magic kicked in." He paused to chuckle. "I was stuck that way for a week. The shala'ni treat those with magic the way Evitankari treats shala'ni: by exiling them. Luckily my skills are subtler than most."

"So how did you...escape?"

"Evitankari sends a ship to Poa to trade once a month. I stuck to the shadows and stowed aboard, curious as to where they were going. They found me, of course, but when they saw that I had magic of my own, they had no choice but to bring me back with them."

"What do the shala'ni have to trade?"

"Narii dust, ironically enough. Or, more appropriately, the raw material used to make the dust."

Roger nodded. He understood why Driff had wanted him to attend that morning's ceremony—and that the elf had thwarted the will of the Council in bringing him. "They didn't want me to see that, did they?"

The elf shook his head. "They didn't. Evitankari needs you on board, Roger. The Pintiri has to be one hundred percent committed to our mission. Some of the others thought you weren't ready to see the parts of elven society that aren't all peaches and cream and shiny, fun magic."

It was the shiny, fun magic that made Roger most uncomfortable, but he kept that to himself. "After today, that commitment might need a little shoring up."

"Understandable. I've convinced the Combined Council that telling you all about how well-intentioned we are isn't going to cut it; we've got to actually show you the good we do for the world. That happens tonight."

Driff turned to go, but Roger called him back. "Wait." He paused, taking a moment to reconsider his decision. It wasn't enough to change his mind. He needed allies, and so far, the enigmatic Council of Intelligence had proven to be the most honest man in Evitankari. "The Evertree...processed...the events leading up to the attack on the Kralak. A man named Greven brought a shipment of unicorn placenta into the city a few days prior." He couldn't believe he'd managed to say that with a straight face. Driff was rapt. "He had papers with a Council seal," Roger added.

The elf took a deep breath, momentarily playing one boot through the wet grass as he processed that information. "That's pretty serious, Roger. You're sure?"

"The woman working customs—Shellae—was killed in the attack. The Evertree showed me all of it through her eyes."

Driff nodded. "I know Greven. He's an excellent buyer, but he cares little about the intended use of the products he brings into the city. He comes and goes often, rarely spending more than a day or two in his home. I'll find him myself."

Roger took a step forward. "If you...uh...need any help..."

The elf shook his head before he disappeared. "I won't."

— CHAPTER NINETEEN —

Talora noticed four things before she opened her eyes: the throbbing ache in her temple, the bumpy motion of the vehicle beneath her, the scratchy rope that bound her wrists tightly together, and the metallic taste of whatever the hell was in her mouth. She was on her back, her hands underneath her where she couldn't bring the fire to bear. Briefly she wondered what the hell had happened, and then it all came back to her: *fucking Cletus.* Her overconfidence had snuck up behind her and bit her in the ass. She promised herself that wouldn't happen again.

Someone was guarding her closely. She could hear his quick, ragged breathing. He smelled like he'd doused himself in a bucket of cologne. It probably wasn't Cletus. His voice, squeaky and nervous, confirmed it. "A-a-a-are you a-a-a-awake? D-d-don't move or I'll shoot!"

Talora's eyes fluttered open. That metallic thing in her mouth was a gun, a black pistol with its hammer cocked, held in place by a greasy hand just past the tip of her nose. She traced the hand into a dingy black sweatshirt. The spindly arm led up to a narrow torso, the neck to a young face with a pointy nose ringed in thick acne. Green eyes stared down at her under the tattered brim of a red baseball cap. By all outward appearances, this young man was human. Talora knew that couldn't be right. There had to be a pixie in his chest or a gnome up his ass, or maybe he had a more powerful cloaking talisman than Jehia. They were inside a plywood cell lit by a single bare bulb dangling precariously from a single wire—the back of Cletus's semi-truck.

"I'm s-s-s-s-sorry," her captor stuttered, looking away from her. "Cletus m-m-made me. He says I'm not to take the gun out until we reach our destination. And then he'll split the reward with me, 75-40."

Talora tried to correct him, but her words came out as gibberish around the barrel of the gun. Somehow, her captor understood.

"I know the m-m-math's not right," he replied. He turned his head to the left, toward the front of the truck. The motion revealed an ear topped with a pointy tip. "Cletus h-h-hits me when I get lippy."

"Are you an elf?" she tried to ask.

He nodded emphatically. "Shala'ni. No magic. The b-b-b-bastards were going to dust me and send me to Poa. My family got me out, sent me to live with the humans and the ex-pats. Not all elves like to live in Evitankari. Not all fae like to live in Talvayne. Sometimes I think P-p-p-oa wouldn't have been so bad."

Talora was confused as always, but she figured it would be best to keep this kid talking. Maybe he'd reveal something she could use. "What's your name?" she asked.

"Pell," he replied. "Cletus says you're Talora."

"Did he tell you where we're going?" She felt the vehicle begin to slow. Had they reached their destination? Were they stuck in traffic? She couldn't tell.

"D-D-Detroit. To the police, for the reward."

Back to the Witch it was, then. Unless the shifters intercepted her first.

"D-d-d-did you really d-d-d-do it?" Pell asked. "D-d-did you really help Evitankari bring down Tallisker's t-t-tower?"

That was an interesting wrinkle. Talora didn't doubt for a second that the elves were just as responsible for the attack as she herself. The Witch was playing Demson and Tallisker. Talora didn't know enough about the world at large to judge if pinning such an attack on the elves was a good idea or not, but it sounded like a dangerous play nonetheless. In response to Pell's question, she shook her head. "I'm being framed."

"Cletus s-s-s-said you'd say that. He also s-s-s-said we don't care whether that's true or not. Cash is c-c-cash."

Cletus said this, Cletus said that. I'm sorry, Cletus made me. Cletus hits me. She wondered if there was a crack there she could exploit, if she could turn Pell against the pixie. He looked haggard and a bit malnourished. At the very least it was worth a try.

"And what do you think about that?" Talking around the gun was starting to hurt her tongue. Saliva flooded the sides of her mouth, prompting a strong urge to spit—but surprising Pell with any sort of sudden movement while his finger was around that trigger seemed like a bad idea.

He shrugged. "It d-d-d-doesn't seem fair. But life's not fair, Cletus says."

"Maybe you could *make* life fair. Help me get away from Cletus and I'll help you."

"H-h-help me what? W-w-w-where would I go? W-w-what would I do? Cletus took me in when no one else would. He's the o-o-only one that gives a shit."

The vehicle came to a complete stop. Cletus's horn joined in with a cacophony of others. A traffic jam, then. That made sense; the attack on Tallisker's tower would've put the authorities on high alert and whipped the populace into a frenzy. Nobody would be getting into or out of Detroit as easily as usual.

Time to try a new tactic. What was it Pell had said earlier? About Poa maybe not being so bad? Maybe Talora could use that. She had no fucking clue what or where Poa was, but she understood the dust well enough. "I lied. I did it. I helped the elves bring down Tallisker's tower." She paused for a moment to let that sink in. "I have friends in Evitankari. Powerful friends. If you help me, I can bring you to them. They can dust you and send you to Poa. It'll be like none of this ever happened."

Pell's hesitation told Talora she had him. He blinked a few times and swallowed, trying to digest what she'd just offered, debating if she could be trusted, weighing his chance of survival if she couldn't. Maybe going to the elves wasn't such a bad idea; there obviously was no love lost between Tallisker and Evitankari, and they'd surely like to meet the woman they were accused of being in cahoots with. At the very least it would be better than fleeing without a direction or a plan.

The truck's engine chugged to a halt. Cletus's driver-side door opened with a metallic screech. Talora couldn't hear his footsteps, but surely her captor only had one destination in mind: the back of the truck.

She opted to play it as if Pell had already decided to join her. "You'll only get one chance at this," she said. "Don't miss." The kid's eyes widened in shock.

A key clicked ominously in the lock. Metal squealed across metal as Cletus threw the big lever that kept the trailer secure. He yanked both doors open and glowered into the trailer. Talora blinked against the sudden wash of light, but her eyes adjusted quickly. Parked cars jammed the city street beyond, many surrounded by frustrated motorists who'd gotten out to stretch their legs or vent their frustrations. The neighborhood's dingy businesses and apartment buildings had obviously seen better days.

"We'll take her on foot, give her to the first cop we find. Get her up, but keep the pistol in her mouth," Cletus ordered. "Back her toward me. Do it right or I'll shove that fucking gun up your stupid fucking ass."

Pell did as he was told, standing and hauling Talora to her feet by the front of her dress. He turned her so she was between himself and Cletus.

"D-d-duck," he whispered as he slowly drew the gun out of her mouth. Talora dropped, banging her already throbbing head on the floor because she couldn't break her fall with her bound arms. Pain radiated through the root of her left antler where she'd landed.

The pistol in Pell's hand clicked dully as he pulled the trigger. The weapon wasn't loaded. A desperate, keening wail exploded through his lips, getting louder with each successive useless pull of the trigger.

"Dumb ass," Cletus growled. He jerked his left hand upward, using his magic to telekinetically hurl Pell into the trailer's ceiling. The elf crashed back down to the floor beside Talora with a sickening thud.

That was all the time Talora needed. Still groggy, she called the fire indiscriminately, incinerating the ropes around her wrists and bringing her hands forward to blast Cletus, setting the trailer ablaze in the process. Her head spun as she forced herself to her feet and scrambled for the daylight, stumbling over the trailer's edge and careening to the asphalt below. She landed hard on her hip, but this time she managed to keep from whacking her head again. The fall had bloodied her knee and scraped the side of her arm, but she was lucky she hadn't thrown herself onto the sedan behind the truck; intense heat rose up in waves from its blackened hood and semi-melted windshield. All that remained of Cletus was a charred mound of flesh at Talora's side.

She rolled onto her back and gazed up through the hazy smoke wafting up off the truck into the blue sky beyond, willing her vision to steady. She ignored the panicked screams and shouts of the nearby motorists. None of them came to see if she was all right. She couldn't blame them.

Her vision cleared a few moments later and she stood up. The ache in her head persisted, but the lingering ecstasy from using the magic made it tolerable. She peered over the vehicles at the snarl of traffic behind the truck. A pair of men ran away frantically at the sight of her. There was a lot of city in that direction. She'd been unconscious for a while, and Cletus had dragged her right back into the middle of the shit storm she'd been trying to escape. Getting out of Detroit again wouldn't be easy; judging from the sirens in the distance, emergency personnel were everywhere, and likely heading in her direction.

She rounded the burning truck, considering the horizon. A pillar of wispy black smoke rose up among the downtown skyscrapers where she assumed Tallisker's tower should've been. She chewed on her lip, considering her options: find help, or try to burn her way out of Detroit. Seeking out the elves, as she'd suggested to poor, dead Pell, felt like a better idea every second. The enemy of her enemy might make a useful ally.

"You look like you could use a friend," said a small voice to her left. Talora turned to find a tiny, demure Japanese woman in a kimono seated on the curb—an exact replica of the geisha the Witch had burned to death in Tallisker's penthouse. A shifter. Talora's first instinct was to summon the fire and turn the geisha into a bubbling puddle of silver muck, but she held it back. If this shifter meant her harm, why would it bother revealing itself when it could've assumed a different disguise?

"I was thinking I'd like to meet a few elves," Talora replied. "Know any?"

"A few. I've been an elf before. It wasn't much fun. Duty this, danger that. I don't think they'd welcome you the way you're hoping they might."

"At the very least, I doubt they'd try to cut me open and eat me."

"Touché. But we're done with that. We no longer give a flying fuck what you are."

Talora rolled her eyes. The sirens were getting closer. Time to get to the point. "That's reassuring. What the hell do you want?"

The geisha stood and smoothed the front of her kimono. "The same thing we've come to realize you must want: the Witch's head on a fucking platter. We were remiss in identifying you as just another one of those faceless lackeys that joins her little cult of personality every few months. You're thinking for yourself. And where there's independent thought, there's opportunity."

The shifter reached into the folds of her kimono and withdrew a tiny vial topped with a black rubber stopper. Its contents glittered neon green in the sunlight. "A nasty bug for a nasty bitch. Genetically tailored to kill the Witch and only the Witch. When mixed with air it'll turn into a gas. One whiff—ding-dong, the Witch is dead."

The geisha tossed the vial to Talora. She caught it with both hands. It was surprisingly warm. "You can't get close enough to her to use it," Talora said.

"She can smell us coming from a mile away. You cannot imagine how frustrating that is."

Talora considered the vial in her hands. There wasn't much in it; she'd only get one shot. The Witch would be expecting the fire— hell, she probably already had a plan in place to counter it—but she would never suspect an attack like this.

For a moment, she couldn't believe she was seriously considering a confrontation with the Witch, but it was a better option than running or trying to hide among the elves. The Witch would never stop looking for her. There was only one way Talora could be truly safe.

She hiked up the side of her dress and slipped the vial into the elastic waistband of her underwear. "I'll do it."

The geisha bowed reverently. "You do the whole world a great service. The Witch and what's left of Tallisker's board of directors are regrouping in a park I think you'll find a bit familiar. Just follow the smoke."

Talora moved through the city quickly, staying low between the columns of abandoned cars. Detroit was far too calm and serene for a city supposedly under attack. Where were the panicked masses fleeing town? Where were the looters? Where were the volunteers rushing to the rescue of their fellow men? The only sound was that of the omnipresent sirens, harsh and jarring. To Talora, they sounded desperate and confused.

A stack of televisions in the window of a used electronics shop caught her eye. All were tuned to the same news report. An older blond woman in a blue dress, styled and primped to the point that she appeared to have been carved out of plastic, steadily read a report praising Detroit's emergency personnel for their quick response to the day's tragedy.

But it was the red line of text crawling across the bottom of the screen that drew Talora's attention. "There is no need to panic," it read. "Remain in your homes until you are told to leave. You did not see any demons, elves, pixies, gnomes, trolls, dryads, gnolls, or other make-believe creatures in the vicinity of the Tallisker building. That white tower did not exist, and the strangeness of any debris is simply an effect of the intense heat involved in the attack. Have a nice day and don't forget to drink lots of water!"

The letters vibrated as they crossed the screens, resonating with power and malice. Looking away required a considerable exertion of will. Was that magic, or some sort of technological wizardry? Talora couldn't tell. She kept her eyes down and continued on.

She encountered a chunk of the tower around the next corner. It bisected the street perfectly, crushing buildings on either side. The front half of a commuter bus stuck out from under it, windows speckled with blood. The smooth white stone showed no signs of explosion or fire; it was as if the tower had just shattered. The rock was too slick to climb, and Talora didn't dare try to crawl through any of the gaps that looked like they might lead underneath it. She'd have to go around.

The next street was packed with police cars, firetrucks, and ambulances. National Guardsmen in black fatigues patrolled the area, rifles at the ready. She'd never make it through that way. Frustrated, she continued on. She soon came upon a familiar stretch of rolling green grass and manicured oak trees. This was it, then. She pulled the vial out of her underwear and concealed it in her palm. Time to make her own way, whether it meant life or death.

"Told you she'd find us here!" the Witch said with a smirk. She was seated atop a very familiar bench, filing her nails.

Beside her, a very distraught-looking Demson smoked a cigarette, his suit rumpled and his hair speckled with white debris. "Wonderful," he snapped, rolling all three of his eyes. "Where's Crim?"

Talora didn't know any Crim, but she had been expecting them to ask about the demon who'd come for her. "Didn't make it," she said. "Shifters."

"Bastards," Demson growled. "As if we didn't have enough problems with those damn elves." The third eye on his forehead flipped open angrily, scouring the park. Irritated blue veins stuck out in its red cornea. "Their disgusting fucking magic is everywhere."

How had the Witch faked that, Talora wondered? She decided she didn't care. Talora continued her approach, trying to seem nonchalant. The vial was a warm, comforting weight in her hand. The glass felt like it would shatter easily against the bench. She would throw it into the wood between the Witch's feet, the gas would waft up into her face, and that would be the end of things. Escaping Demson might be tricky, but the fire—and hopefully his confusion at the suddenness of her attack—would give her a chance.

The Witch eyed her skeptically. "Before you do whatever foolish thing you came here to do, tell me: what was the family name of the three little children in that troll's house?"

Talora couldn't remember. She shook her head. Had the Witch been following her the whole time?

"What about that poor man who tried to turn you in for the reward we posted? There was something different about him. What was it?"

She tried to picture Cletus, but all she could generate was a rather hazy picture of a generic looking trucker. Was there something strange about the way he spoke? Did he walk with a limp? Was he missing any pieces? She closed her eyes and concentrated so hard it hurt, but she couldn't recall more details.

"And Pym. What was it he called you?"

She couldn't answer that, either. The word was right on the tip of her tongue. The King of the Forest was still vivid in her mind, as was the patch of flowers which had spelled out his diagnosis—but the word itself was gone. Her heart sank. *All flames consume fuel of some sort. What do yours burn? You used it alllllllllllllllllllll up!*

The puzzle pieces in Talora's mind suddenly clicked into place. The flames she'd been using so liberally to protect herself had burned through her memories. Likely they'd also devoured everything that had happened to her before she'd woken up in that park. She relaxed her grip on the vial. The Witch's death would mean the end of any chance at understanding. Talora couldn't kill her while she still had so many questions about herself and her past. Her free hand drifted to the locket hanging around her neck and she bowed her head.

"Very good, Talora," the Witch said, tapping the nail file against her chin. "We may make something useful of you yet."

Demson sighed. "About fucking time. All this 'let her find her own way' bullshit was starting to get old."

Talora ignored him. "Can it be controlled?"

The Witch nodded. "We can help each other, Talora. That's all I ever wanted from you."

Talora didn't like the sound of that, but she'd never get anywhere if she burned away everything she learned. The Witch would certainly expect terrible things in return. Talora would wait, and learn, and listen—and keep the shifter's vial close until the Witch was no longer of any use. She chewed her lip for a second, then nodded.

The Witch clapped her hands happily. "Then it's settled! Friends to the end!"

"Oh, that's cute," the demon snarled, his third eye blazing red with anger. "Evitankari's starting shit and you want to dance around and build a fucking clubhouse."

"The elves will pay, Demson," the Witch said, her demeanor suddenly darkening. "But first, we must acquire a bit of leverage."

The Witch's conspiratorial wink sent a shiver down Talora's spine.

— CHAPTER TWENTY —

Roger spent the remainder of the afternoon wandering aimlessly around Evitankari. Though he had a very nice place to live, he didn't feel as if he actually had anywhere to go. No friends, no family, no familiar place to hide and relax and think through the things he had to think through.

So he walked, hands in his pockets and eyes downcast. He left Willowglen and wandered in a direction he hadn't been before, up and over a gentle hill. He stopped briefly to admire the glittering lake to his right, watching two teams of tiny sailboats race around a circle of buoys. When he noticed the robed figures on the shoreline, seemingly directing the air currents with their glowing fingers, he shook his head and continued on.

He stuck to the forests, avoiding streets that looked like they led toward civilization. The few elves he encountered either barely acknowledged him or ignored him completely. At one point he found himself on the edge of farm country, overlooking a seemingly endless field of corn speckled here and there with silos and outbuildings. He doubled back and took a turn he'd previously avoided. He wasn't particularly in the mood to run into Piney.

The events of the last few days replayed themselves over and over again in his mind's eye. Not once did he see where he could've done something different that would've actually improved his situation. His life had become a roller coaster; he was hurtling in a predetermined direction, and the operator wasn't going to let him off no matter how much he screamed and waved his arms and threatened to jump. He cursed the Witch for what seemed like the hundredth time.

An hour later he reached the wall at the edge of the city. He'd seen it in the distance and wanted to check it out up close. A behemoth of blue stone and black mortar, Roger guessed it was at least five stories high. Pointed watch towers sprung up from the wall every hundred yards, lined with cannons and antennae and various other instruments he didn't recognize. What dangers lurked out in the world that necessitated such protection? The entire thing was covered in unintelligible characters written in something like white chalk. Runes, he guessed, the source of the directional wards he'd heard the elves mention. He ran his finger across one that looked a bit like a Z, but the chalk didn't come off. It made sense that the elves would want to protect their defensive spells by keeping them on the inside of the wall, but Roger couldn't help wondering if they were also intended to keep someone or something from leaving.

Continuing on, he turned left down a narrow street into one of Evitankari's pocket neighborhoods. The cobblestones turned uneven, the roofs of the small cottages pitching sharply. Some part of his subconscious had directed him to Old Ev. There was something here that was bothering him, something he wanted to take another look at.

Roger almost missed the turn to Tash Square. He just barely caught a glimpse of the imposing statue out of the corner of his eye, between two squat homes that framed a narrow alley. He approached the stone warrior slowly, almost reverently, waiting for the answer to his question to jump out at him. But there was no commemorative plaque, no sign, no label—just the dark human warrior looming high above the sacrificial pedestal.

Roger waved at an old man leaning heavily on his cane. The bent elf smiled warmly as he shook the Pintiri's hand. He seemed a bit lonely and glad for the conversation.

"I was wondering," Roger said, trying to sound casual, "who that statue is."

"Ahh," the elf said, his smile widening. "That statue is of the Liberator, Axzarian."

Roger gasped. "A-Axzar? The Devourer?"

The elf shook his head like a teacher admonishing his student. "No. Axzarian the Liberator."

"But...are they—were they—the same person?"

The elf thought for a moment, scratching the white stubble on his bulbous old chin. "That is hard to say. The Liberator became the Devourer...but physically, mentally, and spiritually, the two couldn't have been more different."

Roger nodded. Something had changed this Axzarian, something profound. "If that's Axzarian, why is this called Tash Square?"

"Tash was our first Pintiri. He defeated Axzar and brought peace to the world. Tash was a great elf, but he was humble as well; he refused to allow a statue to be built in his likeness. He insisted Axzarian be commemorated instead, so that the good the man did before his turn would not be forgotten. Some say it's also a reminder that even the best of us can fall into the darkness."

It all came back to Axzar—the Ether, the exiled shala'ni, and, Roger guessed, the detachment from humanity. The battle with Axzar's hordes had changed everything for Evitankari and sculpted the society in which he now found himself trapped. It was the elves' Pearl Harbor, their 9/11. It had happened so long ago, but they still felt it. Maybe they couldn't make themselves stop. He felt like he'd gained some insight into the elven psyche, though he doubted it would do him much good.

"Is that all, Pintiri?" the old man asked. "I enjoy the company, but these old bones ache so after the rain."

Roger put on what he hoped was his benevolent Pintiri face. "Thank you for your time, sir. One last thing: is there a decent pub in the area?"

He followed the man's directions—two blocks west, turn right, first door on the left—to Goody Gallant's in the basement of the crookedest, most dilapidated building Roger had seen in Evitankari. The thick stone house listed heavily toward the street, far enough that its steep peak would've protected a small crowd from a rain shower. He descended the stone steps to the heavy wooden door gingerly, afraid that the slightest vibration might tip the whole thing over onto his head. The first thing he noticed when he stepped into the dark, dingy establishment was the smell of heavy ale and strong whiskey and something greasy cooking in the kitchen. *This'll do,* he thought.

Goody's was a wide, sprawling place. Expansive booths lined its walls. Except for a narrow strip for the dartboard in the far corner, every other open space was filled with tables and chairs. Roger kept his eyes down and sidled his way to the empty stool at the end of the bar. The place was surprisingly busy, given the hour. He supposed Evitankari had its fair share of problems to drown lately.

The waitress, a curvy elf with bushy blond curls and bright red lips, greeted him with a smile and more of a view down her frilly, strapless blouse than Roger was comfortable with. "Welcome to Goody's, Pintiri. Name's Byss. What can I do ya for today?"

"Beer," he said, trying hard to keep his gaze from wandering. "IPA if you've got it. And a burger with fries. But I...uh, well, no one ever gave me any money," he stuttered, embarrassed that he hadn't thought that through before heading for a bar.

"Not to worry, sugar. Combined Council's got a standing tab."

Byss returned with a tall stein of golden, frothy beer. That first hoppy sip was exactly what he needed. It warmed his veins and his heart, filling that cold void like it always had when he'd started thinking about Virginia a little too much.

And then the Council of Sorcery sat down beside him and the moment was completely ruined.

"Good choice," Aldern said, a little too chummy for Roger's taste. "Byss brews it herself, and only three times a year. Little extra hops in this batch."

Roger ignored him and took a long swig, draining half the glass. It didn't help.

"Look, Roger, I understand how you can be a bit cross with us. I'd feel the same if our roles were reversed," the old elf said warmly, slipping into wise grandfather mode. "Just know that there was no malicious intent in the decision to keep certain things from you. We weren't trying to sweep our dirty little secrets under the rug. We're trying to ease you into your new position slowly. Give you time to adjust. The Council came to an agreement on this. Driff had no right to go against our decision, and he will be reprimanded."

Roger glared at Aldern, fighting the urge to loudly and obscenely defend the Council of Intelligence. He didn't think the old elf was lying. He couldn't fault his reasoning, either, even though he didn't like it.

"Do me a favor," Roger said slowly. "If there's anything I need to know, just tell me—and don't get too cute with your definition of what I need to know."

Aldern pursed his lips. "Fair enough, but remember that life here in Evitankari is harder than anything you've known. We play for keeps, Pintiri."

"All the more reason to make sure I understand all the rules," Roger said carefully. Could Aldern be the traitor? Was he keeping things from Roger for more malicious reasons than he claimed?

Roger didn't want to risk ruining his meal by thinking about it. Surely Driff was already hot on the traitor's heels.

Byss delivered Roger's order, a quarter-pound burger on a crispy sesame seed bun beside a heaping pile of seasoned steak fries. The delicious smell reminded Roger of his favorite diner back home. At least there were a few things the elves knew not to screw with.

"You want fairy dust on that, hon?" Byss asked, giving an imposing metal cylinder a little shake.

"N-no," he replied quickly, throwing up his hands. "Just plain is fine for me!"

"Eh, suit yourself," she replied, tossing the cylinder aside and moving on to other customers.

Aldern chuckled under his breath. "That's just what they call their special spice mix. Cayenne, chili powder, and a bit of brown sugar."

Roger laughed in spite of himself. "Can't be too careful."

The first bite was positively delightful. It was almost too good, enough so that Roger wondered briefly if the chef had cooked it or just summoned it from thin air using some sort of perfect burger spell. He decided that he didn't care.

"So Aldern," he began, feeling relaxed enough now to broach what he worried might be a difficult subject. "How's the Brooks family doing?"

"Very well, actually. Collecting them was not easy; we wanted to do so discreetly, so as not to call any more attention to them than was necessary. They've been united in our safe house in Connecticut for transport here, using a less traveled route that likely won't be watched. If all goes as planned, they'll be in Evitankari for breakfast tomorrow morning."

Although that wasn't much more than what Driff had already told him, the news that his family would soon be joining him brought a genuine smile to Roger's face. He bit into his burger vigorously, letting the juices roll down his chin without caring one bit. Virginia and the kids would be there soon, safe, and he'd have someone normal to talk to, someone with whom he could try to make sense of Evitankari and its strange inhabitants.

"I'm curious about this Axzarian fellow," Roger said between mouthfuls. He shoved in a handful of fries, which were even better than the burger. "This morning the Evertree showed me a frightening vision of the guy leading a demon army. And then this afternoon I find out that statue out in the square is the same man."

The old elf nodded. "It is nice to see you taking an interest in our history, Roger. Axzarian's tale is an old one, and complicated to boot. Suffice to say that when the truly good fall, they fall extremely far and they pull many down with them in their wake. It was to defeat Axzar, in fact, that we first created the Ether you now carry."

Roger was about to ask for some clarification when his vision suddenly blurred, twisting and swirling and then snapping back into place. He took a deep breath to steady himself, dropping his burger and swallowing a quick swig of the beer. It happened again, but this time when the colors and the room settled he found himself sitting at the head of the table in the Council Chamber. A little man made of wood sat to his left, smiling warmly under a thick mop of green leaves where his hair should've been.

"Hello," the wooden man said.

"Hello yourself," Roger replied. "What the hell just happened?"

Aldern appeared out of nowhere at the opposite end of the table. "To put it simply: I added a bit of glass and spit to your burger. Didn't even taste it, did you?"

Roger fought back the urge to retch. "I have to eat that shit whenever I need to visit the Council Chamber?"

The old elf shook his head. "No. If it works as intended, the effect will be permanent. You'll be able to travel here and back with a single thought, just like the rest of us. You can only return to your exact previous position, however, so be careful."

"If it works as intended?"

Aldern shrugged. "There aren't exactly a lot of humans around I can use for testing."

Roger glared at him. "Never, ever magic me without asking first." The elf's only reply was a smug smile.

"I apologize for the way you were brought here," the little wooden man said, his voice like branches rustling in the breeze. "We have a situation that requires the Pintiri's immediate attention."

"Well, you could've asked first," Roger snapped, still glowering at the Council of Sorcery. "I'll be back in a second." Roger thought about returning to Goody's, and suddenly he found himself back in his seat at the bar. He took hold of his meal and his beer and smiled at Byss. "Um, thanks."

"Don't mention it, sugar," she replied. "Just be careful coming back. You might end up in someone's lap. That's Pike's favorite seat."

Roger stood up, took a few steps away from the bar, and thought himself back to the Council Chamber. He put his plate and his beer down on the table, took a quick bite of the burger, and turned to the little wooden man. "I'm Roger Brooks. Nice to meet you."

"Sorrin, Talvayne's ambassador to Evitankari."

"Talvayne?"

"Royal Seat of His Majesty King Luminad VI, Lord Protector of all Faerie," Sorrin said, beaming.

"Oh. Okay." Truth be told, he really didn't give a shit. If there was a city full of elves, he decided, it was perfectly reasonable that there would be other cities full of other things he never suspected were real. He just wished they'd waited until after dinner to bother him with it.

Aeric popped into existence in the seat to Roger's right. "Ambassador," he said with a curt nod. "We believe we've located Princess Myrindi."

"That is excellent news," Sorrin said with a clap of his hands. "Talvayne thanks you for your assistance—and your discretion."

That set off alarm bells in Roger's head. Now what the hell were these damn elves dragging him into? "Do we know who took her and why?" he asked. He didn't doubt for a second that this was another step in whatever the Witch was up to.

"A particularly nasty group of demons," Aeric replied. "As for why...they've yet to issue any ransom demands, so we have no clue."

"Contact me when you have news," the ambassador said officiously. "The quicker we have her back, the better."

And with that, he was gone.

Aeric turned to Roger. "How are your princess-rescuing skills, Pintiri?"

"You kidding?" Roger asked, angrily devouring the last bite of his burger. "We janitors do that kind of thing all the time."

— CHAPTER TWENTY-ONE —

Talora closed the book and looked up at the Witch expectantly.

"Did you read it all?" the dark woman asked sternly.

"Every last word, Mother," Talora responded curtly. She didn't think this was going to work, despite the Witch's assurances. She'd read the book more to keep herself entertained than to satisfy her psychotic new mentor. It kept her mind off the fact that they were sitting in a gloomy cemetery, alone, setting an ambush for a group of people Demson thought powerful enough to destroy Tallisker's tower.

The Witch sat across from her, leaning back against a thick gravestone. The cherubs carved into the stone on either side of her head did not look enthused by her presence. "Choose a scene from what you just read. Not the first, nor the last. Bring that scene to the forefront of your mind; the words on the page, the crisp feel of the clean paper, the weight of the book, the soft breeze rustling through the trees..."

...the crazy bitch making stupid faces at me the entire time, and the nagging desire to kill her with the vial of death in my pocket. On the way out of Detroit, they'd stopped in the ruins of a swanky department store to acquire some new clothes for Talora. The black jeans,

gray sweater, and blue running shoes she wore would've cost her several hundred dollars. If she had to follow around a crazy woman, at least she could be comfortable in the process.

Talora closed her eyes and did what the Witch suggested, losing herself in the memory. She was back in the cradling roots of the ancient oak tree a few rows of graves away, book in hand, wondering why the Witch had chosen such a sappy story for her and why the idiot main character was killing himself.

"Now hold that image and call the fire," the Witch instructed.

Using the magic had become second nature. That familiar rush warmed Talora's nerves as the fire burst to life. In a way, the sensation was reassuring. It made her feel like somebody who could take control of her situation, rather than a confused woman with no past and an uncertain future.

"Good," the Witch cooed proudly. "Now end it."

It felt so good she almost didn't. How good would it feel to turn the fire upon the woman she still held responsible for her situation? *One day, Witch,* she promised herself as she squelched the flames. She opened her eyes.

"Well?" the Witch asked.

Talora blinked, surprised. She shuffled through the few memories she had, searching for one in particular. "I don't remember how Romeo killed himself. I assume he did it because of something to do with Juliet, and I know how she ended her own life, but...in between, there's just a blank."

The Witch clapped her hands like an excited little girl. "Perfect! Now you get to ask me *one* question."

Talora despised this fucking game; she hated how helpless it made her feel, how much joy the Witch obviously took in messing with her, how carefully she had to choose and phrase her inquiry. She hadn't wanted to agree to it, but she'd take advantage of it nonetheless. Given her situation and the role the Witch expected her to play, there was really only one question that seemed pertinent at the moment. "How did you bring down Tallisker's tower?" She hated herself for asking something so immediate when she should've asked something more relevant to herself on the whole, but she knew that knowledge of her own situation would do her no good if she couldn't survive what was coming long enough to make use of it. She wondered if the Witch had planned this on purpose; how many more times would she shield herself from Talora's more personal questions with a smokescreen of imminent danger?

"I had nothing to do with it and I resent what you're implying," the Witch said playfully. "It wasn't hard for those elves. Not with the numbers they had to work with, all casting in concert. They created a vortex of negative pressure inside the tower and a few similar bubbles along the outside; give all of those bubbles a little rub in the right direction, and...KA-BOOOOOOOM!"

Talora nodded. The Witch was full of shit. She'd done it on her own, and she'd somehow saturated the area with evidence to the contrary. Demson had seemed so reliant on her afterward, almost deferent, ready to give her the world so she would exact revenge on his enemies—exactly the opposite of the cold, calculating, independent power broker she'd first met atop that tower. Talora hated to admit it, but the Witch's ability to manipulate others was perhaps her most frightening quality.

The Witch's head snapped to the left at the sound of an engine approaching. Talora's gaze followed, expectantly watching the dirt road that disappeared into the thick pine woods. She had no clue where the hell they were, which implied that no one but the exact people they were waiting for were likely to show up.

"The problem with elves," the Witch said slowly, "is that they aren't nearly as clever as they think they are."

Sounds like someone else I know, Talora thought. She turned her head, eyeing the short, squat rock that was actually some sort of magical gateway through which she and the Witch had arrived in this forsaken hole, and which they were to try to keep the approaching elves from reaching. The Witch called it a transpoint. Talora still suspected that the Witch had brought them there on her own accord and was, as usual, just playing games. After all, if there were transpoints hidden throughout the world, why go through all the trouble of trying to reach this one?

"They don't expect anyone to be watching this particular transpoint," the Witch said suddenly, as if reading her mind. More likely she had read the absentminded way Talora chewed on her lower lip whenever she was trying to work things out. "And so, rather than risk ambush at any of the more obvious choke points, they come to this one, which they assume will be unwatched."

Seemed like awfully convoluted logic for a group that, as the Witch put it, were the self-appointed protectors of everything warm and fuzzy. "Well, they assumed wrong," Talora replied, just to keep up appearances. She pulled on a floppy black hat and adjusted the veil across her face, assuming the role the Witch had assigned her: a widow grieving for a lost love. More importantly, the hat and veil would hide her antlers long enough for the two of them to get the drop on the arriving elves. When she looked up again, the Witch was gone.

"Have to make her teach me how to do that," Talora grumbled as she stood. She played with the bracelet on her wrist as she cast a nervous glance across the woods surrounding the little cemetery. Pym's trinket, the Witch had reminded her, contained a different message for each individual able to read it—sometimes in regard to the reader's relationship to the wearer, sometimes directly from Pym himself. "I hope you get hit by a bus, you raging bitch!" the Witch had read aloud triumphantly. Talora seconded the bracelet's feelings.

A hearse rumbled to a stop beside the brown, sagging chapel at the edge of the graveyard, displacing a pair of blackbirds that had been watching from the dirt driveway. Talora squared her shoulders and turned to face it, a lone guardian directly between the elves and the transpoint they sought to reach. She didn't expect her ruse to last long—especially given the way her antlers pushed up against the brim of the hat, underneath the veil—but then again, it didn't have to.

The passenger door opened and a towering pallbearer lumbered out, straightening his lapels and glowering at her through a dark pair of Ray-Bans. "Afternoon, miss," he snarled, casually meandering her way. She didn't miss the bulge in his jacket underneath his left arm. "Paying your respects?"

Talora nodded and choked back what she hoped sounded like a pathetic sob, clutching *Romeo & Juliet* close to her chest. "My husband," she whimpered, her eyes on his shoes. "Five years ago today."

"I'm sorry," he said, obviously not meaning it. "You must have the wrong cemetery. No one has been buried here in over fifty years."

Fucking hell. Then what's the hearse for, shithead? Apparently, the elves really weren't as clever as they thought they were.

"His ashes," she stammered. "We scattered them here. He was a historian, and he loved this place so." *Come on, Witch.* Talora's job was to distract whoever came out of the hearse while the Witch spirited the entire vehicle away. She didn't understand why they didn't just blow the thing to hell and pick up the pieces of whatever had been inside.

"Uh-huh," the man said, now a few feet away.

Talora squinted and concentrated, really looking at him as the Witch had directed. When she did so, the slightly blurry areas atop his ears became pointed tips. An elf, all right. The veil wasn't opaque enough to hide her own interesting features if he got much closer.

"Nearest town's five miles away, sweetheart," he said, "and I don't see a car."

She winced inside. This plan was so stupid. That damn hearse still showed no signs of going anywhere. The reason why hit her like a slap in the face: the elf she was speaking with had been in the passenger seat. There was another behind the wheel.

"A friend dropped me off. I like to be alone when I come to visit Kevin. Say..." Her tone became friendlier, a bit coquettish. She stepped forward and took hold of his black tie, massaging it through her fingers. She kept her head down. "Would you and your friend be kind enough to give me a lift back to town? Why doesn't he come out and say hello?"

"He just drives. I deal with the riffraff."

Now he was just being insulting. "Riff—"

His massive hands closed around her shoulders and jerked her up off the ground, sending her hat flying. "What the hell?"

She rolled her eyes and smiled, taking herself back to the book and the tree and soft scratch of the pages between her fingers. "Two households, both alike in dignity..."

The fire flared to life in her hands, hammering the elf like a punch to the chest. Talora landed on her feet, the elf on his back. She pressed the attack, Shakespeare's words streaming unbidden between her lips as she roasted the elf alive. "...what here shall miss, our toil shall strive to mend." His screams ended with the last syllable of the prologue.

The engine of the hearse choked a few times and then rumbled to life. The driver shifted into reverse and floored it. Talora smiled wickedly, lost to the blissful power of the magic. "Gregory, o' my word, we'll not carry coals..." With both hands, she heaved a tremendous fireball up over the hearse. It crashed down into the gravel driveway behind the vehicle. The driver brought the hearse to a screeching halt just short of the roaring bonfire. Without hesitation, the wheelman shifted gears and stomped the accelerator, sending the hearse speeding up over the grass embankment and directly for her. He leaned out the window, pistol in hand, and began to fire.

"To move is to stir; and to be valiant is to stand: therefore, if thou art moved, thou runn'st away." Tendrils of flame lanced out from the fingers of Talora's left hand and vaporized the bullets coming her way like a snake picking off a fleeing meal with its tongue. In her right hand, she gathered a blast the size of a basketball, waiting for the hearse to come a little closer...

Just as she was about to blow the vehicle apart, an invisible force flung her aside and out of the car's path. The vehicle was lifted up into the air and turned onto its side. It hovered for a few moments, its wheels desperately whirling in search of traction. Then it was jerked up and down like a pepper shaker and the elf in the driver's seat tumbled out through the open window. His scream was cut short when the vehicle was dropped on him with a tremendous crash of metal and glass.

"The library's going to be pissed," the Witch snapped.

Talora turned to find the Witch standing behind her, examining a burning page. In her haste, she'd vaporized the book. She let the fire die and pulled herself to her feet.

The Witch sauntered past her and yanked the back door of the hearse away with a twist of her wrist and a bit of telekinesis. A black coffin slid out onto the grass with a *thunk*. "How droll," she muttered as she righted the coffin and gently lifted its lid.

Talora leaned over the Witch's shoulder to inspect the coffin's contents. Inside were a young girl and a little boy, maybe eighteen and ten, respectively. Talora could see their chests rising and falling—they were alive, although heavily sedated.

The Witch reached out and gently tousled the boy's mop of sandy brown hair. "Now we're in business."

— CHAPTER TWENTY-TWO —

Roger thought himself back to Goody's and directly into the path of a hard left hook that sent him tumbling into the elves seated at the bar. One of them poured a beer over his head, then he was shoved back toward his attacker. The room around Roger spun and his skull rang, but he came out swinging and landed a right cross to someone's jaw. He punched out again with his left at a blurry shadow but caught nothing but air. A pair of strong hands took firm hold of his shoulders from behind to steady him.

When things came back into focus he found a prissy-looking elf with long white hair staring blankly up at him from the floor. The entire bar was roaring, cheering Roger on. He was dismayed to find Pike's stool, which he'd moved from earlier so as not to teleport into an awkward situation, empty.

"Well done, Pintiri," came the surprisingly feminine voice of the elf who'd stopped his mad twirl. She spun him around gracefully, as if leading a dance partner. "Next time try not to manifest in the way of my fist."

"That was you?" Roger asked, rubbing his aching jaw. He could feel the sticky beer crusting on his face and in his hair. The boozy stench made him grimace. "Hell of a punch."

The woman was short and slim, seemingly all bones underneath her black sorcerer's robes. Her red hair was pulled tight into a short ponytail. She smiled up at him, her blue eyes beaming. "They never see it coming, sir," she said. "They know I'm a sorceress, right? They all expect me to turn them into a toad or something, and then—wham!"

The man Roger had decked got to his feet and scrambled out the door. The rest of the bar, now full for dinner, returned to their own business. It struck Roger that none of them found it odd that someone had popped into their midst from out of nowhere. He supposed that was just part of living with magic.

"Get yourself cleaned up, sir," the woman said, pointing toward the restroom sign next to the main bar. "You're in no shape to rescue a princess."

"You're Ivree?" Roger asked, recalling the instructions Aldern had given him before adjourning the meeting. He lowered his voice. "Should you be saying that bit about the princess so loudly in public?"

"Hiperian Battlemage First Class Ivree," she said with a sharp salute. "Sorceress-at-Arms of the Gadukah. At your command, Pintiri! Don't worry; nobody cares about that princess bit."

Roger nodded and stumbled to the restroom, flicking a waxy gob of beer out of his ear as he went. Why did Evitankari, and everyone in it, have to be so damn strange?

Goody's only had one bathroom, a cramped unisex with a urinal, a crooked stall, and two basins set into a stainless steel counter that tipped precariously toward the left. Roger took a heaping helping of soap from the duck-shaped dispenser and scrubbed his face and hands until they hurt. He couldn't fit his head under the spigot, so he rubbed water through his sticky hair with his bare hands. It didn't work very well.

He stopped to stare at himself in the cracked and streaked mirror. The haggard, dripping man staring back at him looked absolutely petrified. Driff had come to the Council Chamber after Sorrin left to brief Roger and Aeric on what they were up against. The princess's captors weren't just kidnappers, thieves, rapists, and killers; they were full-fledged demons, monsters who'd escaped from humanity's worst nightmares. Each beast came with its own greatest hits list of atrocities: a bit of mass murder here, some torture and maiming there, all summed up real nice like some outfielder's career on the back of a baseball card. And then there were the pictures and the video clips, right there beside the calm numbers and cold descriptions so the Pintiri and the Mongan would know by sight which demon would try to dismember them and which might try to burn them alive with its acid breath.

The demons were holed up, Driff explained, in the hidden sub-basement of Iki, a Beijing nightclub owned by someone even worse and frequented by lesser demons who imagined themselves just as bad. The club also played host to a sizable human clientele, social climbers and hangers-on with little knowledge of the place's true nature. On the outside, Iki didn't look any more threatening than your typical upscale nightclub with a slightly Asian theme, protected by a velvet rope and a pair of large, angry bodyguards. The first floor was a posh, trendy space covered in metal and red fabric. But then Driff's little projector shifted to show blurry, grainy shots of the VIP areas downstairs, of the cages full of naked, abused humans and animals, of the booths where the tables came equipped with bloody shackles, of the twisted clientele dancing maniacally around the bonfire of corpses in the center of the main floor. And those, Driff noted, were only the rooms for which they had photographs.

Intelligence indicated that Myrindi was likely being held in the dungeons in the lowest basement level. To get to the princess they'd first have to find a way through the nightclub from hell. This was the kind of thing the Pintiri did all the time, Aeric assured him with a smile. Driff merely stuck his hands in his pockets and asked to be excused.

And so, Roger had returned to Goody's because Aldern's spit-and-glass concoction could only take him back to the location from which he'd initially thought himself to the Council Chamber, and then his escort to the city gate had almost knocked his block off because she couldn't behave herself for a few minutes while she waited for him. He wondered how many fights Ivree would start before he finished washing the beer out of his hair.

The blow dryer barely worked and there weren't any paper towels, so Roger left the bathroom still a bit soggy, cringing in embarrassment as he slipped past a woman on her way in. He found Ivree atop a table by the door, doing a one-armed handstand while her free hand directed a stream of crackling blue energy that levitated a pair of patrons and their chairs. Her heavy robes had fallen down around her armpits in a thick tangle, revealing the gray sweatsuit she wore underneath. The word "Luscious" was written across the back of her pants in flowing pink script. The crowd around her was laughing and exchanging money won and lost on whatever bets they'd made.

Roger just shook his head and headed for the door. The crowd let out a collective "awwwwwwww" as Ivree vaulted to the floor to follow. The floating patrons were gently lowered back to the floor.

"That was a new personal best, Pintiri!" Ivree chirped at him as they stepped out into the cool night. The soft glow of the iron streetlamps was like something primal, making Old Ev's archi-tecture seem even older. She inhaled deeply, out of breath. "Seven whole minutes!"

"Congratulations. Which way to the gate?"

"Port's to the north," she said, pointing in the general direction Roger had come from earlier. "One point two clicks."

He wasn't sure exactly how far that was. "Aeric said the Gidookie would be joining us, but he didn't tell me just who you are," he said as they set off.

A group of three drunks smoking beside Goody's steps hollered a few lewd comments in Ivree's direction. She sent their cigarettes sailing off into the night with a wave of her hand. "It's Gadukah. Ga-du-kah," she said slowly, as if correcting a small child. "We are the cream of the crop, the best of the best. When a job is too big for the Pintiri alone, we back him up. Err, not that you need any backup, sir."

Roger laughed. "I'll take all the backup I can get."

She laughed back. "Aye, sir. You should know that we answer to no authority but the Pintiri. We operate independently of the jackasses on the Combined Council. No one can tell us what we can and can't do except the Pintiri. For all intents and purposes, we are above the law."

Ivree stopped when they reached the statue of Axzarian. She raised one hand, shaped her fingers into a gun, and flicked her thumb down. A bolt of lightning burst from her fingertip to obliterate a pair of pigeons roosting on the statue's shoulder, sending feathers and flesh in all directions. "Can't have them shitting on Axzarian," she said as she pretended to blow smoke away from the tip of her gun finger. Roger didn't think it wise to ask if Axzarian would mind being covered in pigeon guts instead. "He's still in there, you know," she continued. "Watching over us all, scaring small children into eating their vegetables and going to bed on time. Devious bastard." They shared another laugh.

Old Ev had finally come alive. Elves were everywhere, hanging out on their stoops or just on the sidewalk, or traveling in thick, boozy clusters to the night's next stop. Roger suspected it was whatever passed for a weekend night with their kind; he'd lost track of the days, and he hadn't thought to ask the elves how they tracked time. They passed a pair fighting with wooden practice swords as a small crowd gathered around them hooted and hollered. Another couple were playing frisbee with a shaggy brown dog, using telekinetic magic to keep the whirling disc zipping here and there.

"It's good to see everybody out and about," he said. "With all that's happened."

"If there's one thing we're good at, Pintiri, it's moving the fuck on," Ivree replied. "Evitankari is no stranger to tragedy, but we deal. Some say it's why we're all so fucked up," she added, crossing her eyes, jutting out her front teeth, and circling her ear with one finger.

Roger nodded. He supposed that made a lot of sense. "If you don't mind my asking, why weren't you in the tower that day?" He couldn't remember the name the elves used for it.

"I told you, sir: we're not beholden to the Council, and so Aldern's bullshit about 'stay in the Kralak this' and 'it's not safe to practice powerful magic outside that' don't apply to me. It's that dumb old goat's fault we put almost all of our eggs in one easy-to-squash basket."

He didn't think that was fair, but he let Ivree's comment pass. Elven society, in the end, was subject to the same fractures and faults and blame-placing as his own world. He felt a bit stupid for not recognizing that sooner.

"And that fucking giant is damn lucky I wasn't there," she continued, not missing a beat. "I would've kicked its ass the minute it looked at the Kralak if I hadn't been hung over off my shit at home."

Somehow, Roger didn't doubt it.

They came upon the wall then, that behemoth of stone that separated Evitankari from the world at large. The runes that maintained the defensive wards took on different colors in the starlight, blue and green and purple tracing across the dull rock like neon. It was a bit gaudy, to be sure, but it was also strangely pretty.

To their right, not twenty paces away, a man and woman were kissing against the wall. Ivree made a throwing motion and a terrible farting sound erupted behind the man. The girl shoved her paramour away and slapped him in the face. Ivree and Roger laughed as the man chased the fleeing woman along the wall.

"You're a bit of a troublemaker," he said.

"Well, sir," she said coyly, looking up at him in a doe-eyed way that reminded Roger of the way his daughter would when she was trying to play innocent. He wondered just how old Ivree actually was. "There is only one person in the city who can tell me when I'm misbehaving..."

Roger laughed heartily. "Just don't magic me without asking first and we won't have any problems."

"Aye, sir!" she said with a crisp salute and a click of her heels.

They stared at each other for a few awkward moments. "So, where's this gate?" Roger asked.

Ivree slapped the wall with her palm three times. "Open up!" she shouted. Something inside clicked, then a three foot wide section began sliding and grinding its way down into the ground.

"That's it?" Roger said happily.

A deep, spine-tingling voice interrupted Ivree's response. "Name and purpose?" it snarled.

Roger turned to face the voice and almost lost control of his bowels. The beast glowering at them from the gap in the wall was ten feet and five or six hundred pounds of pure terror, its sinewy muscles rippling underneath its tight black cloak. It had the long, sloping face of a horse, its mouth full of sharp fangs and a forked tongue. The top of its skull was a crown of short, jagged horns. But by far the most terrifying thing about it was its eyes: it didn't have any, just a pair of empty black holes where they should've been. Roger could feel those empty holes examining, dissecting, and measuring. His hand drifted down to the shotgun at his hip.

"Cheers, Ornock," Ivree said. "The Pintiri and I are off to rescue Princess Myrindi."

Ornock nodded, his tongue flicking in and out between his fangs. "Apologies, Ivree. Pintiri. One can't be too careful these days. Do give Myrindi my best."

Ivree brushed past Ornock, giving his arm an affectionate pat. "You do your job well, old gnoll."

Roger swallowed in a dry throat and hurried after her. "Um, thanks..." he muttered to Ornock as he stumbled past, blushing and staring.

The alley they stepped into was narrow enough that the two of them had to travel single file. The wall loomed above them on both sides, the runes here even denser and brighter. When Roger stepped too close, the hairs on his arm stood straight out and a feeling like static electricity zipped through his skin. After a few close calls, he focused on keeping to the center of the cobblestone path.

A minute or two later the path forked hard to the left. Roger glanced back behind him to make sure Ornock was out of sight, then he tapped Ivree on the shoulder. "What...ah...who...was that?"

"Ornock dia nu li Ulanapai," she replied without looking back. "Guardian of the Path to Port. No one gets past, either way, without his approval."

Of course, Roger thought. *The guard dog.* "But this route is so narrow. How does anything ever make it into or out of the city? I can't imagine this is convenient for large shipments."

"Path adapts itself to whomever and whatever traverses it, to whichever part of Evitankari it leads to or comes from."

Roger scratched his head, struggling to keep up both physically and mentally. Ivree didn't seem to mind stepping close to the wall and its disconcerting discharges. "You're saying I can open one of those...doors...anywhere along the wall, smile at the...uhh...gnoll, and Path will just direct me to Port?"

Ivree smiled brightly. "You got it."

He tried to visualize it, picturing something that looked a bit like an octopus grasping a single point with its twisting, turning tentacles. The whole setup seemed needlessly complex and slightly paranoid. He wondered again what the elves were trying to keep out—or if they were, in fact, trying to keep people in.

The route ahead ended in a solid wall. Ivree slapped it three times, like she had the wall in the city proper, and a six-foot section rolled upwards like a garage door.

"Welcome to Port," Ivree said happily as she led him inside. Roger had been here before, when the Evertree had slipped him into Shellae's memories. Port was a sprawling, towering, industrial warehouse, a behemoth of steel girders and metal plate and concrete. Ivree led him down a wide aisle lined with soaring shelves piled high with all manner of crates, bags, and packages. Elves in black uniforms hustled to and fro like bees in a hive, checking this, discarding that into floating plastic bins that followed along like obedient dogs. Roger watched in awe as a teenage boy telekinetically lowered a huge crate down three stories to a silent landing on the concrete floor, his fingers maniacally waving complex spells in the air before him.

"Everything entering or leaving the city must first pass through Port," Ivree explained, reaching back to drag him along by his arm when he stopped to stare at a giraffe in its cage. "Contraband that can't be returned to its owner is disposed of via singularity."

To their left, a burly elf shoved a couch into one of the plastic waste containers. The couch twisted and distorted, shrinking and deforming as it was sucked inside. It disappeared with a disconcerting slurp and the elf slammed the container's lid shut.

"You throw your garbage into black holes?" Roger asked, incredulous. "Isn't that a bit dangerous?"

"No worse than dumping it in the ocean like you humans do," muttered a worker to their left. Ivree set the commenter's clipboard on fire with a glance and the woman ran away screaming.

"Crossing the street can be dangerous, Pintiri, but I'm sure you do it every day regardless," Ivree said.

"But that's a black hole!"

"In a plastic container," she corrected. "Perfectly manageable."

Their aisle came to an end at the center of Port, a circular area not unlike Tash Square in Old Ev. Five other aisles were evenly distributed around the hexagonal dais at the center, on which stood the wooden pilot box of a sailing ship, complete with a steering wheel. Activity was heavier here. Port workers examined packages and people, marking their comings and goings on their clipboards and dispatching them down this aisle or that. There was a bright blue flash and a pair of elves in combat fatigues popped into existence upon the dais, each with one hand on the steering wheel. They checked in with a nearby official and departed down one of the aisles, nodding to Roger and Ivree as they went.

Son of a bitch, Roger thought. *So that's how we're getting to Beijing...*

"You're late," growled a grizzled old man from his seat on the floor beside the dais. He was surrounded by four heavily armed elves wearing all black. Roger spotted automatic rifles, pistols, swords, a crossbow, and even a bazooka. Aeric stood off to their side, absorbed in conversation with one of the Port workers.

"Apologies, Commander," Ivree said, snapping to attention. "Altercation with some civvies. The Pintiri dealt with it."

The man stood with a groan, his joints obviously creaking, and he spat on the floor. "Commander Rynes," he said, offering Roger a warm, firm handshake, "and these are the most feared fighters on the planet: the Gadukah."

The other four men answered with a loud "Hoo-rah!" The worker chatting with Aeric rolled his eyes.

"A pleasure," Roger said. The Gadukah came in all shapes and sizes, as diverse as their weapons, and they were a mean-looking bunch. Rynes introduced him to the other four in turn. Hirace, the young sniper and medic. Ankh, huge and stoic. Halbert and Balt, a pair of lithe, lean brothers so perfectly toned they looked like they'd been created in a lab. Roger found his prior fear beginning to dissipate. With these men and this much firepower, how could things go wrong?

"Well, men," he said, deciding to at least try acting like the leader he was supposed to be. "Saddle up. We've got a princess to rescue!"

— CHAPTER TWENTY-THREE —

Every nerve in Roger's body screamed as blue light flared around him. When it faded, he found himself clutching the side of a dumpster in a dark, cramped alley, throwing up all over the place.

Rynes clapped him on the back. Roger coughed violently. "Happens to all of us the first time," the elf said helpfully. "Let me know if the feeling doesn't pass."

Roger coughed and spat one last time. "What if it doesn't?"

"Nothing to be worried about, Pintiri," Rynes replied. Behind him, the gigantic Halbert pulled one finger across his throat in a slashing motion. Ivree kicked him in the shin.

Aeric was the last one through. He materialized right in Roger's puddle of vomit. "What's that smell?" he asked.

"Just the transpoint, Mongan," Rynes replied. "Pintiri, the Gadukah communicate via neural link made possible by a complex combination of spells that would likely kill a human." He handed Roger a headset. "This will keep you in touch with us."

For a moment, Roger feared there was going to be magic involved. The headset looked perfectly harmless and a bit flimsy, the kind of thing a telephone operator might wear. He slipped it over his head, adjusting the fuzzy microphone so it would be closer to his mouth. "Test," he said. Something thin and sharp stabbed into him just above his ear canal, sending a burst of electricity tingling through his skull. He gasped and stumbled, but Rynes caught him.

Can you hear me? Rynes's voice echoed in Roger's head, though his mouth didn't move.

Your mother's a whore, came Ankh's voice in a similar fashion. A stream of obscenities whirled through Roger's mind. He wished they'd told him that was going to happen. Before he could mention his annoyance, Ivree's voice was in his head. *We heard that. The microphone's just for show. Keeps us from having to rearrange your synapses into an antenna. Calm yourself and listen.*

Roger straightened and took a deep breath, trying to do just that. He didn't want to look like a fool in front of the hardened Gadukah. Then it came; he could feel them all, almost as if they were other personalities inhabiting his body. Rynes was in there, impatiently waiting to get the show on the road, as was Aeric and his growing suspicion that he'd stepped in something. Ivree was a cacophony of spastic thought while Halbert, Hirace, and Balt were quiet and subdued. Ankh was still trying to convince Roger that his mother was a whore.

"Takes some getting used to," Aeric said, "but it gives us a real leg up."

Rynes kicked in the emergency exit door in the brick building opposite the dumpster. "Nice of the local trolls to relocate the transpoint for us, but the lazy fucks hate heights. Pintiri, Hirace, Ivree—you've got the roof. The rest of you are with me. Shift change at the back door in eight minutes, twenty seconds."

Roger followed the two hustling elves into the stairwell. He looked up and his heart sank; there had to be at least fifteen flights to the top. Hirace and Ivree were moving at incredible speed, having already crested the fourth floor. Roger swallowed his trepidation and hurried after them. He was too old for this crap.

The roof access door slammed open when he reached the eighth-floor landing, huffing and puffing and willing his aching legs to keep going. He stopped to catch his breath, pacing to work the kinks out of his thighs.

Pintiri, came Hirace's thought, *would you like a bit of assistance?*

Roger's pride almost got in the way, but he nodded. His entire body began to tingle like he'd been hooked up to an invisible battery. The pain in his muscles eased and his breath began to flow smoother and easier. Feeling ten years younger, Roger once again began the climb to the top, finishing the last seven floors in half the time it took him to do the first eight.

The feeling dissipated as he burst through the door and onto the roof. He found Hirace seated atop the building's chiller, cleaning the business end of a wicked-looking sniper rifle. Ivree was sprawled out on the roof a few feet away, staring up at the stars and humming to herself.

"What was that?" Roger asked. The extra energy was gone, but he still felt better than he had all day.

"We healers can do a lot more than mend wounds and set broken bones," Hirace said with a wink. For once, Roger was grateful for the magic.

He wandered over to the edge of the roof. They were right across the street from Iki. Colored lights played across the windows of the club's three visible floors like the inside of some demented kaleidoscope. Club hoppers decked out in their finest stood impatiently in a line that wrapped around the far corner of the block. Roger wondered how many of them knew what really happened in there—and how many would never make it back out.

Rynes's voice echoed through Roger's mind. *Ivree, Hirace: clear the building.* Roger could feel the Gadukah tense. His two companions appeared at his side, ready to commence the operation. Hirace raised his sniper rifle and surgically placed a single round through a window on each of the club's three floors. The crowd below degenerated into chaos at the gunshots and the glass raining down, screaming and running in all directions.

"What was that for?" Roger asked.

"Just seeding the clouds," Hirace replied. He popped the used clip out of his weapon and slapped in a new one. "Get ready, Pintiri; if any of those bastards try to escape, it's up to you and me to bring 'em down."

Roger fumbled with the catch on his holster, finally raising his weapon in shaking hands and taking aim at the building below. Sweat rolled down his brow. There were so many people down there; if he had to fire, he hoped they'd all make it clear first. He wasn't sure he'd be able to pull the trigger if there was a chance an innocent might get caught in the blast.

He felt Ivree's mind go suddenly blank and he jerked around to make sure she was all right. The sorceress was absolutely still, eyes shut and jaw clenched. Then an image of a hurricane tore through Roger's mind and a peal of thunder echoed from the building across the street. The kaleidoscope of light had gone suddenly murky, accentuated every so often by the flash of lightning and the rumble of thunder.

Yup, came Hirace's thought, *she started a storm inside that building, using the little canisters of starter potion I fired inside.*

We're in, Rynes broadcasted. *Sub-basement door in sight.*

People poured out of the club, both through the front door and the emergency exits that emptied out into the alleys on either side. Roger flicked his gaze from patron to patron, searching for any that seemed something other than human. They were so far away that it was impossible to tell.

You'll know, Hirace sent through the neural link. *Panicked crowds are one thing; raging demons are a whole other level.*

We've gained access to the first subbasement, Rynes reported. It was deserted, Roger could tell through the link, though the Gadukah found themselves surrounded by the aftermath of the night's revels. A wave of disgust rippled beneath the calm readiness of the elven commandos as they scanned the VIP area for threats. Roger felt Ankh's attention linger on the plaintive cries of one of Iki's victims, then cold detachment as the commando banished any thought of assistance from his mind. Even though Roger couldn't see what was going on, he wanted to throw up. Driff's intel hadn't lied.

Breaching entrance to second level, thought Rynes. *No resistance yet—*

A terrific boom shook the neighborhood and five cries of anguish tore through Roger's mind. He stumbled backward as if struck, his senses struggling to contradict his mind's insistence that he was in great pain. Hirace dropped the rifle and clamped his hands to his head. Ivree wailed.

And then, one by one, the five elves in Iki winked out of his consciousness.

"Are they..." Roger couldn't finish the thought.

"No," Hirace replied. "That was a conscious disconnect, not a termination. They're alive, but they're in a bad way. We sever the link when our own situation could hinder the others. They'll check in briefly once every two minutes when it's safer. Think of it as a psychic homing beacon."

Iki had shifted on its foundation, its left side crumpled like the front of a car in a head-on collision. Smoke rose up from the ruined building to blot out the stars.

"We have to get down there," Roger said. "We can't leave Rynes and Aeric and the others."

Ivree nodded, her spell shattered. "First priority is to finish the mission. We rescue Myrindi, then we worry about the Gadukah."

"But aren't they in the same place, roughly?"

"Not for long," Hirace said. "They'll move her. The entrance the others used was on the ruined side of the building, so they'll come out through the front. It's our job to intercept."

The nightclub shifted again, rumbling as it came to rest against the building across the alley. Roger swallowed in a dry throat. That thing wasn't going to hold much longer. He turned toward the stairwell. "Let's go, then."

"Not that way," Ivree said, peering over the edge of the roof. Beside her, Hirace had stowed the rifle in his heavy pack and drawn a pair of small submachine guns. "Put your arms around me, Pintiri."

Roger didn't like where this was going, but he knew there wasn't time to argue. He took the slender elf by the waist and closed his eyes. She was stronger than she looked, lifting him bodily and leaping over the side of the roof. There was a brief, frightening sensation of plummeting headfirst toward the pavement below as the wind whipped through his hair and clothes, and then they began to decelerate, twisting so that they landed softly on their feet.

You can open your eyes now. She punctuated the thought with a giggle.

He did, one at a time, not quite trusting his other senses. All hell had broken loose on the street around them. People—and many things that looked kind of like people but weren't—streamed out of the ruined club, running every which way in their panic to escape the attack. Hirace's machine guns echoed above the din as he landed beside Roger, shredding a pair of black things that got too close. The medic kicked one in the head to make sure it was dead.

"Hard to believe they were once human," he said, his eyes scanning the crowd. "Myrindi's captors should be making a break for it any moment—"

"What did you just say?" Roger shouted, incredulous.

Hirace looked hurt. "I was going to say that the bad guys should be here soon."

"About the demons, asshole."

Ivree draped an arm around Roger's shoulder. "It's complicated, Pintiri. We'll explain it when we get back to Evitankari."

He brushed her aside. "Explain it now!"

Hirace's machine guns went crack-crack-crack-crack, felling a big toad-like thing with three eyes. Roger drew his own weapon and pointed it at the elf. "Drop 'em!"

"But Pintiri—"

"The Pintiri says drop 'em! Ivree, watch our backs but don't kill anyone."

Hirace did as he was told. Ivree's face fell, but she obeyed. "Whatever you say, Pintiri."

"Hirace, explain," Roger snapped.

The medic sighed and shoved his hands in his pockets. The years melted away from him then, the cloak of military discipline and cocksureness cast aside, and he looked suddenly vulnerable. He actually wasn't much older than Roger's own daughter. "The Council really didn't tell you, Pintiri?"

Roger didn't feel the need to reply.

The elf nodded. "They're good at things like that, that's for damn sure. Must've thought you'd hesitate." He spat on the sidewalk and looked up at the stars. "Here's the deal, Pintiri: humans are not the only source of evil in this world, but they sure absorb a hell of a lot of it. The more evil they cause on their own, the more susceptible they become to outside sources. When they've absorbed enough, well..." He glanced toward the fallen demons at his feet.

Damn the fucking Council! Roger thought. This definitely fell in the category of things he needed to know. He was tired of being treated like a child; he didn't need to be shielded from the big bad world, protected from perceived dangers until he came of age in the eyes of Aldern and the others. He could handle it all, he knew, if only they'd let him.

"Is there any way to reverse it?" Roger asked.

"If it's caught early enough, sure. But when they get this far..."

"Pintiri!" Ivree shouted, pointing down the street. "Here comes the escape plan!"

Three black SUVs hit the far corner hard and rumbled toward the front of Iki, plowing through anyone and anything in their path. Roger couldn't see the drivers through the tinted glass, but the heavily armored panels and the lack of any markings or plates betrayed their purpose.

"Pintiri!" Hirace said, almost pleading. "Roger, the transformation doesn't happen by accident. These things made their choice. Any humanity they ever possessed is long gone. They're a blight upon this planet, Roger, and we're the only thing keeping them in check."

Roger's grip on his weapon wavered. "No bullshit?"

"No bullshit."

He reached out in the neural link, searching Hirace for any trace of deception. All he found was a single thought: *Uncle Pike's going to be pissed.*

Roger lowered the gun and laughed. "Ivree, take out that caravan."

She smiled happily and pirouetted like a ballerina. "With pleasure, Pintiri!"

Ivree snapped her fingers and the cars' engines exploded one after another. The SUVs skidded to a halt and slammed into each other. Roger took careful aim and pulled the trigger. A tremendous boom tore through the night as a pair of blue fireballs slammed into the pile of wreckage and set it ablaze.

"Nice shot, Pintiri!" Hirace cheered.

"Be sure to tell Uncle Pike," Roger beamed, feeling quite proud of himself. If only his family could see him now!

"Sir, they're making a break for it!" Ivree called.

Iki's front door shattered in a shower of metal and glass as a goliath of a creature burst through. It reached out one tremendous arm to swat aside a pair of women trying to run past, then it stepped out onto the sidewalk, its beady eyes searching the crowd. The thing appeared to be made of stone, its body a jumble of crags and sharp edges. Tendrils of gold wrapped the demon's skin in a mineral impersonation of a circulatory system.

Two smaller figures emerged from behind it, a woman and a young girl joined at the wrist by a heavy chain. The woman was very pretty in her red cocktail dress, despite the antlers growing from the sides of her head. Haggard and nervous, she looked a bit like Roger felt. The girl chained to her was definitely Myrindi, the fairy princess, blue and ethereal in a thin white shift. To her credit, she appeared more annoyed than concerned. The stone demon pointed to the right and they took off, the woman dragging the girl behind her.

"That big bastard's no match for you, Pintiri," Hirace said. "Think you can take it down while we rescue the princess?"

Visions of Hirace gunning down the woman in the red dress danced through Roger's head. He didn't care if the others saw them through the neural link. She was still so early in the change; maybe it could be undone. "Negative. You two deal with the big guy; I'll take care of his friend."

He took off after the woman and the princess before the elves could protest. The stone demon came for him, but a volley of gunfire forced it back toward the club. His quarry disappeared around the next corner and Roger picked up his pace.

— CHAPTER TWENTY-FOUR —

After casting a further hex to ensure the children remained asleep, the Witch and Talora buried them in their casket in the shade of a mighty elm beside the graveyard.

"The one place the elves will never look: the scene of the crime," the Witch explained. Talora wasn't convinced, but she didn't protest because she wanted to get that dreadful task over with. Her companion refused to give her a straight answer about who these children were or why they were important. She'd made Talora snap a creepy picture of them with an ancient Polaroid camera and then in the ground they went.

Then the Witch took Talora by the hand, led her to the transpoint, and brought them to China, where a limousine picked them up on the outskirts of a rice paddy in the middle of nowhere. She eagerly read half of *War and Peace* during the four-hour drive into Beijing, right to the back door of Tallisker's night club, Iki. There Demson introduced them to his latest acquisition: Myrindi, Crown Princess of Talvayne. Wherever the hell that was.

The little blue girl to whom they'd handcuffed Talora did not look impressed. "So, you work for the Witch, huh?"

Talora looked up from her book. "For now."

They'd freshened up and had dinner with Demson and several other Tallisker executives at a long table set up on the roof, where they had a great view of Beijing's skyline and the sunset beyond. Someone had loaned Talora a skimpy red cocktail dress that fit a little too well. She decided not to look a gift horse in the mouth, even if it was trying to look down her dress. At least there was room to hide the shifter's vial in the skimpy bra that came with it. Dinner was a tense affair during which Talora ate her fill and kept silent. Two more towers had fallen to elven attack, one in London and another in Paris, and Demson's crew were none too happy about it. Raising an army, Demson moaned, was too fucking expensive. The Witch taunted and teased the demons around her and didn't touch any of the food. Myrindi, who was chained up at the head of the table as the guest of honor, ate everything she could and glowered haughtily at anyone who addressed her.

After the plates had been cleared away, Talora and Myrindi were left in a room on the top floor in the rear of the building while the Witch and Demson went to discuss "grown up things." The VIP suite was all dark wood and red leather and soft, moody light. Bass-heavy club beats thumped around them, muffled by the walls. Talora had been left in charge of guarding Myrindi, and then seeing her to safety when—and the Witch insisted it was when and not if—the elves came for her.

"Head through the floor and Rocky will see you out," the Witch had instructed. "Two rights and then your second left to the backup getaway car in front of the noodle joint."

The princess brushed a lock of thick black hair out of her face and fixed Talora with a piercing stare. Supposedly she was a teenager, but she couldn't have weighed more than fifty or sixty pounds. As Talora understood it, possession of the Crown Princess of Talvayne would keep the Lost Races from aiding their allies in Evitankari when Demson and the Witch finally brought the fight to the elves. She didn't doubt that there was more to it than that.

"She's a sneaky bitch, that's for sure," Myrindi said wistfully. "I made a deal with her to get me out of Talvayne, away from the troll I have to marry. I was where I was supposed to be when I was supposed to be there. So were Demson and his shithead lackeys."

Talora didn't miss the hint. "I'll keep my eyes open."

The princess chewed her lip for a moment; obviously she'd been hoping for more. "You're not like the rest of them. You look a little like them. You smell a little like them. But you're something different. You're...in better control of yourself."

Myrindi may have rightly labeled the Witch sneaky, but she obviously wasn't far from that mark herself. Talora was impressed with how well the girl was handling her situation. "I'm not one of them," she replied, more because she hoped it was true than because she believed it.

"But you could be. With the right push."

A deep vibration rattled the walls and the booth in which they sat. It wasn't the beat of the music; it was something else.

"Was that thunder?" Talora asked.

The princess sniffed the air. Gills opened hungrily on either side of her slender blue neck, exposing the pink flesh inside. "Water..."

The music screeched to a stop as the equipment shorted out. Screams mingled with the patter of rain pouring on the dance floor and the occasional rumble of thunder. The floor shook as the club patrons beat a hasty retreat down the emergency stairwell beyond the far wall of the VIP room. A puddle of water trickled in through the door, streaked with blood and spilled drinks.

"Awww, party's over," the princess said melodramatically.

"Time to go," Talora said. Myrindi rolled her eyes.

She focused on the few bits of *Romeo & Juliet* she had left and gathered a tremendous fireball around her free hand. Myrindi gasped and ducked under a nearby table. Concentrating hard, Talora gently released the energy from her hand and let it float up toward the ceiling in the center of the room, a miniature sun casting ominous, flickering shadows across the walls. Ripples of power washed over her in waves, making her shiver. And then, with an ear-piercing shriek, she slammed the fireball down through the floor. It hit like a meteorite striking solid earth, with a deafening crash accompanied by a black cloud of dust and debris that momentarily blocked out the view. When the smoke settled, there was a ragged four-foot hole in the floor—and a matching gap in the floor below, and another in the floor below that, and another in the floor below that, and so on and so forth until Talora lost count. The debris at the bottom burned bright red.

"Rocky's waiting," she snapped, dragging Myrindi out from under the table and onto her feet. They peered over the smoldering edge. Two floors down, a pair of beady yellow eyes stared back up at them from dark hollows in a squat face. He was the size of three men and seemingly made of brown stone. Gold veins traced every nook and crag of his body as if he'd been draped in a spiderweb.

"Of course..." Myrindi huffed.

"Jump and I will catch you," the demon fluted in a surprisingly high-pitched voice. Talora fought off the urge to laugh.

The building shook and tipped on its foundation. Talora's fireball must've hit something important. Myrindi lost her balance and plummeted through the hole. A moment later the chain at Talora's wrist snapped taut and she was dragged down after the princess. For three beats of her pounding heart she was in free fall, staring face-first down at the hot pile of jagged wood and torn metal in the basement far below. She fell past Myrindi, cradled like a baby in Rocky's left arm, and the chain went taut again. Her armed stopped first, followed by the rest of her body as she flipped one hundred and eighty degrees. She stifled a scream as something in her shoulder popped. Her teeth dug into the tip of her tongue as Rocky hauled her up and deposited her on the rain-slick floor. She fell to her knees, clutching her arm close.

"Dislocated," Rocky tootled. "Don't watch."

Talora closed her eyes as the demon took hold of her bicep with his massive thumb and forefinger. It felt as if someone had closed her arm in a vise. She wasn't able to stifle her next scream as he violently popped her shoulder back into its socket. She flexed it a few times to confirm it was back in place, then opened her eyes and nodded. It hurt—a lot—but she refused to let it slow her down. Rocky smiled and helped her back to her feet. Myrindi ignored them both, picking something out of her fingernail.

"Thanks," Talora said, her shoulder still throbbing. She used the pretense of adjusting her undergarments to make sure the vial was still safely in place, which it was. "Now show us the way out." She had decided earlier in the day that when dealing with demons, it was probably best to be firm, not to show any fear, and not to hesitate.

Rocky nodded and turned on his heel, taking off down Iki's main entrance hall at a breakneck pace. His heavy footfalls shook the floor and left the dangling light fixtures swaying in his wake. Talora shoved Myrindi ahead and the two women hurried after him. They tried hard to avoid touching or having to look at the trampled club-goers sprawled here and there across the ruined marble, especially the ones Rocky hadn't bothered to step over. The floor was slick with rain and blood, and Talora wished Demson's cronies had given her a thicker pair of shoes.

Rocky exploded through the glass and metal entrance and out into the night, swatting away a pair of fleeing women who erred too close. The getaway car the Witch had warned Talora not to count on was a flaming wreck in the street. People rushed away from the building in all directions, screaming and shouting in a language she couldn't understand. Across the street, watching and waiting, stood two men and one woman, all in black military coveralls. The woman and the bigger male had pointed ears. *Elves.* They'd come to raid Iki, just as the Witch had said they would, and their objective was chained to Talora's arm.

Two rights and then your second left to the backup getaway car in front of the noodle joint.

Talora bolted to her right, dragging a surprised Myrindi behind her. "Buy us some time!" she hollered back at Rocky. She didn't look back to see if he had heard.

Myrindi kept pace, chugging along right at Talora's side as they rounded the corner of Iki to complete the second right. The princess even shoved a limping club-goer out of their way. They stuck to the sidewalk, following the herd of fleeing patrons and other night owls. Traffic had been brought to a sudden halt on this one-way street, vehicles abandoned as their drivers fled the danger around the corner. Neither of them looked back, but both could hear the pounding boots and harried shouts of a single pursuer.

At the first left—a narrow alley between a restaurant and a high-fashion boutique—Talora made a snap decision and veered suddenly into the black opening between a pair of empty vehicles. The elves wanted Myrindi. The demons wanted Myrindi. The Witch, she was willing to bet, had some stake in all this. That wasn't a fairy princess chained to her arm; it was a king's ransom, the sort of leverage Talora needed to find out just what in the hell was going on. She could set up a trade: the princess for her past, and when the deal was done she could unleash the contents of the vial.

Myrindi, who'd listened intently to the Witch's escape directions, did not object. "I don't care where we go or what we do," the princess gasped. "Don't give me back to the demons, and don't you fucking *dare* give me back to my father."

Talora nodded without looking back.

The alley was dark and cramped and smelled of many disgusting things Talora didn't want to think about running through. They proceeded single file, slowing slightly to keep their footing on the slick stone. Talora's heart leapt into her chest as the glow of a flashlight flared behind them. Their pursuer had followed them, and he was gaining.

Ahead, the alley forked at a grimy brick wall. Talora headed left without hesitation, ignoring their pursuer's repeated requests that they stop. Myrindi stumbled and Talora glanced back, pulling the girl back to her feet. In the process, she ran square into another brick wall that marked the end of the alley's left branch. Her head slammed hard into the stone, blackening her vision and crumpling her to the ground.

Light flared around them as her faculties returned. Myrindi helped the groggy Talora to her feet, but their attempted escape was over. The only exit was blocked by a handsome middle-aged man in black fatigues, flashlight in one hand, a battered old shotgun in the other. Neither an elf nor a demon. A human. Talora tried to wrap her mind around that and just couldn't. Humans didn't get involved. Would the elves work with a shifter? She didn't know.

"Come peacefully," he wheezed, trying to catch his breath, "and I'll make sure you get the help you need."

As usual, Talora had no clue what this latest annoyance was talking about. Human or shifter, he wouldn't stand a chance against her magic, but she knew she'd never be able to hit him with the fire before he could pull the trigger of his weapon. Leaning heavily on Myrindi, she brushed a lock of hair out of her face and played the last card the Witch had given her. "I have a message for Pentari Roger Brooks."

The man lowered his weapon ever so slightly, his eyes wide. "Do you mean Pintiri Roger Brooks?"

She laughed one tired laugh. "Whatever. It's in the top of my dress."

He nodded. "I'm Pintiri Roger Brooks. Hand me the message."

She reached into her bra and pulled out the greeting card the Witch had insisted she clip underneath her arm. The glittery purple envelope, addressed to Roger in flowing script, sparkled ominously in the flashlight's harsh glow. He glanced down at the shotgun and the flashlight in his hands, then motioned to Myrindi. "Open it and hold it up so I can see it."

The princess sighed heavily, tore into the envelope, and pulled out the card inside. "Missing you" ran across the front of the card in cartoony block letters above a sad-looking teddy bear. Myrindi flipped it open and offered it up for Roger's inspection.

The man's face turned white and his jaw dropped. The Witch hadn't shown Talora the contents of the card; she had no way of knowing if this would help her or hurt her, but it was the only play she had left. Obviously, it had struck a nerve. It was almost a full minute before Roger regained his composure and looked away from the card.

He handed Myrindi the flashlight. "Hold that for a minute."

As he strode past the princess, murder in his eyes, Talora called the flames. Then his hand was in her face, showering her with sparkling silver dust, and the heat in her fingers died away and the world went black.

— CHAPTER TWENTY-FIVE —

P ike lit a cigarette as he stepped out of the Goat's Mistress and into the warm Galworth afternoon. The information Lep had just imparted had left the Council of War a bit perturbed. Tallisker command towers had been falling for the last three days; two more had gone down the night before, one in Los Angeles and one in Moscow. The demons had unloaded their cache of narii dust into reservoirs and pumping stations around the world in an unprecedented attempt to keep humanity docile— cascades of flaming rubble from formerly invisible citadels in the middle of their most heavily populated cities were making the humans a bit jumpy. There were rumors flying everywhere that Tallisker had overdone it and left segments of the population brain dead. Other, more disconcerting rumors posited that the attacks were perpetrated by Evitankari in response to the destruction of the Kralak. And just that morning, hours before Pike arrived and immediately following the return of the freshly rescued Princess Myrindi, Talvayne disconnected itself from the transpoint network without a word of explanation.

The world was going to hell and no one had bothered to tell Pike about it. He disliked being left out of the loop. Stringent security measures controlled the flow of information into and out of Evitankari; only a few very high-ranking members of the Intelligence caste were given access to the Internet and external television and radio channels. Elves returning to the city via Port were immediately debriefed and dusted as necessary. The general population didn't know anything certain members of the Council didn't want it to know—hence Pike's regular trips to visit Lep and Chas.

There was no way Driff could've missed all this; it'd be like not noticing a nuclear blast because you were staring at a firecracker instead. Which meant one thing: he'd taken the information to Aldern—proper protocol, given the situation—and the Council of Sorcery had squashed it, as was within his power as senior member of the Council. But why? What was that crazy old shithead up to?

Pike took a long drag on his cigarette, letting the spicy smoke linger in his throat. Someone with delusions of grandeur was about to make a very big power grab. The traditional players— Evitankari, Tallisker, and, with the kidnapping of its princess, Talvayne—had all been systematically weakened. The door was wide open for someone new to steal control of the game. And if that someone was who Pike thought it was, they were all in a world of trouble.

He tossed what was left of his cigarette aside angrily and stormed off toward the woods. At least his crew had a game plan. Chastity was already off looking into Tallisker's recent activities. Lep had feelers out to every Talvayan ex-pat he'd ever met. That left Pike to figure out Evitankari—a difficult enough task on what passed for a normal day in the elven capital. It all came down to that damn human Pintiri, he thought, unless Roger Brooks was just a smokescreen, in which case focusing his energy in that direction would be playing right into his enemy's hands.

What he really needed, he decided as he breached the first set of ancient oak trees, was help. For Pike, that was no small admission. He hated pretty much everybody in Evitankari and thought he could do all of their jobs better himself—and that went doubly true for the assholes sitting on the Combined Council. But then again, even if there was someone he thought he could trust, the story he could tell wouldn't exactly be the most reputable. *I've got a black market transpoint coded to one other transpoint in Ireland,* he thought sarcastically, *and I use it to regularly visit a criminal ex-pat and his demon wife. They say the world's going to shit and certain members of the Council know it and refuse to do anything about it or even tell the rest of us what's going down. And I can grow wings and fucking fly.*

Galworth's transpoint was a sliver of granite sticking straight up out of the earth in a small clearing a quarter mile out of town. The oblivious locals knew it as the Devil's Finger. Legend painted it as a former site of pagan worship tainted by all sorts of unholy rituals still haunted—of course—by the spirits of those sacrificed in ancient times. Evitankari liked to add stories like that to the local mythology whenever possible as a means of keeping people the hell away from its transportation network. Pike had always thought that liberal use of land mines would be simpler and more effective, but he was glad for the privacy such legends created. He didn't trust the dust and he hated having to use it. They were too dependent on it, he thought, and he often wondered where they'd be if it ever dried up completely. Anything that fucked so badly with a person's mind, whether that person was an elf or just a stupid human, should be saved as a last resort.

Which, as he reached the transpoint, brought his thoughts back to Driff. Here was a man the Council had dusted out of his fucking skull and left to rot on some island in the Pacific. And then he came back, proving the Council wrong, and rode his folk hero status to a position on the very governing body that had condemned him in the first place. No way he was as loyal as he seemed; if he didn't harbor some resentment toward Aldern and the others, well, he was either completely devoid of emotion or really fucking stupid. Hatred was one thing Pike knew he could trust. If his assumption that Driff knew what was going on and had been silenced was true, the Council of Intelligence could prove to be the perfect ally. The elf might even have a few pieces of the puzzle that Pike had missed. He didn't trust Driff as far as he could throw him—the man was a little too secretive for Pike's taste—but he'd have to chance it.

He reached out and touched the transpoint, thinking of his living room...

...and wound up somewhere completely different: someone else's dining room. The bust of Napoleon on which his hand rested was, indeed, *his* black market transpoint, but this was not his home. Someone had moved his transpoint. Panicked, he decided his best bet would be to flee back to Lep's. As the word *Galworth* screamed through his mind, the little statue crumbled in his grasp. Pike closed his eyes and swore. He'd really liked that bust.

There was a familiar smell in the air, noxious and sweet. Blood. On the other side of the room, a crimson trail led into the kitchen beyond. He swore again. Beside the pile of Napoleon's dusty remains was a cardboard box just big enough to hold the little statue. The name on the printed shipping label read *Council of Agriculture Piney.*

Someone had set him up. Someone who knew about his clandestine meetings with Lep. Someone who knew what was going on elsewhere and wanted it kept quiet. And, most importantly, someone inside Evitankari.

Pike took a deep breath and followed the trail. A pair of bloody handprints on either side of the entryway, close to the floor, told him that Piney had still been alive when the murderer dragged her into the kitchen. She'd put up a fight.

The next room was an absolute mess; Pike almost slipped on the blood pooling on the tile floor. Piney's body was propped up in the corner against the refrigerator, apparently eviscerated in a single stroke. Broadsword, he guessed. What was left of her head was on the counter beside the sink, split like a melon—and empty. The sink and disposal were caked with blood and ichor.

Without an intact brain, the Evertree couldn't add Piney's memories to its store. The smoking gun that would've cleared Pike's name was gone. Whoever the murderer was, he was good. He'd never liked the annoyingly bubbly Council of Agriculture, but she hadn't deserved this.

The door to his left exploded in a shower of wood, knocking Pike off his feet and down into the puddle of blood on the floor. When the three commandos breached the kitchen, they found him covered in evidence. He didn't bother fighting off the kick to his gut, or the slap to his face, or the heavy cuffs that soon bound his hands and feet.

When he figured out who had framed him, that person was as good as dead.

— CHAPTER TWENTY-SIX —

A sharp, stabbing pain in the sole of Aeric's left foot woke him suddenly. *Where am I?* he wondered. The last thing he remembered was the searing heat of the fireball coming down through the ceiling of Iki's horrific basement level. Was he dead? Was the inky, impermeable blackness surrounding his bed the waters of the Origina?

No...there was more. He'd been conscious briefly, in the hospital, while a team of healers sealed his wounds and set his broken bones. His injuries had been bad enough, however, to warrant an overnight stay for observation. The healers' magic was powerful, but elven physiology was a complicated thing. They wanted him close in case it turned out they'd missed something. Chyve had put him under with a maternal smile and a quick flick of her fingers.

The bed in which he found himself definitely belonged in Evitankari's hospital. This wasn't the first time he'd been roughed up. The crisp white linens and metal rails were familiar. But where were the walls, the floor, and the ceiling? There should've been a little nightstand to his left, set with a glass of water and a plate of crackers, and a wide window to his right with a view of the city beyond.

He'd been through this once before, he realized, way back in basic training. Elven teachers were big on making their students experience the effects of the techniques they'd be using to do their jobs. He was within the sphere of a nevect, an enchanted grenade of sorts used to create what was essentially a reverse event horizon; light could escape the magic's field, but it couldn't come in from the outside. Typically, nevecti were used during interrogations to isolate a prisoner and hide the people asking the questions, who could see him perfectly fine. The nevect itself, he figured, was probably under his bed.

"Who's there?" he asked. He knew the nevect's field would only last half an hour. If he could stall, he might be able to distract his— what, his captor?—long enough that he'd forget about the field's pending dissolution.

There was no answer. His foot began to feel a bit numb. What in the name of Axzarian was going on?

A very familiar syringe sailed out of the blackness and landed on his chest. The chamber was short and stumpy, the tip little more than a pin. The label on the top of the sturdy plunger read "Caution: Perambyrol" in big block letters above a skull and crossbones. Aeric's heart leapt into his throat. Only the Combined Council had access to Evitankari's perambyrol stores. A slow-moving drug, it would spread from the injection site to the rest of his body at an agonizingly slow rate, numbing tissue as it went— and if it reached his heart, it would cause immediate cardiac arrest. This particular syringe was empty.

"You have approximately three minutes and thirty-seven seconds before your heart stops," a distorted voice, like nails on a chalkboard, announced from somewhere outside the nevect's field. "The dissolution of the narii barriers in your mind will release the counter agent and save your life."

Aeric knew all this. Not unlike yeast, narii dust was alive; it was absorbed into the bloodstream instantaneously upon inhalation, rendering the subject semi-unconscious as it hit the brain and began to colonize. Without interference, it would settle in areas where it wouldn't affect mental function. But when the host was spoken to during its initial colonization period, the parts of the host's brain that reacted strongest to the speaker's words lit up like miniature suns to attract the little beasts. They'd wall off the relevant neurons, removing the host's access to the memories therein. Neither magic nor surgery had proven effective in excising these colonies; attacking them in any way caused the release of the enzyme narimose, which would spread through the body and shut down the host's major organs. Those who'd been dusted could break the paths naturally with enough effort, but doing so would release the enzyme and kill them. Strangely, narimose and perambyrol, both deadly in isolation, cancelled each other out. Their molecules would bond to form an inert compound that later would be passed through the host's urine. The administration of perambyrol, combined with a forced remembrance, was the best means of un-dusting a dusted individual—and even that process could only claim a thirty-six percent success rate.

Understanding the science was the easy part. Accepting the revelation that he'd been dusted, forcing himself to remember, and breaking the narii barriers wasn't so simple. Like anyone who'd ever been dusted, Aeric had no clue what had been taken from him or why. He'd never felt so helpless, so afraid. Even if he survived... what if the memories he unlocked were something terrible, something better left buried? Would he even still be himself when it was over? What did his interrogator want with the information he was trying to restore?

"What am I looking for?" Aeric asked, his voice cracking.

"You had a sister."

"I did?"

"You had a sister. She was a pretty little thing with long dark hair and big brown eyes."

Aeric searched his mind frantically. His entire foot was numb and he could feel the poison working its way up his shin. He was an only child. He'd always wanted siblings, but his parents had thought one was enough. Or had they?

"Rayn was your sister's name. Rayn was a talented girl—smart, funny, the head of every class she enrolled herself in. Rayn could've been anything she wanted to be."

Aeric's thoughts raced, but nothing the voice told him sounded even remotely familiar. He closed his eyes and concentrated harder than he ever had in his life, thinking so hard it hurt. Salty tears streamed down his face and onto his neck and chest, soaking into the collar of his hospital gown. The name Rayn meant nothing to him. He could feel the perambyrol in his thigh now, racing hungrily toward his hip. When it hit his chest in another minute, he was done for.

"Rayn could've been anything she wanted to be. She wanted to heal. Rayn wanted to give of herself to help others. She had a talent for using the magic of her patients to augment her powers; where other healers would've aged months or years, Rayn aged mere minutes. She was the most powerful magic user Evitankari had seen in centuries."

Aeric's heart raced, beating so hard he suspected it was trying to burst from his chest and escape the cold death heading its way. Sweat streamed through his pores, soaking the sheets. He still couldn't remember a sister, or even anyone who could perform the type of magical feats the speaker described. His hip went numb.

"But that wasn't good enough for Evitankari. Rayn, it was decided, couldn't be wasted on something as basic as medicine. She was to be a battlemage, the best of the best, a demon hunter with the power to bring Tallisker to its knees and establish Evitankari as the world's preeminent authority. Rayn balked at the idea, refusing to become a weapon. The Council decided to dust her into compliance."

There, Aeric thought, finding the empty spot in his mind where the memories—or some memories, at least—were surely locked. *There it is.*

"You couldn't let that happen. You freed Rayn and took her into hiding. You were on the run, but you were together and you were happy."

He lost his grasp on the walled-off part of his mind. He never would've disobeyed the will of the Council. Their word was law and what they decided, though not always pretty and not always popular, was always for the best. He would never actively work against them, even for his family. The greater good trumped the fate of one individual. He lost the feeling in his abdominals. The memories his interrogator wanted didn't exist, Aeric knew, and that meant he was as good as dead.

"But in the end, you were betrayed by someone you both trusted implicitly: Rayn's lover and your best friend, a man you'd both grown up with, a man who may as well have been family, renounced his loyalty to Evitankari and sought you out. You welcomed him with open arms. Together, the three of you could face anything. Until he dragged Rayn kicking and screaming back to Evitankari and left you for dead."

Something in Aeric's mind finally shattered and he bolted up into a sitting position. The memories came rushing through him like a tidal wave. He and Rayn on the playground, he in the swing, she using her magic to hurl him up and over the crossbar; in math class, passing notes back and forth, Rayn shifting the chalk particles on the blackboard to make them spell dirty words; birthdays, holidays, milestones, fights and reconciliations—all the things a brother and sister, two peas in a pod, would've experienced, enjoyed, and suffered through.

And then the bad times. Rayn coming home in tears when her admission to Medicine's top program was preempted by Council order. The Gadukah stealing her away in the middle of the night.

Aeric lying paralyzed in the room next to hers, powerless to free himself from the grasp of whatever sorcerer was supporting the commandos. Their daring escape from the Kralak and through the city streets. Their time in exile in Spain, hidden in a community of trolls, and then in Brazil, lazing on a beach owned by elven ex-pats who'd made their fortune in the coffee business.

The tearful reunion with Pike. Pike and Rayn kissing in the ocean, framed in a pink and red sunset. Pike's blade slicing through his back. Rayn sobbing wildly as Pike dragged her off. Then the Pintiri came for him. Evitankari never wasted an asset, especially one talented enough to break someone out of one of its most heavily fortified compounds. The dust in his nostrils as they robbed him of his spirit and his sister...

Blood rushed to Aeric's face and he shook with rage. How could the Council have done this to him? How could he ever have become such a patsy, such a follower, an unthinking, unquestioning lap dog for the powers-that-be? All that was gone now. He wasn't Aeric anymore—or maybe he was Aeric again for the first time in years. Regardless, a more important question washed away all other thoughts: where was Rayn?

"Thank you," Aeric said to the blackness. "Whoever you are."

"You are welcome, Mongan. I'm glad you came through."

Aeric snorted. "Show yourself. I won't bite."

A chuckle was the only response.

Whoever his mysterious benefactor was, he wasn't taking any chances. Aeric couldn't blame him. "Fine. So, what's the deal? Why go through all this effort?"

"Evitankari needs you, Aeric. And it needs you in one piece."

He rolled his eyes. "Give it to me straight. No more bullshit. What the hell do you want?"

"What I want doesn't matter," the voice replied. "You are free to act in your own best interests."

"How will that serve Evitankari's needs?"

"Damned if I know. Rayn hasn't told me that part. If you'll pardon me, Mongan, I still have much to do."

Footsteps, then a door closing. The voice was gone.

Rayn. Aeric was glad she was still alive, and happier to hear that she was conspiring against those who'd wronged them both. He leaned back in his bed and pondered the pile of bodies he was about to create. Evitankari, he mused, certainly would be a much better place without the people on his hit list.

— CHAPTER TWENTY-SEVEN —

T
he room in which they'd confined Talora was a ten-by-ten cube equipped with a twin bed, a sitting area with a table and a pair of chairs, and an old television atop a squat white bookcase. Natural light streamed in between the baby blue curtains on the window, reflecting warmly off the soft green wallpaper speckled with smiling yellow duckies. The television, devoid of controls, was tuned to a pair of happy puppets singing a song about friendship and sharing. Talora sat on the bed in a white cotton hospital gown, picking crud out of her ragged toenails.

Roger watched her through the one-way glass in the room's mirror, seated on a hard plastic chair in the dingy, cramped observation space. He'd been there for most of the morning, just watching, with no idea what he was looking for. An orderly in white fatigues with some sort of wand strapped to his hip brought her a spartan breakfast of scrambled eggs and potatoes. She ate some and left the rest on the table. Then she stared out the window for awhile, her gaze glassy and unfocused. She tried to turn off the television but couldn't find any buttons or a cord to unplug. Defeated, she'd returned to the bed and her own thoughts. Half an hour ago an orderly had returned to Talora with a piece of jewelry: a gold locket she'd worn around her neck in China. Roger doubted the elves had done that out of the goodness of their souls. They were looking for a reaction. Talora accepted the locket gently, then hung it around her neck and returned her attention to the window.

There was nothing about Talora that stood out, nothing that shed any light on Roger's situation or why she'd been involved with his family or helped him better understand this strange, hidden world he now found himself such a prominent part of. He'd expected a demon, even one so new to the path, to be more otherworldly, somehow above and beyond anything resembling humanity. The antlers on her head were strange, sure, but to Roger they weren't any weirder than some sort of silly hat.

The greeting card rested in its cheery envelope on his lap. He hadn't been able to look at it again; he didn't have to. The image of that strange woman lying between his comatose children in that silver coffin, smiling as if nothing was wrong, had burned itself into his brain. Whenever he closed his eyes, there it was.

But that still left the question of Virginia's whereabouts. Was she safe somewhere? Had the elves separated her from Ricky and Samantha intending to confuse anyone looking to snatch his family away? Or was the Witch playing another game? Driff had taken the card briefly to run some tests but hadn't learned anything useful. It contained no traces of magic, malicious or otherwise, and he found no fingerprints other than Roger's. The Pintiri wasn't surprised.

The door to his left creaked open, admitting Aeric. The heavy bandage wrapped around the elf's head was the only sign that he'd been injured. He'd looked to be on his last legs when Roger and Hirace had pulled him out of the ruins of Iki the night before. Aeric handed Roger a coffee in a styrofoam cup, which he gladly accepted.

Roger decided to get right to the thing bothering him most. "Aeric, where the fuck is my wife?"

The elf shook his head. "We have no idea. Your children were questioned—gently—before we attempted to move them from the safe house to the cemetery. Neither knew anything about Virginia. Your daughter claims she was just gone one morning. It was the day after you found the Ether. Samantha couldn't reach your wife's cell, so she filed a missing persons report. She did the same for you when you didn't answer. The police found no trail...and neither did we."

Roger's heart sank. He couldn't imagine how lost and scared Sam must've felt when both of her parents dropped off the face of the earth. One more thing to thank the Witch for. "And you weren't going to fucking tell me?"

Aeric's eyes suddenly grew distant, like he was somewhere else entirely. "No, we weren't. We're a bunch of fucking assholes, Roger, and when we decide a piece of information's going to do more harm than good, we bury it for as long as we can."

The elf's candor was like a slap in the face, but Roger appreciated it.

Aeric continued. "Whatever the hell is going on, you're the center of it. Every single bit of it is trying to weaken you. If you let it, you lose. So do your wife and kids and all the rest of us."

Roger knew Aeric was right, but that didn't make it any easier. There was an ache in his heart where his family should've been, and it had gotten worse by the day. "Maybe you should just dust me. Make me forget. Just enough to take the edge off."

"Fuck you."

It seemed like a good time to change the subject. "How are you feeling?"

Aeric smiled. "Like they dropped a building on me. The others are up and about, but Ankh's right ear is gone for good. He refuses to let them regrow it. Says it makes him look like a badass."

Roger was glad. The Gadukah were good people. "Myrindi's safely back in Talvayne?"

"Sorrin picked her up bright and early this morning." His attention shifted to Talora's room. "Anything new?"

"Nothing. She's—Aeric, she's so normal. If it weren't for those antlers I'd never guess there was anything different about her. Are we sure she's what we think she is?"

The elf nodded. "Chyve checked her out personally. Besides the antlers, the bones in her face have shifted and elongated, and there's a growth at the base of her spine that might one day become a tail. It's likely she became a demon so recently that the big changes are yet to come."

Roger took a long drink of the bitter coffee, letting it warm his bones. That feeling that something strange was going on was back. He was tired of that feeling.

"Listen, Roger," Aeric said hesitantly, suddenly like a child confessing a wrongdoing to his father. "I wanted to apologize for the way your life has changed. If I'd done my job correctly, I'd be the Pintiri and none of this would've happened to you and your family. I'm sorry."

Roger hadn't been expecting such an admission of guilt. It took him aback. How could he possibly respond to Aeric's apology? He stared down at the steaming coffee for a moment, formulating a response. "Honestly, Aeric, I've never blamed you for what happened. It's that woman from my kitchen. She's pulling everyone's strings: yours, mine, Evitankari's. She's five steps ahead and all we can do is try to keep up."

"Thanks, Roger. That means a lot."

But Roger didn't hear him. His attention was locked to the woman in the cell, his own words resonating in his ears. Realization struck him like a slap in the face. Driff had interrogated Talora earlier, but she either didn't know much of anything or wasn't willing to share. Maybe the Council of Intelligence had taken the wrong approach.

"It's the same for her," Roger said, rising. "She's not a part of the conspiracy; she's a pawn, just like us."

Aeric grabbed his arm as he brushed past. "Be careful in there. We still don't know exactly what we're dealing with."

Roger pulled aside his jacket to show Aeric the shotgun holstered at his hip. He hadn't been as sure of anything since he'd arrived in Evitankari. The elf nodded and let him pass.

The hallway outside the observation room was white and sterile, the air pungent with disinfectant. This wing of the Demonicam was home to lesser evils, Chyve had said, those deemed sane enough and safe enough to house unrestrained. All but Talora were in the last stages of their rehabilitation. Each cell was adjoined to an observation room, and each was guarded by a single docent in a white smock. The man standing guard at Talora's cell raised an eyebrow at Roger's request, but he opened the door anyway.

The door locked behind him with an ominous click. Talora didn't even look up at him. He stood there awkwardly for a moment, waiting for an acknowledgment that didn't come, and then he took a seat beside the little table, clutching the card so tightly his knuckles turned white. She continued picking at her feet. He tried one of the fried potatoes left on her plate from breakfast.

"All the magic in the world, and they still can't make hospital food taste any good," Roger said cheerily. Talora didn't respond. A bit of grime came free from underneath her toenail and she flicked it aside.

Roger leaned toward her, staring at the floor. "I first met that strange woman in my own kitchen," he explained somberly. "She asked me if I would help her change the world. Next thing I knew, well..." He patted the weapon at his hip. "Here I am, living with a bunch of elves. I'm still trying to find the hollow tree where they make the cookies."

When he looked up he found her staring right back. Her brown eyes were wet and sad, but still hard and defiant. In that moment,

Roger found her unspeakably attractive. Embarrassed, he looked away.

"I woke up on a park bench with no memory of who I am or how I got there," Talora muttered. "She asked me the same question about changing the world. Then she offered to look after me. I had nowhere else to go, so..."

Roger smiled softly, trying to hide his elation. At last, things were making some semblance of sense. "There was an attack here, on the elven city. A giant. It destroyed an important building and killed a lot of people. We think she was involved."

"She didn't mention anything to me about a giant," Talora said, "but I wouldn't be surprised. The others—the demons—were all very afraid of her. They called her the Witch."

Of course, Roger thought. "Did she show you what was in this envelope you gave me?"

She shook her head, her antlers swishing through the air. "She told me it would save me if I got caught. Can I see?"

He offered her the envelope. She hesitated, then gingerly took it and carefully removed the card inside. She examined it for a few moments, her eyes wide and her breath heavy. "We ambushed the escort party as they arrived at the transpoint. We killed the elves. The Witch put a stronger hex on the children to keep them unconscious."

Roger's heart leapt, although the thought of magic being employed on his children made him feel sick. "That's my family."

She slipped the card back into the envelope and handed it back to him. "I'm so sorry. They're beautiful. And they're safe. We buried them under a big elm at the edge of the cemetery."

That brought Roger to his feet. Before he could thank her for the information, the intercom on the wall crackled to life. "I'm on it, Roger," came Aeric's voice. "Driff organized the extraction; he'll know the exact location of the cemetery."

Roger paused, wondering why Aeric had stopped him. These were his fucking kids they were talking about; he wanted to be the one to bring them safely to Evitankari. Then he looked back at Talora and Aeric's unspoken message became clear. The Mongan and the Council of Intelligence were more than capable of recovering the Brooks children, but only Roger could keep Talora talking. Like it or not, he had a job to do. He could trust Driff and Aeric to do theirs.

"Thank you, Talora," Roger said as he sat back down. "You remember nothing from before?"

She frowned. "Nothing. I know what things mean and what things are, and I immediately understand how to do the things I need to do...but any sort of past, any knowledge of how I know the things I know, just isn't there."

He pondered that for a moment. It was certainly a new wrinkle. What was someone, most likely the Witch, trying to hide from Talora? Did her condition somehow make her more useful? He'd have to remember to ask Chyve if there was evidence she'd been dusted.

"I want you to know," Talora continued, "that I did the things I did because I didn't know what else to do." A pair of tears streamed down her face. Roger could tell she was fighting hard to hold back more. "The Witch said she'd take care of me, and I—I didn't know if I could make it alone. I was planning to rid myself of her as soon as I found a better option."

He looked away, at the puppets singing merrily on the television. He'd spent the entire night and most of the morning hating Talora, wishing the worst upon her, but now he actually felt sorry for her. Watching her now, he saw a version of his own plight staring right back. It was like he'd told Aeric: the Witch was driving the bus and everyone else was just along for the ride.

"Say—is all this happy-go-lucky crap helping?" he asked. "Do you feel any less demonic?"

The sound Talora made was half sob and half laugh. "Not at all. Those frigging puppets make me want to light something on fire."

Roger laughed back. An idea struck him then, one that wasn't without a fair bit of risk, but one that could prove extremely fruitful all the same. "Here's the deal, Talora: I'm going to find the Witch, I'm going to rescue my family, and I'm going to give that bitch what she deserves."

"Sounds good to me."

"Promise not to do anything evil?"

"Only to the Witch," she said with a smirk.

Roger stood and knocked on the door. "It's the Pintiri," he said. "I'm checking Talora out of here. She'll be living in Merrowood with me, under my protection. I'll take full responsibility for her."

Surprisingly, it was Council of Sorcery Aldern who opened the door. The old elf stared at Roger reproachfully for several agonizing moments, clearly about to issue a harsh reprimand of some sort. Then Aldern reached out, wrapped one stick-like arm around him, and leaned in close where only Roger could hear him. "Great idea, Pintiri!" he whispered conspiratorially. "We'll play along and catch her at whatever game she's playing!"

Roger swallowed in a dry throat. That was not what he had in mind at all.

— CHAPTER TWENTY-EIGHT —

His name was Tash. For a brief moment that didn't seem right. His name was Roger. It always had been. And he wasn't so short and slim. And what the hell was the heavy thing he clutched to his chest as if dropping it would be the end of him? Why was his hair long enough to brush the base of his neck? Why were his pants so tight?

The Evertree solidified the scene then, walling off the bits of Roger trying to fight through and leaving only Tash. He stood in the Great Hall of Oad, the receiving room at the base of the Kralak and the only space in the great tower non-mages were permitted to visit. Upon entering, Tash had wondered if it was really a room at all. The Great Hall had no walls, no floor, and no ceiling, and it seemed to travel forever in every direction into the sparkling depths of outer space. They were surrounded by stars in all their glittering glory, by binary systems and dusty nebulae and distant, blossoming galaxies. Tash recognized a few of the constellations, mostly the ones beneath his feet or directly above his head, but the rest were foreign. Evtankari's sorcerers had carefully cultivated a reputation for the mysterious and the fantastic; those few outsiders allowed into their tower weren't allowed to forget it.

The burden in his arms was a sword. His master's sword. He was squire to Gowert, a man renowned as the greatest elven warrior. No one, especially Gowert, liked that this was only the case because Axzar had spent the last few years slaughtering greater elven warriors. As Gowert's squire it was Tash's job to carry the sword, and sharpen the sword, and clean the sword, and be seen but never heard. He loved that sword as if it were his own child. A pompous, self-important ass like his master didn't deserve such a grand weapon. Fireheart, Tash called it in the privacy of his own daydreams, as Gowert hadn't seen fit to give it a name of his own. Fireheart should've been wielded by a man who led others into battle rather than dispatching them to fight and die for him, by a man who didn't reposition himself to avoid the fiercest melees, by a man who challenged his nation's greatest enemies head-on rather than wandering the field to dispatch of the wounded and the weak. Or at least Tash thought so, anyway.

Gowert liked to brag that he had personally killed two hundred and sixty demons since the beginning of Axzar's uprising five years ago. Tash suspected that at least two hundred of those would've died soon anyway, and the others had merely caught Gowert unaware and left him with no alternative but to stand and fight.

Tash stood beside and behind his master. Gowert dwarfed him by about two heads, maybe three. He was a mountain of a man with a thick skull and a bulging belly to match. Tash did not envy the manservants responsible for getting Gowert into his golden armor, which Gowert refused to have altered even though he'd outgrown it years ago. That armor glittered in the starlight, making the big man radiant, like some kind of supreme being come from on high to save them all from the rampaging horde. The thought of the stupid, shit-eating grin the big ass surely had on his face killed that illusion for Tash right away.

Two men and a woman approached from the opposite side of the Great Hall of Oad. Ancient Proct, the High Mage, moved forward slowly, kept upright by a gnarled cane and the attendant guiding him by his other arm. A bent, twisted shell of his long-removed youth, Proct was in charge of Evitankari's sorcerers and was, by all accounts, the best magical mind the city had ever seen. His milky eyes were blind, and yet he always knew his surroundings and the names of those present. Beside him came Princess Sinta, youngest—and last—of the Atlantean royal family, resplendent in a long green gown that accented her blue, crystalline skin and long black hair that almost touched the floor. Her proud bearing and slender form were that of a statue, of the perfect woman chiseled from stone by the world's finest sculptor. Tash caught himself staring and looked away.

Surrounding them all were a few dozen of Evitankari's finest dignitaries, mostly representatives of the Combined Council. They stood in a rough circle, one person deep, watching with grave faces and knowing stares. No one in the room dared hope that the magic to be bestowed upon Gowert would bring victory to the forces of good. They'd watched in horror as Axzar decimated the realm of man, sank Atlantis, sent the fairies into hiding, and then turned his army upon the world's last true bastion of civilization: Evitankari. And then they watched as the Devourer slaughtered their finest and turned aside wondrous new spell after wondrous new spell, as the great black horde closed around the city and left the elves with no escape. The demon army would be there soon, they all knew, but none of those privy to the specifics would admit just how soon.

Proct and Sinta stopped a few strides from Gowert. The High Mage's young attendant bowed and took a few steps back and to the side, mirroring Tash's position. The two pairs took a moment to size each other up before Proct's scratchy, creaking voice cut through the silence. "Sir Gowert, today we bestow upon you the greatest fruit of elven and Atlantean labors." The pitch of his voice steadily rose and then fell as if directed by the motion of a metronome. "Today we grant you the power to destroy the Devourer. Axzar shall fall before the Ether!"

One of the stars directly above the four elves began to fall, slowly growing bigger and brighter. It became a little golden urn the size and shape of a pumpkin, embossed with a combination of swirling elven runes and blocky Atlantean characters. All eyes traced its descent to the floor at Gowert's feet.

"Open it," Sinta instructed, her voice soft and sweet but also confident and strong. "Take what's inside and accept your position as our Pintiri: the light that splits the darkness."

Gowert sank to his knees dramatically. "It is my honor and my privilege," he said in a tone that implied the honor and privilege actually belonged to those lucky enough to witness his greatest moment. Tash rolled his eyes.

The big elf reached forward and took the urn in his hands, slowly twisting the lid and lifting it away. Brilliant golden light streamed out through the opening. Someone in the audience gasped. Tash leaned around his master, trying to get a closer look.

And then the Ether zipped up and out of the urn, heading straight for Tash. The golden orb slammed hard into Fireheart, knocking the young squire flat on his backside. Screams echoed through the chamber as the weapon's blade suddenly erupted in blue fire, burning away the scabbard and a strip of Tash's clothing but leaving his skin untouched. Tash tossed the weapon away, more frightened of what Gowert would say and do than of the wild magic that had leapt into his arms. The flames died out as the sword clattered to the floor.

A sharp crack rang out through the Great Hall of Oad as Proct slammed the tip of his cane into the invisible floor to silence the roaring crowd. "Experimental magic can be unpredictable," he said calmly. "Gowert, please pick up your sword and summon the Ether. A simple thought will do the trick."

Gowert glared daggers at Tash as he snatched the sword away. He squinted and grimaced in concentration, but the flames didn't come. Gowert took a deep breath and scrunched his face even tighter, putting all his mental effort into calling the fire. Tash thought he looked rather constipated. Still nothing. Someone in the audience began to sob.

One of the politicians in attendance stormed out onto the floor, shaking his head. He was a tall, spindly man with polished skin and perfect hair who looked he hadn't done a day of honest work in his life. One of the merchant class, Tash decided. "This is simply unacceptable!" the politician shouted, waving his finger in Proct's face. "All the resources we poured into this project, all the time you wasted on it, and this is the great and powerful weapon that'll stop Axzar? I will see to it that the Combined Council removes you from your position *immediately!*"

Proct didn't reply. The old man was crestfallen and defeated. He looked as if he'd prefer to die right then and there.

The audience exploded into a flurry of angry shouts and cries of ruin. "It's over!" one woman shouted. "We're done for!" cried another. "We never should've left our fate in the hands of those crazy wizards!" a man called to a chorus of agreement.

Gowert whirled on Tash, raising Fireheart as if preparing to cut his squire down. "This is your fault, you little shit! What did you do to my sword?"

Tash stared up at the bigger man, his heart in his throat. How the hell was this disaster his fault? He'd taken great care of Fireheart, just as Gowert had instructed: polishing it to a glistening sheen, carefully honing it to its sharpest. If any of that had conflicted with the magic, it was Gowert's fault for requesting it, not his. But Tash had learned the hard way that standing up to his master only made the beatings worse, so his protests died in his throat.

Sinta strolled nonchalantly past Gowert and snatched the sword from his grasp as if it were a loaf of bread he'd stolen. She pulled Tash to his feet and pressed Fireheart's hilt into his hand. "You can call it," she said confidently, as if it were the most obvious statement in the world.

Tash stood still in shock for a moment, not believing the Atlantean princess would lower herself to speak to a simple squire. Then he noticed the scowl on Gowert's face, the burning blue eyes that seemed to say "Don't you fucking dare." Tash smiled and closed his fingers around the familiar grip. If he could summon the Ether, Gowert wouldn't be able to touch him anymore. Sinta let go and took a step back.

A single thought brought the Ether raging to life around Fireheart's blade, brought silence to the Great Hall of Oad, and sent Gowert storming out of the building, through an invisible door that swung open at his approach and slammed shut when he was through. Her mouth agape in shock, Sinta sank to her knees. She stared up at Tash with a look of such awe that it summoned a hot blush to the uncertain squire's face.

"You will be our Pintiri," Sinta whispered softly, her eyes wet with tears. "You will be our light that splits the darkness."

The scene suddenly melted. Sinta's beautiful face twisted into a grotesque blob, her eyes and lips and hair sinking into her blue skin and spiraling into a nondescript mass that blended into the swirl of nothing beyond.

Older memories don't manifest as quickly, a familiar disembodied voice explained somewhere in the depths of his mind. For a moment Roger was standing by the Evertree, disoriented and a bit nauseous, and then the world snapped back into view and Tash was once again in charge.

The young man swallowed nervously, his gaze glued to the black sea of smoke and death washing over the horizon. The horde had breached Evitankari's wall and the elven defenders were slowly falling back toward Willowglen. From his perch atop the hastily erected observation tower he could make out two riders in the distance, inside the line, riding hard in his direction: Princess Sinta, gallantly baiting Axzar to the ambush point. They'd reach his position in five minutes, maybe less.

A slender hand clamped onto his shoulder, somehow warm and reassuring even through his heavy plate armor. Rentas had been his constant companion since his departure from the Great Hall of Oad. She was a fine warrior, the only woman who'd been on the short list of potential bearers of the Ether. The two of them had been shoved together on the idea that she was the best to improve his swordsmanship. She was similar in size and preferred a blade almost identical to Fireheart. Rentas and Tash had spent most of the last few days sparring, at first with wooden practice swords and then with the real things. Truth be told, he didn't stand a chance against her. She knocked him on his ass every few minutes. But whereas other teachers would've grown frustrated or given up completely, Rentas always pulled him back up to his feet with a smile and a few friendly words explaining how she'd gotten the better of him. She was one of the few people in Evitankari who didn't look at him like he was some sort of leper. He didn't have the courage to ask her why.

"It's about that time, Pintiri," she said somberly. She and the others involved in the ambush had taken to calling him by the Atlantean term Sinta had used for the Ether's owner. Her small, young features were very attractive even though she'd shaved her head completely bald, Tash thought, although he'd always preferred women with long hair. "What say we prove all the stupid politicians wrong and save the world, eh?" she added.

Tash smiled and nodded. "And then we'll all get statues and a big parade!"

Rentas giggled, a sweet sound that made Tash blush. "You can practice your heroic poses later, Pintiri. Right now, all we need is your courage."

He shifted uncomfortably. "I'll try."

"Don't go getting cold feet on me now," she growled, her expression suddenly dark. "You will kill Axzar. You're the only one that can."

Her words somehow made him feel both better and worse. He could do it, he thought; but if he failed, that was the end of everything. Nothing left on the planet would be able to stand against the Devourer and his horde. If the light that splits the darkness were to be extinguished, dawn would never come.

The wooden ladder shook wildly with each step down to the next rung. Tash's knuckles were white around its sides. Falling from a ladder would be a rather terrible way for a Pintiri to die. Planting his feet on solid ground had never felt so good.

The rest of the ambush team awaited them on the road below. Five of Evitankari's finest greeted Tash and Rentas with expressions of grim resolve and confidence. His Gadukah, Sinta had labeled them, his pillars of strength. Three were big, beefy warriors in full plate, a variety of nasty weapons strapped to their belts and backs: Henk, Yarik, and Rolf. Middle-aged Gir was their battlemage, a chunky man in a black robe. The healer, a slight blonde girl named Enri, couldn't have been more than twelve. Tash concentrated hard, fighting to keep still the nervous left leg that wanted to bounce up and down, to keep his gaze from drifting noncommittally to the cobblestones. These men and women were here to fight and die, not just for Evitankari, but for him. He couldn't bear the thought that they wouldn't think their sacrifice worth it.

"Four minutes," Rentas said sternly. "You all know your places."

Everyone nodded but no one moved. Their attention shifted to Tash. They expected him to say something. Something inspirational. He said the first thing that came to mind.

"One shot," he said, his voice quivering ever so slightly. "Get me one clean shot on the bastard and we'll all be fucking heroes."

Yarik smiled a big, gap-toothed smile and slammed his helmet's mask down over his face. "Hoo-rah!" he shouted.

"Hoo-rah!" the others echoed.

The group dispersed into the forest on either side of the road. Tash, Rentas, Yarik, and Enri took cover on the north side, Henk, Rolf, and Gir on the south. The battlemage separated himself a little bit, heading back west a few dozen yards toward Evitankari. Axzar would feel the magic emanating from his position. The thought was that the others would have a better chance if they came from a different angle.

The next three minutes seemed to take three days. Tash's breathing was ragged, his heartbeat like repeated claps of thunder. Though it was a relatively cool spring day, sweat soon covered every inch of his skin. He couldn't keep still, shifting his feet or his arms every few seconds. Fireheart was an ominous weight on his hip, a tremendous force threatening to pull him into and under the soft forest floor to suffocate in a shallow grave. He couldn't do this. Even with the Gadukah at his side, even with the Ether at his call—what chance in hell did he have against a creature like Axzar? How could he succeed where dozens of other, greater men and women had failed? He wasn't a warrior; he was a glorified manservant. He knew more about maintaining weapons than using them. What the hell was he doing in those woods, playing soldier and pretending to be the man that would finally best Axzar?

His face must've betrayed his thoughts. Rentas sidled over to him and took his hand in her own. When he looked away from her piercing blue eyes, she grabbed his chin and forced him to meet her gaze. There was confidence there. There was hope. There was faith that he could do the job.

"You weren't our first choice," she said softly, "but you're the only Pintiri we've got. You'll do."

Tash knew she was right. She had to be. The only other option was oblivion, for him and her and the Gadukah and everyone else. And he wasn't ready for that. He opened his mouth to thank her, but the sound of hoofbeats on cobblestones cut him off. Rentas released him and moved back to her own position.

Sinta stormed past first, a blue and green blur atop a gorgeous white mare. Axzar came next, six lengths behind on his terrible black charger. Tash's heart caught in his throat; he'd seen images of the Devourer, but no reproduction could've prepared him for Axzar's overwhelming presence. It was as if the sun's light dimmed around him, as if he sucked the very air out of his immediate vicinity. Tash inhaled deeply to steady his nerves and took firm hold of Fireheart's hilt. *I can do this. I have to.*

A thick section of road between Axzar and Sinta suddenly exploded upward, spraying dust and stone in all directions. Axzar's charger reared back on its hind legs, screeching wildly as its rider violently yanked back on its reins. Gir's next spell called forth a thin, sharp spire of rock from directly underneath the horse's stomach, sending it up and through its flesh and then through its rider's thigh. The horse and its master both roared, the charger rearing back even further but failing to free itself. A gout of black flame formed in Axzar's left gauntlet, swirling like a miniature storm. He flung it back toward Gir's position. The blast wove its way cleanly between the tree trunks as if it had eyes and a mind of its own. Gir's scream told Tash all he needed to know about its accuracy.

The Gadukah burst from the woods, descending quickly on the Devourer. Axzar suddenly stood in the saddle, pulling himself clear of the stone spear, and then leapt to the ground to meet the attack. He moved to parry the wild swing of Yarik's war hammer, but the demon lord's injured leg gave out and he crumpled to one knee. Yarik's weapon caught him clean across the face, denting his helmet and dropping the him to the ground like a sack of potatoes.

"Pintiri, now!" Rentas screamed as she kicked the Devourer's sword out of his slack grip.

Tash stumbled to his feet and plowed through the brush, tripping over a tree root but somehow maintaining his footing. Axzar lay prone and dazed, Rolf straddling his chest and holding his shoulders to the cobblestones with his heavy knees. The other warriors looked on, their weapons ready for any sign that the Devourer had regained his faculties and was preparing a counterattack. Countless times in previous battles the elven forces had thought they'd killed Axzar, only to watch his wounds heal and his armor mend as he popped back up to his feet and murdered his surprised opponent. The Gadukah weren't taking any chances.

Tash skidded to a halt a few paces from Axzar's blazing skull. Blue flames exploded around Fireheart's blade as he raised the sword over his head in a two-handed grip, ready to drive the heavy weapon through the demon's helm and into his twisted brain. Tash brought the blade down with all his strength, swinging for himself, for the Gadukah, for Sinta, for Evitankari, and for all those Axzar had wronged.

His blow never landed. Axzar's fiery crown suddenly exploded outward, blasting Tash with intense heat that knocked him off his feet and sent him sprawling. He dropped Fireheart and screamed, clutching his charred face as if trying to keep his features intact. The pain was blinding, deafening, all-consuming. Rolf's shriek echoed as if from somewhere far away. Tash was vaguely aware of the battle raging around him, of the heavy footsteps and the screech of metal on metal and the screams of the wounded and dying. But he couldn't focus; he was beaten, ruined, useless. His eyes wouldn't open. They'd been fused shut by the heat. He tried to scream, but it came out as a weak gurgle around what was left of his tongue, teeth, and lips.

It was over. *Just kill me,* he thought. *Don't make me listen to their deaths. Don't make me suffer here. Just end it!*

Suddenly someone's hands took his own, jerking them away from the remains of his face. The fingers around his were small and soft but they held him like a vise. Enri. *Get away!* he tried to shout, but what was left of his mouth twisted his words into a series of unintelligible grunts. *Get as far away as you can or he'll kill you too!*

"Shhhhh," a soft little voice whispered in his ear, slicing through the sounds of battle. "Relax and let the magic do its thing."

Warmth washed into him through his hands, racing through his body like electricity from a lightning bolt. His back arched upward as Enri's power wove its way painfully through his face, briefly illuminating every damaged cell, every crying neuron. He felt the meat in his face shifting, repositioning, growing to replace that which was lost. The black crust on the surface fell away like the rind from a piece of fruit as fresh, clean skin pushed its way through. His nose centered itself on his face once more, sprouting a new tip. His eyes solidified and expanded, shoving his renewed lids painfully open. The blinding sunlight was the prettiest thing he'd ever seen. When his vision cleared he found Enri smiling down at him, suddenly taller and thicker and more mature looking, a beautiful young woman of about twenty-five.

"Now kill the fucker," she said as she pulled him to his feet and handed him his sword. The hilt was a slagged mess and the blade was bent, but he doubted the Ether would care. He'd never felt so fresh, so ready to take on the world.

A slight feminine moan knocked him back into reality. He whirled to find Rentas impaled on Axzar's sword, her feet dangling a few inches off the ground. The other elven warriors were down. Yarik had been cleaved clean in half. Rolf's body lay to

Tash's left, but his head was on the opposite side of the road. Henk tried weakly to crawl away, leaving behind a thick trail of blood from a deep gash in his chest. Axzar shoved Rentas off his sword and chuckled, turning to face Tash.

Something inside him tightened. He was all that was left. Their only chance. The Ether burst to life around Fireheart, brighter than he'd ever seen it. "Come on," Tash growled, beckoning Axzar with a quick wave of his fingers.

A cascade of purple lightning suddenly poured down on the Devourer, making him stand up straight and stiff. Tash turned to trace it back to its source: Sinta's fingertips. The Atlantean princess stood a few feet to Axzar's left, her face screwed tight with intense focus as the magic streamed forth from her hands.

No further instruction was necessary. Tash summoned the Ether and lunged forward, swinging Fireheart in a sweeping blow with all his strength. Despite the damage to the blade, Fireheart slit Axzar's chest plate as if it were made of paper. Blue flames trailed in the sword's wake. Axzar didn't scream until the weapon came free from the other side of his torso. The blue fire exploded outward from every seam in his armor. The Devourer's howl set Tash's heart fluttering...

And then Roger was back in Willowglen, stumbling away from the Evertree. The force of being expelled from Tash left him disoriented and dizzy, and he fell into a sitting position in the soft grass.

"Thank you," Roger muttered, his head in his hands. Aldern had insisted on taking Talora on a solo tour of the city, leaving Roger to his own devices for the afternoon. He'd been both curious about Axzar and in need of something to take his mind off of his family, so he'd come to Willowglen to get the information he sought straight from the horse's mouth. His curiosity was more than sated.

"Something wasn't right about that," the Evertree said thoughtfully. "You shouldn't have disconnected so violently. Only one thing causes that."

Roger didn't have to ponder that one long. "Tash was dusted. They took his greatest moment away from him."

The Evertree's face nodded. "That is the greatest mystery among all of my stored memories. The men responsible either had themselves dusted before they died or did not join their comrades in the waters of the Origina."

Roger dragged his fingers down his face and sighed. He'd come to Willowglen seeking what he thought would be a simple answer. As usual, everything he did led to yet another mystery.

But this was a mystery he could worry about later. There were more pressing puzzles that needed his attention: the pretty demon woman with the antlers, the state of his family, and what the Witch had in store for them all.

— CHAPTER TWENTY-NINE —

Roger met Talora and Aldern in Tash Square.

"...and that's how you could subvert the directional wards, if you really wanted to do it!" the Council of Sorcery declared with a dramatic bow. "Oh, hello, Pintiri," he added when he noticed Roger's approach.

Roger nodded to both of them in turn. Talora sat atop Axzarian's foot, chewing on her nail in pained boredom. The Demonicam's staff had given her a pair of blue jeans, a plain white T-shirt, and a pair of sneakers. Roger almost felt bad having left her in Aldern's care, but the old elf had insisted.

The Council of Sorcery straightened and turned to go, beckoning them both to follow. "One more stop, now that the Pintiri has joined us."

Talora stuck her tongue out at Aldern's back. She pulled herself off the statue with a heavy sigh and approached Roger. "Now I know everything I ever would've wanted to know about crippling Evi-wherever-the-fuck-we-are. I can poison the water supply, turn the food foul, sabotage the generators, vaporize the market, corrupt the path to Port, and even give the gnoll that guards the wall a rampant case of the shits," she explained in a tone so even, so matter-of-fact, that Roger couldn't help smiling in spite of his discomfort.

"I'm sorry," was all he could manage.

"You should've left me with the happy-sunshine brigade," she snapped. "Your friend is fucking insane."

Aldern wasn't really his friend, but Roger couldn't quite bring himself to correct her. "This is true. And it's never a good idea to keep the crazies waiting."

They followed Aldern in silence down a path Roger had taken before, one he recognized immediately even though he'd only traveled it once. The thought of their destination set him at ease.

"...and no tour of our great city would be complete without ending at the world-renowned Goody Gallant's!" Aldern announced as he yanked the pub's heavy wooden door open and held it for his two companions, his long white beard flapping in the cool evening breeze under his fake smile and piercing green eyes.

Roger looked at Talora and shrugged, leading her inside. Goody's was packed, the air thick with conversation and alcohol. Elves milled about everywhere, some seated in booths or at tables or at the bar, others standing in knots around the perimeter. A few waved or nodded in the newcomers' direction, but Roger didn't recognize any of them.

"I need to use the ladies' room," Talora said.

She was past him before he could point it out, disappearing into the thick cloud of elves. Several of the patrons cast disapproving looks in her direction, but the sight of the Pintiri and the Council of Sorcery kept them from acting.

Aldern put a hand on Roger's shoulder. "The Combined Council has a permanent reservation on that empty booth in the corner," he explained. "Let's take a seat and have a chat."

Roger's aching knees thought that was a great idea. He groaned as he slid into the wooden bench, leaning heavily on the thick old table. "Doesn't anybody in this town drive?"

Aldern looked at him as if he'd tried to tell him the sky was purple. "This nut's proving tougher to crack than I expected," he said as he slid in across from Roger. "I served up every juicy target in Evitankari on a silver platter. She didn't care about any of it!"

"Maybe you were a little too obvious," Roger replied tentatively. "Or maybe she isn't some sleeper agent planted here by the Witch."

Aldern shook his head. "These are dangerous times, Roger. We can't afford to be naïve."

Roger rubbed his eyes and took a deep breath. Talora had put it correctly: the Council of Sorcery had gone insane. He'd surely been a bit cracked before Roger arrived in Evitankari, but the fall of the Kralak had pushed him over the edge.

"Or...maybe that's exactly what we need," Aldern said, almost to himself. "You take over from here, Pintiri. I expect a full report in the morning."

And with that he stood and wandered out of Goody's. Roger buried his aching head in his hands. For the umpteenth time that day he wondered how Evitankari managed to get by with people like Aldern at the helm. Had the previous Pintiri been such a strong leader that he'd willed all the cracked, disparate personalities on the Council into operating as a coherent whole? Roger doubted it, and he hoped that sort of work wasn't in the job description. That pair of shoes would be way too big for him to fill. Worst of all, the Council of Sorcery hadn't given Roger the chance to ask about his children.

A few minutes later Talora returned with two pints of stout. "I put it on your tab," she explained dully. "Where'd the old fart go?"

Roger stroked his chin and considered the frothy beverage she placed in front of him. "Home."

"So he figured that if he stopped watching me like a hawk and left me with you I might get careless and spill the beans about my secret mission to destroy this dump," she said, raising her glass.

"That's about the whole of it," Roger replied with an awkward smile, clinking his own beer against hers and taking a swig.

They stared at their beverages awkwardly for a few moments before a familiar voice sliced through the surrounding bar chatter. "Pintiri!" Ivree squealed as she barreled into the booth and slammed into Roger's shoulder. Some sort of bright pink concoction sloshed up and over the rim of her glass. She was wearing a red, strapless dress that left little to the imagination. "Are you on a date? Hirace says you're not, but I think you are."

Roger blushed, but Talora just rolled her eyes.

Hirace and Ankh strolled over and saluted lazily, each carrying a tall stein of black brew. Hirace winked at Roger, obviously enjoying the scene Ivree was causing. The big pink scar where Ankh's ear should've been really did make him look more badass.

"Wait a minute," Ivree said, her glazed expression suddenly settling into an icy glare. "That's the woman from Iki. How the hell did she get out of the Demonicam?"

Roger nodded. "She's under my protection. This is Talora. Talora...this is my...uh...personal commando squad, the Gadukah." It struck him then just how different the current incarnation was from Tash's crew. He wasn't sure what to make of that.

Ivree snapped to attention, spilling her surprisingly warm drink all over Roger's leg. "Hyperion Battlemage First Class Ivree, at your service!" she squealed.

Hirace and Ankh introduced themselves like normal people and slid into the booth beside Talora. "At ease," Roger muttered a few awkward moments later when Ivree was still saluting. He wanted to go clean up in the restroom, but he didn't dare risk making Ivree move again lest she drop the rest of her drink all over him.

"You guys did a hell of a job rescuing that princess," Talora said haughtily.

"The advance team didn't expect the upper floors to come crashing down on their heads," Hirace replied. Ankh pointed at his new scar and smiled.

"Anyone heard anything from Driff or Aeric?" Roger asked.

The Gadukah all shook their heads. "Should we have?" Ivree asked. Roger responded by draining half of his beer.

"So, what's your story, Talora?" Hirace asked. "Tallisker ain't exactly the nicest people to be hanging around with."

"I...didn't really have anywhere else to go at the time," she muttered.

"Crazy-ass Aldern's gone," Ivree slurred. "And we report only to the Pintiri."

"We're also in a crowded bar," Talora growled. "And you elves have big ears."

"I only have one," Ankh said with a belch, looking quite pleased with himself.

Ivree rolled her eyes and pulled a rather nasty-looking dagger from somewhere in the back of her skimpy dress. Something dark and dangerous flashed in Talora's eyes, and for an instant Roger found himself very much afraid of the strange woman seated across the table. She relaxed as Ivree began carving a circle of runes in the tabletop. When the elf finished, she held her left hand out over her work and mumbled a few words Roger didn't recognize. The runes flared blue with power and all the chitchat around them suddenly evaporated.

"No one outside this booth will be able to hear us for three hours," Ivree explained. "If you lie, that rune is going to scream bloody murder. Now spill it."

Talora shrugged, defeated, and started talking. When she finished an hour later without triggering the rune's bullshit alarm, no one was quite sure what to say. Hirace stared into what was left of his third beer, swirling the thin foam around and around so it made a little spiral. Ivree was face-down on the table—asleep or in deep thought, Roger couldn't tell. Even Ankh seemed a bit contemplative. Talora chewed on a fingernail, probably rethinking her decision to tell her story.

Roger decided to break the ice. "The Witch has been busy."

"There's more to it than that, Pintiri," Hirace said. "Outside of last night's raid, has the Council informed you of any overt activity against Tallisker or its subsidiaries?"

Roger shook his head, suddenly angry. "They haven't told me shit. And I'm really fucking tired of it."

"Not our style," Ankh said.

"Not your style?" Roger shouted incredulously, rising from his seat. "The Council's been hiding things from me since I got here."

Hirace raised one calming hand. "That's not what he meant, Pintiri. He means that we would never attack one of their command towers so blatantly."

Roger sat back down, mollified but confused. "Why not? Aren't those demons the bad guys?"

"The worst of the worst, Pintiri. But over the years we've come to an understanding."

"An understanding?" Roger couldn't believe his ears. Leave it to Evitankari to take what should've been a simple battle between black and white and repaint it eighteen shades of gray.

"We don't attack the towers, and they stay out of Evitankari. They recognize that some of their number are a bit...unhinged... and they look the other way when we rectify the situation. Oftentimes they even encourage and assist us."

"So you clean up their messes," Roger growled. "Like that time one of them got a little too ambitious and kidnapped the fairy princess. Great. What else?"

Hirace looked suddenly uncomfortable. "We provide the raw nari'imide ore. They refine it into narii dust and distribute it to the human population when necessary."

Roger's jaw dropped. "Evitankari is working *with* the demons to keep humanity in the dark? How?"

"Tallisker controls the world's water supply," Talora said speculatively. When Hirace nodded to indicate that she was correct, she continued, "and the media. You take a drink of water, then you sit down to watch TV or listen to the radio...and whatever you saw on your way to work or in your backyard or in the neighbor's house that you shouldn't have seen just melts away."

Roger drained the last of his beer and looked to Talora. If she had an opinion on all this, she was hiding it well.

"It all goes back to Axzar," Ankh said. "The Devourer's evil was infectious—he could turn a shala'ni or take control of a demon with a snap of his fingers, instantly driving them violently insane. He was able to create a psychic network of sorts with those who'd already turned, gradually spreading his influence from one corner of the globe to the other. He was the only thing holding the horde together. It was, in effect, an extension of his will, and he exerted absolute control over any demon or shala'ni trapped in his web. When he fell, the demons dispersed. Most of them turned on each other. The rest were easy to track and kill.

"But there's always evil in the world, Pintiri, and the next generation of demons recognized the failings of their predecessors. This realization brought about a phenomenon never before seen in the world: a group of demons aware enough to exert a modicum of self-control. Rather than go for the big kill, they began to work from the shadows. Evil became much subtler.

"What we see today with Tallisker is the latest incarnation of a centuries-old model. Starving a village to death by cutting off its water supply or providing arms and security forces to a genocidal dictator satisfies their needs just as well as raping and pillaging.

Directing tragedy from atop their ivory towers keeps them safe and keeps them sane and has allowed their influence to reach places it otherwise wouldn't have. They've learned that there are more opportunities for evil in a stable world than in one that's already gone to hell."

Roger was stunned. Talora asked the question he couldn't bring himself to voice. "If you elves are so high and mighty and moral, why are you working with them instead of cleaning them out?"

Ankh's attention returned to what was left of his beer. Hirace smiled sadly and answered for him. "Most of us wish we would. We could have, easily, a few hundred years ago, but the Council of the time thought it more prudent to wait for this new movement to fizzle out on its own. Demons are notoriously unstable, and the Council thought it only a matter of time before they turned on each other and brought down their burgeoning little empire. But now...there are too many of them and too few of us. They have the resources of the world at their disposal. They could turn humanity on us in the blink of an eye and we wouldn't stand a chance."

"Sounds to me like they've got all the chips," Talora said. "Yet Evitankari's still standing."

Hirace nodded. "I've wondered about that myself from time to time. They could police themselves, or maybe cut a deal with Talvayne or one of the ex-pat communities, or—hell—even draft a group of humans to do the job. But they don't, and I have no idea why."

"So, if Evitankari isn't bringing down the towers," Roger said, "who is?"

"Shifters?" Ankh suggested.

Talora shook her head. "No. Demson was absolutely convinced the magic involved was elven. The Witch was a little too happy to hear about it. She's behind it all—she's playing Tallisker and the shifters both."

Ivree sat up and rubbed her eyes. "That's the part that makes absolutely no sense," she mumbled. "Shifters. The type of sudden cellular reconfiguration you're talking about is impossible. Anything with a nervous system complex enough to direct that type of change would be incapable of dealing with the resulting pain. It would pass out mid-shift and probably die in the process."

"I know what I saw," Talora said darkly.

"No one's disputing that," Hirace said quickly. "But these shifters are either something new or something that's been very secret for a very long time. Talora, do you still have that vial?"

She shook her head. "It was gone when I woke up in the Demonicam. Driff asked me about it during the initial interrogation, but I said nothing."

"The Council has to know," Ivree said. "About all of this. Driff is too damn thorough to have missed a bunch of fallen towers."

"Which means that they are, in fact, still keeping things from me that I need to know," Roger said sadly. "The Council of Intelligence and I are going to have a little conversation."

"Bad play, Pintiri," Hirace said. "What they don't know you know can only work to your advantage. If you press them, they'll only deny it or give you half of the story. Or dust you."

Roger banged his empty glass on the table. "What the hell do we do about all this?"

"We wait," Ankh said. "We watch. We listen."

"And you keep that headset we gave you close, Pintiri," Hirace added. "We'll be there for you when the shit hits the fan."

"In the meantime," Ivree continued, "we all get fucking plastered on the Council's tab!"

— CHAPTER THIRTY —

Talora moaned and rolled over. Her head throbbed, her dry throat ached, and her stomach felt as if someone had poured a gallon of battery acid into it. She did not know if this was normal. Was she the kind of drinker who had to deal with terrible hangovers after every night out, or had she legitimately overdone it? She suspected the latter.

The sheets were cool and slick on her skin—silk, she assumed. Her hand, Talora discovered, had landed on something soft and warm. Something breathing. She closed her eyes tighter and sighed, then she rolled out of the bed as quietly as she could. On the other side, Roger shifted once and then was still. Thankfully. She slipped quickly into the jeans and T-shirt she'd left on the floor, picked up her sneakers, and darted out of the bedroom, gently closing the door behind her with a barely audible click.

She swore at herself as she put her shoes on. What the hell had she been thinking? She hadn't thought she was desperate enough to fall into the arms of the first man she'd decided she could trust. Roger had a certain charm and all, but this was no time for ill-conceived romance. Not while she was stuck in a strange city populated primarily with scheming bastards and manipulative lunatics. Not with the Witch still out there. Her memory of events after their departure from Goody Gallant's was only bits and pieces; she could only hope that Roger's was even worse. He'd certainly been just as drunk, if not more so. Thinking about that last round of shots that maniac Ivree had gleefully forced upon them made her gag. She hoped the effects of the liquor hadn't led her to reveal any of the things she'd strategically avoided while telling her story under the auspices of the truth rune. Roger and the elves didn't need to know about Crim, or the Witch's implication that Talora had done all this to herself.

Talora found her way downstairs, then staggered through the foyer and into the dining room. Roger had given her the grand tour the night before, slurring happily as he showed off the fucking palace—his words, not hers—the elves had given him as a home. It was a nice place, she thought, but it wasn't nearly as extravagant as he'd made it out to be.

Walinda was in the dining room waiting for her, lounging lazily atop one of the chandelier's arms. The pixie had been none too happy to see that Roger had brought home company. There'd been more than a hint of judgment in the raspberry she'd spat at them before disappearing down the hall. "I suppose you'll be wanting breakfast, then?" she called down in her squeaky little voice.

Talora collapsed into one of the chairs at the dining room table, too hung over to care about Walinda's attitude. "Breakfast would be good. And aspirin."

Walinda's light flared red as she fell from the chandelier and floated off toward the kitchen. "Yes'm. Nobody goes without in Merrowood—not even demonic harlots."

Talora shook her head and waved one hand dismissively at the departing light. Why did everyone in Evitankari have to be so fucking strange?

The better question, she decided, involved what she was going to do with herself now that she was in Evitankari. She was safe enough for the time being, she supposed, under the Pintiri's protection, but lounging around Merrowood trying to make peace with a floating Christmas light wasn't going to get her any closer to discovering what the hell had happened to her—or, she corrected, what she had done to herself, if the Witch were to be believed. Maybe one of the elves could help. Ivree had recognized the bracelet Pym had given her, and she seemed trustworthy despite the numerous ways she knew to be annoying. Maybe she could point Talora in the right direction.

Roger's uneasy stomping down the stairs snapped Talora out of her contemplative mood. Despite everything she'd dealt with since waking up on that park bench, she didn't feel ready to face the awkwardness that was sure to ensue. Here was a situation where she actually kind of cared what someone else thought. That was a new one.

Roger stumbled into the dining room with his hand over his eyes and the right side of his hair sticking up at a crazy angle that suggested he'd been electrocuted. His brown robe hung at a ridiculous angle off his slumping right shoulder. It took him two tries to pull out the chair at the head of the table, and then he collapsed into it as if he'd been shot.

"Good morning," Talora muttered.

"Morning," he replied. "I feel like shit."

"Me too."

Walinda came humming back into the room, her red light bobbing merrily and two plates of breakfast and two cups of coffee trailing behind her. The food and drink settled gently into place in front of Roger and Talora, accompanied by two sets of silverware that suddenly zipped in from the kitchen when Walinda realized they were missing.

"Good morning, Pintiri," she chirped. "Anything else I can get you?"

"No thanks."

"Then enjoy. And, since you warned me not to magic you without your notice, I should tell you that I put a little something extra in your coffee to clear out the effects of last night's revelry."

Roger replied with a weak nod and Walinda fluttered back into the kitchen. He eyed the coffee warily, but Talora dove right in and downed half the mug.

"Magic you?" she asked.

He sniffed the coffee suspiciously before taking a short sip. "Aldern tricked me into eating glass and spit as part of a spell," he said. "Where did you sleep last night?"

Talora fought back a sigh of relief. If he didn't remember, she wasn't about to remind him. "I woke up on the bathroom floor."

In the kitchen, one of the cabinets slammed violently shut. Talora jumped in her seat and smiled awkwardly at her scrambled eggs.

Thankfully, the doorbell cut through the uncomfortable silence. Walinda zipped through the dining room on her way to the foyer.

"Early for a visitor," Talora muttered, glad for the change of subject.

"Ivree probably needs bail," Roger said.

Talora heard the front door open and close, and then Walinda reappeared in the entryway. "Pintiri, Mongan Aeric to see you."

Roger raised one eyebrow. "Oh."

"Will you see him now?" the pixie pressed. "He assures me it is a matter of utmost importance."

"Yeah. Send him in."

Aeric stormed into the dining room and collapsed into the chair beside Roger. He looked like Talora felt: beaten, abused, and downtrodden. His normally crisp uniform was disheveled, dirty, and torn, his face streaked with grime and sweat. He locked eyes with Roger and frowned.

Oh no, Talora thought, stifling a gasp. *What happened to the kids?* Judging by the ghostly pallor that fell over his face, Roger was wondering the same thing.

"Daddy?" a small voice squeaked from the living room.

Roger bolted to his feet. "Ricky?"

"Dad, is that you?" asked an older, feminine voice.

"Samantha?"

Aeric burst into a big smile. "I couldn't resist. Sorry we didn't bring them to you last night. Chyve wanted to keep them for observation to make sure the Witch didn't hide anything nasty on them. They're clean."

Talora suddenly felt uncomfortable. She wiped her mouth with her napkin, set her silverware on the edge of her plate, and headed for the kitchen. Roger didn't even notice.

"I'm so glad you guys are all right!" his voice echoed from the living room. "Have you seen your mother?"

"No," his daughter replied. "We were hoping she was with you..."

In the kitchen, Talora found the liquor cabinet and grabbed the biggest bottle of whiskey she could find. The sliding door was already open and she slipped outside onto the patio behind Merrowood. The day was beautiful, warm and sunny. Walinda sat atop a nearby picnic table, smoking a tiny cigarette. Talora sat down beside her, cast away the top of the bottle, and took a long swig.

"Well, that's awkward," Walinda chirped after a few silent minutes. "And far too easy."

Talora frowned. "How so?"

"Do you really think the Witch just left those kids there, knowing you could tell Roger exactly where to find them?"

"How did you know—"

"Girl talk. Ivree and I go waaaaaaay back. She's never been able to keep her big trap shut when she's had a few drinks. Drunk dials me every time she's had a few too many. Anyway, that happy reunion back there is probably just a repositioning of leverage. Shit's about to go down."

The red light flared around Walinda and she lifted off. She stopped to hover beside Talora. "I won't tell him about last night if you won't," the pixie said. Then she flitted back inside.

Talora took another drink and stared out at the horizon. Merrowood sat atop one of Evitankari's tallest hills, and the patio had a great view of the city. She picked out all the places she'd been shown yesterday, naming them one by one and considering their significance.

Aldern had it all wrong, she decided. Anyone looking to destroy the elves needn't concern themselves with the market or the airfield or the food supply. Evitankari's biggest point of failure, she knew, was about twenty feet behind her, celebrating his reunion with his children.

Or so the Witch obviously seemed to think. Talora had never known the Witch to be mistaken.

She needed to simplify things. She needed to clear her head and make sure she'd be ready to do whatever was necessary when the time to fight inevitably came—and she reckoned it would come sooner rather than later. Hopefully, by then, she would know which side she should be fighting for.

Talora closed her eyes and lost herself in the previous evening, beginning with Roger's drunken—but chivalrous and charming— offer to escort her home after they left Goody Gallant's. Focused on those memories, she called just enough fire to light a few fingers and burn away the experiences that would only make her decisions more difficult.

— CHAPTER THIRTY-ONE —

They'd shoved Pike into the deepest, darkest, dankest cell in Evitankari. He knew this because he himself had tossed plenty of criminals into it. The cell was a twelve-by-twelve hole with no light, no fresh air, no bedding, and a tiny, disgusting crack in the corner where he was expected to do his business. It reeked. Every inch of his body ached where the elven security forces had worked him over. The cold floor wasn't helping.

And yet, inside, Pike was nice and warm. His lust for revenge burned hotter than the sun. When he found his way out—*when*, not if—someone was going to lose his head. If only he could figure out exactly who that someone was. He hated to admit it, but he was at a bit of a loss.

The iron door opened with a heavy, grating squeal. One set of boots entered the cell before the door was shut again. A small hand lantern flared to life, momentarily blinding him. When his vision cleared, he found himself staring up at an uncharacteristically concerned-looking Council of Intelligence Driff.

"Fancy meeting you here," Pike croaked, his throat dry and cracking. "Come to read me what's left of my rights?"

"Last night, someone broke into Council of Agriculture Piney's home and surprised her in her dining room. The assailant, wielding a broadsword, opened her up from hip to shoulder with a single stroke, then dragged her, still alive, into the kitchen. There she was beheaded with that same broadsword—a perfect replica of your own. Her brain was removed and shredded in the garbage disposal," Driff explained, his voice quivering. "Earlier that day, she'd received a package from an unknown sender. Inside was an illegal transpoint used by the murderer to enter Piney's home. This transpoint, however, was rigged to fail upon its attempted second use, leaving that traveler trapped inside the home—and set up as the murderer. Piney's neighbor heard her scream and called Security Services."

Pike had been wondering how Security Services had been alerted so quickly, but he doubted that was the whole truth. He would've been amazed if that neighbor hadn't been dusted into believing that was what she'd done.

Driff continued. "The follow-up investigation revealed a half-empty jar of unicorn placenta stashed in your basement beside several other materials required in the conjuring of bottle giants. DNA found in your garbage disposal was matched to Greven, a trader known to specialize in rare and illegal goods. Records reveal that both those raw materials and the transpoint found in Piney's home were purchased from the aforementioned trader using a Council seal."

That, Pike thought, *is fucking ballsy.* Whoever had framed him for Piney's murder was also trying to stick him with the attack on the Kralak. He had been planning to kill the fucker really, really slowly, but this was going to require something special.

"Tell me you didn't do it," Driff said.

Pike laughed. "Fuck you."

The Council of Intelligence opened his mouth to say something, then thought better of it. Pike had never seen Driff look so unsure of himself. Maybe there was something to his theory about what was going on after all. Even if there wasn't, he had nothing left to lose.

"I know what's happening out there," Pike said. "I know Tallisker's towers are coming down. I know Talvayne's cut everyone off. I know shit's about to go down."

Driff hesitated. "And I know you were set up."

Pike laughed again. "Finally, someone in this fucking city with some fucking brains."

What Driff said next made Pike's jaw drop. "There's a transpoint in the bottom of the privy. The closest active transpoint to Talvayne is outside a little village named Rio Rojo. Talvayne itself is five clicks due west. I'll hold down the fort here, but I need someone I can trust to figure out how the fairies fit into things. The timing of Myrindi's kidnapping was too convenient."

There was no way in hell Pike was going to Talvayne, but he kept that to himself. He'd go to Lep and plan his next move. "What the fuck is a transpoint doing in the privy?"

"I put it there a long time ago," Driff said. "Insurance."

The light clicked off. The cell's door was opened after three knocks, and then it was closed right behind the departing Council of Intelligence.

Pike didn't hesitate. He took a deep breath and lunged for the privy, reaching down through the shit and the piss and groping blindly for his one shot at freedom.

— CHAPTER THIRTY-TWO —

The ringing doorbell startled Roger out of his seat on the couch. Beside him, Samantha glanced nervously toward the foyer. He had just finished explaining what had happened to him since the Witch's appearance in his kitchen. Ricky had listened to his story in dumbstruck wonder, but Sam hadn't taken it nearly as well. She didn't seem to believe a word he said, and she'd challenged him outright on the more outrageous pieces. Having Talora, Aeric, and Hirace there to corroborate the chain of events somehow made her more suspicious, like it was a lie they were all in on. Roger supposed he couldn't blame her; she had no memory of being taken by the elven team (the first time Roger had found reason to be thankful for the dust), and he imagined being in a strange place with people claiming to be elves, a moody woman who looked kind of like a forest animal, and a father who said his crappy old shotgun could shoot magic fireballs would shake even the most confident individual.

Roger had to remind himself that it had taken him several days to become adjusted to his new reality. He supposed it was a minor miracle the children had been willing to travel across the city with Aeric, posthypnotic suggestion or no, and that whatever Chyve had done to them during "observation" had been dusted away—although he made a mental note to insist that the Council never, ever screw with his children's memories ever again.

The bell chimed once more. Walinda flitted into the room. Samantha cringed closer to her father, but Ricky smiled up at the little red light. "Are you home, Pintiri?" the pixie asked.

Roger took a deep breath. "I think I probably should be." He'd decided earlier—and the others had agreed unanimously—that he should keep himself between his children and the other crazies in Evitankari for the time being. "Hirace, can you take Sam and Ricky upstairs?"

The medic nodded. He'd been the first of the Gadukah to respond to Roger's summons. The others were on their way. "Come on. We can check out the whole city from your father's room."

Ricky sprang right up and wandered over to the big elf happily. Samantha, however, didn't move. The bell rang again.

"Sam..."

"I'm not going anywhere with that...thing."

Hirace feigned a hurt look and rubbed at the tips of his ears. When he let go, they were perfectly round. "What about now?"

"Fuck no."

"Whoever's on the other side of that door," Talora said slowly, "is probably twice as strange as Hirace."

Samantha chewed on her bottom lip as Roger had seen her do countless times when she was mulling something over. She'd picked up the habit from her mother, and it tugged a little bit on Roger's heart. "Fine," she finally growled. Hirace led the Brooks children into the foyer. Walinda lingered until they reached the top of the stairs and then zipped out to answer the door.

Roger looked over to Talora and smiled. She'd handled that well, and he almost asked her if she had children of her own—and then he remembered that she wouldn't know. "Thanks," he said.

She nodded very softly, her attention back on the cup of coffee she'd left on the table.

Walinda returned. "Council of Intelligence Driff to see you, Pintiri."

"Thank you. Bring him in."

Driff looked like hell. His clothes were wrinkled, his hair was a mess of cowlicks, and the heavy bags under his eyes made Roger suspect he hadn't slept in a while. He took a deep breath before he spoke. "I hope you had time to enjoy your family, Pintiri. The shit's hit the fan."

Coming from the usually unflappable Driff, that was a jarring statement. Roger stopped trying to hide his own level of stress and leaned forward, rubbing his face and creasing his brow. "Coffee for our guest, please, Walinda. Driff, have a seat."

"I take it black," the Council of Intelligence croaked.

Walinda took off for the kitchen and Driff sat on the couch beside Roger, taking Samantha's place. "Do you want the good news, the bad news, or the terrible fucking news?" the elf asked.

Roger didn't like where this was headed. He traded a nervous glance with Aeric. Talora didn't seem fazed or even all that interested. Roger thought he'd broken through her shell in Goody's last night, but apparently that had just been a product of copious amounts of alcohol. "Start with the good and work toward the terrible."

Walinda returned, levitating a cup of coffee that she gently lowered onto the table in front of Driff. He drained half of it with one long, unsteady gulp. "We've caught our traitor, Pintiri. It was Pike. We found him in possession of all the materials needed to create the bottle giant that destroyed the Kralak."

Somehow, Roger felt like he had known it all along. Who the hell else could it have been? Pike was a violent lunatic—just the type to do something extreme when he didn't get his way. A genuine smile spread across Roger's face. "That's great news!"

Driff shook his head. "We caught up with him in Council of Agriculture Piney's residence. We were too late to save her. We also found evidence tying him to the murder of Greven, the merchant who sold Pike the necessary materials on a Council seal. Council of Economics Granger also went missing last night—we're not sure if Pike was involved, but there's a good chance he was."

Roger's spirits fell as quickly as they'd risen. Two lives—perhaps three, depending on Granger's fate—were lost because he and Driff hadn't been able to put the pieces together. And one of them was a person he liked and respected, one of the few elves who'd immediately welcomed him to Evitankari. "At least we got the fucker."

Driff sighed and looked away. "That's the bad news. He escaped."

Roger's jaw dropped. Talora finally looked like she was paying attention.

"How'd that happen?" Aeric asked.

"We have no clue. The guard that brought him breakfast this morning found his cell locked and empty. He must've had help."

Roger almost didn't want Driff to continue. What could be worse than that? There was a psychotic murderer on the loose, a terrorist who'd unleashed a tragic attack on his own people—and Driff had news even more dire to deliver? Somewhere, Roger thought, the Witch was giggling like an evil little schoolgirl.

"Which leads me to the real purpose of my visit today," Driff said sadly. "Port has been cut off from the transpoint network and the city has been surrounded by a demon army the size of which hasn't been seen since the time of Axzarian. The demons in charge have called a meeting with the Combined Council. We're to meet them in Tash Square as soon as possible."

Roger leaned back in his seat. "Well." He didn't have anything else to add.

Driff burst out laughing. "That about covers it."

"She's about to make her move," Talora said thoughtfully. Her demeanor suddenly darkened. "You're not going without me."

"I've got your back, Pintiri," Aeric said firmly.

"The more, the merrier," Driff growled.

"Then it's decided," Roger said, his voice shaking. "When she shows herself, we shoot the bitch."

Leaving his children so soon after getting them back was one of the hardest things Roger Brooks had ever done. He explained the situation to them as calmly as he could—which meant his voice quivered and he found it hard to look them in the eye—and then he said his goodbyes. Ricky understood. This was all a Saturday morning cartoon to him, except this time his father was the hero, and the hero always comes through. Samantha wouldn't even look at him and she didn't return his embrace.

Aeric and Driff led the way to Old Ev. Roger and Talora trailed a few paces behind. The Pintiri couldn't take his mind off Ricky and Samantha. If he didn't make it, what would become of them? Would the Gadukah be enough to protect them? Visions of twisted demons pouring into Merrowood haunted him. What could he do to ensure that wouldn't happen?

Halfway to Old Ev, Roger stepped forward beside Driff and put a hand on his shoulder. "You've got a way out of the city, don't you?"

Driff hesitated for a moment, then nodded. "Several. I'm no fool."

Roger had been counting on that. "If it all goes to hell, I want you to be the first one out of Old Ev," he explained. "I want you to get to Merrowood as quickly as you can and get my kids the hell out of this place."

It was Driff's turn to look pensive. Roger wondered if he'd insulted the elf by asking him to back out of a fight. The Council of Intelligence stopped walking and sat down in the middle of the street, laughing like a maniac. The others halted and stared down at him.

"What the fuck is so funny?" Roger demanded.

Driff took his glasses off and wiped his sweaty face with the sleeve of his overcoat. "I can't do this anymore, Roger," he said with a sad smile. "It was one thing to deceive the dirty sons of bitches who dusted me and tossed me aside like yesterday's trash. That felt good. But it's something else entirely to fuck with you. You haven't done anything wrong. Your children haven't done anything wrong. This is...this is so fucked."

When the others stared at him, dumbfounded, he continued. "Did you know I have a wife and kids of my own, back on Poa? Everything I've done, I did it for them. I didn't want my children to grow up slaves, prisoners held for crimes they never committed. It's not right. So, I signed up with the Witch. We all did. Mages from Poa brought down Tallisker's towers. That's right—not every child those bastards dusted and exiled is shala'ni. Sometimes a child is taken to punish a family or to exert political pressure. Like I was." Driff stopped and took a deep breath. "She's using Tallisker to wipe out Evitankari—and when it's done, the city will belong to the shala'ni."

He put his glasses back on and stood, facing Roger with tears in his green eyes. "But I'm done with that and I'm done with her. Not this way, Roger. Not this fucking way. How am I supposed to look my family in the eye after everything I've done? How can I explain to them that their father's a lying fucking murderer?"

Roger's brain whirred to assimilate everything Driff was saying. He felt like a damn fool; the one man in Evitankari he trusted without question, the only elf he'd decided was honest beyond reproach, had played him like a fucking fiddle. He'd been so ready to accept Pike as the traitor, but the real enemy had been right under his nose all along. Rage roared up inside of him like lava erupting from a volcano.

"You're right," he snarled. "This is pretty fucked." Roger sent the Council of Intelligence sprawling with a right cross to the chin. He drew his shotgun from the holster at his hip, cocked the hammer, and trained it firmly on the prone elf. Neither Aeric nor Talora moved to stop him.

Driff adjusted his jaw and looked back up at Roger. "I deserved that. I definitely deserve an Ether shot to the fucking head—but if you kill me, I can't tell you where your wife is."

Roger's grip on his weapon faltered, the barrels quivering wildly. Driff knew where to strike. "After what you told me, why the hell would I believe a single word you have to say about Virginia?"

"You may not," he said, his attention shifting to Talora. "But she might, and she might be able to talk you down."

Roger shifted his feet, suddenly uncomfortable. "If you've got something to say, just say it."

"I'm not the only one here who's spent time on Poa. There are ruins on the island, old and mysterious. You were there, Talora, investigating those ruins for the Witch. Occasionally, you had a visitor, a demon named Crim. A Tallisker executive, very close to the top. But you didn't go by Talora back then, and your face was longer, your eyes a little closer together, your hair more of a dirty blond, and you had a small dusting of freckles across your cheeks. No antlers. The evil inside you, remember, twists its bearer to satisfy its own image. I almost didn't believe it when the Witch told me, but seeing you now—your mannerisms, your bearing—there's no doubt."

Talora frowned and chewed on her lip, deep in thought—and Roger gasped. Virginia did that all the time. Could it be? Was it possible? Or was it just another trick? Roger examined Talora closely. He hated to admit it, and he didn't want to believe it...but he could almost see the resemblance, given the changes Driff had described. Chyve had found evidence of recent changes to Talora's facial structure, after all.

More importantly, how could he ever know for sure? If she'd been constantly running off to Poa, what did that say about their marriage? How the hell had she accomplished that? What had she been looking for in those ruins? He couldn't make sense of it.

"Prove it," Talora spat. Her hand drifted to the locket around her neck. Roger didn't remember Virginia owning any jewelry of that sort. Where had she gotten it?

"Roger," Driff said. "Have you tried to read Pym's bracelet?"

He hadn't; he didn't think that he would know how. It was magic, and he was just a dumb human.

"Those bracelets are ancient, powerful magic," Aeric said. "According to legend, they describe the reader's relationship to the bearer—past, present, and near future."

Roger still hesitated. He trusted magic about as much as he trusted Driff at this point. He wasn't sure he wanted to know the truth. He'd always assumed Virginia was a captive somewhere, confined but unharmed, and that their reunion would be full of joy and relief. But if Driff's claims were true...

"Just fucking read it," Aeric growled. "We've got places to be."

Talora wanted to know. She strolled up to Roger, a purposeful look on her face, and raised the bracelet to his eyes.

"Cross your eyes and focus, like you're trying to look through it," Driff instructed.

Roger did as he was told. Curvy green letters suddenly sprouted from the thin wooden band like leaves sprouting from a tree. His voice cracked as he read the first sentence out loud. "The love of your life." He couldn't bring himself to voice the second line. If the magic of the bracelet worked as advertised, no one else would ever know he'd kept it to himself.

Talora dropped her arm. In her eyes Roger found more curiosity than emotion. He was something interesting to look at, like a rare species of bird or—perhaps more appropriately—a man with a disgusting disfigurement. He opened his mouth to tell her he still loved her, but she silenced him with a finger to his lips. Another familiar gesture.

"We deal with Tallisker and the Witch first," she said softly. "Then we figure this out."

Roger initially didn't like it. If something happened to one of them, they'd never get the chance to do anything about what they'd just learned. But he recognized their relationship as something they weren't going to sort out very quickly—and the woman responsible for twisting their once-simple lives into a complicated knot was waiting for them. With the Witch gone, Roger and Talora would have all the time in the world.

He wanted to embrace her and tell her everything was going to be all right, but he just nodded.

"I've got one more thing to offer," Driff said. He'd moved into a sitting position, his legs crossed beneath him. "I know where your memories are. But I want something in return."

Roger snorted. "Of course you do. You're a real piece of shit, Driff."

The Council of Intelligence looked legitimately hurt. Roger couldn't believe it; after all the lies, he expected—what? Sympathy? Camaraderie? Understanding? Roger could relate to Driff's desire to do anything for his family, but he couldn't forgive the elf for helping to hide Virginia.

Driff reached into his pocket and withdrew a small vial of green liquid sealed with a black rubber stopper. "I'm supposed to shoot Aldern," he said grimly. "She'll never see me coming."

"How do you know what that is?" Talora asked.

Driff smiled sadly. "A shifter offered the same opportunity to me once. I flushed the vial down the toilet."

"So what? You kill the Witch and it's all better, and we skip off into the sunset and live as best fucking friends forever?" Roger snarled.

"There's no making it better. Being the one to end it doesn't make me the hero. It makes me the idiot who woke up too fucking late, which is really the best I can hope for at this point."

"The Witch's attention will be on the three of us," Aeric said. "Driff's our best shot."

And the deal he's offering is my only chance to really get my wife back, Roger thought. It was a chance he had to take, but that didn't mean he had to be stupid about it. "Aeric, take his gun."

The Mongan did as instructed. Driff held the side of his coat open so Aeric could easily pull out the silver pistol inside, then stood so the other elf could pat him down for other weapons. Aeric didn't find any, and he stashed the gun in his belt. Only then did Roger holster his own weapon.

"One wrong move," Roger said darkly, patting the stock of his shotgun, "and I get to be the fucking hero."

— CHAPTER THIRTY-THREE —

The remainder of the short walk was quiet and tense. Driff kept his gaze on the ground, his expression sour. Talora looked like she'd seen a ghost; she hadn't let go of that locket yet, either. Only Aeric seemed unaffected, whistling to himself and walking with an almost jaunty stride. He'd been so serious and boring up until that morning. Had the stress of the situation made him crack? Was it some kind of coping mechanism?

Roger decided to leave them to their thoughts; he had enough to think about. The message on Pym's bracelet had burned itself into his eyes. He saw the world now through a filter of green letters. "The love of your life," he'd read aloud, before the next sentence had stolen his voice. "But maybe not of hers." He wondered if that was a statement on Virginia's past or Talora's future. Did it depend on the outcome of today's confrontation? On the recovery of her lost memories? Or had she already given her heart to another, either during her double life trekking off to Poa or in the aftermath of her transformation into Talora? It was too much. He hated her for it, even though he still loved her.

It's all that fucking Witch's fault, he reminded himself every few steps. Though he hadn't seen the Witch since that fateful night four days ago in his kitchen, her presence had loomed ominously over his every waking moment. Because of her, he'd lost his house, his life, and his family, and he'd found himself trapped in a city full of lunatics, many of whom treated him like a second-class citizen. Most of all, he realized, he hated her for the ways he'd been forced to change. He'd started looking for ulterior motives in even the simplest words and actions. He'd become paranoid and jaded. Life after Virginia left had been almost unbearable, but life in Evitankari was exponentially worse.

A crowd had already gathered in Old Ev, filling Tash Square. It parted as the foursome approached. Roger searched the elven faces as they passed, finding a mixture of curiosity and concern. A few, mostly small children, looked up at them with glimmers of hope shining in their eyes. Evitankari had been through a lot, he realized, and it wanted to know just what was going to happen to it next. He was surprised to find himself hoping that he wouldn't let the elves down.

What was left of the Combined Council—Aldern and Chyve—awaited them in the center of the square, just beside Axzarian's right foot. Across from them stood a trio of demons in sharply pressed suits. Behind them stood another fifty of the evil beasts, all armed to the teeth with various weapons. Roger took a deep breath and went to stand beside Aldern. The old elf didn't even seem to notice his arrival, so set was his angry expression toward the interloping demons.

One of the well-dressed demons stepped forward, the red eye in the center of his forehead blazing angrily. "It's about fucking time," he snarled, heading straight for Roger. "Just what the fuck are you trying to pull?"

Roger took a frightened step backward. Aldern stepped between the two. "Demson, calm down and back off. You haven't even told us what this is about. Cutting Evitankari out of the transpoint network and surrounding us with an army are two very extreme ways of starting a conversation."

Demson raised his hands in sarcastic supplication and rolled his third eye. "I'm sorry, I didn't realize this was amateur hour. Playing dumb is not going to help you. You started this shit, not us. Or did you think we wouldn't notice a few fallen towers literally dripping with the signature of elven magic?" He leaned around Aldern to point at Roger. "I bet it was *his* fucking idea! Damn humans are so fucking ungrateful."

"My idea?" Roger croaked. "I didn't even know any of you people existed until four days ago!"

"Bullshit! You thought you could pull a fast one on us, but *nobody* fucks with Tallisker." He paused to let that sink in. "Didn't they tell you how the world works, human? Didn't they tell you that *we* are in fucking charge, and that *we let* Evitankari exist because it suits us to do so?"

"It wasn't us," Aldern said slowly. "Although I admit I took some small pleasure at the news."

Roger stifled a gasp. What kind of game was Aldern playing? These demons obviously weren't the sort of people you want to mess with.

"Fuck you, you ancient piece of shit!" Demson screamed. Aldern snapped his fingers. The demon's mouth continued to move, but no sound came out. He gave up a few moments later, crossed his arms, and pouted like a child.

"I know you're here, Rayn," Aldern called out. "I've played right along with your little game. I let your Pintiri stay. I let your little lackey run around the city with him. My patience is wearing a bit thin."

"L-let me stay?" Roger stuttered. "What do you mean?"

"Oh, use your head," the Council of Sorcery snapped. "Come on out, Rayn. Let's settle this like adults."

A familiar giggle wafted through the square. Roger cringed.

"Up here, boys!" the Witch called out.

Everyone in the square looked upward. The Witch sat atop Axzarian's left shoulder, kicking her feet in the air. She responded to the attention with a regal wave and a maniacal grin. Roger took a deep breath and drew his weapon. The squad of demons on the other side of the square responded by brandishing their own. Beside Roger, Aeric returned the Witch's wave.

The strange woman giggled. "Aldern! You are *such* a stupid old fart. Even after all these years you're still deluding yourself into thinking you can get the better of me. Let's get this over with." She slid off of Axzarian's shoulder and gently landed on the cobblestones. "Better than a broomstick, eh?" she said to Roger with a wink. She spread her arms wide and shoved her face forward. "Come on, fuckers, I'll give you the first shot!"

Roger was sorely tempted to take that offer. He held back when he noticed Driff circling around behind her.

Aldern's hands burst into mitts of crackling green energy. "Last chance, Rayn," he replied. "The things we did to you in the past were wrong. I see that now, and it tortures me every day. But Evitankari will still have you if you're willing to come back."

Roger's brow furrowed in confusion. The Witch—Rayn—had grown up in Evitankari? And Aldern was somehow responsible for what she'd become? He willed Driff to move quicker, to release the virus and be done with it. Aldern could be the distraction; it was about time Roger knew something the old bastard didn't.

The Witch shook her head and clicked her tongue. "Two wrongs don't make a right, Aldern. They make me."

Aldern, trying to catch the Witch off guard before she finished speaking, thrust his hands forward and sent a beam of green energy spiraling toward her. She countered with a blast of her own, black as night. The spells collided somewhere in the middle, the two colors scratching and clawing against each other as they fought for dominance. The two sorcerers stared each other down, sweating profusely and gritting their teeth as they poured power into the fight, but they appeared to be an even match. Screams rose up from the crowd around them as the elven onlookers scrambled for cover.

This is it, Roger thought as he aimed his weapon at the Witch. *You've got five seconds, Driff.* He could no longer see the Council of Intelligence in the crowd. He didn't like that. He counted down in his head, slowly and steadily, and when he reached zero he took a deep breath and pulled the trigger.

Something hard crashed into the side of his skull, sending his shot careening off into the sky. Roger dropped his weapon and went down in a heap, his vision blurry and his head aching. *Driff,* he thought. *The son of a bitch came back around behind me.* But when the world swirled back into focus and he was able to lift his head a moment later, he looked up to find Aeric, his face grim, pressing the Council of Intelligence's pistol between Aldern's shoulder blades and pulling the trigger. A gout of blood and gore exploded from his chest. The old elf collapsed to his knees, his features wide with shock, but still his beam of energy did not cease. The Witch's black magic rushed through Aldern's green and then suddenly the Council of Sorcery was ablaze in a heap on the ground. She let the magic die and bowed dramatically.

All hell broke loose. The elves in the crowd who'd brought their own weapons dove into the fray, throwing themselves at the Witch and the demons. Talora rushed to Roger's side, her hands burning with hot fire. Chyve knelt beside Aldern and pressed her hands to his raw flesh, sobbing and pouring healing energy into what was left of the Council of Sorcery. Somehow the Witch's laughter echoed over it all, childlike and chilling.

"Get up!" Talora shouted at Roger. "We have to get the fuck out of here!"

But Roger still wasn't in control of all his faculties, and he was transfixed on the scene before him. Chyve's hair withered to straw and her skin wrinkled as she gave Aldern all she had. Her eyes rolled back in her skull and she fell dead by his side. The Council of Sorcery, still horribly burned, began to crawl toward Axzarian's foot. He reached into his seared robes and withdrew a partially melted medallion from his tattered, smoking robes.

"Someone stop him!" Demson's voice called out over the din. And then the demon was beside Roger, wrenching Talora away from him. "This is it," he said sternly. "This is what you were made for. Turn your magic on that statue. Remove Evitankari's hold over us. Do it now, or so help me—"

He never finished. The Witch appeared behind Demson, took his head in her hands, and snapped his neck with one sickening twist. She tossed him aside like yesterday's newspaper. "I am so glad *that's* finally over with," she said, her voice dripping with satisfaction.

A hail of bullets pattered the cobblestones around Aldern, but none hit their mark. He pressed the medallion to Axzarian's toe and stopped moving. A deafening roar echoed through Old Ev, shaking the ground. Cracks spiderwebbed across the monument with tremendous pops and snaps.

"Every generation, a few of us are born who can hear him," the Witch explained, her eyes wet and sad. "It's enough to drive anybody a little batty, especially when the Council *makes* you listen because they think they might learn something. Evitankari never wastes anything that might be useful—even *him*."

Axzarian's left arm fell away first, then his right, then his chest split and plummeted down to crush the bodies of Aldern and Chyve.

The Witch smirked. "They wanted Axzar? Now they've fucking got him!"

The fire flared to life in Talora's hands, but the Witch squelched it with a single sharp clap. "You were a good little ruse, my dear. Those Tallisker fucks wouldn't have come anywhere near this thing without you. But now we've got things to do. Come along."

She waved a few fingers in front of Talora's face. Her body suddenly went rigid, her eyes wide and her hands clamped to her sides. As the Witch turned to leave, Talora followed.

A feeling of intense cold washed over Roger, ending his attempt to stand and fight. He'd never been so afraid of anything in his life. The last thing he saw before the shockwave hit was a man in spiky black armor, the top of his head burning brightly, floating in the air where Axzarian's statue had once stood.

— CHAPTER THIRTY-FOUR —

Roger hurt. A lot. Every fiber of his body ached, inside and out. The air around him was heavy, as if he'd been submerged in a thick bog. And then there was the fear, hot and stifling, that kept him curled up in the fetal position on Evitankari's hard cobblestones, his eyes shut so tight he worried they might burst. Something was out there. Something black as night, something merciless, something that fed on fear and pain like a plant absorbing the rays of the sun. He could feel it siphoning those things from him, healing itself, mending its body and its dark soul.

Footsteps shook the earth, heading away from Roger. The pain and fear lessened with every quake until, finally, he was able to think clearly once more. Ivree's supposed bedtime story had turned out to be true: Axzar had indeed been watching over them all from within that statue. Whatever sorcery had initially bound the Devourer was surely what they'd wiped from Tash's memories. Had anyone on the Council other than Aldern known the truth? Demson surely knew. Was that what kept the peace between Evitankari and Tallisker, then? The threat of mutually assured destruction? It was insane, but Roger wouldn't put it past those crazy assholes.

Talora. The Witch had his wife. The thought sprung his eyelids open, rolled him onto his hands and knees, and pushed him to his feet. Tash Square was a mess. Bodies littered the ground around the smoking crater that used to be the statue of Axzarian. He was relieved to see that most of them were moving. A trail of smoldering footprints as big around as Roger's head led out of the square along a residential street, toward the city wall. Roger bent down and picked up his shotgun. There was no sign of the Witch or her passing; he hoped she'd gone with Axzar.

A familiar voice made Roger turn. "I didn't think he'd actually do it," Aeric said, clearly in shock. He was on his knees, Driff's pistol dangling limply from his fingertips. "That bastard Aldern couldn't bear to lose."

Roger and two other elves, burly soldier types, closed on him. He kept talking, rambling like a madman. "But I gave him what he fucking deserved. For me. For Rayn. She's my sister, you know. Fuck, what the hell has gotten into her? She was always so focused on helping people—"

Roger cracked him across the jaw with the butt of his shotgun. Aeric's eyes rolled back in his head and he collapsed to the ground, unconscious.

"Lock him up somewhere," Roger instructed the two soldiers. Giving orders felt strange, but with every other member of the Combined Council dead, missing, or working for the Witch, he was the last authority figure left. He wasn't doing it for Evitankari; he was doing it to protect his family. "If you find Council of Intelligence Driff, arrest that son of a bitch too."

He didn't wait to see if they obeyed, instead turning and taking off at a dead sprint along Axzar's trail. The Devourer hadn't been particularly careful with his feet, carelessly walking through any elves or demons lying in his path. Roger tried not to look down as he vaulted the charred, ruined bodies, some of which were still alive. The wall wasn't far; if Axzar joined with the army of demons outside the city, there'd be no catching him. It had only taken Tash one shot with the Ether to stop the Devourer. Roger could handle one shot.

He remembered the headset when he reached the first row of homes that framed Tash Square. It was a reassuring weight in his back pocket. He could contact the Gadukah and maybe summon one or two for backup. They could distract Axzar and get him a clean shot. But the crushed, tangled mess of metal and wires he pulled out didn't look functional. He cast it aside and continued on, swallowing his fear. What choice did he have?

The wall loomed at the end of the street, its runes glowing white hot. The magic was working overtime. Axzar studied it intently with the Witch and Talora at his side. Roger banged a hard left down a side street, planning to circle around and take them unaware. Charging straight in would likely be suicide, but it would still be two-on-one unless he could free Talora from the Witch's spell. Or should he take Axzar down first? The elves had created the Ether to stop the Devourer, after all, and it had proven effective at doing so. Axzar first, he decided. Slowing his pace, he tried to hide the sound of his footsteps as he traversed the two blocks to the wall. He stopped at the final corner and pressed himself tight to the building, taking a moment to listen.

"I told you this wasn't going to work!" the Witch shouted like an angry parent scorning a small child. "The elves have had thousands of years to perfect their fucking wards. They're stupid, but they're good at this rune crap. You're supposed to hang out here, using that psychic jibbery-joo you do to drive the world's demons batshit insane and ruin any diabolical plans they might have toward pretty little Evitankari, and then they bring the Pintiri 'round and—POW!—back in the statue you go! Maybe this time they'll pose you better."

Axzar replied with a bone-jarring snarl. Judging by the sound, he was the closer of the two. Axzar first—one shot—and then another for the Witch...

Roger's muscles suddenly seized up as if a giant hand were crushing him, and then he was yanked out around the building by an invisible force. It released its grip and he fell forward, rolling to a halt at the Witch's feet. He lost his grip on the shotgun and it clattered to the ground a few feet away.

"Oh, look!" the Witch cackled. "It's the worst Pintiri ever! Hello again, Roger, you good little distraction you! The Council's dead, Tallisker's fucked, and I'm about to unleash a force of unstoppable evil upon that shit stain you people call a civilization. I was going to send a card, but since you're here—thanks for helping me change the world!"

The Witch's telekinesis took hold of him again, pinning his arms to his sides, forcing his legs straight, and lifting him a few inches into the air. He could see Talora in his peripheral vision, motionless and rigid. Behind the Witch, Axzar turned to consider him. The death's head helmet betrayed no emotion, but Roger felt the malice there nonetheless.

The Devourer's voice exploded like the crack of thunder. "Kill him."

The Witch shook her head. "I told you, Axy-waxy, he might still be useful. He's such a good little pawn. Why free the Ether so the elves can make a new Pintiri when we can have a Pintiri of our own? Maybe he can help us with our little wall problem—"

She never got the chance to finish. A small glass vial appeared out of nowhere, bursting to life from the shadows along the wall and then careening into the side of the Witch's head. It exploded beside her ear in a puff of green smoke, rancid and sour in Roger's nostrils. The Witch's eyes went wide with shock and fear as she inhaled it. Roger's feet dropped to the cobblestones, his muscles suddenly his own again. The Witch clutched her chest and spasmed as if shot in the back. She stood rigid for just a moment, and then acrid black smoke wafted up from her skin as her features began to melt. With a bloodcurdling scream, she launched herself into the sky like a rocket, disappearing over the wall.

Roger didn't waste any time, ignoring Axzar's furious roar. He dove back the way he came, landing hard on his shoulder and scooping up his weapon. Sitting up, he pointed the shotgun in Axzar's general direction and pulled the trigger. The pair of bright blue fireballs struck Axzar in the shoulder, blowing away a chunk of armor in a shower of black metal and bloody flesh.

But the Devourer still stood. Strings of bone and sinew sprouted from the wound, rebuilding his ruined shoulder and the armor that protected it. Axzar's right hand twisted into a spike, sharp and deadly, and he strode confidently toward the Pintiri.

Roger's jaw dropped and his blood turned to ice. Why hadn't that worked? A single slash from Tash's blade was all it took to stop Axzar the first time. Had the Ether weakened with age? He fired again, this time blowing a hole in Axzar's stomach through which he could briefly see the wall. The wound began to mend itself almost immediately. The Devourer kept coming. The big demon stabbed out to his right with the spike almost nonchalantly; Council of Intelligence Driff suddenly appeared, impaled through the shoulder. Roger sent a blast high over Axzar's head as the demon stooped to push what was left of Driff off his spike.

A bright flash caught Roger's attention. Talora had summoned the fire. Roger wanted to scream at her to run, to get away, to let him deal with Axzar so she could live, but she turned the magic on the Devourer before he got the chance. Axzar halted, writhing in pain as the flames coursed up and down his body, melting his armor and his flesh. Somehow, he retained his shape.

Roger fired again and again, blowing away a leg there, an arm here, even the side of Axzar's head. Despite the fire and the Ether, the flesh grew back. He kept pulling the trigger, willing the magic to work and despairing that it wouldn't. As she'd explained in the pub, Talora only had so many memories; when she burned through them all, they were both as good as dead.

Book after book flickered out of Talora's mind. What remained of *Romeo and Juliet. A Tale of Two Cities.* The *1992 Farmer's Almanac.* It was a good thing she was such a fast reader, she thought morbidly.

When those were gone she turned to people she didn't like, piling on the names and faces and willing the flames to burn hotter. Cletus. Pell. Demson and his Tallisker lackeys. The shifters. Aldern. Aeric. Driff. Even the Witch.

Next went places and events. Waking up in the park with...who was it again? The Tallisker building. The forest and Pym. The rest stop, the back of that guy's semi-truck, the streets of Detroit. The cemetery. Who was that in the coffin? What coffin? What the hell had she been doing there? China. In the alley, fleeing with that girl. She was green? Red? Blue? Some color she shouldn't have been. The Demonicam and its annoying fucking television.

But it wasn't enough. Axzar healed as quickly as she and Roger could take pieces out of him. She was running out of fuel. The flames weakened and the Devourer continued his slow approach toward her husband.

He was all that was left. The one person who'd shown her any legitimate kindness. She'd tried to burn away her memories of Goody's and their night together that morning, but in the end, she hadn't been able to make herself do it. That evening with him was the only time she could remember being truly happy. Burning it away to save herself the sorrow of revisiting it had seemed like a waste. Now it was all she had left.

Talora's memories of Roger didn't simply catch fire. They exploded, hotter and brighter than the sun. Treasured memories, she realized, were more powerful. Burning them was a sacrifice and the magic responded in turn. The flames became lightning bolts, dancing and crackling as they ensnared the Devourer and stopped him once again.

Roger's next shot took Axzar in the face. The two magics mixed in a white-hot swirl. Axzar dropped to his knees, his flesh burning out through what was left of his neck and dissipating into the sky as thick black smoke, sour and cloying, until all that remained was a scorch mark on the cobblestones.

Roger rushed to Talora and hoisted her into his arms, holding her tight. Axzar and the Witch were finished; they'd done it!

"It wasn't just the Ether!" he shouted. "It was the combination of the Ether *and* Sinta's magic! That's what they hid from Tash!"

Talora pushed him away, her face confused and afraid and panicked. "What the fuck are you talking about?" she snapped. "And who the hell are you?"

Roger felt like he'd been shot. He knew immediately what she'd used to power that last burst. *Fucking magic,* he thought. *No good, dirty, goddamn, motherfucking magic.*

A raucous cheer exploded all around them. Elves poured into their intersection from every side street, mobbing the two of them, hugging and shouting encouragement and patting them on the back. He wasn't simply the human Pintiri anymore; he'd proven himself, and now he was *their* Pintiri. And it didn't mean a damn thing to him because of what his wife had just sacrificed.

Neither Roger nor Talora protested or fought when the crowd hoisted them upon its shoulders. Against the wall, Roger saw a pair of medics tending to Driff, closing the wound in his shoulder with their healing energy. The fucker was going to make it.

Someone kissed his cheek. He turned to find Talora beaming at him, smiling like a little girl. "I remember now," she said. "I left myself two things: I'm Virginia and you're my husband. That's all I remember. I think that's a good start."

He couldn't help smiling back.

— EPILOGUE —

The pain of death was nothing new to Axzar. The problem for his enemies had never been killing him—they'd managed that a few times—but in killing him slowly and painfully enough to keep his soul from immediately jumping to another body before they could bind it. An Atlantean Serat working in concert with the Pintiri had been their ultimate solution, and here it was again.

As his flesh turned to white-hot plasma and evaporated into the sky, Axzar waited for that familiar embrace of cold, hard, unforgiving stone. How often had he dreamed about it in that damn prison, locked away for millennia? But that touch never came, and soon his mortal form was gone, naught but microscopic particles of ash aloft on the wind, and his soul was free.

The Serat didn't know how to bind him. Not like that damn Sinta Talora.

Incorporeal and undetectable, Axzar rushed over Evitankari's wall. The Witch had been right; even the wall couldn't stop death, and she'd put the proper tools in place to make it happen. He blasted toward the demon lines beyond. Searching. Examining. Tasting. His horrific death had left him weak, barely able to keep himself together.

There! Two shells, just as the Witch had promised. Humans, innocent and pure. Blank, corruptible slates into which he could carve himself. But...

Oh, that bitch...

Both were back in Evitankari. Trapped inside the walls he'd just escaped. He had no choice; he could feel himself dissipating, his grip on reality loosening. Back to Evitankari it was, then. The little boy didn't put up a fight—how could he, against one as strong as Axzar?—and in turn the Devourer showed a little restraint. The boy was young enough that there was room for two. An effective disguise, if Axzar played his cards right.

Things would be different this time. He would rest. He would slowly learn of the modern world in which he suddenly found himself. He would find a way out of Evitankari, and then he would draw his enemies to him rather than rushing headlong after them. Years locked in stone had taught him the harsh lesson of his own vulnerability.

Safely grounded, Axzar reached out to touch the demons outside the city. *Disperse,* he told them. *Retreat. Our time shall come.*

Yes, this time would be very, very different.

READ ON FOR A SNEAK PEAK OF THE FIRST CHAPTER OF *DIARY OF A FAIRY PRINCESS*, BOOK 3 OF THE DEVIANT MAGIC SERIES.

— CHAPTER ONE —

T his is the worst hiding place ever," Myrindi snapped with the sort of melodramatic huff only a spoiled teenaged girl can manage. "You assholes suck at this rescue shit."

"Take it easy, Princess," Lep said soothingly. A big bear of a man, the elf's head almost scraped the low stone ceiling of the ancient storage room they'd ducked into. "We'll be safe here."

Her dark eyes narrowed and her blue cheeks flushed purple. "Why can't we be safe somewhere with some natural light? My tan's going to go straight to hell in this hole and vitamin D deficiencies have always been hell on my mood."

"But you don't really tan, you navy blue," Lep replied, his beefy jowls quivering. "And you're safe."

"My stylist warned me that prolonged exposure to cold, damp places could lead to discoloration of my highlights."

"But you're *safe*. And you're a water nymph. Cold and damp is your natural habitat."

"And how can I *possibly* keep up with the Kardashians without a television? Kanye's new single drops tomorrow."

"But you're safe."

"And I was supposed to be at Tachel's sweet sixteen half an hour ago—"

"Shut the fuck up!" Pike roared, stepping between the two of them. Although not nearly as enormous as Lep, Pike nonetheless was large enough and in good enough shape that most people wouldn't want to mess with him. His plate armor shone the color of fresh blood in the soft light thrown by the single flickering halogen in the corner. A huge broadsword was strapped to his back. "And you, Lep, I don't know what kind of perverse pleasure you get from riling up this little bitch—"

"Little bitch?" Thin as a rail, Myrindi shifted her weight back onto her heels, stuck one bony hip out to the side, and crossed her arms over her chest. The simple white shirt she wore hung loosely from her narrow shoulders. The gills in the sides of her slender neck fluttered angrily. "Little bitch? Do you know what happened to the last Rot-licking asshole who spoke to me that way?"

Pike rubbed the top of his shaved head as he considered her question. "Absolutely nothing."

Myrindi squinted right back at the burly elf. "Fine. Technically, you're right. But that guy's on my list and he *will* get his."

From her seat beside the tiny room's only door—a hunk of dented metal that had seen better days and much better paint jobs—Chastity cleared her throat loudly. A pretty young woman with bright red hair and pale skin spattered with freckles, she was dressed conservatively in sandals, a pair of ripped blue jeans, and a gray T-shirt sporting the Irish flag. She looked more like a tourist on holiday than a commando on a rescue mission. "Hey, you know what's kind of hard? Maintaining a magically cloaked door while a bunch of dumbasses argue about stupid shit like a bunch of five-year-olds kicking dirt at each other on the damn playground."

Pike took a step closer to the tiny princess and stuck his finger in her face. "Exactly. So if you don't shut your trap, I'll shut it for you."

A shadow detached itself from the wall, taking the shape of a gnarled old troll as it inserted itself between Pike and Myrindi.

"You shall not threaten the Princess," Froman growled, his deep voice seeming to fill all the empty space in the small room. Knobs and warts and whorls pocked his scaly, yellowish-green skin. Under a loose black robe typically stocked with all manner of tools, weapons, and supplies, he wore a black chainmail shirt over black jeans with a pair of combat boots.

Pike glared down his nose at Myrindi's protector. He had a couple inches on the troll, but Froman outweighed him by a good hundred pounds. "Keep her quiet."

Froman let his angry gaze linger on Pike one moment longer, then he took the princess's elbow and led her to the back corner. "He's an ass, but he's right. The more noise we make, the greater our chances of being discovered," he explained gently as he motioned for Myrindi to take a seat atop a short pile of wooden pallets.

She wrinkled her little nose at the offered seat, but she sat nonetheless. Her sore legs needed a break. She figured she'd done enough running that day to keep her personal trainer off her back for at least a week or two.

"I'm going to go stir crazy in here, Fro," Myrindi whined. "Developing young minds like mine require appropriate stimulation. I can't believe I let you talk me into leaving without my tablet."

"I've got something even better than that infernal device," Froman replied happily. His wide smile transformed him from a rugged, untamed beast to a cartoon ogre ready to burst into song. He reached inside his robe and produced a leather-bound journal. "I grabbed this before we fled your chambers. Thought you might want it."

With a mighty sigh and an eye roll that would've made most observers immediately dizzy, Myrindi snatched the journal and opened it up to its first page. "Fine."

Dear Dumb Fucking Diary,

I can't believe I've been reduced to writing my life's story in the back corner of a janitor's supply closet. In case you haven't heard, I'm Myrindi XVII, Crown Princess of Talvayne, and I do not often frequent dirty, dingy places like the one in which I now find myself trapped. A janitor's closet is for mops and buckets and poor people who want to fornicate when they're supposed to be at work.

And as for you, Diary, suffice to say that you and I wouldn't be spending this quality time together had I entertainment options beyond reading the labels of various cleaning supplies, counting cockroaches, or giving Pike the Royal Stink Eye when he isn't looking. I've avoided you for thirteen years, after all, so don't you start thinking we're friends all of a sudden. We're just temporary acquaintances, kind of like people matched on dating shows. Fro gave you to me on my third birthday. Apparently it's tradition for Talvayan Crown Princesses to keep a journal no one else ever reads. Fuck that noise. You are kind of cool, though. This whole "think about what you want to write and the words just appear" thing would've been super useful during my penmanship lessons. Learning cursive never helped anybody.

But that's enough about you, Diary. I'm the star of this here memoir; you're just part of the supporting cast. I'd put you on the marquee just below Fro but way, way above Pike. Take a powder. And get some lotion. You're looking a bit chapped.

In medias res openings have always seemed a bit cheeky to me, so the inspirational, heartwarming, perfectly written story of my life will start at the only logical place: the very beginning. As the cells of my little fetus brain flared to life, I couldn't help being struck by how fucking pink my surroundings were. Mother's uterus really needed an interior decorator—and a thermostat. It was like a troll's armpit in there, except it smelled a little better. Sorry, Fro.

I spent the ensuing four months floating, absorbing nutrients, and listening. There was a whole world beyond my dark, poorly decorated prison, and it was full of loud, obnoxious ass-hats. Most of Mother's time was spent listening to the inane requests of bitchy people who needed more room for their goats, less noise out of their neighbors, or the continued support of the crown in bringing their experimental cheese-based geomancy project to fruition. Mother rarely replied to these petitions, leaving Father to do the majority of the work—and make the final decision, which struck me as a bit odd. Why bother putting Mother through all that if she couldn't really contribute? I got the general impression that she was just an accessory, a pretty pair of earrings stuck crookedly into the gangrenous ears of a governmental apparatus that thought it was the coolest cat on the block but in reality didn't have a clue how tragically unhip it really was.

Sorry about that, Diary. Didn't mean to go all nerd-burgers on you. I'll tone it back down.

There were also lots of what I would later learn to be parties. At the time, I had no clue what Mother had wandered into. What the Rot was all that noise and fuss and hullabaloo? The rare people who stopped being ridiculous for a few moments to offer their congratulations or a few words of encouragement confused me even more. Mother was saddled with a great responsibility, apparently, and she was fulfilling it with the grace and dignity befitting someone of her station. Maybe she'd been named den mother of a troop of pretentious girl scouts. Maybe it was her job to guard the nuclear football. Maybe it was something as simple as cleaning the pool or sweeping the stairs. No one explicitly said, so I had no clue that yours truly was actually the reason for all the chatter. Ah, to be that young and naïve again...would actually suck sweaty elf taint, come to think of it.

Sometimes the outside was quiet. These times were exceedingly rare, but Mother put each and every one of them to good use. When no one else was around, her soft, scratchy voice worked a mile a minute as she described the world and her role in it. She told me about being princess and becoming queen and knowing her death wasn't far off. She told me about Talvayne, our home. She told me about the deadly Rot surrounding the city and the magical network of transpoints that connects us to the rest of the planet. She told me about the billions and billions of humans and the sorcery used to keep them oblivious to the existence of fairy folk like us. I committed every single syllable to memory, reciting them to myself when the outside became too raucous for my tender little ears to deal with.

And then, after months of unbearable warmth in the unfurnished efficiency unit that was Mother's womb, my birthday finally came. Mother's insides quivered like a teenaged pop star loaded up on cough syrup cocktails. I knew it was time for me to be born, but I would've held onto something had I known exactly what that entailed. As I was shoved violently out into the world through the fleshy canopy of Mother's woo-woo, a single cry burst forth from my lips.

"What the fucking fuck?"

It was too bright. It was too cold. My brain was far too addled to focus on anything. Mother was crying. And—worst of all—some stranger had his hand on my ass.

"Put me down, you plebeian neanderthal!" I roared.

"Congratulations, Your Highness," the stranger said as he offered me to Father. "A beautiful new Talvayan Crown Princess!"

"The man's got good taste, but he's copping waaaaaaay too much of a feel," I added.

"Yes, yes," Father replied as he deftly avoided the doctor's attempt to hand me off. Lard Ass is not the type of man to hold angry, sticky newborns. "See that she's cleaned up and vaccinated and all that. The nanny will take care of the rest."

"Yes, Your Highness."

The doctor set me down gently on something soft and absorbent. As my eyes adjusted to the harsh fluorescent light of the birthing room, I suddenly found myself face-to-face for the first time—and the only time—with my mother. She was beautiful, both for a wood nymph and for someone covered in sweat and leaking blood from all her orifices. But still. She was a perfect angel, a petite beauty with girl-next-door good looks carved in wooden skin and trimmed in leafy green hair. When our eyes met...well, that's the only time I've ever cried. Seriously. I fucking swear. I was just pretending all the other times. Fuck you, Diary.

"I love you, Myrindi," she muttered as she breathed her last breath.

"Love you too, Mother," I wailed, "but I was really hoping you'd name me River or Bailey or Zoe or something a little more modern and hip, you know. Mother? Mother!"

She'd been telling me for days that she would die delivering me, that it was just the way life goes when you're Queen of Talvayne, but I hadn't believed her. It sounded too horrible to be true. I'd hoped Mother was just nervous and scared and too caught up on the worst-case scenario. I'd been wrong, and it made me wish I'd spent more time with her—you know, even though I'd technically never *not* been with her. I just always assumed we'd have all the time in the world to be best pals. Nope. My mother was dead.

And Lard Ass hadn't even said good-bye. Thought I'd point that out in case you needed further proof that he's a total tool shed.

— ACKNOWLEDGEMENTS —

Thank you for reading my book. I hope you enjoyed it as much as I enjoyed writing it. Sometimes it was a big pain in the ass. Sometimes I wanted to throw it into traffic and take up knitting instead. But all the work was well worth it and there will be more.

Sometimes you write something and you're so convinced it's awesome that you miss the obvious problems with it. Mad props go to Daniel Gooden and William Ward for their editorial contributions. And a big thanks to Jeremy Mohler for his work on the book's original cover.

For more by Scott Colby, check out www.deviantmagic.com.

— ABOUT THE AUTHOR —

Frustrated with the generic, paint-by-numbers state of modern fantasy writing, Scott Colby is working hard to give the genre the kick in the pants it so desperately needs. Shouldn't stories about people and creatures with the power to magically change the world around them be creative, funny, and kind of weird? Scott thinks so.

Check out deviantmagic.com for more from Scott Colby.